The Human Inside

To my friends and family.
Without them, literally and metaphorically,
none of this would have been possible.
Amanda A., Taegen R., Meghan M., thank you.
To Kiden, your smile was unwavering
and your will never gave in.

THE HUMAN INSIDE

by

Y.T CHENG

BookVenture Publishing LLC
1000 Country Lane Ste 300
Ishpeming MI 49849

www.bookventure.com
Hotline: 1(877) 276-9751
Fax: 1(877) 864-1686

Ordering Information:
Quantity sales. Special discounts are available on quantity purchases by corporations, associations, and others. For details, contact the publisher at the address above.

Printed in the United States of America.

Library of Congress Control Number	2016943177
ISBN-13: Softcover	978-1-944849-82-5
Hardcover	978-1-944849-83-2
Pdf	978-1-944849-84-9
ePub	978-1-944849-85-6
Kindle	978-1-944849-86-3

Rev. date: 09/24/2016

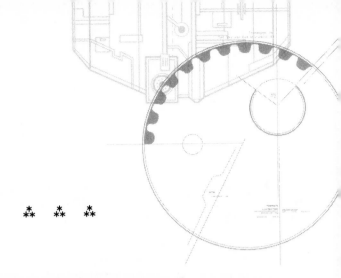

                    * * *
                   ** ** **

Amborg Industries, or A.I. Industries for short (Not to be confused for artificial intelligence), was initially and still is a place dedicated to science. There are several things that aren't known to the public though despite its popularity. For instance, no one knows where it's actually located. It is a kept a secret by every single person on the staff or security list. Employees are personally interviewed by Dr. John Kendrick himself who greatly values loyalty. Remember that name. His name is probably the very reason this story is written. Anyway, anyone affiliated with A.I. Industries lives on site, room and board, all expenses paid. The job applications keep coming in from every college graduate as well. If you manage to land a job, then they enter a new world where they are allowed to work with a very special group of individuals. These individuals are not exactly normal. Not anymore. Dr. Kendrick prefers to call them a very special group of… children. Young adult or teenagers would probably be more politically correct. They are not affiliated with law enforcement or any private military organization but they were created for a few reasons. Evolution to the next level and to fight for humanity. Although that might not be specific enough for most audiences, let us return to the specifications at A.I. Industries and what the company does. We will get back to the special individuals, the characters of this story in a bit. Promise.

The first thing to learn about A.I. Industries is that it's not a school to the common population despite the fact that one section of the complex is made up entirely of classrooms. One then might assume it's a private school and they would be partially correct. It

                                  5

is in fact a school that teaches everything. Well... everything about the known world that is. These classes range from philosophy, art, music, physics, and etcetera. Pretty much, any class elective you can think of, there is an eighty six percent chance they teach it. If you're wondering what the students there are like, well, then you're about to know.

They are known to the public by classification, known to each other by their name and numbers, and known by their own individual stories. If you had the time to sit through their life stories, which would literally take forever, then Dr. Kendrick would be able to explain how special each of them are. What are their names? They have regular first names but their last names are numbers. These individuals are named for the company that made them. They are known as, you guessed it, the amborgs.

It does sound like a weird name to give to a group of people that are and have been special for generations. Dr. Kendrick, when he came up with the idea, hoped it would be iconic while admitting it was a peculiar but unique name. In fact, it wasn't even spelled the way it is now. Originally, the word amborg was a combination of the words anthropological cyborg. It was supposed to spell "anborg" but because of a typographical error thanks to a news reporter, a typo was put into the broadcast making the word amborg. Interestingly enough, the name just stuck and everyone became used to the accidentally edited title. Even several of the lead scientists preferred it that way. To this day, Dr. Kendrick believes that amborg is actually a lot easier to say. Even they don't care what you call them.

If it hasn't already been made clear already, an amborg is one of the next levels for the human race. When you combine anthropology and cybernetics together it results is a half-human half-robot hybrid. The amborgs look human but are equipped with the advanced capabilities of a computer with minimal flaws. Also, they have the strength and the abilities a cyborg usually has. Initially though, there were problems with the first group amborgs. But eventually, with the coming of the second group amborgs, they overcame these issues. This is that story. Where to begin though is the real question? So have fun. Welcome to a new world.

Access granted. A.I. Industries files opened for viewing. Enjoy your session.

The not too distant future:

Most of the staff was not on duty during the evening hours. Which made it fairly convenient for Mandy Walker, one of the senior instructors and technicians at A.I. Industries. She disliked being interrupted by loud noises or any distractions when she was about to give lessons. Her footsteps echoed across the hallway as she walked to her designated classroom. She spotted one of the guards down the hall chatting with a custodian. They both looked at her, smiled and acknowledged her presence, to which she smiled back before entering the room labeled 312. As she walked over to her desk, she entered her password into her computer and a 3-D screen projected up in front of her. She checked the time on her watch and the clock in the room as she took her seat. She was exactly five minutes early for her private tutoring session. But even as she wondered what she'd have time to do in that short reprieve, there was a chime at the door.

"I guess I'm not the only one who likes being somewhere early," Mandy sighed as she stared at the door. She cleared her throat and said loudly, "Come on in!"

The door opened and a tall figure walked in. Mandy smiled at the young female amborg who walked in with a very neutral expression. She had always been envious how the amborgs managed to look young no matter how long they lived after their cybernetic enhancement. Shoving this thought aside, Mandy motioned for her student to sit in the front row instead of her usual seat. Hesitantly, the young amborg looked at her seat to the one in front but promptly sat down.

"Good evening Mrs. Walker," She said without even flashing a smile. This made Mandy sigh a little.

"How many times have I told you Sarah," She said cheerfully, "One, call me Mandy. Two, remember your human etiquette classes? Always remember to smile every now and then. But to continue with a proper response, good evening to you as well."

"I apologize," Sarah looked downwards but then shifted her eyes back up to Mandy. "Everyone refers to you as Mrs. Walker during your classes. Personally, I also believe that smiling is redundant as I can find no correlation with that action to happiness at all. Perhaps my programming is malfunctioning."

"No one's perfect Sarah. Even when someone has computer programming in their brain," Mandy said as she grabbed a data-pad and synchronized it to the screen at the front of the room. "In the classroom setting, it's Mrs. Walker. I agree. But when it's just us, I prefer if you used my first name. Kind of like how I use all of your first names. Just like Dr. Kendrick does for all of you."

"But our first names are informal," Sarah frowned. "Amborgs have numbers which are shorter and faster to say."

"Also true. Yes," Mandy said. She had learned to be patient with the amborg's observations and continued to smile. "It is but I feel it's much better to do exactly that and a better way to get to know you if I use the names you were born with instead of just using your numbers. Your numbers are your nicknames and last names. I completely understand that among amborgs, your numbers are best known to your friends and family. I happen to be one of the few oddballs who likes using your real names. You mustn't forget who you've always been. Even with a supercomputer in your brain, you're still born a human."

"Very well. If that is your choice. Also there is a flaw within that statement. Amborgs do not forget. Our long-term memory is entirely accurate."

"It's a play on words Sarah," Mandy smiled, "But then again, that was always something I dealt with early generation amborgs when I was still only a technician. And actually, it's one of the minor subjects I'm hoping to be able to teach you in this lesson. I'm sure you've heard of Amborg David 117? The very first amborg that I actually chose to be partnered with?"

"Of course. His reputation is very well-known and he has a list of many great accomplishments over several years of working at A.I. Industries. There are possibly thousands of data files that hold all of his deeds in terabytes of information."

"Very good," Mandy then opened the file that she had prepared on her screen and made sure it was connected to Sarah's monitor. "Nice to see that long-term memory working perfectly."

The blank but curious expression that Sarah gave her made her clear her throat and she went back to her screen.

"Anyway," she said confidently, "I thought that a look into some of the video files and reports that 117 and I made so long ago would give you some insight into how even the slowest of amborgs could discover their full personality and arsenal of human emotions. You remind me so much of him that in a way, I have a hunch this might help teach you something. Computer, unlock files 367810 dash 117 please. Password, 'My Friend David.'"

As the files began to play, Mandy looked up quickly at Sarah who was waiting curiously for the files to run the playback.

"Alright," She said to the silent amborg, "Let's begin."

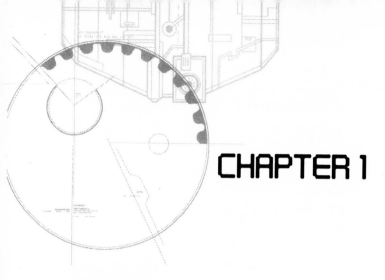

CHAPTER 1

"May I call you John, sir?" A young high school senior asked inquisitively. The atmosphere of the room wasn't supposed to be intimidating at all but he found it very scary to be where he was.

"Well we'll see about that," The person he was interviewing sitting across the table was fiddling with his glasses. This man turned out to be Dr. Kendrick himself. He smiled pleasantly, "Now why don't you tell me what you're writing about? Your name is Brad, is it not?"

"Yes sir, Dr. Kendrick... Oops!" Brad fumbled and dropped his pencil which fell and made a mildly loud tap on the smooth steel floor. He clambered out of his seat and bent down to the floor to pick it up. Upon retrieving his tool, he rose too quickly and smacked his head into the edge of the table.

"Sir? Do I look that old?" Dr. Kendrick raised his right hand and examined it carefully as Brad casually took his seat again massaging his head. "Hmm, curious. I see a few wrinkles starting to show but I doubt that's a definite sign."

Brad bowed apologetically. He wasn't sure if it was from the pain but he leaned forward and dipped his head in respect as he sat back in his seat. In his tense state however, he accidently dropped the pencil again.

"Uh no sir. I meant..." He stammered as his eyes quickly darted under the table to see where the pencil rolled but Kendrick chuckled calmly.

"Calm down," He said reassuringly which made Brad sit back up straight in his chair. He was still nervous but at least he had managed to stop fidgeting. Dr. Kendrick looked him over once before continuing, "There is nothing to be nervous about. Forget for a moment of what I do for a living. Treat me like you would anyone else you meet."

As he said this, he bent over and picked up the pencil which had rolled over to him. He placed it on the table and rolled it over to Brad who pinned it down with one hand. Dr. Kendrick smiled.

"Then you'll see how there's no need to be nervous. Take a deep breath."

Brad took a deep breath and coughed a few times, straightened up and prepared to write.

"Thanks Doctor."

Dr. Kendrick looked Brad over for the second time, stood up and went over to the window that overlooked a large field.

"Before we begin, I'd like to ask why you decided to write your essay about my work. Sure, it's flattering but not normally what someone of your age range normally is interested in. It's usually college kids who really have the levels of enthusiasm that you have displayed. Never before have I met a high-school student as passionate as you. Especially one with such entertaining and very excellent credentials."

"Well," he fidgeted a bit more but looked at the Doctor's silhouette, "I think that your work in cybernetics is very amazing. Not a lot of my classmates really care but I do because it's bigger than all of us and I want to be a part of that. Most of my friends just want to graduate but I was hoping to get better insight into what you do so I can show them how what you've done has helped the world they live in. Everyone knows how famous you are but they just don't know about you and the amborgs. The real inspiration to me is seeing them. Teenagers that look almost like me doing great things and I want to learn about that. It was like someone granted my wish when you agreed to let me come here. Opportunities like this are like gold but it's really making me edgy because I want to savor everything about this."

"Well, I did have to reply to your letters at some point," Dr. Kendrick admitted bluntly. "Reading them was a nice way to pass time. After the eighty-seventh letter, I figured I knew you to the point that it merited a response. You mentioned in several of them that you were hoping to one day sign on to here after your schooling was finished. Which position are you considering? Artificial Intelligence Development? Drone Research? Technician advancement?"

"Umm, actually I was hoping to be submitted for cybernetic augmentation. To be one of them."

"Don't take this the wrong way but unfortunately, no."

It was probably the fastest that Brad had ever been turned down. Dr. Kendrick sighed and placed his elbow on the glass and stared out at the clouds.

"I know you're going to ask why," He said turning to face Brad who was piling up questions in the back of his mind, "I've seen that look of confusion in your eyes before and I'm going to tell you it's dangerous. I appreciate the fact that you're willing to volunteer for it but I refuse that here and now."

"But why?" Brad wrote the words, 'dangerous' on his notepad. "I figured that the augmentation procedure was perfected after the third group's success."

"True," Dr. Kendrick nodded, "But still, no. The reason being that you have other priorities. Mmm, or rather, you have more important responsibilities and you shouldn't throw your life down a path that is in my opinion irreversible."

"More important than an amborg's responsibilities? What could be more important than being a scientifically enhanced robotic organism capable of... a lot?"

"An excellent question actually but there's a really complicated answer," Dr. Kendrick placed a hand on Brad's shoulder and gestured towards the door, "I can tell you for sure that it won't be easy to explain here. Why don't we take a walk around and make it a personal tour?"

"Into the facility?" Brad's eyes lit up, "Seriously? The facility itself?! You mean I'll be You're an allowed to see them?"

"Well... not too much, just enough for you to understand."

As they left the room, they proceeded left and walked down the hall. Brad looked on the wall and saw numbers etched into the wall. Before he could ask the significance, Dr. Kendrick stopped and activated a console which immediately lit up.

"Who's online?" He asked to no one in particular.

The console lit up and a female voice entered the room.

"Greetings Dr. Kendrick, CEO of Amborg industries, head of the science and the r&d division, representative to multiple law enforcement detachments worldwide, official consultant for the United Nations and Creator of the Amborg. Artificial Intelligence Serina is available and reporting."

The console flashed another light and immediately began to project the form of a three-dimensional figure into the air from the wall. A holo-figure of a young dark haired girl in average clothing appeared and smiled. She waved which made Brad's eyes widen.

"Ah Serina! Perfect! I was going to ask for you myself anyway," Kendrick smiled, "This here is Brad and he's going to be going on a special tour with us."

He pulled Brad forward, who had begun to slink backwards. He straightened up and extended a hand. But then he remembered he had just offered his hand to a holographically projected figure and retracted it quickly.

"Wow... Uh I mean," He gaped at Serina as she pulled a holographic top-hat out of nowhere in particular and tried it on. "You're an A.I.?"

"Bingo! You must be the student prodigy." She winked.

"Serina here was actually one of the original test subjects who volunteered," Dr. Kendrick explained. Serina gave a slight look of disgust and threw the hat away. The hat disappeared into thin air and she looked back at the two of them with a huge grin.

"Well what happened?" Brad asked with concern.

"The short answer is I died!" She replied casually continuing to smile. "But before I was completely brain-dead, Dr. Kendrick managed to take my data and convert my knowledge to an A.I. So you could say I was an Amborg who didn't quite actually make it."

"That's... interesting?" Brad shuddered and looked at anxiously. Serina created an orb of light in her hands and juggled it around playfully.

"It's alright Brad, we're not trying to scare you off," Dr. Kendrick said reassuringly, "But just be aware that this is what potentially might happen if things don't go the right way. That's one reason you need to think carefully about augmentation. It will be next to impossible to go back in certain cases. Are we ready to move on?"

"Umm...," Brad stared at the floor and looked at the open page of his notebook. He had stopped writing and wasn't sure what to put down.

"Say yes! I'm kinda getting bored here," Serina piped up after the awkward silence, "Heh sorry. It's just we rarely get visitors other than the usual security guards, scientists, and the custodians."

"Yes!" Brad piped up, "I mean, yes I'm ready. I've been waiting my whole life for this."

"Ok Brad," Dr. Kendrick moved over to another door and opened it, "Once we go through here, you're going to see something really epic. I hope your heart is prepared for what you're about to see."

"Amborg residential area," an automated voice announced as the door hissed open. Serina floated along the hallway with them as a light emitter followed her from the wall so she could remain projected for the two of them to see. As they continued down the hall, the projectors in the wall lit up in sequence to keep Serina from disappearing.

"Here's my favorite part of the tour," She said enthusiastically. "Or rather, all of it is my favorite."

Brad could not believe what he was seeing. He was actually in the place where the amborgs lived. An actual behind-the-scenes up close tour just for him. He wasn't sure whether to feel excited or faint from all that he was trying to take in with his eyes. There was one question building at the tip of his tongue. One that he had hoped to ask Dr. Kendrick since he was a child but there were far too many filling up.

"Dr. Kendrick," He said taking several breaths to clear his head. "All of this is amazing. I have a million questions!"

"I'd assume so otherwise I'd think you're crazy if you claimed you only had one," Dr. Kendrick winked. "What's on your mind?"

"Well, for starters, where did you get the inspiration for all of this?"

"Would you believe me if I told you I had a dream about it? If the spirit of Dr. Martin Luther King would permit me to use that type of phrase under these circumstances, then that's the simplest answer I can give you to start."

Brad scribbled the word 'dream' onto his notebook pad but then found himself drawing a question mark next to the word. Was this the whole truth?

"So you're saying that the reason that the amborgs exist today," He spoke, lifting his pencil and pointing it at Dr. Kendrick, "It's because you dreamt about it? That sounds like a cliché right out of a children's storybook. They have been helping the world for so many years and this all started from a single thought?"

"How else is it supposed to manifest into something great?" Dr. Kendrick replied with a curt smile.

He pointed into the window of one of the labs and Brad looked inside. One of the amborgs was with a security guard teaching one of the caretaker drones a few things. Brad watched as the amborg grabbed a coffee mug but when the drone tried to reach out and grab its own mug, it shorted out and fell over. Brad looked back at Dr. Kendrick who chuckled nervously and motioned for the group to keep moving.

"There were rough patches but at least, my ideas came to light and became reality when people said it couldn't be done," He said as the entered another hall. "It did start from something small. All big things start like that. Look at the way people or animals are born, how we design buildings, go somewhere, assemble armies, start families, go to college, make money, or help others. These are all things that start from the most basic and abstract thoughts in our mind. It just takes a great deal to develop it into something epically fantastic for the world to idolize."

"You're not going to write that down?"

Brad turned and saw that Serina was gazing at his notepad. He had only written a few notes but had stopped when Dr. Kendrick had begun his explanation.

"Uhh," He muttered, "Can you repeat that again Doctor?"

"Just write down 'dreams equals outcomes,'" He replied thoughtfully, "It is the choices of every single individual, be it amborg or human, that decides the final outcomes of whatever it is they put their minds too. Good things yes. But always remember that there are bad things all the same. I would be lying if I told you that we live in a perfect world. Even with all my contributions."

"What exactly did you see in your dream doctor?" Brad asked as they stopped outside another room.

"Well, it's better to show you a tidbit of what I dreamed."

There was a number labeled in bold grey paint and illuminated by neon lights on the door. Brad read the number and saw the number 33 printed on the metallic door. Dr. Kendrick raised his hand and knocked on the wall just to the right of the door. Seconds later, the wall faded away and Brad gaped at what he was seeing. In place of a blank wall now sat a window frame of transparent glass revealing the room on the inside. On the other side stood a taller than average teenager who smiled and waved back at the group. Brad noticed that the other boy was wearing a jacket with the number 33 printed across his left chest pocket.

"This is amborg 33," Serina said as the amborg inside turned away from the window. They watched him sit back down at his desk and resume his activities. "He seems to be enjoying his hobbies."

Dr. Kendrick watched as 33 lifted a model car in his hands and held it up for them to show. Both he and Serina gave him a thumbs-up and 33 turned back to his modeling kit.

"Years ago, the amborg was a fresh idea in my mind," He explained as he motioned for Brad to step closer to the window. "I wanted to change the way we were treating the world and its inhabitants. So I thought, why not give it people who could be the change? I figured, why not put electronics inside someone and upgrade them? Unfortunately, several people said that this was too radical. They were right. After all, at the time, I was limited by the technology that was available to me. But I believed in what was possible despite the risks."

He nodded to Serina who flashed a bright blue. A set of images appeared on 33's window. It showed a young boy lying on a table and some specialists were around him readying some surgical machines. The images faded before it could reveal anything gruesome which was good since Brad was starting to feel queasy.

"33 was one of the lucky ones you see," Dr. Kendrick explained as they watched 33 slowly grab different parts and glued them together. "Then again, every amborg is lucky after they undergo enhancement. Obviously, my original proposals for these projects weren't well-received. Naturally, I was on my own for a while. Nowadays, everyone is falling over each other to try and get in on the action at A.I. Industries. Almost all of the ethical concerns brought up back then have mostly or completely faded into the history books. Almost."

"But Doctor, if no one wanted to support you in your proposals, how did you get where you are now?" Brad asked as he kept writing down notes. Every now and then, he would look up to peer into 33's room to make sure he wasn't missing anything as well. "I mean, A.I. Industries is one of the biggest companies worldwide. It was the amborgs that kick started all of the popularity and pretty much made this place what it is now."

"Very true," Dr. Kendrick agreed. "Before however, it was definitely not a similar story. Which is why I have to give credit to my ancestors and my parents. Most of the initial research, equipment and funding came from my own personal expenses and family fortune. I would have been broke if the amborg projects hadn't succeeded. Also my reputation was also in serious question."

"How so?"

"Well, because of the death rates."

Brad saw Serina's luminescent hand fly straight over her mouth. She cleared her throat and looked down, avoiding the stunned gaze from Brad. Ashamed, she looked up nervously at Dr. Kendrick but he merely smiled.

"Sorry," She said quickly, "You really didn't need to know that."

"It's alright Serina. Sometimes the best way to tell the truth is to say it like it is," Dr. Kendrick shrugged, "You just saved myself from having to find the words for it."

"Death rates?" Brad said questionably, "I was under the impression the death rates were extremely low. Well obviously, you can't make someone cybernetic without drawbacks but wasn't it ok? When the first group amborgs appeared, we were told that all of them had survived the procedures with minimal negative effects."

"The media never really changes does it?" Dr. Kendrick said amusingly. "It has been a while since I stepped off the grounds. Do they still say that sort of thing?"

"Seventy-eight percent of the statistics I found claim that the second group had no casualties whatsoever," Serina pointed out. "I just love when people assume they know the truth."

"The point in this case Brad is that you shouldn't be so quick to get your information straight from secondary sources," Dr. Kendrick added. "As much as the news likes to make it sound child friendly, unfortunately the reality of it is much more harsh and upsetting to me. There was a high risk for failure and the public didn't care about dead test subjects. They only liked the stories they could make up from it. Too many lives were lost. But the real truth is they all chose to do it. Amborgs became a symbol of hope to a very chaotic setting in this country as well as many regions around the world. What people don't really know is that they also carry a heavy legacy in order to honor the fallen."

"They chose to do it?" Brad asked with concern. "Sounds very harsh."

"Oh yes," Dr. Kendrick admitted. "As more and more amborgs came into being, I developed the ability to safely keep them alive. At great cost. Other scientists accused me of defying ethical codes of conduct. Many claimed I was manipulating with human lives in order to accomplish my goals like a tyrant but that wasn't so. Every person I found for the amborg projects were orphans, children that the world turned their back on. Crippled, so young to be cast aside and struggling for their own survival on the ground they lay upon. I took it upon myself to offer them an opportunity to have a life different than their current ones. Of course, I couldn't take in all of them which was an added consequence. I offered these teenagers the opportunity to advance forward and gave them all the chance to do great spectacular things. I interviewed them myself and asked them the big question if they wanted to volunteer. Every one of them who have survived to become an amborg or passed on accepted these terms. They knew the risks, had nothing to lose, clung to their hope and I admired even to this day the courage they showed me. The human will inside of them was strong which was heartbreaking but something I could respect."

An eerie silence filled the corridor as Dr. Kendrick looked down sadly. All anyone could hear was the sound of their footsteps. Serina stopped smiling, closed her eyes and bowed her head.

"They will be remembered," She whispered. "Brothers and sisters who will rest in peace and their memories will not disappear."

"Thank you Serina," Dr. Kendrick nodded as he pushed his glasses up his nose. Brad was filled with remorse.

"You interviewed them, understood them, and really learned about who they were," he said, "It must have been very personal for you. I'm sorry."

"It's alright. You should have seen when the government brought me in for a hearing," Dr. Kendrick explained, "I was initially charged with intended manslaughter... but then my Amborgs fought for me. Not literally of course. They banded together and argued how their lives were better and that they chose this kind of life for themselves voluntarily. They absolutely refused to allow me to be locked away. Now that I had amborgs with me, they claimed that the future would be worth the costs inflicted. My biggest regret probably was trying to mass produce them. It's still a regret but seeing them in action makes me feel better. Remember kid, life is precious. We don't really notice that until we lose it."

"Wasn't there also an incident with the military as well?"

Brad thought for a moment and then remembered something he had read about a few years ago. Something about the amborgs appearance and performance in the field had led to the U.S. military coming about. Dr. Kendrick merely nodded when the subject had been brought up.

"Yes there was Brad," he said, "Although, let me correct you. It wasn't actually an incident. It was more of a rebellious choice. The top brass in the government wanted the amborgs to be commissioned into service with the military. They figured the Amborgs could be used to bring down all sorts of enemies."

"What was wrong with that sort of thinking?"

"They wanted to use us like cannon fodder," Serina said with a huff. "There aren't a lot of military people that I trust but I have tons of code that draws the line whenever we get labeled as weapons."

"Blunt as usual Serina," Dr. Kendrick shook his head with a small chuckle. "From my perspective, I said at the time that their descriptions of them as weapons was demeaning and I refused to let them take control of the kids. The military witnessed their strength, skills and abilities and wanted to exploit that without even trying to understand that amborgs continue to retain their feelings about humanity. They aren't mindless machines that just take orders. They have every capabilities as a commander leading an army but individually, that's their choice."

"Ah. So you drew the line," Brad stated his thought aloud. Kendrick nodded.

"One that must never be crossed," He described. "Well it's a line I personally drew. Amborgs have their own individual free wills and choose what they want to do. They can set their own boundaries and then choose to do whatever their hearts desire. It really depends on what you ask each of them individually. Believe me, they do have their opinions."

As Brad listened, Dr. Kendrick pulled a small hand-held rod from his pocket and pressed his thumb onto the end. It lit up and showed a few video postings and newspaper articles. Several of them were about the amborgs and what appeared to be personal media interviews of them.

"Nowadays, there aren't that many conflicts for the amborgs anymore to resolve anymore. If the military had taken them, I shudder at the idea of what would have happened to them in peacetime," Kendrick scrolled through all of the different videos and stopped it at a certain clip. Brad stared and watched a video of an amborg carrying two crates to a transport. "But I'm glad they have lots of fun working on their hobbies and doing other things for society in their free time."

Another video popped up to see a few amborgs feeding homeless people sitting on the sidewalk. Brad then saw the image change to a video of an amborg working in the hospital. Then it changed to show a group of amborgs assembling a small building faster than any construction crew Brad had ever seen. He was about to ask Dr. Kendrick what sort of things they did for recreation when the videos then switched to a different scene. It showed an amborg who looked like they had just been put on fire. Another amborg was in the background with a fire extinguisher and appeared to be laughing.

"Ah, that would be 9 and 8," Dr. Kendrick said rolling his eyes, "They've been pulling pranks on each other for as long as I can remember. And their devious little imaginations continue plotting up another humorous stress reliever. It surprisingly doesn't get old."

The video image changed again and revealed a female amborg trimming a few flowers. Then it revealed a male amborg flaming a steak. Another image showed a pair of amborgs fixing a car engine. Then it showed an image of a familiar face.

"That's 33 right?" Brad said excitedly and pointed at the amborg who was in the middle of assembling a model with one hand while piecing a puzzle with his other. "He really does love puzzles and complicated set-ups."

"Yes he does," Dr. Kendrick smiled. "Watch this next part."

Brad watched as the video of 33 showed him picking up a piece of tubing looked at the instructions and carefully attach the piece to another and began to slowly glue it together. He set the pieces down to dry and grabbed a lego set. He rapidly took it apart in his hands within seconds and slowly began to piece it back together as if he had just opened the box.

"Do you notice how slowly he is building the model?"

Brad nodded as he watched 33 smile at his handiwork.

"When he first started on the models, he'd always build them so fast that it took all the fun out of it. Eventually, he learned patience and slowly found the fun in working slowly the way model toys was designed to be made."

"Wow, that's really neat." Brad said in awe as the three of them continued on. The trio found themselves at another fairly large door. The words 'GYM' was printed in bold black ink on the door frame.

"Welcome to the training facility!" Serina piped up and the three of them stopped outside another door. Smiling again, she bowed and waved her arm towards the entrance as it slid open to allow them inside.

"Amborg Industries Gymnasium," A small bodiless voice announced as they stepped inside. "Welcome Dr. Kendrick, A.I. Serina, and VIP guest. ID confirmed."

"I'm not all that special though," Brad muttered with an embarrassed look as they stepped inside.

The door opened to reveal a massive gym. Brad looked up straight at the ceiling and was amazed at how high it was. There was probably room to fit a ten story building. Mats lined the walls and there were a few crash test dummies on the floor. Some of the equipment along the walls included hand to hand weapons for training purposes. Apart from the few vacuum bots scooting across the floor, there wasn't anyone in sight which made it convenient for Dr. Kendrick.

"Hmm," He said observantly scanning the area, "It doesn't look like we have anyone using the gym... well for starters, Serina, go and find him."

"Him?" Serina floated towards the two of them, "Who are you referring to? There are tons of guys in the facility doctor. It'd be helpful and I could save eight whole minutes of scanning the entire database."

"Number 117 Serina," Dr. Kendrick chuckled, "Just checking to see how well you're paying attention. Also be a dear and request some refreshments. I'm guessing we might be here a while."

They went to the corner of the gym where there was a large stack of fold-up chairs. He pulled up a chair and motioned for Brad to grab one as well who nodded and picked one up. Serina responded to the doctor's instructions nodded and then did a loop de loop in the air and emitted sparks of light from her palms. The light show illuminated the gym very brightly like a star erupting in the night sky causing Brad to gaze in wonder as he followed Dr. Kendrick towards the center of the gym.

"Absolutely doctor! Number 117 it is!" She squealed delightfully and disappeared into the wall.

A blue light emanated off the panel where she had practically jumped into. The panel connected to similar light projectors that ran through the hallway corridors. With a flash, she moved from one emitter to another and then the light flew off towards an exit on the other side of the gym. The light reached the door and then disappeared like magic.

"Now Brad, have you ever seen an amborg?" Kendrick turned to look at Brad who was still gaping in awe at what he had just observed. Shaking his head to gather his thoughts, Brad sat down slowly with one eye focused on the wall where Serina disappeared into.

"No I can't say that I have," He replied calmly without looking at the Doctor. He began to scribble a few notes in his book, "Do the A.I.'s here always behave so eccentrically?"

"Some of the time," Dr. Kendrick took his glasses off and wiped them off using the edge of his jacket. "For a group of computer based programs, they can do wonders that would leave you drooling. In Serina's case, well... She's definitely a special case."

"I'll take your word for it," Brad chuckled as he wrote a few notes about Artificial Intelligence. "Serina seems to be a very outgoing A.I."

"Yes she is." Kendrick placed a few fingers under his chin. "She's one of the best ones that probably ever set foot on this good planet. Adventurous, full of humor, brave, quick... those don't even begin to describe what other features there are about her."

"I can tell," Brad stopped writing and immediately remembered something else. "Is she as special as 117?"

"Nice guess. Why do you ask?"

"Well," he stared Kendrick and continued his observation, "You specifically asked for him or her, and with such intensity that obvious, I don't think it was by random choice. Seems like that amborg made a huge impression on you."

"Very good," Dr. Kendrick applauded, "He is a very special amborg indeed. Even though they're all special to me, I have great admiration. Err, well, everyone has great admiration for him."

Dr. Kendrick looked over his shoulder at the door but nothing happened. Kendrick sighed patiently and turned back to face Brad.

"But I think to really connect with that story," He smirked, "I believe he can tell you that himself. Want to hear his story personally directly from the mouth?"

"Directly from his mouth?" Brad's smile faded, "I thought that amborgs only could communicate with us through the specially designed wrist bracelets. Aren't their speech patterns gone instantly after the cybernetic augmentation?"

"Yes, that is very true, but 117 specifically learned how to speak again."

"Verbal speech??" He exclaimed, "But I thought the augmentation procedure disabled the use of the vocal chords permanently!"

"Also true, you see when I first met 117, he had a very sincere voice. All of the amborgs whose voices were recreated electronically through the bracelets were identical but of course, it always felt strange to me," Dr. Kendrick looked over his shoulder again but the door remained shut. "So imagine my surprise when I first heard his voice again. It wasn't the computer monotone that follows from the transmission of the bracelets. After a whole year of being an amborg, and fighting the bad guys, he found his actual voice and shocked me. Because his sound wasn't coming from the watch, it was coming from his own throat again."

"How did all of it happen?"

"His vocal chords adapted and by some miracle, they restructured in a way that I never anticipated," Dr. Kendrick said with a look of glee on his face. "It truly was something amazing that I never saw coming. Complete and total immersion with his upgrades and suddenly, he was speaking again. Not entirely but he's working on it. Soon after, they all began developing their voices again as well."

At that moment, the door opened and two people walked in. Actually it was technically only one since Serina was a miniature light glowing next to who she arrived with. She waved her arms majestically at the figure behind her.

"Well say hello to amazing!" She exclaimed with a wink

She stepped aside and the amborg walked forward. Brad gaped at the six to seven foot tall cyborg. The number 117 was printed into his jacket on his chest which glowed a bright green. Slowly, he raised his arm forward and extended it for Brad who continued to stare upward at the modified human being before him.

"Pleasure... To meet you," 117 said slowly. Speaking from the mouth did have a toll. Brad noticed 117 was wincing with pain and his neck twitched with each word. In order to remedy this, 117's wrist bracelet lit up, flashed in a sequence of lights and another voice with a more electronic tone sounded out finishing his introduction.

"I'm David 117," The lights on his wrist flashed as the words projected out for everyone to hear. "At your service. Speaking is very strenuous. I was in the middle of attending an seminar when Serina called. May I inquire to your designation... correction. Sorry. I mean... What's your name?"

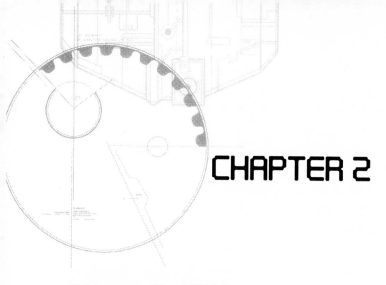

CHAPTER 2

Eight years earlier. 2127 July.
Amborg Evaluation Center.

"Amborgs report to selection room. Technicians are standing by. Numbers 35, 82, 27, 43, 297, and 117. Prepare for inspection and formal mingling."

Many of the technicians wore lab-coats or suits for the inspection. Although Dr. Kendrick's orders had said that it should be a casual pot-luck setting, many of them still felt it was necessary to look their best. A few of them were about to meet their first amborgs. But for all of them, they were hopefully about to select their future cybernetic partners after this was over with.

Overlooking the room below where all the technicians and amborgs would be gathering together was a small observation center. The windows were viewable from both sides and the room contained several seats for important guests. In this case, several business executives were touring the facility under invitation from the public relations staff. The head of PR was one of Dr. Kendrick's closest friends by the name of George Ramirez who was showing the visitors the facility with his daughter Thalia.

"Daddy, can I pick an amborg?" She asked curiously as she placed both hands on the windows of the observatory and peeped down. The amborgs hadn't arrived yet and she was just as anxious to see them like the people below.

"No sweetheart, only technicians get to pick an amborg," George said to his little girl. "Now come over here. You said you wanted to welcome the visitors."

"Ok daddy," She replied as she ran over to his side and waved to the panel of executives. "Hello everyone! My name is Thalia. Tall-ee-uh. You spell it with an 'h' after the T and before the first A in my name. This is my daddy and we're both going to be your tour guides for the afternoon!"

A few of the executives chuckled and waved back. Some of them clapped for Thalia's introduction as she gestured for her father to speak up. George then stepped forward, bowed his head in acknowledgement and then spoke.

"Well you heard it straight from the child's mouth," He said with a smile. "As you can see, ladies and gentlemen, my daughter will be joining me as I give you the local rundown of what will be commencing today. Now you already had a tour of the research and production center with Dr. Kendrick but since he's currently unavailable for the rest of the day, the two of us are here to help let you be introduced and better acquainted with the other children of the facility."

Everyone walked to the glass at George's signal and peered into the room. Inside, they watched as a door opened and a group of amborgs entered the room. The technicians and everyone in the observation room stared for a few seconds. Finally, one technician stepped forward and introduced himself and the rest of the crowd in the room below began to converse. One of the executives coughed for attention and then raised a hand.

"So what exactly is the selection, Mr. Ramirez?" She asked which prompted everyone to face Mr. Ramirez.

"This is the event where a technician is assigned to an amborg or rather an amborg is assigned their human partner for operations for future endeavors," George explained. "A moment where the amborgs are allowed time to bond with normal human beings who are prepared to be friends and their partners in a sense."

"Why pair one of the amborgs with a human technician?" Another person asked, "Isn't that supposedly less efficient? Like ehhh... asking a janitor to keep a supercomputer oiled and properly maintained?"

"To answer that sir," George chuckled. "First, a supercomputer is never oiled, it is liquid cooled. At least that's what I know about the one at the Leibniz Supercomputing Centre in Germany when it first debuted in 2012. Second, pardon me for saying it like it is but they are not maintained by janitors the last time I checked."

Everyone laughed including the man who asked the question. Bashfully chuckling, he muttered an apology and then George continued to speak.

"Nevertheless, that is a fair comparison and it also generates many questions," he said nodding in agreement. "Why put an ordinary human at the hub of another human being with the calculating speed of a super computer at all? The reason is it's because the technician is able to provide human instinct into what an amborg sees. The amborg takes to the field while the technician remains here on the A.I. Industries compound and monitors them carefully. The technician is in charge of monitoring the amborg's well-being, mental state, physical prowess, and occasionally, helping them with basic human behavior and decision making."

"Why would the technicians need to help the amborgs with... basic human behavior? Amborgs are superior to us in so many ways. Aren't they?"

"That is actually partially untrue. Surprisingly, most of the amborgs have trouble with dealing with certain issues," George explained. "It used to be that someone was torn between two choices. Should they save the bus full of children or defeat the person causing the destruction to escape? Normally an amborg is actually capable of doing both. But several of them have actually developed significant problems making choices. They sometimes become indecisive, the calculations don't compute to them emotionally, or in the time it takes for them to map out every possible contingency, because they actually do think about it, it's most likely too late. That's also why the technician is there for the role of being a guide. The person who provides hints if the game becomes too difficult. They keep an eye on their choices and to become the little voice in their heads. A mentor, teacher, or the manager of the buddy system. Many of the amborgs lose or are slow to use their own instinct in certain situations. Therefore, the technician helps them adapt and undergo a type of therapy or whatever they choose to call it in order to make it easy for them."

"Is the selection random?" A female executive inquired curiously.

"No it is not," replied George, "The technicians end up choosing which amborg they'd like to be paired with. Like I said earlier, this is when they are allowed to bond. A time for them to get to know one another. Amborg or technician. They'll become a team when they go into the open world. Because we try to teach the amborgs to feel secure and comfortable with whoever they feel close to. Or rather, the technician most compatible is the way they like to describe it."

"So why not have a team of technicians working with a single amborg?" The same woman looked at George who smiled back.

"Picture yourself as an amborg," he replied, "You can't speak through your mouth because of broken vocal chords after augmentation. Instead, a signal from the CPU that your head sends to a bracelet which reproduces your voice is all you have in order to communicate. A basic walking computer with several outlets but technically only two ears and one brain. Do you really want fifteen people talking into your head at the same time? Too much activity on any computer system will increase the chance for an overload or a crash. In the mind of an amborg, it has a similar principle because it's not good mentally. It is also difficult to describe or even imagine. You do have to admire the bravery they have to submit to such a sacrifice."

The woman then closed her mouth, nodded in understanding, and turned back to the window to look back down below. Thalia walked up the window and pressed her hands to the glass. As she began to scan the room below, George began to describe some of the amborgs below.

"Below us," he said indicating two of them, "You'll see these amborgs from the Second Group. Except for 27 over there. Regretfully, he lost his technician in an automobile accident a few weeks ago so he's attending the selection sessions. He actually requested time to grieve for his lost partner but now he's back for more I guess."

"What does you mean by Second Group? Is 27 different from the others?" Another executive interrupted.

George looked carefully at the person who asked the question. This particular executive looked to be very young from the rest of the entire group. His suit was much shinier by the look of it and brand new compared the other two people he stood between. Their clothes looked very tattered and worn out. Definitely someone not aware or knowledgeably experienced.

"Our project began a year ago with over one hundred and two volunteers specially selected by Dr. Kendrick. Forty eight survived the initial augmentation process. But we lost eighteen more soon after leaving only thirty survivors who became official amborgs. These thirty survivors are referred to as the First Group."

Several of the executives began to mutter and whisper to each other. Many of them turned their heads when George finished and gave looks of intense curiosity. Realizing he had everyone's attention again, he spoke up.

"A few months ago," he continued, "We successfully made another thirty amborgs. For security reasons, I won't say out of how much. The death toll still hangs but now we have developed safer methods to ensure a lower casualty rate. These next amborgs have been designated the Second group."

*** *** ***

Down in the selection room, 117 stood in earnest. He looked at 43 who stared back. Although both made no emotion or showed any response, they secretly were having a private chat in the back of their heads. As long as they stood in range of each other, they could send messages back and forth without the possibilities of anyone eavesdropping. Unless another amborg was allowed into the loop. 43 stared at 117 and without opening her mouth, her voice rang clear in the back of his head.

"What are you thinking about?"

"Based on the previous selections," he replied sending a reply to her computer, "The probability of being selected during this one remains the same. A minimal chance."

30

"Do not be negative 117. A technician will select you today," 43's voice rung clear as day in his mind. However, her attempt at reassuring 117 was unsuccessful.

"No 43," he replied while shifting his mouth into a frown. "This has been my fourth selection and no one has chosen me. I calculate a low probability for selection today."

At that moment 43 walked over and stood on his right. She was many inches shorter than him but still had the height to allow her to lean towards him as if she was about to whisper in his ear.

"Calculations do not factor for them," Her voice spoke earnestly, "I know someone will choose. This is... a prediction. From what I have perceived in human behavior."

"Since when do you make predictions?"

"We're amborgs aren't we?" 43 shrugged. "Isn't it our job to make multiple calculations and predictions? That last one was a calculation for you. To lift your spirits if you will."

"Is that so," 117 stared blankly at a technician who was interacting with 27. He watched the technician place a hand on 27's shoulder who reacted with a smile on his face. From what he could guess, this technician was possibly exhibiting sympathy however it felt so unfamiliar that 117 disregarded this prediction. As he did so, he heard 43 speaking to him again.

"Look up in the observation room 117," She informed him, "It would appear you have a young admirer."

* * *

"Daddy, that one looks sad," Thalia pointed a finger at the glass. She spoke loudly enough for all of them to hear and George walked over. "Do you see? The boy amborg who's talking to that girl amborg."

George knelt down by his daughter and looked. A couple of the executives, overhearing the conversation, also looked at where Thalia was pointing. Despite her age, George had no understanding how she could sense that type of feeling. Must be from her mother's side, he guessed.

31

"Amborgs don't get sad Thalia," He said plainly. "They're basically computers. So emotions aren't really a priority in their programming. Why do you think he's sad?"

She made a small humming noise which meant that she was thinking really hard about her answer. After a couple of seconds, she spoke again.

"Because he hasn't been chosen," She replied softly. "That's how mommy looks when she's sad. Look at his face. He's waiting for someone."

George looked at 117. Now that she had mentioned it, he could also see what she was talking about. He looked around briefly and realized that the whole room had gone quiet. Everyone had stopped to look and listen to the conversation too. George could also see through the window that 117 was looking back up at them. He must be wondering why we're singling him out, he thought, I wonder what's on his mind?

* * *
** ** **

"It would appear there is more than just one."

Noticing the number of eyes that were trained on him, 117 nudged 43 to tell her of this correction. After seeing three pairs of eyes fixed on him with his peripherals, he didn't have to guess that all of them were watching. Without making a noise and standing perfectly still, he could hear the exact number of people sitting up in the booth above. By his count, twenty eight people were possibly staring.

"43, perhaps returning to your original position is appropriate," 117 said as he tilted his towards 43. "Multiple people are now monitoring me."

117 looked up at the glass at a little girl who was pointing at him. Running a facial recognition into his database, he realized it must be Thalia, daughter to George Ramirez.

"Curious," 117 said, "I wonder if Ms. Thalia is selecting me? At least that would be a first."

"117, I doubt a technician could place that young."

"I was attempting to subtly make a joke."

117 turned to look at 43 who was tilting her head in confusion. Suddenly she arched her head back slightly and then nodded.

"Oh. Pardon me. I failed to recognize the attempt," She replied dubiously.

"No apology is necessary," 117 said in confusion. "There has been no insult detected."

At that moment a door opened and a teenage girl walked through the door. Despite how young she looked, she wore the same uniform that the other technicians were sporting and entered the crowd.

"That, is a young technician," 43 noted observantly at the late arrival, "Although I have been wrong on a few occasions."

The new arrival was panting heavily and joined the other technicians. Over the course of the next twenty minutes, she walked around and took a deep look at each amborg. Finally, she stood in front of 117 with a smile on her face.

"Well?" She asked in a plain but demanding voice. 117 stared blankly back at her.

She was obviously waiting for a response. But her one word question was confusing him slightly. Her tone of voice suggested that she was expecting an answer but she had also used a strange word from his perspective. He stared and thought hard about what he wanted to say. Finally, his CPU sent a signal and linked up with the silver bracelet worn on her right wrist.

"I do not understand," He admitted as his voice projected out of the silver band loud and clear for the young lady to hear. "Well? A word for of inquiry to examine one's physical or emotional well-being. If that is indeed the context you are indicating, then I am... well. That is my response."

She stared back at him and then suddenly began to laugh which confused 117 even more. He had never encountered such a strange person.

"Pardon," He interjected, "What is funny?"

After a few moments, the technician stopped laughing and then straightened up.

"I was under the impression we were introducing ourselves," she smiled and patted him on the shoulder really hard which made him stare at where she had struck with a puzzled look. "In that... context was it? I was trying to see what kind of response you'd make. I'm Mandy. What do they call you?"

"Amborg designation number 117," He replied. It is a pleasure to meet you Mandy."

Mandy had extended her arm out but 117 didn't move. He was still contemplating about what the pat on his shoulder meant.

"No silly!" She said impatiently, "I was asking for your name. Your real one? I know you have a number but you have a name too. Don't tell me you don't know how to shake hands."

At these words, 117 held up both hands and shook them rapidly at a tremendous speed. A small buzzing noise began to sound from the rapid movement. A normal human would have shaken their hands clean off. But to an amborg, it was a very simple feat. Unfortunately, 117 knew this was wrong when Mandy placed a hand to her forehead and shook her head.

"No no no," she chuckled, "Copy me. Take your right hand, hold it out and hold my hand. Now close your fingers but don't do it too hard or you'll crush mine. I know how strong you amborgs are so be careful."

As 117 slowly wrapped his fingers with hers, he looked directly at her.

"Before I chose 117 as my number, I was designated with the name of David. Last name: Classified."

"It isn't classified David," Mandy sighed. "We just respect your privacy and your family names which is why it is not mandatory for you to share your last name. Don't act like we locked it away from you."

She released her hand and put it on her hip.

"Another thing. Was? What do you mean you were designated as David?" Mandy let go of his hand, "You still are David. I know we just met but do know that we'll be doing a lot of things together. After all, 117 is going to be weird to say consistently when you're in the field. Which is why I like David more. It suits an amborg with your looks. A six foot tall human being cybernetically upgraded. It's interesting how you have not been chosen in four selection sessions. To me, that makes me think you're someone unique. Am I going too fast?"

"When I am in the field?" 117 repeated for clarification, "Who are you referring to? Someone unique?"

"I'm talking about you David," She replied happily, "I'm your technician, David 117, and we got a lot to learn together! But for an amborg, you sure are surprisingly slow…"

"Slow?" 117 repeated skeptically. "My programming operates at full capacity enabling rapid calculations in the exabyte range. If my calculation speed is not in question, I am perfectly capable of withstanding or exceeding normal human parameters in the field based off of training simulations. My speed is equal to that of the other amborgs."

"Yeah David," Mandy sighed, "But I am indeed talking about a different version of slow. But we'll… slowly get to that later. For now, I'm your technician and you'll be taking instruction from me. Understood?"

"Understood Ms. Mandy."

"Just call me by my first name David. I prefer just Mandy."

"Very well… 'Just' Mandy."

"Oh boy."

"Understood Ms. Mandy."

Back above in the observatory, Thalia smiled very brightly which caught her father's attention. He looked down at 117 and saw a young woman speaking to him. He then returned his gaze back to Thalia who pointed excitedly down at the room below.

"Look daddy he's happy now," She smiled. "It's going to be alright for him now."

"You know sweetheart," George replied beginning to form a small smile, "I think you might be onto something."

He stood and turned to the others. All of the executives, satisfied with this portion of the tour appeared to be ready to move on. Possibly since the exciting bits were over and finished with. They all began to huddle around the exit.

"So, would everyone like to continue the inspection? It looks like we're all finished here," George asked all of them. "Dr. Kendrick would like to meet with you once we finish the tour to give a concluding statement. Our next stop is the medical center."

The large group of executives began to file out the door that was indicated. George turned around and motioned for Thalia to follow. She turned away from the glass and walked towards her father but then stopped. She quickly ran back to the glass and waved her hand at 117. Down below she saw him look back up at her and tilt his head. The woman standing next to him also turned to look up and began to wave to Thalia. Thalia then saw her nudge 117 in the side and then he also began to imitate her. Having successfully signaling her farewell, she then turned her back on the glass for the second time and ran over to her father. The two of them left the room and then followed the line of waiting executives to the next section of the facility.

*   *   *
** ** **

Present Day
Classroom 312

Mandy hit the pause button and the video stopped. Sarah looked up from her screen with a blank look. Evidently, it was time for a little bit of commentary.

"Is there something wrong Mrs. Mandy?" She asked. "That was a video log of you all those years ago wasn't it?"

"It really was wasn't it? A long time ago I mean," Mandy smiled just as she did in the video which caught the attention of Sarah who recognized the similarities. "Some things still haven't changed either in the present. That's why I stopped for a bit. Do you notice anything that caught your eye for a bit? So far?"

"This lesson focuses mostly on amborg 117 like you mentioned previously," Sarah said observingly, "But I fail to understand. You also clarified before the presentation that he was the first amborg you paired with. That is common knowledge to everyone. Why show the footage of your first meeting during the selection?"

"Because you just had the opportunity to see what you've heard about all this time," Mandy smirked. "Tell me something Sarah. What is the difference between hearing stories about someone versus being there to actually see it happening?"

"Wouldn't the experience of being there as a full on witness increase the genuine feeling of what really happened? Exaggeration of certain details is a variable that occurs when one tells a story which mostly results in a very inaccurate repetitive deal of misunderstandings."

"Yes absolutely."

Mandy scrolled the video back a bit and it showed the picture of her shaking hands with 117. She looked happy and very enthusiastic but the same couldn't be said for 117. Sarah looked at his confused and innocent looking expression and began to see what Mandy was trying to teach her.

"He was helpless wasn't he?" She said presumptuously.

"Not entirely," Mandy corrected her. "I would say he was a little lost when I first met him. You see, all the records portray his accomplishments. His profile tells you all about his personality and what he's like. But when you see him interacting or even speaking. You get another piece of the puzzle that makes him... him."

"When you first met him, was he not living to your expectations?"

"Actually, when I first met him, I thought he needed someone to guide him," Mandy replied zooming the picture on 117's face. "It wasn't that he wasn't living to my expectations. It was just the way he acted differently. Oh sure, the Second Group had all the same equipment installed inside their cybernetics but he had this aura about him that just made him stand out to me. To me, it felt like he was stuck in between trying to be an amborg and be himself. Naturally, all the other amborgs had difficulties adjusting and they all coped with it at their own paces. But with 117, I chose him because I felt like he was the one who needed my help specifically. Now do you see why you remind me of him so much?"

"Am I failing the exams in your class Mrs. Mandy?" Sarah asked with a little bit of concern in her voice. She suddenly began to look afraid.

"No of course not," Mandy quickly reassured her, "You're one of the best students in the class. But sometimes you just have that aura that tells me you're a little lost. Caught between your upgrades and your normal life. We don't have technicians paired to amborgs anymore which is a disadvantage with amborgs who have problems. At the same time, they all can cope and so will you. Is that clear Sarah?"

"Yes ma'am," Sarah said with a sigh of relief. "Are we continuing the lesson? I would very much like to proceed to the part of the lesson where you talk about the high school student Brad."

"All in due time Sarah. Commence video log again at the last pause."

The computer chimed once and the video began to play again.

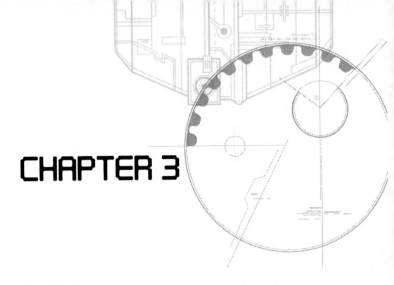

CHAPTER 3

2127: Amborg Industries Gymnasium

"Attention all personnel. Next stage of testing will now commence. All personnel stand clear of the temporary firing range. Next group of amborgs, ready for ballistics testing please."

The gymnasium had been retrofitted for many different uses. The vast room was being used to conduct experiments and physical exercises for the day. Almost all of the amborgs were undergoing multiple tests with their technicians on hand who were evaluating their performance. Practice dummies and sparring bots stood in various spots while a large shooting range occupied one corner. However, instead of dummies or paper targets, the people firing weapons were shooting amborgs. Mandy walked with 117 to one of the shooting stands with an annoyed look on her face. The sight of watching security troops and military inspectors shooting at unarmed people for test results was simply not what she called a good day.

"It's sick what they do to you in order to get results," she pouted as she moved out of the way to let 117 walk down range so he could position himself, "Why on earth do they have to shoot so many firearms at you? I get that all of you are willing to do this but it feels like assisted suicide…"

"Do not be alarmed Ms…"

117 turned his head and saw her glaring at him.

"...Mandy," He quickly corrected. His voice spoke calmly out of her bracelet. "An amborg's exo-skeletal structure is designed to withstand every known weapon in existence from a standard firearm minus a superheated concentrated blast or tactical nuclear explosion. Bombs are also unknown since testing is not the advisable option. It is highly improbable that I will be destroyed from a simple ballistics test."

"You know that's not what I mean David," Mandy called out to him in annoyance as the soldier next to her fired a round from a nine millimeter pistol. The bullet struck 117 right in the forehead but nothing happened

She had covered her ears just in time as the sound went off. Even though there were other guns being fired on the makeshift shooting range, it was too loud for her ears when she stood too close. Mandy looked down the line and saw all the amborgs obediently standing still as bullets plastered them. It wasn't a shooting range, it looked more like a gallery at a carnival.

"I mean from where I'm standing," Mandy called out to 117 and lowered her fingers, "All I can see is a six foot unarmed human being shot at repeatedly. That just seems wrong!"

"But I am not a human Mandy," 117 replied. "I am an amborg but I still am confused how this is still making you feel angry."

This didn't make Mandy feel better at all. She stared at him and made sure he could see her expression clearly.

"I know you are an amborg," She snapped. "But from my own eyes you should be aware that I have concerns about this. You should be able to at least understand the ethical implications and morals currently in place right now. Also you should... HEY!! What do you think you're doing with that?!"

She was now staring hard at the soldier who had just shot at 117. He had switched weapons and had jumped from a small handgun to a really huge rifle. Taken aback, he clenched the fifty caliber sniper rifle and looked from her to 117.

"Following the proper testing procedures miss," He said nervously as he turned to look at Mandy again. "All amborgs need to be tested if they can withstand even our most powerful guns. Those are my orders."

"Well Sergeant," Mandy said angrily. This definitely had crossed the line. "Are you always blindly following orders like this?? Can't you grab some of the material used to make their exo-skeletons and shoot at THAT!?"

From down range, 117 watched, startled as Mandy stared straight into the soldier's eyes. Despite the huge rifle in his hands, she was definitely intimidating him. She pointed at the rifle and then at 117.

"Can't you see how wrong it is to purposely use... that," She said, "That weapon on an innocent looking biologically enhanced human? A fifty caliber would blast a regular person's head off as well as the ones behind them for Christ's sake!!"

"I'm sorry you feel that way, but I'm under orders..."

The sergeant looked at 117 for a minute but then looked back at Mandy.

"It's not like this is the first time I've seen someone else feel this way before," he explained as best as he could while trying to hold his own composure. "AND, it's not like I haven't done this only once. I've fired every known firearm they've given me and these amborgs take it. No emotion, no damage, no nothing. Of course it's wrong to do it just for test results but they can withstand it."

"Did you hear what you just said?" Mandy asked. Unfazed, she stared hard at him and shouted, "They aren't playthings for the military that you can abuse!"

Other soldiers along the firing line lowered their weapons and were now listening to the argument. Although her gaze did not stray, Mandy could tell that several of the amborgs were beginning to pay attention to her. 117 continued to stare. Out of his peripherals, he saw 297, 57, 92, and 93 stop their two ton medicine ball exercises. All of them stared curiously.

"Get Kendrick here and he'd agree," Mandy continued very sternly. "Frankly I don't know why he authorized this sort of thing but they aren't just machines, not entirely, they are humans who are changed. You still need to treat them normally and equally. They should not be labeled as livestock for slaughter."

On one part of the gym, amborg 999 stopped doing pushups and looked up as well. Her spotter, amborg 917 placed a hand to steady the cargo container she had on her back and they stopped mid exercise to watch as well. Several first group amborgs stopped their track relay activities and allowed the weights they were carrying fall to the ground with a clatter.

The soldier took a breath, and then looked at 117, who remained silent. All of the amborgs being tested on the shooting range stared from each other, wondering what to do. Finally the soldier turned back to Mandy.

"Well what would you have me do?" He asked politely. "If I don't do my job, well I'm screwed. I have orders. I hate having someone yell at me unless it's my C.O. What can I do?"

"Ask him."

"What?"

"Ask him how he feels," Mandy repeated. "Before you take the next shot, you ask him how he feels about getting shot at without trying to avoid or dodge the bullet like the matrix. Get his permission and make sure he's ok with it. Go on," She said enunciating the last few words, "Ask David what's it's like to be a target for the rest of his life."

Baffled by her request, the sergeant lowered his rifle and turned to face 117. The recent turn of events was now being watched by everyone in the gym. The technicians and regular personnel had forgotten about the tests and were wondering what would happen next. Placing the rifle on the stand, the barrel was aimed down range at 117 but before he leaned forward and put his eyes to the scope, the sergeant stood straight and called out to 117.

"Amborg 117," he said respectfully, "Permission to discharge a fifty caliber rifle round for ballistics testing? Is it ok?"

117 stared back with a little twitch in his head. After a brief pause, a response came through, out of both Mandy's and the Sergeant's bracelet.

"Permission to proceed, granted," 117 nodded. "You may fire when ready Sergeant."

The soldier turned to look at Mandy for confirmation who reluctantly but silently nodded. He leaned forward and leaned his shoulder into the rifle butt while she lifted her fingers again to her ears again to prepare for the noise. Taking a deep breath, he looked through the scope, down the sights, and took careful aim. The safety was switched off and he pulled the trigger after a few seconds.

The shot rang out through the entire gymnasium like cannon fire. It seemed louder now that everyone wasn't going about their own business. The bullet instantly struck 117 directly in the chest and created a giant puff of smoke. The force of the impact caused him to bend a couple of inches forward and Mandy saw him get pushed back a couple of feet from the impact. With the smoke dissipating, all that remained was a blast mark all over his A.I. Industries jacket. Looking carefully, Mandy saw a hole next to where 117's heart was but it didn't look like he was hurt too badly. The sergeant switched the safety back on, lowered the rifle and he called for a ceasefire even though no one else was shooting. He walked over to 117 who was straightening up from the force of the bullet.

"Are you all right?"

117 looked at the ground and then looked up at the sergeant as if nothing had happened.

"Damage assessment; Struck by fifty caliber sniper round at a velocity of three thousand feet per second," He recited slowly, "Force of impact at twenty-three thousand four hundred and thirty two pounds. The impact has pushed me back roughly three inches from where I was originally positioned. Structural and circuitry undamaged. All systems functioning within the proper parameters."

"Next time, just say you're fine," The sergeant smiled and then walked back to the firing line.

Everyone else then began to go back to their own business. As noise flooded the gym again, Mandy walked up to 117.

"You should always have your own voice David, always," She said, "Don't let anyone take your right to defend yourself away from you. You're not a complete machine that just runs entirely from your programming. You have feelings too. I want you to use them."

"Have I offended you Mandy?" 117 asked with concern.

"No it's all right David, I shouldn't have yelled," She explained as she led him towards another part of the gym. The next amborg who came up after 117 moved downrange and she heard the sergeant ask them for permission before readying the next test which made her feel better. "By the way, when he asked you for permission, did you really think about your answer?"

"Of course Mandy, after hearing your discussion, I took all of the factors into contemplation. The alloy that all amborgs are made of, the maker and designer of the rifle, the amount of force that I could expect from the bullet, the soldier's previous records, your tone of voice, and Dr. Kendrick's reports on all of the test subjects. This is only the first of a few factors I thought of before reaching my decision."

"How long did it take for you think of all that?"

"About three point seven two seconds," he replied, "And that, is a long time for any amborg."

"Hey 117!" 917 transmitted a message. "You want to do some pushups? 999 says she's done and will let you have a turn with the cargo container."

"You still need to finish your physical test on the relay race too," 297 added as he ran by.

117 looked at Mandy who sighed and eventually, she gradually gave him a smile.

"Go finish what you need to do," She replied. "Don't keep your family waiting."

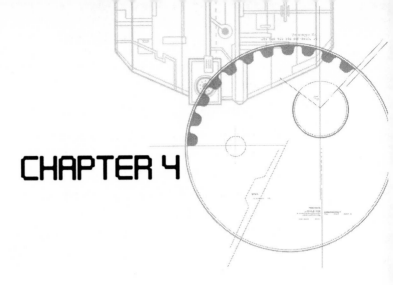

CHAPTER 4

2127 September
Los Angeles, California

"Attention, amborg deployment requested by many officials of the Los Angeles urban districts. Multiple gang-related activity reported. Local police forces unable to contain and military response time has been delayed. All amborgs stand by. Emergency Status."

117 sat inside his deployment pod and gazed out the window briefly. There were a few clouds but he could see the columns of smoke along the skyline as he listened to the computer's initial pre-deployment scenario briefing. His memories of his old home were blurry but he knew that this was the type of setting that he had struggled for his very life before Dr. Kendrick had found him. Now here he was, getting ready to step back out in the world for the first time as an amborg, saving innocent people caught in the crossfire. As the briefing ended, Mandy's voice spoke in the back of his head.

"Ready for your first operation David?" She asked loud and clear. "I suppose it's technically our first operation together. But luckily you get to do the heavy lifting and I've got my coffee back here in my cubicle."

"Isn't questioning my readiness redundant?" 117 answered as he tilted his head. "I have been ready for this and am operating under normal parameters. I predict many positive outcomes as well."

"David, just say you're ready..." Mandy mumbled bitterly. "I'm already nervous enough."

"Did I say something to make you nervous?"

"Obviously yes 117," Mandy answered as the pod's thrusters activated and he felt the speed dropping. "It looks like both of us are asking redundant questions today."

There was a loud kroom as the pod touched down on the ground. The door clamps hissed and unlocked allowing the door to swing outwards. 117's harness automatically came undone and he leaped out. Landing on his feet, he looked around and surveyed the immediate area.

His landing zone was in the middle of a parking lot with a few vehicles. Taking particular note of a group of children playing on the wreckage of a destroyed car, he nodded and waved a hand at their stunned faces. 117 stepped forward and transmitted a signal to his pod.

The engines roared and with a loud burst of flames, it flew up just like a rocket and shot off back into the air. 117 watched it shoot out of sight before beginning his walk. His HUD, which was on almost all the time began to chime and suddenly, Mandy's face appeared in the upper right corner of his display signaling a phone call.

"Alright David," She said, "Checking your sensory data. Eyesight, hearing, taste... Well only if you actually eat some food. Uhh, implants are running really well since your last checkup. Primary CPU and main functions are green. Perfect as usual. Sensor and GPS are running right... about... now. Sound systems, video connection is streaming. Great graphics. I now see what you see. A set of eyes and voice in the back of your head. Standard procedure says I have to ask this even though it's obvious... Can you hear me?"

"I am reading your communication line loud and clear Mandy," 117 replied, "All systems are green."

"Oh good," Mandy replied, "I was afraid I'd have to check the volume control."

"Sarcasm is still not my strongest suit," 117 replied in his neutral tone. He looked around and didn't see anything suspicious so he continued walking. "What is my current objective?"

"Ok David, here's what's up," Mandy said informatively. "Heavy assaults from gangs all over the West Coast are flooding in like crazy. Los Angeles is one of the worst places to be living in right now. A lot of violence and outbreaks have been happening over the last few months. The precincts here and in a lot of the major cities have requested more amborg deployments than usual to help calm the situation which leads to more bad news."

"That totals over one hundred cities," 117 calculated really fast as he turned a corner. He could hear several shots now as he progressed slowly and gave his conclusion. "There aren't enough amborgs to respond to so many deployment requests."

"That's right David," Mandy replied grimly, "Which is also why you're even being deployed today instead of one month from now. It's so bad that Dr. Kendrick authorized the release of the Second Group early even with the First Group working overtime. But it also might mean we'll be sharing that same workload soon. So far, the First Group is scattered up in Washington and Oregon but if we're lucky, you might encounter a veteran amborg who finds time to kill. Until that happens, we take care of California which is the state that has the highest record of amborg deployments so far. Hopefully that's not too intimidating or stereotypical. It's actually not an entirely bad place to live."

117 came to another corner and looked around it cautiously. The street was deserted, possibly because people were hiding in the safety of their homes or had already evacuated. He could hear loud speakers coming over thirty meters to the northwest blaring out a series of alarms. From what he knew from the city emergency plans, the broadcast alarms were signaling for the people to remain out of sight.

From A.I. Industries, tons of information was being uploaded to 117's HUD from Mandy's computer system. She was rapidly typing the keys on her keyboard like there was no tomorrow. Tons of information was being entered into her system and being displayed from 117 in perfect synchronization.

"Who is it that I am seeking out Mandy?" 117 asked as he spotted his destination.

"Calm down you walking GPS," she replied with a chuckle. "I'm getting to that. I got a ton of stuff to go through and the cops are really flooding the com-lines. They really need your help and it's my job to prioritize where to send you. You're looking for the chief of the precinct. Dr. Kendrick wants you to report to her before you go running around."

"What is your assessment of this operation?" He asked as he scanned the area in front of the police station. Seeing no one around, which puzzled him, he walked up the steps to the entrance which was badly boarded up. "How is my current performance?"

"Well you've been deployed to Los Angeles for your very first op," Mandy said with slight discomfort. "Sending you out will be good experience for you. You're doing fine so far David. Watch the ceiling."

117 looked up and stepped aside as one of the ceiling tiles fell down. It broke and shattered across the ground next to him. Suddenly, he was now aware of all the bullet holes and make-shift barricades sitting in the middle of the entrance hall. Mandy chuckled from the back of his head.

"Wouldn't want a decapitation by tile now would we?" She said, "Now let's see, according to these files, the chief's name is Captain Jennifer Bradley. Wow, she's got quite a rep. Apparently she's been dealing with a gang called the Splatter-Bugs, how original, for the last five years so I'm assuming she'll tell you where to go to take on these guys. If you ask me, she'd probably give us the worst part of the mission to take care of. Ha ha. Oh shit. There goes my coffee."

117 heard the sound of what apparently was a mug falling over on a desk in his head. Disregarding the noise, he kept walking.

"Hmm," He muttered as he looked around, "Shit. A slang term and noun for feces or a contemptible worthless person, object, or thing. Where do you see shit Mandy? I cannot identify anything in the area to associate with that term. A rag would also be sufficient in wiping up the mess."

"That's not what I meant David," Mandy stammered, "Ouch! That's hot! Oh never mind. Just go find the Chief."

Several police officers looked his way when 117 walked in. But things were so hectic, they ignored him and promptly went about their business. Every single officer was walking around with body armor which caught his attention. Nevertheless, he walked down the aisle through the middle of all the chaos while everyone was scrambling around. Despite there being so many empty desks, it seemed like there was already enough people running around to fill the whole room including damaged police drones. Phones were ringing, people were shouting and sirens were blaring from the garage which sounded like it was one floor below. To a normal human, 117 was amazed anyone could hear each other through all of this. He promptly switched his hearing to mute out the noise and continued his search for the Chief's office but it was rather difficult with all of the doors missing off of several offices. But as he walked by one, he could hear a woman shouting.

"I don't care if it's dangerous! I was born in the middle of this, raised by this municipality, molded and devoted to keep fighting! I've been in the field against orders because for the last week, there hasn't been any time for any of us to stop the damn raids all over the precinct because I keep getting a whole bunch of academy noobs who've barely graduated with average skills who get their heads shot off after being here for only a couple of hours. Participating in the streets with my men and women is risky but I'd rather lead my officers instead of in my office. Stop telling me a lucky crook is going to get me because of my recklessness. I'd like to see them try! I had one woman show up who survived at least a week and then I learned her name properly but that went south because we lost her twenty two minutes ago! So you'll excuse my attitude and my disregard for your orders but I have to be on the streets three minutes ago to make sure I don't lose another one of L.A's finest! Excuse me while I try to save city hall which I still think is on fire!"

There was a loud slam as 117 heard someone's hand slamming down on what he assumed was the phone or what was left of one at least in this place. He looked at the office without a door and looked inside. He immediately knew he was in the right place when he saw the name Chief Jennifer Bradley badly smeared and printed in black ink on the side of the wall. It almost looked like someone had crudely dipped their fingers in ink and painted it on without the brush. The name was written just above a destroyed bulletin board which 117 noticed had a lot of requisition orders for several miscellaneous items including a new door, new wall, new stationary, and more jars of black ink. His attention then drifted over to the middle aged woman standing over her desk or rather, what was left of it, who looked up at the doorway.

"Well FINALLY!" She shouted. "Look who's finally here!"

Forcing a lot of sarcasm and joy into her voice was immediately detected by 117 who stared completely bewildered at her appearance. She was wearing body armor just like the officers outside but there was a bandage on her right cheek. Her left cheek was covered in black ink as well as her hands and there were several holes in her shoulder sleeves from either being too badly torn or from what looked like fire damage. 117 only had time to speculate about what this woman had been through when she marched around her desk and made a very big welcoming gesture.

"You'll have to pardon the blown up door," Chief Bradley said with a very angry look, "A Splatter-bug raid is what we have to thank for no privacy nowadays. Can I get you anything? How about some motor oil or whatever you guys eat? Come in, come in and take a break! God knows I haven't lost any more people while you've been casually strolling to get here!"

Taken aback by the questions the chief was asking, 117 quickly linked his CPU to her bracelet before she could comment about why he hadn't said a word yet.

"I do not require anything Chief Bradley," He said hoping that this would pacify her apparent rage. Seeing that it wasn't working, he quickly continued to talk. "It was my understanding that you requested an amborg and you needed tactical support. Have we misinterpreted your request?"

From the back of his head, he heard a slap and a groan from Mandy. He briefly looked at the upper corner of his HUD and realized that Mandy was still on the line. From what he could tell from the slap, he concluded that Mandy had done a face palm. Chief Bradley didn't look pleased as well.

"No shit wise-guy," She said growling under her breath. 117 detected sarcasm again and listened without saying another word. "I sent that request an hour ago for crying out loud! What'd you do, stop for drive-through?! Shut up. I don't want to know. Come here, look at this map, and let me show you where you can be useful!"

He silently followed her over to the wall where a holo-map was shining. However it was sputtering and barely able to maintain its image. To fix it, Chief Bradley slammed her fist into the side and then the image cleared up. It showed the area around the precinct and there were several red dots blinking. As 117 observed the dots, he privately sent Mandy a message.

"Have I offended the police chief Mandy?"

"No David, she's just stressed," Mandy replied reassuringly. "Women at her age can get really tough when they're pushed especially with what she's been through. But she's fairly tough based on what I can tell about her initially and her records. Just follow her instructions and don't worry about it. You'll learn how to interact with tough people soon enough. But I definitely don't think she likes it when you ask rhetorical or dumb questions. Be more direct and don't let her catch you saying anything stupid."

"Hey tin head! Bring whatever's going on in your head back to now!"

Switching his attention away from Mandy, 117 immediately turned back to the chief and perused the map casually for the third time.

"Where is my presence required?"

"Right here, bozo!" She said extending a finger and pointing it at a location on the map which was at least a few miles north of the station. "Splatter-bugs have got this area pinned down from the north, a couple civvies down, five of my men wounded and two of my nut-jobs are taking on a whole goddamn mob with low ammo three blocks east from that position. If we try to move in to help, we get sent back with more people hurt or killed. Some officers and emergency crews have set up a barricade here but they can't hold. Every block we take, I lose good men and women and... Where do you think you're going?"

117 was already heading to the door before she had even finished.

"Situation understood," He said, "I'll handle it. Or as humans say, I got this."

"Wait a minute," Bradley called following 117 out of her office and waved her hand to signal someone. "Take Sergeant Johnson here with you, he's fairly new but he needs experience either way. I'd rather he be fighting with an amborg rather than get killed with another newbie they send my way."

A young officer wearing a safety vest with two pairs of assault rifles ran up as she said this. One of the rifles slipped out of his hand and fell to the ground with a clatter.

"That is..." Bradley said shaking her head, "If his own stupidity doesn't get himself killed."

We are both new at this, 117 thought silently as Johnson struggled to pick up the other rifle.

"Anyway, he'll do the job right, I hope," The Chief said when Johnson straightened up, placed the rifles on another desk and smiled which didn't reassure her feelings at all. "But... While you're here, try to keep him and everyone else alive. That's asking a lot but I'm sick of seeing too many new faces and writing anymore condolence letters. Johnson, I want you back here by tonight."

"Yes ma'am," The young officer replied.

"It's Captain."

Chief Bradley nodded grimly and gave a thumbs-up to 117 who dipped his head in acknowledgement. With that, she walked off down the hall, snatching a shot-gun from a nearby desk and was immediately flanked by another pair of officers. Left alone, 117 and Johnson weaved their way outside and found themselves outside on the streets again. Finding north, the two of them began to run at a slight pace. Seeing that Johnson was struggling to keep up, 117 slowed down to keep the same speed as him.

"Sorry we don't have a vehicle," Johnson panted as he struggled to maintain a good pace. "But with the way things are, all of the vehicles have been destroyed or already been put to use."

117 was perfectly alright with running to his destination. Although he had concerns as to why Johnson was having trouble to run. He should be fresh from the academy so his physical training should be up to date, he thought.

"Not a problem Sergeant," He replied linking up to Johnson's bracelet, "But I am amazed that you are struggling to maintain a pace when police academy training does put emphasis on endurance and physical training."

"Oh well that's because of how fast they've been rushing us out into the field," Johnson explained in between breaths of air. "To be honest, I was only halfway finished with school when I was sent back to L.A. The whole time I was at the academy, what we should have learned in the classrooms was instead devoted to training for field operations. It's almost like they were teaching us to skip all the legal stuff and just wanted us to kill the criminals because there are too many to arrest. Besides, I hate running even though they had us do a ton of miles at the track. It's funny, even after all the intensity at the Police Academy, nothing could ever prepare you for this."

"Perfectly natural feelings," 117 stated observingly, "Especially since both of us are participating in our first mission."

"Actually, this is my second, hey slowdown will you?"

Johnson's voice sounded so frantic that they stopped at a corner so he could take a break. 117 scanned the area and listened to all the background noise. Shots rang out, ambulance and police sirens were blaring in the distance and the shouts of people were in the air. But despite all of what was heard, Johnson still felt optimistic.

"My first mission," He said slowly to 117, "It was with… amborg number… 5. Do you know him? We had a bunch of units driving on a raid that time and he rode on top of the police car like it was nothing."

"I have only heard of his exploits," 117 admitted. "Never met him before."

Many of the First Group Amborgs had already done a great deal of accomplishments while he had still been recovering from cybernetic enhancement. Before 117's initial training, several amborgs had amazing reputations that was often discussed by many A.I. Industries staff. But with so many distress calls, they were often away for long periods of time. They only returned when they needed to recharge their implants and equipment.

"The amborgs don't really have a lot of time to interact with each other except for when we collaborate about our mission reports," 117 explained. "Because of how many amborgs there currently are, we are limited from many social activities most humans typically participate in. Although we are kept away from each other, we are always busy helping around in places where we are needed."

"That's pretty amazing," Astounded, Johnson stared in awe at 117. "I bet you guys wouldn't mind a vacation anytime soon though right? It must get tiring doing what you do all the time."

"We do not have vacations," 117 said with a puzzled look. "If we are not in the field, we spend time recharging our energy levels and working nonstop."

"But that's pretty unhealthy even if you're only part-human," Johnson stated bluntly, "I'm all human and already wish I was on vacation instead of a place like here."

"Your feelings are precisely what we were built for," 117 replied. "So your fear of death can be alleviated."

"Well, if you're ever in L.A. more often, then we need to teach you how to relax."

* * *

They arrived at a makeshift barricade and found a crude but small tent which 117 saw was a triage center based on the torn Red Cross on the side of the canvas. It was sitting behind the wrecks of several destroyed cars piled on top of one another making a perfect barricade from all the flying bullets. 117 peered briefly into the flaps of the tent and saw paramedics helping a group of civilians. But there didn't seem to be any other officers guarding the wounded. He now understood Captain Bradley's dilemma from when they first met. Innocent lives risking it all with virtually no help.

Automatic fire filled the air along with the shouts coming from police, the EMTs, families, and possible gang members. At least his noise filter was working. 117 immediately knew his first task. He ran to the edge of the barricade and looked around the corner. As he did so, he felt someone bump into his back which meant that Johnson had followed.

"Sergeant Johnson," 117 looked forward only to withdraw his head when bullets began to strike at his cover. "I can hear four civilians trapped down the street. If you look over my right shoulder, they are on the other side of the road behind that wreckage. They are being suppressed by gunfire twelve meters in that direction. We need to pull them back behind this area."

117 felt a hand on his shoulder. Johnson stared at where he was pointing and then ducked down.

"You're nuts! How am I supposed to get over there? I mean, I know you're bulletproof and I can hide behind you to get there but you can't block all the bullets with four people behind you coming back," Johnson looked in disbelief at the ground between the barricade and the trapped civilians. "What if after we got over there then I lay down some suppressing fire and give you cover?"

117 however had ran back up the street as Johnson took a peek down the road. He grabbed a car, flipped it onto its side and lifted it over to the gap in the barricade. Johnson stared as 117 jogged back with the wreck as if it was paper.

"It would possibly be more ideal if I cover you Sergeant, there are too many weapons firing at us and you would hardly be able to shoot anything," He said preparing to take the car out into the open. "I will use this as a shield and draw their fire. You make sure no one strays into the line of fire."

"Oh right, we can do that," Johnson said. The lack of effort from carrying the car had him in a daze but he snapped out of it and waited for 117's signal. Suddenly, another flash from Johnson's bracelet spoke 117's next command.

"Walk with me."

The instant they stepped out into the open, the car-shield was instantly struck with multiple bullets. 117 knew that the top was being shredded to pieces but it didn't matter. They eventually made it to the trapped civilians and 117 held the car in place while Johnson began rounding up the terrified people. Johnson immediately urged them to their feet and soon, they all huddled around 117. Checking to make sure there was no one else, Johnson tapped 117 on the back.

"Ready!" He shouted and 117 nodded.

At the signal, he lifted the car slightly and they all began making their way back. The trip back seemed longer since 117 carried the car as slowly as he could to prevent the people behind him from falling back too far. Johnson made sure all the civilians stayed centered around 117 away from the edges of the car. Once they were safe behind the barricade, some of the paramedics escorted them to the triage tent and 117 lowered the shield and carried it back to where he picked it up. Johnson looked at the car and could see the damage. The entire top had been shredded all the way down to the chassis. All that was left were wheels, and a couple of seats.

"Man I hope that guy's insured," He joked as 117 lowered the car. But before it touched the road, there was a slight snap as 117's arms shot up with a piece of metal in his hands and the wreck slammed into the ground.

"Insurance accommodation for bullets. I doubt they cover this much damage," 117 said as he threw the piece of metal away. Johnson opened his mouth but then closed it and stared.

"I'm only guessing," 117 said when he noticed the young officer staring with a questioning look.

"Right," Johnson replied in a concerned voice. "I'll take your word for it. Hey where are you going?"

117 turned to look back.

"Defend the area and protect the civilians," He ordered, "I am proceeding to support the cut-off officers. Once I have ensured their safety, I will send them here to support you. Are you there Mandy?"

"What's up David?" Mandy's voice spoke up as 117 continued walking. Johnson, immediately heeding his order, ran off and was beginning to help around the safe-zone. "Wow, they really tore that guy's car apart. You got any more footage for me to watch?"

"My eyes are recording and broadcasting live Mandy," 117 pointed out as he walked east down another street. "You should be able to see what I see."

"I know David," Mandy sighed, "Just pretending to be lazy. So far, your broadcasts don't show anything out of the ordinary. I was just not talking to let you develop your social skills with Johnson. It was nice to see you getting along with someone without me speaking in your head."

"Am I improving?"

A couple of bullets struck 117 in the shoulder but he shrugged them off casually and kept walking. Mandy chuckled and then spoke to him calmly.

"Socially? I'd say yes," She said. "But dodge the bullets at least. You can't let your reflexes get sloppy while learning how to develop people skills."

"Understood," 117 nodded, "Send calls for back-up to arrive at this location, multiple civilians unprotected, and we need transports to pick these people up."

"Roger that David," Mandy replied, "Oh by the way, 43's tech just notified me. She's in the area if you need or want some help."

"I am fine Mandy," 117 responded, "Unless if 43 wants to help. Then I have no objection."

⁎⁎ ⁎⁎ ⁎⁎

Several blocks away.

"I NEED BACKUP NOW!! DO YOU HEAR?! MULTIPLE SPLATTERBUGS!! IT'S JUST TWO OF US!! CAN ANYONE RECEIVE?!"

"We copy Harrison but right now there's no one to spare! If you can hold for a few more minutes, we'll get you help ASAP. What's the situation now?"

"Can you hear the noise and the intensity of my voice? I already told you about the situation!" Harrison shouted in disbelief. He looked over his cover, took aim and fired a few rounds. "It's EXTREMELY HOSTILE you idiot! We cannot wait a few minutes! Hello?! ANYONE THERE?!"

A bullet suddenly struck Harrison's radio barely missing his flesh. The shot had destroyed the frequency selector and whip antenna. All that came out was static from the receiver now. Furious, he ducked down and ran back to his colleague who was desperately checking his pockets. Several more bullets began crashing down on them as they huddled together.

"Harrison, I'm almost out," his partner panted peering over the hood of the squad car, "I got one round in the pipe, and seven in the mag. How much you got?"

"One full clip left and my revolver," Harrison took aim through the window of the car and pulled the trigger but it merely clicked and failed to fire.

"Crap! My guns jammed!" Harrison threw his gun down and took his revolver out of a secondary holster in his belt. "Our standard issues are useless! Looks like this is it for us Lewis."

Lewis took a breath to take in the moment and grasp his partner's words. Harrison pulled back on the hammer of his preserved antique and also inhaled deeply.

"Harrison?" He heard his partner say, "Partners to the end. Right Harrison?"

"You kidding?" Harrison said with a smirk, "I always hated you kid."

"Thanks sir," Lewis chuckled as they both lifted their weapons. "You always were an old windbag."

"Always... Now. Lewis. On three ok? One... Two..."

"WAIT!"

Lewis suddenly grabbed Harrison's hand, interrupting the count.

"What's wrong?"

"Is it one...two...three and then we jump out?" Lewis asked with a very confused face. "Or do we jump out on three?"

"Does it matter?" Harrison stared at his partner in disbelief but suddenly realized how serious he was so he quickly dropped the question and said, "We'll count to three and then jump out."

"Oh ok... Thanks."

"You're welcome. Now...Together...One...Two..."

"Wait!"

Harrison flinched but managed to stop himself from leaping out for the second time.

"What now?!"

Lewis pointed at the silver revolver in Harrison's hand.

"When did you get that?" He asked curiously. "I have never seen you with that before."

Harrison rolled his eyes. "I got it from my old man damn it! Still works perfectly. Now will you shut up and let us do this?"

"Ok got it."

"Ready?" Harrison double-checked nervously. "I swear to god, I almost want these gangsters to shoot me... Or blow me up before you at least."

Lewis shrugged once, thought silently for a moment but then nodded. Harrison didn't count but continued to stare at his partner as more bullets struck their car. Lewis nodded once, paused, then nodded again but then stopped to think again. In his mind, Harrison was already unsure if he wanted to die with such a mediocre partner. Finally, Lewis nodded much more firmly for the third time and then Harrison prepared to give the count again.

"One...Two...Three!"

The two of them jumped out from behind the squad car giving off the loudest war cry they could muster. Just as Harrison managed to fire one shot out of his six-shooter, many more shots rang out.

Someone had opened fire with an automatic rifle from a distance. Instantly, many of the figures in the two officer's sights began to drop to the ground. To both of their surprise, all of the splatter-bugs they saw were falling to the ground either screaming or dead silent. After a few seconds, the two of them stepped out even further from their cover to observe the mess.

"WHOA," Lewis exclaimed in awe, "Did you do that? What kind of ammo was that? Nice shooting."

"I only fired one shot..." Harrison shook his head slightly. He eyed his revolver curiously and at the bodies sprawled across the street, "That... was definitely not me..."

"What's that up there?" Lewis pointed up at the top of the nearest building and then grinned, "Oh hey! It looks like our back-up came."

Both of them gazed at the figure at the top of the building. Instantly, it jumped and fell three stories and landed on both feet in front of them. He landed with an almighty thud, creating giant cracks in the street,. Both officers stared dumbstruck at what they saw. Lewis' smile disappeared and his mouth fell open.

"Uhh, Lewis, I think our back-up, isn't human..." Harrison said to his partner who closed his mouth but still stared wide-eyed at their savior. "It's an amborg."

The cyborg stood up and they could see the number printed on his jacket. His number was 117. It... He straightened up and walked over to the pair and linked up with their bracelets.

"What is the current situation?" His voice spoke but neither of the two officers answered. Finally Harrison spoke up when Lewis only stammered. The amborg then turned away with a focused look and then turned his head to acknowledge the officers again.

"My apologies," 117 said. "My technician was just privately informing me of my lack of manners. I forgot to introduce myself. I am amborg 117."

"Oh uhh well, I'm Harrison," Harrison then pointed at his partner. "And this is Lewis. Nice to meet you. Always a pleasure meeting you upgraded kids."

"Introductions aside," 117 continued, "What is the current situation?"

"Well uhh, we have five wounded, and some dead civilians we didn't get to in time... We weren't able to sweep the area properly for survivors," Harrison reported. He also had forgotten how fast and straight to the point the amborgs usually were. "We got ambushed when we arrived in this area you see. A lot of people here..."

Not taking his gaze off of 117, Lewis finally spoke up.

"Thanks for helping us out," He replied with a relieving sigh, "We owe you big time. Otherwise we probably would be like everyone else."

"You are welcome," 117 replied ignoring Lewis and his awkward remarks. "Both of you are uninjured? I took the liberty of running bio-scans of the two of you but I have been told it is more reassuring to ask directly."

Harrison holstered his revolver and picked up his pistol from where he had dropped it.

"No just a few scratches but we're fine," He said quite comfortably. "Hey you wouldn't mind checking up on my nicotine intake from my bio-scan would you? My wife says I might be dying soon but I keep telling her with all these raids, who has the time to light up. Am I right?"

117 tilted his head and didn't respond. Oh right, Harrison just remembered, they aren't too good with small talk. Before 117 could say anything out of their bracelets, he turned his head sharply and looked to the right.

"Stand firm! Three hostiles still remain," 117 said as he whipped around.

Seconds after 117 pointed this out, there was a gunshot. Instantly, David's arm shot out and held it in front of Harrison's face. At the same time, his other hand reached back and grabbed Lewis' sidearm. Yanking it smoothly from his holster, 117 pointed, and instantly shot off a round immediately in the direction from where the shooter was. Someone in the distance screamed which made Harrison and Lewis' eyes widen. But Harrison wasn't staring at where 117 had shot his partner's gun. He was fixated on 117's hand. Nestled in between his left thumb and forefinger was a bullet. Based on the direction it was facing, it would have gone straight into Harrison's head which made him shudder.

"Correction: Make that two," 117 reported. "One second late and Officer Harrison would not have to worry about dying from smoking anymore."

117 threw the bullet away and handed the gun back to Lewis who took it back with a little apprehension. 117 stared and was puzzled by Harrison and Lewis' expressions.

"That was a joke," He explained to the officers. "Was that poorly timed?"

"No no! It wasn't at all," Harrison stammered after staring blankly at where 117 had cast aside the bullet that almost claimed his life. "I owe you one again it seems. You kids know how to do things with a flair."

"You are welcome again," 117 nodded, "Thank you for the compliment Officer Harrison. Excuse me for a moment. Initiating scan. Completed. Two hostiles are in retreat but the area is secure temporarily. Support units may now proceed to your location. Estimated time to arrival, approximately four minutes. Forgive me for leaving but I am needed elsewhere."

"Leaving already?" Lewis asked nervously. He looked around at all the wrecked buildings as if a python was about to strike suddenly from above.

"I am more efficient with making the city secure if I return to my mission parameters in other parts of unresolved combat zones," 117 said reassuringly. "You are safe Officer Lewis."

"Well thanks again," Harrison said. "Lewis, let's go check on the wounded. Let's get them ready for the paramedics when they get here."

"Got it partner."

Lewis instantly ran off and knelt down by a wounded officer and 117 bid Harrison one last nod before turning away to leave. Suddenly Harrison called out to the amborg's retreating figure.

"Hey wait a moment 117," He called, "You need a weapon?"

"Concern appreciated but unnecessary officer Harrison," 117 smiled, "I am well prepared. Stay safe."

And before Harrison lost sight of him, 117 ran off and was around the corner in seconds.

"Damn," He muttered as he jogged over to Lewis who was checking the pulse on an unconscious officer. "Kids get the best stuff these days."

** ** **

"Next time David... Just say thank you. If someone is trying to offer you help and you refuse it, acknowledge that at least. Don't get cocky."

"Oh. I will try to remember this Mandy."

117 walked into another intersection and stopped. The gunfire was now further away. Checking his GPS and listening to the surrounding environment, he slowly walked forward and tried to scan for the two people he had been tracking. If they escaped, it would be a problem.

"Mandy," He said in his mind, "Requesting second support. Those two hostiles seem to have disappeared."

"On it David," Mandy replied. "Strange, their trail points several meters that way but... wait. I'm picking up something. I can hear something. Filtering it out. It sounds like... DAVID! Incoming!"

Mandy's warning had come too late. 117 managed to hear what sounded like a loud whoosh. Before he could identify what he had heard, he felt something strike his chest and then there was an explosion.

Blasted off his feet, 117 flew backwards and landed on the street. Heat washed over every part of his body but it dissipated rapidly. He blinked once and sat up slowly. His HUD was blaring alarms which he muted. Quickly he assessed the damage. The heat from the explosive had burned and seared his jacket but his endoskeleton structure had successfully protected him.

"David!" He heard Mandy cry. "My screen is scrambled! Answer me! Are you alright?!"

"Diagnostic check initiated," 117 replied as he got to his feet. "An RPG missile launcher. Struck in the upper abdomen at a force of three thousand pounds at a velocity of two hundred and ninety one meters per second. Point of origin located. It would appear that the weapon caused minimal damage."

"Would you please just say you're fine next time David?" Mandy snapped. "Finally, the video feed is restored."

"Perhaps I should have these burn marks examined," 117 said taking note of the hole in his jacket. The skin underneath was badly burned but not causing too much pain. "Permission to retaliate against the hostiles Mandy?"

"Well, I'd be pretty pissed if someone tried to get away with shooting an RPG at me David."

"Noted," 117 nodded, "Engaging hostiles."

He traced the location of the shooter to a building on the corner ahead. The second floor window from where the rocket had been fired was boarded up but he could identify a hole just large enough to shoot through. The gangsters had to have taken careful aim through a hole that size. To do so with such stealth and avoiding my senses is very impressive, 117 thought as he analyzed the footage of what happened. He would have to report about his findings later.

He walked up to the entrance of the hideout and opened the door slowly. From above the floorboards, he could hear two people arguing and frantically attempting to come up with a new plan. From the sound of it that is.

"Aw man," Someone shouted. "It didn't work!! Quick give me another one!"

"That was the last one idiot!" The other one snapped.

"We're in trouble man, how do we stop one of these guys?!"

From below, 117 looked for the stairs to the next floor. At the same time he looked up and did a scan of the room above. Based off their voices and the clattering from upstairs, he identified where the two of them were. Looking up, he scanned the infrared and found them huddled together trying to throw some furniture together. One last fortification for one last stand.

"Perhaps I should have accepted a weapon from Officer Harrison Mandy," 117 said in his mind. "At least I could wound or incapacitate them from down here to avoid walking into a trap."

"True," Mandy replied into his head. "But from what I can hear, they'll probably just scream and make more noise if you shot them from below. You could just walk up and ask them to surrender nicely."

"A very polite plan Mandy," 117 nodded and proceeded to walk towards the stairs.

"No that's not... Oh never mind."

He heard Mandy sigh as he stepped up the stone steps.

"We really need to work on your sarcasm detection when you get back," She groaned as he stepped up to the door. He raised a hand and was about to open it when he suddenly had a thought.

"Mandy, I am noticing a slight problem," He said.

"What is it?"

"Only law enforcement officials, military personnel and employees of Amborg Industries are equipped with the bracelets for how amborgs communicate."

There was a pause and then Mandy responded.

"Why is that important right now?" She said impatiently. "I keep telling you to tell me things before you go out into the field. You might want to take care of those guys before we discuss what's going on in your mind David."

"Sometimes certain issues only become relevant when it is happening in the present," 117 said observantly. "But the right thing to do is offer the enemy a chance to surrender. You did say so yourself earlier when suggested I directly walk up to them and ask. I can walk but I cannot ask them. My vocal chords are useless and there is no way to have you speak for me given the distance between us. Offering the chance to surrender is not possible."

117 paused. His hand was resting on the door but he hadn't moved it. On the other side, it was completely silent.

"Without a bracelet in close vicinity," 117 explained to Mandy, "I cannot, using my voice, ask them to peacefully come in."

"You also need to remember that these people chose this path," Mandy said after a few seconds. "Sometimes refusing to accept the hand of surrender means turning over your life into another's hands and then you hope that they can help you. People don't take that hand because they're afraid and their pride just doesn't want to admit the consequences of their life choices. Some people are beyond redemption."

"But you have taught me that redemption is possible for everyone," 117 stated adamantly, "Everyone or thing deserves help of all forms."

"I did," Mandy sighed in agreement. "But you have to be careful of those who may betray your trust. There's a lot of things you need to consider. So use your own instincts and judgements about what you feel is right. Now go get them. Understood? I definitely think we can talk about this later."

"Understood."

One of the first things that 117 thought of was breaking the door down. However, he felt that it'd be easier to just be polite. He opened the door and stepped inside casually which caused a panic from the occupants of the room. Both of them remained huddled but 117 could see they were carrying what looked like wine bottles. Molotov cocktails, he thought, primitive but effective.

"Ok you stupid amborg," The gangster on the left shouted. "Can you handle the heat?!"

117 lifted both of his hands and motioned them downwards so the two could see clearly. He softened his facial expression and tried to look less aggressive to ease the tension but as he originally thought. The gangsters couldn't understand his silent game of charades.

"What are you doing? What's that mean? Don't play with us! We will burn you! We'll burn this whole building down. If we die, then we die by our own means!"

No one has to die though, 117 thought. Things weren't getting any better so 117 decided to try something different. He opened his mouth and made an attempt to speak. But no words came out. The air that he expelled from his lungs only made a quiet whine which only made the gangsters panic.

"Hey man! Quit messing with us! We aren't afraid of you!"

Sensing that there was no hope for continued negotiations, 117 prepared for their attack. However at that moment though, the wall behind the splatter-bugs blew open and someone else leaped into the room. Panicking, both splatter-bugs turned and threw all four bottles at the arrival who instantly lit up in flames. However, the figure walked in unfazed and with a few punches, sent both of the gangsters flying out the window. 117 immediately saw and picked up a fire extinguisher sitting in the corner and immediately put out the flames on his savior. The flames had burned the clothes slightly but 117 recognized who it was.

"Thanks 117. I didn't know they were armed with Molotov cocktails until after I entered the room. Oh well."

43 patted her shoulders and ran her hands across her arms and wiped her mouth. She looked around and found a broken mirror and inspected herself. The flames had burned her face but she merely shrugged it off.

"It's great to see you," she smiled. Walking up to 117, she looked him over. "We have not had much contact since the selection."

"The feeling is mutual 43, it has been… empty without your optimism and praise," 117 replied warmly. He set down the extinguisher and quickly scanned her. "Your skin has signs of severe burns. Are you all right?"

"I am perfectly fine. Nothing a little trip to the amborg medical center cannot fix," She replied calmly. "Maybe 6 will help and let me keep some burns as battle scars. That will make me look slightly more badass right?"

Laughing she reached up and undid her ponytail. As she straightened her hair and began tying it up in a bun, she looked at 117's wound.

"I think you had more of an experience than I did though," she observed. "What was it? Ah, wait… An RPG?"

She put her hand to his chest and examined the wound. It pretty much spoke for itself from 43's quick analysis. 117 nodded as she finished tying up her hair.

"It was," 117 looked at her uniform, most of it had been burned but could be fixed. Several black marks were all over from where the flames burned but nevertheless, she was indeed acting as if she hadn't even been set on fire, "Why are you here?"

"I was actually right behind you after you saved those two police officers," She explained with a grin. "They could not stop raving when I asked them what happened. About how you swooped in, killed all of the splatter-bugs and saved the day. I am paraphrasing though."

"An overstatement 43," 117 replied with his neutral tone. "The day is not over and one cannot necessarily save a day specifically. Unless the scientific community perfected time travel."

"I made the same observation. Still humorous."

As both of them walked out of the building, 117 couldn't help but notice something different about 43. It had only been a couple of months but she was exhibiting many different patterns of new behavior he hadn't seen before. He linked up his signal to her mind and spoke.

"43," He said, "This might be just a visual malfunction, but I believe your posture and movements have changed. Also your speech pattern has altered slightly. Is this a wrong assumption?"

"I think the phrase is, correct me if I am wrong," She replied. "And yes. Your assumptions are correct. You noticed."

She stopped and turned on the spot in a three hundred sixty degree spin and then stopped to face him after she had done one twirl.

"My technician is the one responsible," 43 winked. "She has been educating me. Or rather, she has and is providing plenty of etiquette and explicit instructions on how to behave as a woman or as a young female teenager progressing to adulthood. Very insightful."

"Oh. Mandy has also been educating me since the selection," 117 said as enthusiastically as he could. "So far she has been repetitiously pestering me in an attempt to teach me to speak normally with decent and a fairly basic vocabulary. Unfortunately it is not succeeding."

"No kidding," Mandy muttered from the back of his head.

"I can tell," 43 said softly. "You always were a strange one 117. Tell me, what do you think of my hair?"

117 took a casual glance and replied.

"Your hairstyle selection is that of what is commonly referred to by humans as a low hair bun. Worn occasionally by women or girls with the appropriate length which some, most, or all of the hair on the head is pulled away from the face, gathered and secured at the back of the head with a hair tie, clip, or other similar device, and allowed to hang freely causing minimal swaying."

"If you like it, 117, just say so," 43 rolled her eyes and placed a hand on her hip.

"I believe I was," 117 said flustered. "Although your ponytail was much better."

"You might be right," 43 nodded and undid her bun. "This was a really fast and crude attempt anyway."

Her hair fell down and then she grabbed her hair band and tied it up. She pulled the ponytail and let it dangle over her right shoulder down her front for 117 to see.

"What do you think?" She asked again. 117 stared and then replied a second time.

"Your new selection is what is commonly referred to as a ponytail. Worn frequently by women or girls which some, most, or all of the hair on the head is pulled away from the face, gathered and secured at the back of the head with a hair tie, clip, or other similar device, and allowed to hang freely from that point. It's resemblance to an actual horse/pony's tail is where the name derives from. In your case 43, the ponytail removes most of the hair from covering or obscuring your facial features. And it also provides you with a high sense of fashion."

"So you included those last two sentences because you prefer this hairstyle?" She asked in an amazed voice. "Wow. I need to wear ponytails more often for you then."

"You appear to have already assimilated proper human speech," 117 said crestfallen. "But while we are on that subject, I will alter my earlier answer. Yes I do like it this way."

"Thank you 117."

As she thanked him, she walked up and kissed him on the cheek. Dumbfounded, he lifted a hand and ran it where her lips had been.

"What was that for?"

"Well, I had two reasons to thank you. One was for the lovely and descriptive compliment," She said as she began walking up the street. "And the second was for putting me out when I was on fire. I had just remembered and wanted to do that. My technician told me a kiss was an acceptable thank you reward for heroism. In some circumstances. I hope it was not disrespectful."

"You are welcome 43..." He stuttered as he transmitted the message to her head. "No disrespect was detected. I am alright with the circumstances."

"You coming along?" She asked. "Chief Bradley still needs us."

117 quickly ran up and walked beside her. At that point, Mandy decided to chime in.

"Well don't mind me," She joked in a very obvious tone of sarcasm. "I'm just in the back of David 117's head being a third wheel along with 43's technician who apparently can get her to learn seduction faster than I can teach 117 how to speak Basic English. Anyway, having fun lover boy?"

"Mandy, were you listening to the whole encounter?" 117 asked nervously. Even though he wasn't human, he could feel the blood rushing to his head. It seemed to burn hotter than the RPG blast.

"Of course David," Mandy scoffed. "I'm your technician. What else am I going to watch and listen to when you're deployed? I think you have more pressing issues beside the fact I'm in your head 117. It looks like someone's got a crush on you."

117 looked up at the sky. He didn't see anything except for clouds and the blue sky above.

"I cannot see anything that might crush me Mandy. Please interpret."

"Basically, she likes you David," Mandy said teasingly into his head. "Looks like her technician is teaching her some very interesting things. Definitely has got you hooked."

"Improbable, there is no chance of attraction. Amborgs don't have feelings," 117 looked at 43 who was a couple steps ahead.

"So explain how there's so much blood flowing to your head. Interesting readings. David, 43 may be an amborg but both of you still have human qualities. You aren't total robots you know. Feelings are bound to pop up. I think it's kinda cute. You two were found together by the good old' doctor, underwent the same procedures together, and... one thing led to another."

"I am uncertain though Mandy," 117 said slowly in his mind. "I cannot determine whether or not I have a similar interest in her."

He began running some serious calculations about the conversations and the relevant data but it wasn't helping. Mandy sighed and then spoke again.

"Ok... well, what do you think of when you look at her?" She asked intellectually.

117 took a quick glance and then formed a statement.

"Her ponytail aforementioned with the description I used earlier. Her posture and her methods of walking are very fluid and very different than when I remember. Now, it seems as if her motion helps her to blend in as a regular woman. She has also adopted the human capacity to smile which also attracted my attention. Among humans, it is an expression denoting pleasure, sociability, happiness, or amusement. . Her speech patterns and her choice of vocabulary has drastically changed. She has progressed to the point where she probably has become close to perfect."

"David, how long did you look at her??"

"1.84 seconds," He reported, checking the time index, "Shall I continue?"

"No thanks 117. You can keep that to yourself."

* * *

From her monitor back at A.I. Industries, Mandy watched as 117 stopped talking and began to run after 43. She could see his built-in radar, GPS tracker, and vitals on her systems just like a regular first person video game only it was through the eyes of another real person. Just as Mandy was about to take a break from the operation briefly, she heard someone enter the cubicle. Frantically, she attempted to straighten everything out as she turned to look at who had dropped in. She became even flustered when she realized it was her boss.

"Oh... hello Dr. Kendrick," She mumbled meekly. "Can I help you? You'll have to pardon the mess. I don't get visitors and well, it's not like there was a routine inspection today."

"That's quite alright," Dr. Kendrick replied with a chuckle as he watched Mandy continue to put things in a straighter format. "I actually came to see how you and David 117 were doing. I always did notice he was a late bloomer in certain fields with his cybernetic upgrades. Any problems whatsoever?"

"So far, I can list several," Mandy sighed as she looked back at the monitor. "The current one being that he clearly likes her and can't talk properly."

"In time Mandy, in time."

Dr. Kendrick looked at the monitor and assessed 117's readings which seemed to be in order. He adjusted his glasses and then patted Mandy on her shoulder.

"You two are a compatible team," He said solemnly. "117 listens to you fairly well so I don't think it'll be long until he gets a good grasp on certain issues."

"Thank you doctor."

As Dr. Kendrick turned to leave, he suddenly stopped and then looked back to ask one more question.

"By the way, how is your fiancée?"

Mandy looked at Dr. Kendrick and then back to her own monitor. She then turned her chair and pulled herself closer to her desk.

"He's fine," She said with a dim expression. "I just haven't heard from him in a few weeks. They haven't sent me a message about his whereabouts yet."

"Will this affect your performance? He's military isn't he?"

There was a large sigh as Mandy looked from the monitor back to Dr. Kendrick who still had his back to her.

"No," She stated firmly. "I understood the risks of making that kind of attachment with him when he was called to duty. There are many different kinds of things that are bound to happen. And I know in my heart that I have prepared myself for the worst. So I will not let it get in the way of my job and with 117."

"I'll take your word for it this time Mandy," Dr. Kendrick, "But you should know that no matter what you read about or watch in the films, it won't always prepare you for the worst until it really happens. Take it from someone who knows. Also I have thirteen majors and psychology is one of them. I can tell when someone hides behind words. It's ok to share what's really on your mind. Trust me, it's easier that way. Tell 117 I said that alright?"

"You're the boss," Mandy replied with a smirk. "Please don't psychoanalyze me sir. The amborgs already do that around here."

"I guarantee nothing," Dr. Kendrick winked and then walked out of the cubicle. He shut the door behind him as he left.

"After what you've been through Dr. Kendrick," Mandy silently spoke, "I know exactly what you're talking about."

She then typed into her keyboard and opened a communication channel with 117. A green light flashed in front of the microphone to show that he had picked up the call.

"Ok 117," Mandy said into the tip of the microphone. "Keep this in mind when you get back. I really need to teach you how to talk to women. Now get back in the game. It's not over yet."

117's voice suddenly replied from the speakers.

"What game are you referring to Mandy?"

"Nothing. Just carry out the mission."

"Affirmative."

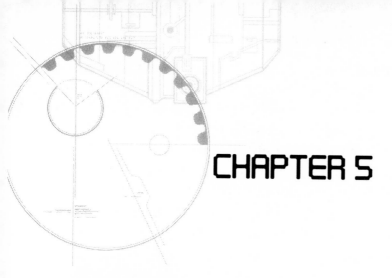

CHAPTER 5

2127, Late November
Several weeks later: Twelve successful operations
A.I. Industries: Amborg Residential Area

It was very quiet and peaceful on the premises which was a first. Whenever she wasn't working, Mandy preferred walking the long way through where the amborgs resided to get back to where she stayed. On any normal weekend, she would usually just breeze past the rooms of the cybernetic teens but this time, she was taking it all in and paying much more attention. Mostly because it was the first weekend in four months she'd actually be returning to her real home off-site for some vacation time. It would be fine unless if world war four started or something.

As she turned into another hall, she looked right outside and saw the main complex across one of the courtyards. Most of the research and development was done there under direct supervision from Dr. Kendrick. Even the amborgs weren't allowed there as well which made it seem ridiculously classified. It would be a long walk to get to the transport pad but Mandy felt she'd rather make a few more turns to pass the time slowly. Part of her wanted to go home and see how it had changed after a few months but she felt more attached here.

"This place is already home enough," She muttered as she clutched the folders she was carrying. "We're all just one big family living in a country house with a lot of toys and jobs to keep us all well-financed and entertained."

"A very astute analogy. May I use that in potential future conversations of interesting subjects?"

Mandy heard the voice come from her bracelet, whipped around and found herself looking up at a familiar face. It was definitely one she was well acquainted with.

"Amborg Johnny 5!" She exclaimed happily. "It's so nice to see you again!"

"It is a pleasure Miss Mandy," 5 nodded cheerfully. The first group amborg smiled pleasantly as her bracelet lit up and recited his thoughts. "Is it not your weekend off? You should be on your way home by now. Unless you really believe that this place is also your home now."

"Well, gratefully I am looking forward to the time off," Mandy shrugged, "But at the same time, there's kind of no point in leaving for two to three days and then be back here. I just wanted to take one long walk before I just plunk down on my bed."

"A trip down memory lane then?" 5 inquired humorously. "Even so, you still seem to be carrying a great deal of work for someone who just ended their shift."

"You won't believe how many reports I've been filing," Mandy slouched. The folders had begun to slip and she needed to readjust her arms to keep them from falling. "I still can't seem to get these done... Are you heading back to your room?"

"Yes I am. I am also participating in the ritual that humans often call down time."

5 looked at the folders briefly before speaking again.

"It is not such a surprise that your reports are enormous," He said. "117 has been accomplishing quite a handful of tasks. You really are an excellent team. However I must go now, I must prepare for a meeting with Dr. Kendrick later after I return to my room first for a charge."

"Thanks 5," Mandy said blushing a little. "117 deserves the credit more than I do though."

"Please," 5 raised a hand. "You both deserve the same amount of credibility for being one of the best teams."

Uttering a quick farewell, 5 disconnected from her bracelet and walked off. Mandy couldn't believe she had bumped into one of the original amborgs. She had met 5 by accident when she first arrived at A.I. Industries and had gotten lost. Luckily a few of the First Group amborgs helped to get her back on track and she got to know a few of them. Normally they kept to themselves or just weren't seen that often by other technicians. It was a total achievement for new personnel just to meet even one of the first ten amborgs.

That wasn't right, Mandy thought. Amborg 3 was one of the first amborgs to pursue an interest in cooking. She always interacted with everyone, human or cybernetic alike. Amborgs 8 and 9 also had a penchant for playing pranks on each other which was witnessed by almost all the employees. Mandy only needed to meet with 1, 2, 4, 6, 7 and 10 to meet the requirements of "The Top Ten" employee achievement which actually was created by members of Dr. Kendrick's staff who have admitted that they don't know all the amborgs personally.

As Mandy tried to remember what the prize was for meeting the first ten amborgs, something caught her eye. Down the passage way, she saw two figures at the other end of what appeared to be a giant memorial. Mandy walked down the hall looking closely and realized they were all a collection of photos. Some holographic but most of the wall was covered by actual pictures. However what got Mandy's attention was the fact that several of the photos had been torn and repaired, burned around the edges, or damaged to the point where you could barely make out the people in the image. It was as if they had been pulled out of a house fire.

The two figures turned out to be amborgs (Ryan) 35 and (Katie) 57 of the Second Group. The same as David, Mandy thought. Although the two amborgs before her were enhanced at the same time as 117, she realized that she never really bothered to learn about them. Deciding that now was the perfect moment to change that, she walked up to them. They looked her way when she had started to walk down the hallway. 57 was the first to link to Mandy's bracelet and 35 followed with his greeting.

"Good evening Miss Mandy," she said, "We were posting additional photographs on the memorial in honor of... our friends."

Before Mandy could reply however, 57 walked off rather fast leaving behind confusion. 35 didn't say anything as well. He mumbled a fast apologetic good-bye and walked away after 57. He stopped, turned to give Mandy a very passive look but resumed his course and walked on. The link from their CPUs terminated and Mandy's bracelet went silent.

"They are mourning, do not feel guilty."

Mandy jumped as her bracelet spoke again. She whipped around and looked up at 117. How he had managed to walk up so quietly was completely beyond her. For the moment, she checked to see if her heart was still pounding.

"David!" Mandy exclaimed as she almost dropped her folders. "Don't do that!"

"Do what?" He asked with an innocent but puzzled expression.

"The sneaking around thing," She replied in a very aggravated tone. "Even when you're home and not deployed, do you guys always have to be silent?"

"It is a part of our nature. Very effective too. 917 believes many of us are possibly descended from ninjas."

Mandy groaned. Obviously, this was something they needed a lot of time to work on. She then looked back the memorial to relieve her anxiety and focused on the picture that she had seen 57 hang up. It was a picture of a teenage girl who bore a striking resemblance to the female amborg she had just encountered. A smile was etched onto the figure in the frame. 117 then spoke out of her bracelet before Mandy could even ask who it was.

"That is 57's sister," 117 stated as Mandy looked deeply at the photo, "I believe she was a year younger than 57. Dr. Kendrick rescued them from the streets of L.A. She did not survive the biological enhancement process. Death occurred one hour into the process. When 57 regained consciousness, her sister was alive for eight minutes. But she has never fully been able to process what happened."

Mandy looked along the wall, all of them had pictures of someone smiling or teenagers with determined looks on their faces. Several more had images of some of the amborgs, before they were changed, with their family members. Others contained children and many other family heirlooms also were displayed. The whole memorial was dedicated to people that were related in some ways to the surviving volunteers that were now amborgs. Mandy then thought of how 35 hadn't said anything and ran off just like 57.

"What about 35?" She asked.

117 pointed at another photo to her right. The photo showed three boys all with their arms around each other's shoulders. 35 was easily recognized in the middle with a wide smile on his face. Another picture taped over it showed a picture of a couple that Mandy assumed was 35's parents.

"His older brother developed a serious and violent reaction to the bio-enhancement," 117 explained. "Dr. Kendrick failed to anticipate this and there was nothing that could be done. We discovered that some of the formulas contained ingredients that he was allergic to. As for the younger brother, he did not survive the plating surgery when his exoskeleton was altered."

Mandy struggled to hold back tears and took a few deep breaths. How? She wondered. How was it possible that with all the technology and the brains that went into this idea, how did so many people who volunteered… how did so many die?

"How do you do it?" She asked 117. "Shutting out feelings like that?"

117 paused briefly and then replied.

"All I can say is, all of the amborgs currently living, not just 35 and 57, work this out as much as we can. Sergeant Johnson once asked me why we never have rest and relaxation. Most of us spend our free time thinking about loss but never delve on it for long. We may never know our true feelings again. What we do remember is everything. For some reason, emotions do not factor. Sorrow, anger, envy, remorse, guilt. Even positive emotions are difficult. We can only imitate every time Dr. Kendrick encourages us to try over and over again. He says our feelings are not shut out, as you say, but we are all working to unlock them again. We aren't necessarily shutting them out. We just have problems working them out."

Mandy, barely understanding a quarter of what he said, nodded in understanding anyway. 117 spoke of emotions as if they were nearly in his grasp but it seemed as if the amborgs could never fully understand emotion anymore. They could only mostly experience it from a cold, hard, new perspective. What was it like to fully devote yourself to become an amborg? When you had nothing to lose? Mandy decided to change the subject.

"Have you lost anyone?" She asked calmly, "Anyone you cared about or knew?"

Mandy looked at 117. His eyes looked down and back at her. She wasn't sure if this was making him sad. Without answering, he pointed at another photo a few feet to the right and Mandy stepped forward to take a closer look. Two people were in the photo, a man and a woman. They looked too old to be amborg test subjects. The couple were holding each other in a joyful embrace and smiling at the camera. Mandy reached out a hand to brush an overlapping picture out of the way when something amazing happened.

The photograph turned into a small video screen and the image moved. The man turned his head and kissed the woman on the cheek making her blush and close her eyes with a smile. It was the only scene that played and then the photo reverted back to the original scene and began replaying. Mandy looked back at 117 who gazed at the moving image with a dazed look. He appeared to be sad but she couldn't tell.

"My parents," 117 explained as they watched the couple embrace each other again. "I have no family left. 43 and I both lost our parents to violence and gang attacks. We both struggled together and kept each other safe. And then, a man strolling along the district with a group of guards saved us while we were begging outside of a café on a bright sunny day. He provided an opportunity for us and gave us the choice for a different life."

"Dr. Kendrick."

"Correct Mandy," 117 nodded, "To this day, I remember being aware that I had nothing left. I do not know how the others felt when they volunteered or when they were offered the same choice as me but when I woke up and knew that things were different, it was a new beginning. I was... happy to see that 43 survived. But we were also both... very quiet when we knew how many didn't survive. We all wish they could have lived in our spare calculations. But now, we stand here alive and we fight for our memories and for them."

The two of them pondered silently and then Mandy decided they should leave. She motioned for 117 to follow and they continued down the hall. Getting to the transport pad had suddenly disappeared completely from Mandy's mind. Soon, they found themselves outside 117's room.

"Would you like to come in?" He asked politely, "A change in atmosphere might prove to be a solution to how you must be feeling."

Mandy blinked, she had never actually seen where David lived. Why not? It's not like her transport was going anywhere anytime soon. She stepped inside and looked around.

It was a simple room. A closet for uniforms and civilian clothing, a computer terminal (HA, computer for a computer, she thought), a circular chamber with 117 written on the glass, a bed, and some other standard furniture. There were also a few photos all over the walls. All in all, it looked perfect and all tidied up.

"Wow. It looks nice," she nodded approvingly, "It looks better than the dump I live in."

"Thank you," 117 sat at the computer which came on automatically, "Please make yourself at home."

He held up his finger and a slot opened up. Mandy sat next to him and stared. 117 put his finger in the slot and the computer screen switched to another screen. A camera opened above the monitor and scanned 117's face. A green light and a beep sounded and the computer unlocked itself and opened to 117's desktop. Moments after the desktop opened, 117 initiated a link to his computer and then began to do something.

"Data transfer complete," The computer responded.

"Data what?" Mandy curiously looked at the screen. "What did you do?"

"5 has been helping me obtain old movie records from the 20th century," 117 said typing a few keys. "There is one in particular that I have taken a liking to."

The computer screen was lighting up and all sorts of images were appearing.

"Do you know the television series, Star Trek: The Next Generation?" 117 asked Mandy.

"I think I have David," She replied thoughtfully. "A famous actor named Patrick Stewart was Captain Picard or something. My dad showed me lots of those old shows from back then. He was really into records and stuff like that. There's actually a lot of stuff that people have forgotten but they really have to see."

"I am very fascinated by the character they refer to as Lieutenant Commander Data," 117 said as he brought up a picture for her to see. "Brent Spiner put on an amazing performance by my understanding. An android completely built to learn from humans. His desire to be like the humans. His observations over the years aboard the Starship Enterprise. In my spare time, I have been trying to monitor and learn by example from him. Star Trek touches on several human issues that is very interesting to watch."

"That's neat David," Mandy suddenly checked the time and stood up to leave, "Listen, I have to get home. I'd love to stay but I really need this weekend. I should have left sooner I guess."

"One moment Mandy," 117 quickly brought up something on the computer. She looked at the screen

A quote had appeared in white letters which said:

Where belief is painful, we are slow to believe. -Ovid

"David, what's that you're looking at?"

"I found a very particular quotation by a long forgotten roman by the name of Ovid."

"Interesting quote," she remarked, "Are you looking up all these things in your spare time? Don't you sleep?"

"Sleep is not required," He replied earnestly, "Can you please assist me in interpreting this?"

Mandy sighed. Who could resist helping a teenage cyborg with the curiosity of an infant?

"Sure, why not? But make it fast."

"Thank you," he said standing up, "Mandy, is it alright for people to develop their own beliefs?"

"Of course it is. It's perfectly alright."

"But Ovid's quotation puzzles me," he looked at the screen with a puzzled look, "If a belief is painful, how does it inflict pain? And how would people be slow to believe?"

Mandy laughed at how literal he had taken the quote.

"David, it's not talking about actual pain," she explained, "At the time, Ovid was saying that new beliefs are hard especially when you're the only one of few who believe in it. Not a lot of people like change, which is why we're slow. At least I think that's what he meant."

"In that case, I have a belief."

"What is it?"

"I wish to be more human," David stared calmly at the photos on the wall, "It is my belief that I can learn to be like a human again with a few cybernetic attachments. Commander Data was a robot built from scratch and he is working to become human. In a way, I feel that as an amborg, I was remade and reborn with the ability to learn all I can and I believe I can be like that."

"Well David," Mandy smiled and placed a hand on his shoulder. "That's something I can believe too. As well as for everyone."

"Did I interpret that correctly?"

"Heh. I don't know David. Hehe, I don't really know."

The door slid open at that moment and (Carter) 297 walked in. As tall as 117, he kept a reserved but strong look on his face. From what Mandy had heard, 297 was another amborg slowly making a name for himself as a fighter and also had a flawless record. He had also been a close friend to David when they first went into service cybernetically. He linked up with Mandy's bracelet so she could hear what he said next.

"117," 297's voice filled the room. "Would you be interested in joining the rest of the 1st and 2nd group for dinner?"

"I didn't know you guys ate food," Mandy interrupted when she heard 297's question. She looked at 297 who shrugged casually. "Well I mean… I've never seen you guys eat anything before."

"On occasion we do," 117 said straightening his jacket, "Again, it is also not a requirement for basic function but the food that numbers 3, 7, 9, and 13 make is excellent for making our olfactory and gustation senses provide nice results for data analysis. If we end up going to a restaurant for food on a mission, for example, undercover, it can provide us with proper camouflage incognito. Many technicians suggested it may help us blend in if we are out for a long period of time."

Mandy was stifling a laugh which confused the two amborgs. Mandy looked from 297 to 117 and could tell they were secretly transmitting a message. Obviously, they had no idea how to respond to the current situation.

"Sorry," She cleared her throat. "I was just laughing because even when you guys try to blend in in public, it doesn't work. I mean sorry, I can still spot you guys from a mile away if you tried to hide in the open."

"Our performance seems to be lacking more than we thought," 297 noted observingly. "Perhaps we need to have another eight hour discussion."

"And next time," Mandy added, "Include some actual humans who know how to teach whatever you discuss during your meetings. Eight hours? Wow you guys have too much time."

"It is our most efficient time for a meeting," 117 stated.

Mandy sighed.

"Well I won't get in the way of that then," She said trying not to burst out in laughter again. "297 will you go on ahead? I have something to ask David."

"Certainly," 297 nodded, "But make it quick, the main course is spaghetti tonight."

Without another word, 297 turned around, disconnected from Mandy's bracelet and then left.

"What did you want to ask?" 117 asked as the door closed.

"Well it's about your numbers," She looked at the number 117 on his jacket, "The first group is all numbered one through thirty. But then they allowed the second group the choice of picking a number. Well… can I ask why did you pick 117?"

"That is the last three digits of the apartment building 43 and I stayed in front of before we came here. Therefore, in memory of our old home, we chose the number 43117."

"Oh I see," Mandy paused briefly then spoke up, "Funny, I thought it was because you were a Halo fan."

"It is a very good game Mandy."

"Sorry David. I'm not a gamer girl so I automatically piss off a lot of people when I say I probably will never see how good the games you play are. I never knew you could be so sentimental."

"You taught me how to act that way."

"Is that what it is?" Mandy asked. "An act?"

"No," 117 replied. "My feelings in this case are genuine."

"Well I'm going home David. See you next Monday."

"Of course Mandy. Unless trouble breaks out," 117 replied with a small grin.

"Was that a joke David?"

"Unconfirmed... was it a good attempt?"

"Try smiling or something when you say the punch line next time," She said giving an A-Okay sign with her fingers. "For homework, try working on smiling."

** ** **

Taking this to thought, 117 proceeded to the mess hall. When he entered, there was an abundance of noise. Many staff members including Dr. Kendrick were all enjoying the amborg cooked Spaghetti. Even the security guards had decided to loosen up and have some food. 117 scanned the crowd and saw the face he was looking for but then Dr. Kendrick walked up to him.

"David, my boy!" He happily clapped his hand on 117's back, "I was afraid you weren't going to show up. You have got to try this! Out of all the food that 3, 7, 9 and 13 have made, this spaghetti is the best! Not that their other recipes were bad but I haven't eaten anything so scrumptious in my entire life! But I also wanted to tell you that I'm currently working on something in R&D and I want you to be one of the first amborgs to try it. An early look at what I have planned for Christmas so to speak."

"Of course Dr. Kendrick," 117 replied, "May I ask…"

"Hey Doc!"

Dr. Kendrick and 117 both looked at one of the tables where a security guard held up his plate and all the other people at the table cheered.

"We should make Friday spaghetti night!" He shouted which made everyone nearby laugh and Dr. Kendrick couldn't hear 117 anymore.

"Sorry David!" He shouted in order to make himself be heard. "It'll have to wait. Go grab something to eat. It's nice to see you here."

"It is nice to see you Dr. Kendrick," said 117. "A pleasure as always to see you and everyone else in high spirits. If you will excuse me, I will grab some food myself and I will consider your request about the R&D situation."

He walked up to the table where the four amborg cooking team stood distributing the food. All of them turned when 117 approached and linked up to their heads.

"Ah 117!'" (Missy) 3 exclaimed, "Glad you arrived! We have been very successful with this particular recipe. Today 13 learned how to make individual pasta strips for the noodles. He has never been so fascinated by the methods the Italians used to perfectly make the dough just right."

She passed him a plate and a fork and 117 immediately scooped some noodles and put it in his mouth. The four amborgs paused briefly to observe as he chewed and swallowed.

"Very impressive," Said 117 after a few seconds, "The sauce is very acidic and the spices cause a great feeling of warmth throughout my circuitry. Also the textures of the noodles are not too thick or soft but very filling. The metal on the fork probably altered my initial taste-test so I cannot be entirely certain."

"Look at him!" (Gary) 7 piped up, "He still cannot work up the basic grammar to even tell us flat-out that he likes it."

"Oh give it a rest 7," 3 replied slapped 7 on the shoulder, "If I remember correctly, it took you a year to even get a basic understanding of the differences between peppers. You made the mistake of feeding 22 a chili pepper containing extreme levels of capsaicin months ago. The results were amusing and otherwise fantastic but she swears her performance has faltered by point zero zero two one percent ever since that incident."

"I remember that perfectly," 7 responded innocently, "You would think that with all the biological enhancements and upgrades, the vanilloid receptors in our mouths would be able to resist the pain that the capsaicin ingredient elicited."

"22 already had a severe allergy to certain spices before she went through the biological enhancement!" 3 retorted with a very annoyed look. "Clearly it translated and adapted over after her cybernetic enhancement. She also still hates you."

Leaving the two of them to their quarrelling, 117 grabbed his plate and proceeded to the table where 43 was sitting. She smiled when he sat down next to her. He felt even warmer for some reason when he looked at her.

"Busy day? What's on your mind?" She inquired as she twirled her fork into her own plate.

"The day when we were rescued," He replied taking another bite and a stray noodle flung sauce onto his cheek. She picked up a napkin and wiped his face.

"What brought that up?"

"I showed Mandy the Hall of Commemoration," he said taking her hand.

"Oh..." 43 stopped and looked at him with a serious look.

"I'm sorry if that initiated any residual memories," 117 apologized quickly.

"No no it's fine," 43 turned and stared at her plate again. "I just haven't really thought about the day we were found. Not for some time."

They both paused for a few minutes. 117 looked around. The thirty amborgs from the first group except for the four cooks were all talking to others. Many research assistants were really enjoying the meal. Lights all over the room were flashing as the different AIs of the building were watching the party. Finally 117 looked 43 in the eyes.

"I would like to request a favor 43," he said.

"Just one?" She smiled cheekily.

"For the moment."

"Ask away. Anything for you."

"Can you teach me to smile 43?"

"What?"

43 raised her eyebrows.

"Well," 117 looked around, "I think it would be convenient to finally educate myself in that manner. You are aware of how terrible I am with that process."

"Same old 117," she sighed, 'Always making the simplest objectives the most complex ones. Let's see what we can do."

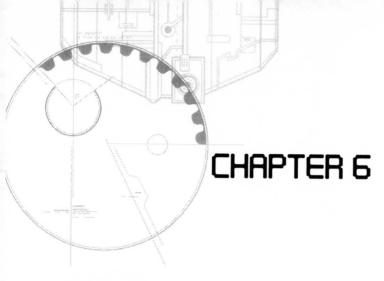

CHAPTER 6

Five days later
Giuseppe's Fine Cuisine

"Captain Bradley, you may want to consider changing your expression to something pleasant. Otherwise you risk giving away our identities."

"Shut up tin-head, you're not supposed to be talking... at all!"

"Captain please calm down, you really are scary when you get angry."

117, Sergeant Johnson and the captain were sitting in a small booth. Despite her loud retort, every other customer continued their meals and conversations. The restaurant was bustling with activity but the three of them maintained a small profile. The atmosphere shifted when the owner, Giuseppe walked up with an electronic tablet.

"Ah Ms. Bradley, going undercover again?" He spoke casually.

"Oh shucks, and I tried so hard to look like a damn civilian," Bradley looked back at the owner angrily.

"You're tone suggests sarcasm Captain..." 117 said which got him elbowed hard in the side.

"Quiet."

Unconcerned, Giuseppe, dragged his finger over the mini-screen and walked away.

"It'll be the usual then," he muttered cheerfully, "Followed by the occasional drop-in of bad guys. I'll go get my shotgun."

Bradley stood up causing Johnson to flinch. 117 picked up his glass of water and offered it to him.

"I'm going in the back to...freshen up," She said very sourly, "You two keep an eye on the place. If there's any trouble, just scream real loud. That means you Johnson."

As she walked away, Johnson let a huge sigh of relief and downed the cup of water that 117 had passed over to him. 117 stared and saw that sweat drops were slowly descending down his head.

"Is the Captain always angry about something?" 117 looked towards where she had gone. Johnson turned to look, then leaned forward and whispered.

"Yeah, she's always been like that. Tough and very pissed. I'm telling you, if looks could kill, then the captain gets the prize."

Giuseppe came back with some drinks and put them on the table. He gave Johnson another glass of water and a beer bottle, placed a martini glass full of something green in Bradley's spot and a third one in front of 117. He then drew up a chair and sat down with them.

"All right, my indestructible friend," Giuseppe said cheerfully as he pointed at the glass in front of 117. "Try one of these new formulas that I just invented. I want to see if you like it."

"Is it ok for a...'Cough' person of your type to drink alcohol?" Johnson asked 117. He looked at the drink which was fizzing quite loudly than any martini that any of them had ever seen before.

"Well I learned that it is polite to... accept things when they're offered," 117 said courteously raising the glass and nodded his head at Giuseppe. "Amborgs typically do not consume alcohol but as you say, there is always a first."

Without any delay, he drank the entire thing within seconds. Nothing seemed to happen at first, until all of a sudden, 117 coughed, turned his head and made a face. Steam then erupted out of his ears. He felt as if he had been hit by a hammer. Johnson nervously looked around to make sure no one had seen anything but apparently, no one paid any attention to what just happened.

"Are you crazy?" He whispered harshly to Giuseppe who was chortling. "You killed him!"

"That statement is… incorrect," 117 burped. "Normally, I would have scanned the drink but most of my amborg functions have been shut off temporarily to maintain my human disguise."

Giuseppe laughed even more.

"So that's what happens when you consume alcohol?" He chuckled as he maintained his composure. "Oh mama mia. I wish I had a camera."

"What if someone had seen?" Johnson asked, "We're supposed to keep a low profile during a stakeout!"

117 coughed again and a smoke ring came out of his mouth. His eyes drooped.

"I am fine sergeant," He said reassuringly out of Johnson's bracelet. "Although that drink was… more potent than I anticipated. Also the ingredients were… weird."

"So what did you think? You like?" Giuseppe looked at 117 with great interest. Clearly, he had never seen anything so amusing before. "Your sister 18. I believe she was the one last time who asked I make some special drinks for you kids."

"It seems to me that drink has triggered some really negative impulses through-out my circuitry. I believe the taste resembles tar," 117 stared curiously at Giuseppe who was listening intently. "It is my recommendation you do not distribute this to the local population. Reviews of your restaurant could be catastrophic."

"Don't worry son! It was just a joke! Besides I did put tar inside that drink," Giuseppe smiled. "Combined with large amounts of alcohol."

"Why you would purposefully feed a terrible drink to an amborg?" 117 glanced at the empty glass with concern.

"Because I've been trying to find something nice to feed you little lab rats!" Giuseppe explained, "Everytime one of you amborgs come in undercover with some cops, it's very good that you look inconspicuous. But you'll draw attention if you don't order food or even look like you're enjoying a drink. So lately, I've been trying to find a drink formula that you amborgs might like so you will fit in."

117 held up the empty glass to Giuseppe.

"You could have just given me a plate of spaghetti," He said as Giuseppe grabbed the glass, "But I'll have some more of this formula. I am... not driving home tonight."

"Another tartini and one plate of spaghetti it is!" The Italian said joyously and walked cheerfully into the kitchen. Johnson at the moment took the opportunity to speak up.

"Hey buddy, is it safe to be talking?" He leaned forward and whispered. "I mean, won't it give you away if you keep talking out of my bracelet? The tip-off we got this morning seemed serious but it might be worse if an amborg is discovered in plain sight."

"Do not be alarmed Sergeant. I took that into consideration," 117 looked around, "The restaurant is creating enough ambient noise so that our conversation cannot be heard by anyone."

"Oh yeah? Tell that to the guy in the corner."

117 looked at the reflection of Johnson's water glass. In the corner of the restaurant, to his five o'clock, was a man who was facing their booth from a corner seat near the window.

"Oh," 117 looked up at Johnson, "I cannot perform a facial recognition. His hood and cloak are masking his features perfectly. Very suspicious."

"Well can't you have your tech do something? A computer scan or 3D construction from the security cameras?"

"You have seen too many movies, Johnson," 117 looked at some of the photos on the wall, "Besides, we do not have evidence to suddenly arrest a man for just wearing a hood in a restaurant. Also, Mandy is not at her cubicle either."

"Wait...what?" Johnson looked at him with shock, "You mean, you're operating in the field without your tech?"

"Yes... Mandy is away for the week," 117 replied. "She is spending time with her fiancée. A... real looker from what she described. Dr. Kendrick ordered her to take more time off apparently. When she came back from her weekend leave, she was instantly shipped off-site again from A.I. Industries."

"So why are you here?"

"I thought that the police department requested an amborg…" 117 stared at Johnson with a questioning look on his face. "As for why, I am here assisting in a stakeout based off an anonymous tip Sergeant."

"No. I know that," Johnson looked around cautiously. "But why you specifically? I mean did you do something wrong and now you're here because of something you did? You spilled something on Dr. Kendrick and your punishment is working without a tech?"

"Not at all. It was my turn," 117 explained. He also decided to practice 43's lessons and smiled as best as he could but he was still struggling with his jaw muscles.

"You guys take turns?"

"Affirmative," 117 returned his face back to normal when he couldn't make any progress, "We came up with a roster back at Amborg Industries so everyone could go to any deployment a fair and equal number of turns. It was my turn today to come to Los Angeles."

Before they could continue, the hooded figure stood up and instantly moved right next to 117. Johnson jumped and 117 immediately turned to face whoever it was. He had moved with such speed that 117 was amazed no one else had noticed. There was definitely something wrong. But the figure looked 117 in the eye and he could see a faint smirk.

"Keep up with me if you can."

His tone was dark. He had a deep voice but 117 could tell it was an old man but before he could register this, the figure reached out and grabbed Johnson by the shoulder. The young officer was picked up and effortlessly thrown from the booth into another customer. The customers all turned their attention to the sudden uproar. Before anything else could happen, someone fired a shotgun. 117 looked and saw Giuseppe behind the counter with his hands on the trigger. He had the gun pointing upwards when he had fired the shot and lowered it so the barrel was aimed at the hooded figure.

"I'm not afraid to use this," Giuseppe shouted bravely. "Leave the customers alone! My family is ready to fight back if you continue to make trouble! Go now!"

The figure laughed and ran out of the restaurant causing several customers to fall into Giuseppe's line of fire. He quickly raised his shotgun to prevent from shooting an innocent person when Bradley instantly came running from where the restroom was.

"WHAT'S HAPPENED?!" She demanded while she ran over to Johnson who was feebly stirring from the wreckage of the dining table he had been tossed into. The little boy and his mother seated there were both checking to see if Johnson was alright.

"I will deal with this," 117 was already out the door, "Take care of the Sergeant."

⁎ *⁎* *⁎*

117 ran out into the street, when all of sudden, the same voice rang out in the dark street.

"Follow me if you dare boy, we have much to discuss. Think of this as a test. That anonymous tip off to the LAPD is now being played out for real."

Tracking the direction of where the voice came from, 117 immediately dashed into an alley. Following the stranger's voice, 117 stopped. Something was not right. The voice analysis indicated he needed to change direction and go straight up. Before he was able to leap onto the roof, he heard another sound as the mysterious attacker's voice rang out again.

"Let's see how well you do now. But finish quickly before I get too far away."

Three figures instantly appeared and surrounded 117, the first one moved and tried to punch him the chest. 117 retaliated by slapping the arm out of the way and punched him directly in the chest. He flew several yards, hit the wall and did not get up. The second person took that moment to aim a blow right on the head. What happened next was very surprising. 117 felt a lot of force from that single hit that it took him a few seconds to recalibrate. Trying to ignore the lucky hit, he beat off the last two ambushers very quickly and continued after the stranger. He looked up and climbed the ladder onto the roof of the building nearest to him. All the while, he kept trying to remember what the person hitting his head had done.

"What's the matter?" The old man called out from every direction. "Dazed? You're not going to let that stop you are you?"

117 instantly turned towards the direction of the voice without hesitating. His guess was spot on because he could see the outline of someone jumping over the rooftops and followed suit. Each rooftop was cleared easily as he leaped after the figure. Finally, after he crossed what must have been the fifteenth roof, the voice spoke again.

"Not bad!" The man called, "Try this next one!"

The instant 117, jumped across towards the next roof, more assailants jumped out and were flying towards him. Calculating fast, he landed on the next roof and turned around and opened his arms. The first attacker, not able to slow down in time, was caught in a bear hug by 117. As soon as he clenched his hands, 117 leaned backwards causing the enemy in his arms to career forward head-first into the ground. A loud thud and crunch sound followed as the man's skull was shattered at the speed. Maneuvering quickly, 117 rolled away and got to his feet. When he straightened up, the last two attackers stopped and looked at each other. Using this to his advantage, 117 picked up the guy on the ground and threw him at both attackers. And then he quickly tore after the hooded figure once again who shouted back at him.

"What's the matter?" He shouted. "Can't take the pressure? If you want to catch me, then you need to prove how good you are! I expect the amborgs to do better! Have fun with this next hurdle!"

On the next roof top, gunshots rang out. Another assailant with a rifle had entered into the fight. Easily ignoring the bullets, 117 ran in and engaged in close quarters. The rifle-man extended a bayonet out of the rifle and tried to stab him. Quickly side-stepping out of the way, he brought his arm down and tore the weapon in half. Then, he elbowed the man and kicked him square in the chest. As the hooded figure flew off into the darkness, someone hit 117 right on the back of the head which threw him into a state of disarray. Growing slightly concerned, he was now confused as to where these attackers were getting so much strength to fight. He felt someone kick him in the stomach and was sent falling off the rooftop. Flipping himself in midair, he landed on the pavement with a giant crash and instantly straightened up to look around.

"Need to send a call for help," 117 muttered in the back of his mind. "I have never encountered these gang members before. Probability of defeat is increasing."

"All right, that's enough of that now."

117 turned around. At the end of the alley was the hooded figure. This was the one, 117 thought, this was the man who threw Johnson back at the restaurant. The man was already assuming a defensive stance. It was a showdown.

"You got past that a lot better than I originally thought," The man called out to 117. "But you're definitely not good enough against me and my people as you've already realized. Against me, you won't able to win."

117 walked forward. The man lifted a hand and beckoned.

"Show me what you got amborg."

117 charged. He threw a fist but the hooded man dodged quickly and hit him right in the rib cage. Dodge? That wasn't it. The man looked like he had disappeared completely. So fast that he couldn't see it. 117 couldn't believe it, but he had felt pain for the first time in his life. Clenching his stomach, he tried to look for the mysterious attacker.

"This man is too fast to be human," He thought as another blow struck his back, "I'm at a disadvantage."

117 desperately tried to continue fighting but he was too slow. He was taking too many hits to his head and was disoriented from the rain that was now falling. He briefly saw the hooded man pulling a knife out and the next thing he knew, he felt it pierce right into his back. A knife had punctured his skin. Only one type of metal had the capabilities of doing this. 117 needed to escape but he was being forced down onto his knees.

"Do I have your attention now?"

117 blinked as he felt the knife twist in his back. He wanted to cry out in pain but he couldn't. The man had also not spoken with

his voice. Instead it was a transmission going through his head. A communication channel had been initiated by this assailant. 117 felt the knife being pulled out and then, the man was suddenly standing in front of his eyes. 117 stared in shock as the man pulled his hood back. It was an old man, much older than he expected standing before him. The unhooded man leaned forward and smiled.

"This knife is one of the only designs capable of inflicting any severe damage to the amborg exoskeleton," He said smugly. "I'm sorry I put you through all that and this my boy but you should know that these weapons are in the open. The amborgs are no longer the invincible beings to roam this earth. The rats have found a way to fight the exterminators now. Fortunately, I'm a rat-lover. And I'm showing you a sample of what's coming."

117 coughed and could only stare as the man continued to speak. He reached around and put his hand on 117's wound.

"I bet you're really surprised," He said showing his hand covered in blood to 117. "Still don't recognize me?"

For the first time in his life, 117 was very angry and in more pain than he could have imagined. He looked right into the man's eyes, opened his mouth and let out a cry.

"WHO... Arrrree.... You!?"

The old man smirked and let out a loud laugh.

"He speaks again," He exclaimed. "What an accomplishment. Tell me. Are you afraid? Well don't worry. You aren't going to die today. There is still hope for you and your siblings. Perhaps we can avoid you being humiliated even further."

He smacked 117 right on the head and it became too much. 117 fell on his side into the wet pavement. He could tell that he was still bleeding but his readings had been scrambled badly that he couldn't perform a diagnostic. He felt helpless. The rain had created large puddles and 117 found half his face lying in the mud of the pavement.

"The amborgs are in danger," 117 heard the old man say, "It would be wise to take into consideration that you aren't the mightiest anymore. Did you honestly decide to live your life assuming you were the best? David. Give this warning to the fair doctor. As an old acquaintance and friend, demons from the past are about to wage war and everyone will be caught in a massive crossfire. You must warn him and get ready. It's time to decide if you and everyone else are ready to face death in the eye. May not seem like an issue but it is. I guarantee one of you will die if you don't listen. From an old man to his grandson, I really hope you'll make the right choice David. Ah, I believe your friends are coming now."

Before 117 closed his eyes, he could see the feet of the old man retreat into the darkness. Grandson? He had definitely heard correctly. But it wasn't possible. He had no family. As he faded, he saw someone else step over him yelling. Blue and red lights flashed and gunshots were being fired. He could make out the loud voice of Captain Bradley.

"Hey! Stay with me! 117!"

Captain Bradley was shouting orders but that's all that 117 could hear. Feeling exhausted, he shut his eyes and everything went dark. A lot of things are happening to me, he thought. Without any calculations or anyway to stay awake, 117 fell unconscious for the first time as an amborg.

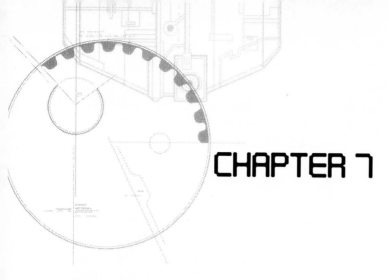

CHAPTER 7

2135
Gymnasium

An alarm caused everyone to jump. Brad dropped his pencil and bent down to pick it up. Dr. Kendrick stood up and looked at Serina who had been lounging on the arm rest of his chair.

"Serina, go find out what's going on," He said adjusting his glasses. "How strange. That's an internal breach alarm..."

"I'm on it."

Serina gave a quick thumbs up, turned bright blue and then leaped towards the wall. She became a light in the wall panel and they watched her zoom across the surface and then out the door.

"Are we in any danger?" Brad asked nervously as he instinctively moved and stood behind 117. His amborg narrator had stopped telling the story when the alarm went off and looked like he was deep in concentration.

"Negative," He said reassuringly.

The strain of talking with his voice made 117 cough and he then switched to his own bracelet. It was the first time Brad noticed that 117 was wearing an A.I. Industries amborg bracelet except it looked different than the one he had been given.

"What kind of bracelet is that?" He asked 117.

"This is a bracelet that Dr. Kendrick designed especially for the amborgs," 117 said holding up his wrist for Brad to see. "Remember when he approached me and wanted me to volunteer for a project? This was what he was designing at the time."

"Especially since you brought up the issue 117," Dr. Kendrick nodded approvingly. "You see, I wasn't too big on the idea of allowing asylum or extending an olive branch to gang members since many of them committed crimes I could never have forgiven. But during his first operation, I heard about 117's willingness to offer redemption to his enemies in his initial report. So to make it more convenient, I designed these custom bracelets only for the amborgs. A little more expensive than I wanted it to be but at least they can speak literally for themselves instead of having to rely on the standard issues."

"They're custom made?" Brad asked curiously.

"Unfortunately yes," Dr. Kendrick shrugged. "There's only so much a genius can do. I had to actually create the bracelets so they could be linked specifically to the owner. They had to be much more durable and strong just like the amborgs than what law enforcement and military officials were using. Uh. Unless you forget about the part where we just told you 117 got stabbed. So... they're almost durable. 117 didn': get his bracelet when he first encountered his grandfather because I chose to reveal them as gifts during Christmas later that year. So naturally, communication during that particular battle was complicated."

"So that man was his grandfather?" Brad asked with uncertainty. "How does that make sense?"

"Hold on Brad," Dr. Kendrick, "Let's wait for 117 to stop concentrating with the others. It isn't actually proper etiquette to forget about the person who was actually there."

"Speaking of proper etiquette," 117 replied after Brad and Dr. Kendrick waited patiently for a minute. "According to number 8, I found out what caused the internal breach. In this case, it actually was a breach from internal housing within the residential area."

"Let me guess," Dr. Kendrick sighed, "Did 9 pull another prank?"

"It would appear so."

"They are the two amborgs who love following crude but amusing behavior patterns," Dr. Kendrick explained to Brad, "You could describe them as the residential pranksters."

The two of them continued to watch as 117 sat quietly. Whether or not he was actually listening or chatting with 8 was something that neither Brad nor Dr. Kendrick could tell. Finally, after a few minutes 117 looked up at the two of them again and his bracelet flashed.

"It appears that 9 has set 8's sheets on fire and set up a miniature mud volcano outside the entrance of 8's quarters," He reported. "Hang on, the feed is a bit fuzzy. Ah, it looks like that 8 has pulled the fire alarm and also drenched himself in gallons of mud. Apparently he declared an internal breach and the alarm was triggered. I should go and assist in making sense of the problem. If I return, I will finish the story. Until then, I believe Dr. Kendrick and Serina will be able to do it in my absence."

Bidding the doctor and Brad a quick farewell, 117 walked out of the gymnasium. As the door closed behind him, Brad turned to the Doctor. The alarm had stopped and now everything was quiet.

"So…" Brad muttered, "How does the rest of the story go?"

"He did leave rather abruptly didn't he?"

Dr. Kendrick sighed and stretched his arms above his head.

"Well Brad," He muttered, "Do you have enough to write about your essay?"

"Perhaps I can write an article or publish my essay to scholastic journals," Brad said thoughtfully. "This is something exclusive that I believe should be shared. But it seems we lost our main character."

"Maybe another witness to what occurs next will be helpful?"

The voice came from Brad's bracelet but both of them turned to see Number 5 entering the gymnasium. There were mud stains all over his clothes.

"Johnny!" Dr. Kendrick exclaimed and waved for him to come closer, "I take it you were just at Number 8's residence?"

5 waved back but with a look of confusion.

"I am afraid you are mistaken doctor," 5 replied, "I just got back from a deployment and the people I arrested laid a trap which involved slowing me down by throwing me into a mud hole. Has something happened to number 8?"

"Another prank," Brad piped up, "Courtesy of Number 9."

"Those two never quit," 5 drew up a chair and sat down, "I swear, all these years, they come up with new ways to humiliate each other. It does not really affect us since we stopped caring but at least it's funny every time."

"You mean to tell me that you haven't been interested?" Dr. Kendrick raised an eyebrow. 5 returned his gaze and it slowly turned into a soft smile.

"Of course I am," 5 said with presumptuous tone. "I just wish I had their creativity."

The three of them broke down laughing. For 5 however, he was imitating the movement of someone laughing but his laughter instead was projecting out of his own bracelet.

"Why do they keep pranking each other?" Brad asked looking curiously at 5 who returned a smile back at him.

"Who knows?" The First Group amborg replied, "They change their reasoning every time."

"Ah yes," Dr. Kendrick nodded thoughtfully, "Last month, 9's excuse was that 8 was a stuck-up dirt-bag."

Dr. Kendrick put a lot of emphasis on the last word which caused Brad to burst out in laughter again.

"If you think that was funny Brad, wait till you hear about this one," 5 said cheerfully, "I remember the time that 8 soaked all of 9's underwear in meat. When 9 deployed into a combat zone later that day, practically fifty dogs were all chasing and attacking her. All the soldiers, police officers, and even the gang members stopped fighting to watch."

Brad and Dr. Kendrick needed a few minutes to collect their thoughts. The idea of an amborg actually scheming and humiliating another was downright cruel but the thought of it was too humorous. Finally, after what seemed like a giant expulsion of air, 5 then calmed them down before speaking again.

"Anyway," 5 spoke out of his bracelet and coughed up some mud, "I believe we should continue with 117's story. Brad seems anxious."

"Am I?" Brad took a couple of breaths, "I think I'm still jumpy from the alarm."

"That's alright kid," Dr. Kendrick leaned back, "Now then, I think a good place to start is... right. Let's start when we first brought him back."

*** *** ***

2127
Amborg Medical Facility

"He'll be fine. I'm just debating whether or not I should tell him."

"Well you aren't telling me, so that must mean it's something big. Damn it Doctor, he almost died, surely you can tell me what's going on. I'm his technician and I can maybe break the news to him. He isn't going to be entirely fine. Not after something like this."

"No. I've made my choice Mandy. Not until he wakes up. Call 43 up here now, she deserves to know as well. I'll tell all of you but for now, we wait."

117 blinked, he could see two shadows standing in front of the curtain. Whether he had woken from the loud conversation or just jolted awake, that didn't matter. He analyzed the voices and realized it was Mandy and Dr. Kendrick. He observed his surroundings and looked up. It was the medical facility back at A.I. Industries. As he looked up, one of the A.I's appeared and stared down at him. The A.I. flashed a smile and disappeared into the wall.

"Doctor, he's awake," 117 heard a voice say from outside the curtains.

Someone immediately pushed back the curtains. 117 looked and saw Dr. Kendrick enter, followed by Mandy. He walked over to the side of the bed and sat down while she made her way to where his head was resting.

"David, can you hear me?" She asked warmly.

He wasn't able to respond. 117 tried synching up with her bracelet but nothing happened. The connection was faulty. The bed automatically was elevating him to a sitting position but even while sitting up straight, 117 was unable to reply or communicate. He tried opening his mouth to speak but nothing came out.

Dr. Kendrick drew a glowing stick from his pocket and without a moment's notice, stuck it inside 117's ear.

"Don't worry," He said reassuringly, "I believe your processor was damaged. I just need to reboot your systems and that should fix your connectivity issues. Initiate system reboot, command clearance Kendrick Omega three beta one one seven."

117's head shot backwards and slammed into the wall. Mandy leapt backwards in shock. Dr. Kendrick, slightly startled, watched as 117 pulled out of the wall and looked around in a daze.

"System recalibrating... calibration complete. Testing...," 117 spoke urgently, "Dr. Kendrick, I have important news to report."

"I know David, calm down," Dr. Kendrick held up both his hands and motioned for 117 to sit back, "Two things David, I need you to relax and be patient a bit longer. Also I'm going to need that back."

He pointed to the left of David's head. 117 raised a hand upwards and felt that the glow stick was still in his ear. He pulled it out of his head and handed it back.

"Sorry," He said as Dr. Kendrick took it back cautiously. 117 turned around and stared. "Doctor, was there a hole in the wall behind me earlier?"

"I wouldn't worry about it," Dr. Kendrick replied in a concerned voice, "Right now, we just need to wait for... ah here she is."

He was saved the trouble of explaining the hole when 43 instantly ran in. She knelt down next to Mandy and instantly clutched 117's hand. She turned to the doctor who gave a reassuring nod in response. Sighing in relief 43's shoulders relaxed a bit but she still stared at Mandy and Dr. Kendrick with an apprehensive look.

"Doctor, what is going on?" She demanded, "You did not permit anyone access to see 117 until now. Why?"

"I had reasons 43," Dr. Kendrick said angrily which caused 43 to become silent. Mandy also didn't say another word. Startled, even 117 remained quiet. Dr. Kendrick sighed and then lowered his voice. "And as I promised," He said calmly, "You shall have answers."

Dr. Kendrick leaned forward and breathed deeply before speaking to 117.

"117 do you have any recollection of your parents? Specifically your father?"

117 returned his gaze with a confused look.

"My father? He was a lawyer," 117 replied attempting to access his childhood memories. But it was difficult since memories before the cybernetic augmentation weren't able to be recovered. Dr. Kendrick shook his head.

"No, that was a cover," He said as he pulled out a holo-device, "He was actually one of my senior technicians."

"He worked for you?"

117 sat up straighter. This was definitely not something he expected hear.

"Yes, he was the reason why I went looking for you when he died. I took it upon myself to make sure you were kept alive for his legacy. But I'll tell you what's even more important," Dr. Kendrick brought up another image from the device. It showed two men, a man greatly resembling 117 and...

"The hooded man!" 117 exclaimed. He suddenly could feel his emotions returning, "What is this?!"

"Easy David!" Dr. Kendrick raised his voice again. When 117 had sat calmly back down in his bed, he lowered his tone again, "This will shock you David 117 but that night was real and what that man said to you was also the truth. That's your grandfather. Is this the man that showed himself to you?"

An eerie silence loomed over the four of them instantly. 117 stared in disbelief at what he had just heard. But the longer he looked at the image, he knew it was not a lie.

"How?"

117 looked again at the hooded man in the floating image smiling with his father.

"I know it's crazy but it's the truth. Your father, and 43's father as well were technicians here at Amborg Industries and they were some of my closest friends. I cared deeply about both of them that I promised to take care of the two of you if anything happened.

Most of the amborgs now, were all selected because I was able to learn about them in my travels or by cosmic coincidence, I found them when they needed to be found. You and 43 are children of A.I. Industries personnel, along with only a few others. That is one of the closely guarded secrets I keep on site. Some would accuse me of favoritism but I'm upholding a promise to your parents."

43 looked at Dr. Kendrick in shock.

"The day they did not come home," She said, "I remember my parents left me with 117 and they said they would return."

Doctor Kendrick turned to look at 43.

"The technology that we were dealing with was theoretical but we knew it was possible," He explained solemnly. "However, this research was also being competitively chased after by other corporations and people wanted to place their bids on my work by any means necessary. This facility at the time was one of the securest places to be but I couldn't always keep both your fathers here the whole time without making you suspicious. They always described how bright you two were growing up and there were several occasions where you began to notice how long they were away from home."

Dr. Kendrick brought up another image. It was a projection of a family portrait. In it, 43 and 117 saw younger versions of themselves as children. What was surprising was that both their parents were in the background as 43 and 117 were playing in the photo.

"That night it happened, 117's parents contacted me and said that there was a threat on their life. They said that 43's parents were arriving to take them to the military for protection. Both 117 and 43 were left in a safe house while they attempted to reach the safety of my facility but they were ambushed and killed."

Dr. Kendrick closed the image and put the device back in his pocket.

"Which brings me to your grandfather 117," He said, "I don't believe that he and your father were the closest. He described him as arrogant, naïve, quite brash in his methods and problem solving. I also think 'untrustworthy' was a commonly used phrase as well."

117 felt the ache in his back suddenly get worse. There was definitely no question about that, he thought angrily.

"Your grandfather asked if he could take responsibility for caring for you," Dr. Kendrick said softly. "He said he felt sorry for not having a better relationship with your father and the rest of your family but I refused because of your father's wishes. But I did send him updates about how you were from time to time and in return, he agreed to keep his distance. I wanted to give you a better life which he's proven wrong with a single blade. His actions are very unorthodox…"

"Well we can add 'stabbing grandchildren in the back' to that list of actions," 117 replied grimly. "It is very comforting to have a family reunion where one gets stabbed as a welcome present."

"Now you use sarcasm properly?" Mandy asked in a surprised tone.

"Please Mandy," 117 replied, "I'm not having a good day…"

"Anyway," Dr. Kendrick interrupted, "He's made an appearance which tells me he wants to reach out to you. I don't know why he decided on these results but he hasn't killed you. He's trying to tell you something that only you can resolve. All I know about him is he runs a secret vigilante group which has connections in the criminal underworld all over the country. Your father even allowed them access to some of the earliest pieces of technology we built here which is why they displayed such powerful abilities. Similar to your skills as an amborg but less sophisticated. Why? I don't know but they fight crime at night and believe the police system isn't good enough so they employ their own measures. They employ very strong military tactics faster than the army and no he is not batman by the way. If that made sense, please tell me before I get even more confused and ramble too much."

Dr. Kendrick at that moment took a massive breath of air from speaking so fast. 117 returned his gaze and contemplated what had just been said. It didn't take too long to finish updating all of the information that had just been revealed.

"That was very clear doctor," 117 nodded reassuringly but then sat back, "I think…"

"What I want to know," Mandy asked, "Is how a knife was able to penetrate 117's exoskeleton?"

"Because the armor plating of an amborg can only be penetrated by a weapon made specifically of the same material," Dr. Kendrick brought up an image of a knife on one of the wall monitors, "And we have found traces of LTO alloy left from the knife deep in the wound. Lutetium, Titanium and Osmium are the strongest metals on this planet. Scientists have found a way to actually mix them together making them stronger which was the same concept but altered slightly when I incorporated it into my work. Originally, it was going to be used to create new structures and change the building industry but of course, scarcity of resources, low funds, and poor stability rates made it unviable for large scale projects. But for the human exoskeleton, I figured it could be used to provide the amborgs with a great defense. But it appears that this formula has made it possible to create weapons fatal to the amborgs on an offense."

"Doctor," 117 sat up once again, "There are weapons out there that can kill us?"

"I'm afraid that the answer is yes..."

Dr. Kendrick took off his glasses and fiddled around with them. Mandy and 43 both became quiet again. Shocked at the revelation, it seemed as if everything had just changed. 117 however, decided not to sit around and wait for a worse outcome. He pressed a button on the wall and a computer screen floated down from the ceiling in front of him. He entered his passcode and eleven dots showed up across the U.S. All of them were orange which indicated that an amborg had been deployed in the field for a long time.

"Doctor, who is in the field right now?" 117 looked at the dots with great concern.

Dr. Kendrick looked up at the map and quickly surveyed it.

"All of the first group are on stand-by or deployment. Those dots are one to five, sixteen through nineteen, and eight and nine."

"Call them back now."

"What?"

Moments after Dr. Kendrick asked the question, one of the dots on the map flashed and become a dark red. 43 also looked at the map and put a hand up to her head.

"Doctor," She said, "I'm receiving numerous reports of attacks in Los Angeles. Very heavy assaults. Requests for military support have been confirmed. Amborg in distress."

"Doctor, when was the last time an amborg activated a distress signal?" 117 looked at Dr. Kendrick who was gaping at the blinking red light.

"Never before…" He muttered, "It looks like it's 5. He's in trouble."

"Call everyone in the field back," 117 commanded. "Whoever has been out for a long duration of time, call them back now."

117 immediately then got out of the bed and began to stagger to the entrance. Mandy and Dr. Kendrick attempted to move and stop him but they stopped when 43 stepped forward and blocked his path.

"What do you think you're doing?" She demanded.

Sensing that she wasn't going to budge, 117 looked right into her eyes.

"I'm going. Don't stop me."

He tried to move forward again but she remained rooted between him and the entrance.

"Then at least let me come with you," she protested as she gently put her hand on his cheek. He ignored the look on her face which had begun to sadden.

"No," 117 firmly said taking her hand off his face, "Stay here. I will be back later."

And he stepped out the entrance. Amazingly, 43 had stepped aside. Just before he walked out of range from Dr. Kendrick's bracelet and 43's CPU, he said one last thing.

"I'm going to get some answers and there is only one man who can do that."

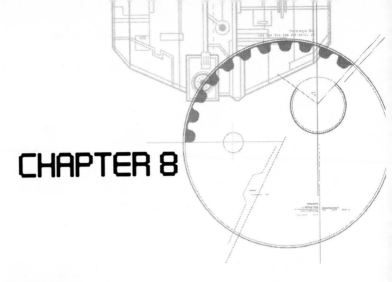

CHAPTER 8

Los Angeles Rural District Fourteen

"Help us! Help! We're trapped in here!"

Listening to the cries, a U.S. soldier crawled his way through the remains of a bombed out home. He made it to a door which appeared to be stuck and banged on the door as loudly.

"This is the U.S. Military! I'm trying to break through!" He shouted as loud as he could but then, out of the corner of his eye, he saw his bracelet light up.

"Move!" A voice from his bracelet instantly projected. The soldier turned around and moved out of the way just in time to see an amborg punch through the door. The door stayed in place but the amborg's arm had punched a hole through. He retracted his arm and the door was ripped back out.

At that moment, explosions outside of the building shook the building. The ground shook really hard and the soldier was knocked off his feet. As he struggled to pick himself up, the amborg extended its hand to him.

"Get up soldier," He said through the soldier's bracelet a second time. "We need to get inside."

Not questioning the command, the soldier immediately grabbed the hand but then was instantly tossed into the air and felt himself flying through the destroyed door.

"Oof!" He shouted as he landed next to a group of children. They all stared at him in bewilderment and were suddenly at a loss for words. The man noticed their frightened expressions, grinned and tried to get on his knees.

"Calvary's here kids," He said as positively as he could and tried to ignore the pain emanating from where he had landed on.

At that moment, the amborg jumped inside with them and sat down. He was carrying something long and he placed it in his lap. The soldier then turned to see which amborg it was. It was hard to read the number on his jacket in the dust so he then looked down at what he had brought. His stomach lurched when he realized what it was.

"What?" The amborg asked shrugging. "You never saw a detached leg before? It looks more painful than it actually is. We still need to be positive for the kids so keep smiling."

"Pardon me for staring," The soldier replied. He looked casually over to the kids and gave them a thumbs up as well as a forced smile.

"I said be positive," the amborg said impatiently. "Don't force it or they will instantly realize you are psychologically manipulating them and it is statistically not healthy for the development of children. Let it flow naturally."

Annoyed, the soldier turned his back on the kids and frowned at their one-legged savior.

"Flow naturally?" He whispered in a tense voice, "Have you seen the immediate surroundings? It isn't psychological manipulation when we're in the middle of a warzone! It's only a lie when you say out loud that it is…"

"No one's perfect," The amborg said holding up his leg above his head.

For a minute, the soldier thought that the amborg was going to attack but then his bracelet flashed again.

"Hey kids!" The amborg said cheerfully, "Want to see the leg of an amborg? Don't be concerned. The bad guys and I just had a disagreement and they tried to steal my leg but I got it back."

The kids, who had remained silent the whole time, moved forward slowly and then the amborg passed his leg to them. They all stared in wonder at the cybernetically altered body part. Fully distracted, the amborg then spoke normally to the soldier and held his hand out.

"What is your name soldier?"

"Lieutenant Palmer," Taken aback by the amborg's sudden change in attitude, the soldier grabbed the hand and shook it curtly. "Are you sure you're alright? Which number are you?"

"Johnny 5 at your service," The amborg replied with a smile. "Yeah I'm fine. It was much more painful when it got ripped off. That will be twice in my life now that someone has taken my leg from me."

Palmer looked back at the kids and realized another interesting detail about the leg. It was all robotic. No bones, blood or regular human anatomical parts. It was a prosthesis.

"So that's not a human leg?" Palmer clarified with 5 who nodded.

"Yes," He replied, "I lost it when I was a kid. Spent a few years walking on whatever I could make into crutches. That leg is one of the greatest gifts from Dr. Kendrick that no money can buy. At least, it is a very treasured gift that I can never repay. Then gangsters stabbed me and pulled it off... I really hope it can be fixed."

"Well, you still need help. Is there anything I can do?"

Palmer instantly began checking his pockets for something that might help but 5 held up a hand.

"No thanks. I'm good," He said reassuringly, "They didn't get any vitals or biological parts. My right leg is a complete machine attachment. They just tore it in a place where it actually can be torn. Actually, they used some sort of special knife. I was surprised when they got in close and managed to stab me."

"Mr. Amborg?" One of the kids crawled over. "Could you show us how your leg works?"

While 5 distracted the children, Palmer decided to take the opportunity and call for help.

"Mayday, mayday, can anyone copy? Transmitting on all military and emergency frequencies."

He spoke into his radio as calmly as possible. Glancing over at the children, he saw that all of them were still fixating on the leg which made him feel relieved. At least they didn't have to try and understand his adult conversation. Suddenly the radio crackled and a response came crackling through.

"I copy your transmission, please identify yourself."

"This is Lieutenant Palmer from the twelfth guardsmen division," Palmer replied, "I need an immediate evac right now from my location. I got separated from my teams and I am currently tied down. Track my location from this transmission and send help. To whom am I speaking to?"

"This is the F.O.B. We have isolated your signal and are tracking you. You seem to be twelve clicks out from our nearest unit. How many to pick up?"

"I have five kids who need to be extracted out of here along with an amborg."

The radio static intensified. Palmer, tuned the radio and tried to clear it. Finally, the person responded but he could barely make out the sound.

"Lieutenant, if there's an amborg, I'm pretty sure you're fine if you hunker down for a while," The person on the other line said calmly. "Currently our transports could be sent elsewhere to help those less fortunate."

"Listen. We kind of are the less fortunate," Palmer said as loud as he could. He held the radio closer and briefly glanced at the kids out of the corner of his eye. They hadn't heard how worried he was getting but he was beginning to feel very anxious. "The amborg is crippled and we are on the defensive. Repeat, we are completely on the defensive and hiding for our lives from Splatterbugs. My rifle is blown to pieces and all I got is my knife. I could really use something here!"

The static was now getting louder and Palmer tried to make out the words coming through. He gave the radio a small slap and tried to listen. The kids, were now playing tug-a-war with 5's leg. How much fun are they having? He wondered. Suddenly, a few words came through his radio.

"...fzzt say again?" The radio spat out, "...zzhh amborzz... crippled? Repeatkzzt... Support...zzft...ot...available! Hold your position! If you read... we will try to get to you!"

A hand instantly appeared out of nowhere and grabbed the radio. With a giant crunch, 5 clenched his fist and destroyed the radio. The noise instantly died away which made Palmer stare in shock.

"What did you do that for...Mmmph?!"

5 held up a hand and placed it over the Lieutenant's mouth. With his other hand, he held up his index finger to his own lips and made a gesture for silence and then pointed outside the doorway. Palmer, disgruntled at being forced to keep quiet, listened carefully.

A few voices could be heard from outside in the other rooms. The look on 5's face told Palmer that they weren't friendly. Splatterbugs, he guessed as 5 removed his hand and they both silently crawled towards the kids. As silently as possible, he slowly drew his knife while 5 motioned for the kids to quiet down. Nobody dared to make a noise.

"It doesn't look like anyone's here," They heard someone say from the other room, "Let's head over to the next place. Nothing to hunt for here."

"I thought I heard something though when we walked by," Another voice spoke. "It was probably just my imagination. Hey dude! Check this out!"

"What is that? It's a photo. Whoa! Looks a picture of some hot chick. Wonder where this one's hiding?"

Palmer gasped and checked his breast pocket. It was empty! Shoot, he thought, I lost Ellie's photo! I got to get that back!

He instantly lifted himself up but 5 held him back.

"Well, don't hog it all for yourself, give it here," The first voice spoke again, "Don't clench it! She's a hottie."

"Finders keepers," the second voice taunted.

"Achoo!"

Palmer froze. Both he and 5 whirled around to see one of the children with her hands over her mouth. He wished that he hadn't heard it and he hoped that whoever was outside hadn't heard. The little girl clenched her mouth and looked scared.

"I'm sorry!" She whispered in a horrified voice. 5 and Palmer listened. But there were footsteps running towards them. Damn! Palmer thought angrily as he lifted his knife.

Someone came around the corner, peered into the hole of the wreckage and saw them hiding in the opening where the destroyed door had been earlier. Palmer could see a wide grin appear on the gangster's face.

"Hey! What do you know?" The gangster said cheerfully, "Looks like we got some lost birds! Hey I found some people here Joey! Fresh kills for us today!"

"Yeah that's great," A second splatter-bug joined the fray. Palmer recognized his voice. It was the one that found his photo. "Kill them and let's get out of here already!"

Both of them crawled through the gap and pointed their guns at Palmer and the children. ("Oh sure, ignore the amborg," muttered 5). Palmer, instantly lowered the knife, tossed it towards the two gangsters and held his arms up. He slowly inched across the ground to try and shield the children as best as he could.

"Smart move soldier," The splatter-bug who found them smiled as he grabbed Palmer's knife and threw it behind them out the door and of anyone's reach. Suddenly, he looked over and noticed 5.

"WHOA! Are you kidding me?!!" He exclaimed with a gleeful attitude. "That plan earlier must have worked!!"

5 rolled his eyes as the man continued to taunt him.

"HEY AMBORG!!" He said in a sing-song voice, "How's it feel to lose a leg? Is it annnyyy fuunn??"

"Come on man," The other one said nervously. "I don't like tight spaces. Let's just get this over with and get back outside. I want to look at this picture some more."

"Ok ok. You take the kids," The splatterbug stopped grinning and then pointed his gun at 5's head. "I want the amborg," he snarled. "This is for all my friends that you kids locked away and killed."

The bracelet on Palmer's wrist lit up and 5 finally responded.

"Trust me pal, you're risking your life," He said smugly.

"What you talking about?" The splatter bug asked with a confused look. 5 smiled.

"I am saying it's not nice to point guns," His voice lowered to a whisper out of the bracelet which made Palmer suddenly look at him with a concerned look.

There was a sudden blur that flew past Palmer's eyes and into the splatterbug standing above 5. He saw a knife in the man's back and 5 had put his hand in front of the barrel of his gun.

The smile on the splatter-bug's face instantly faded. He opened his mouth but nothing came out except for faint whisper. He pulled the trigger and the gun went off into 5's hand who didn't seem fazed at all. Palmer expected the other one to attack immediately but when he looked at the spot where the other splatterbug had been, he saw that he had been pinned down by a new arrival.

The second splatter-bug tried to fight back but their savior punched hard into the back of the man's head. There was a loud thud as the gangster went limp and didn't move again. Palmer looked back at 5 who threw the dead splatterbug aside and spoke in a taunting manner.

"Also, here is another piece of information about amborgs," 5 said casually, "We are also bulletproof to a certain degree. So I wish you all the luck in attempting to kill me with a simple firearm."

"For an amborg without a leg," Palmer's bracelet lit up and another voice spoke. "It is very strange that you did not engage them sooner when you clearly could have. It would have remedied the situation very sooner."

"Well 117," 5 shrugged as he unclenched his fist and threw the bullet that he had caught off into the rubble. "I was not about to give away your position by telling them. It would have been an even bigger waste of time. Savor the fact that you just rescued us like a total badass and enjoy the moment."

The second group amborg looked around and gave a thumbs up to 5. Since the coast was clear, Palmer stood and walked over to the dead splatterbug and retrieved his knife. He then walked over to 117 who was still kneeling on the gangster he had tackled previously.

"Move!" Palmer said angrily, "I want that picture back!"

Without replying, 117 stepped off the unconscious man, flipped him over and searched his pockets. He quickly pulled a small photograph out and then extended it out to Palmer who snagged it back. He looked at it and then sighed with relief when it was the right photo.

"Objective retrieved Lieutenant," 117's voice spoke out from Palmer's bracelet, "You should consider not carrying personalized materials that will easily fall to the ground during combat. I suggest not carrying them at all."

As Palmer pocketed the photo and sealed it, he looked 117 in the eye.

"Look Mr. 'I don't have feelings'," He said beginning to feel tense again, "When you're in the middle of dying, the last thing you probably want to see is something pleasant. I don't know how you stay calm but for those of us who have actual feelings, it helps sometimes."

He shoved past 117, who had side-stepped out of the way quickly. He bent down and picked up the dead splatterbug's gun and ammunition while 117 motioned for the children to proceed outside.

"Might as well," he muttered as he reloaded the gun and then helped 117 lift 5 up. "Not like I'll find my own gun soon."

As the three of them began stepping out after the kids, he stopped and shook his head.

"Thanks," He muttered quietly, "I guess I owe you one."

"Interesting how everyone owes me so much but they aren't specific," 117 replied humorously.

"Wow," 5 did a chuckling motion, "The first joke that I've ever heard him say and he sounds like an extorting capitalist."

Making sure that 5 was properly balanced and secure, they made their way out at last. The kids all remained quiet but at least they weren't scared now that it felt safe.

"You look... great," 117 commented as they made their way down some steps.

"It looks like you took a beating too," 5 said with concern. "When I heard what happened to you, I stayed alert but I took a hit too. Imagine that, you carrying my leg in one arm and me in the other with Palmer."

"It was an LTO knife," 117 explained as they waited. The small party heard a rumbling in the distance and looked right. It looked like a pair of vehicles were heading their way.

"LTO? In the shape of a knife?" 5 said with a surprised tone. "I'm not surprised but who could have the technology to keep the reaction of forging those metals together and keep it stable? Especially with a tool so small?"

"That is what I am here to find out. Mandy has been scanning for patterns the whole time since I arrived."

The rumbling grew louder as two military transports suddenly came closer. They pulled up and immediately opened their doors. A few soldiers exited and secured the area. Palmer left 5 to 117 and immediately ushered the kids inside the armored jeeps as fast as he could. While he did this, 117 set up a private communication with 5.

"Also there is one more thing," 117 said informatively, "The person who stabbed me is my... grandfather."

"What?" 5 asked with a stunned look. "You would not make up something like that but you are also incapable of lying so... huh. Is he a long hated relative?"

"Not exactly," 117 replied. "His methods were unorthodox but he is apparently alive and we have to find him. So I wanted to ask if you see him, please do not try to kill him. He might do more damage even if he notices your current state. I am sending you a photo and video references from when I encountered him."

"Aww shucks. And I worked so hard on my bambi eyes. Hmm, looks like a charming old man," 5 said as he received the upload. "How does he get so much strength? Steroids? Oh wait, I see. Cybernetic implants. Primitive but effective."

"He probably looks better than you do," 117 remarked, "Your new look must have cost you a leg."

"Very poorly phrased. If I lost my arm too, then the joke would have worked. Your first one was better."

"Ah. Of course. It must have cost you an arm and a leg," 117 recited from his joke database. "I'll try that joke again some other time."

Minutes later, Palmer ran back to them and helped carry 5 again.

"Ok guys," He said cheerfully, "The three legged race is over. We'll have you back at the F.O.B. safe and sound."

"Actually Lieutenant," 117 replied, "That won't be necessary. We are remaining behind to finish another important objective."

"You can't possibly stay out here!"

Palmer's protests were cut short when one of the soldiers came up and spoke.

"Sir! We have to leave now! Reports are saying this area is about to get overrun! We're sitting ducks!"

"Go!" 5 said urgently. "We will stay behind and distract them."

"Are you sure?" Palmer eyed 5's leg with concern.

"I am still combat ready," 5 winked. He grabbed his leg back from 117 and held it up. "This does make a great club and I'm not alone this time."

After a few moments, Palmer sighed and then ran to the door of the transport.

"Good luck!" He called out as the door closed and the vehicles drove off leaving the two amborgs behind arm in arm.

"Just so you know," 5 warned as the two of them maneuvered so they were standing back to back. "Based on the number of enemies I am detecting, this is exactly how they cornered me. When I tried fighting them off, in the chaos, one of them managed to knife me."

"Well, like you said," 117 looked down and discovered that there was a rifle in the rubble. "You aren't alone this time."

117 kicked his foot toes first into the rubble and the force sent the rifle flying upwards which he caught in his arms. He aimed it around in a one hundred eighty degree angle and scoped the area in front of him.

"Enormous group of hostiles detected surrounding us," He said. "I can hear some assembling in the nearby streets. And the ones I see are definitely carrying knives. Confirmed Mandy?"

"Got it David," From her module, Mandy was cycling through the cameras, "I'm connected to 5's technician and we are now presenting to you data on the splatter-bug's locations. I have every faith in both of your abilities but to a normal human scenario, I have to inform you that this insanely suicidal."

"Data confirmed," said 5. "At least we are both almost still in one piece. Synchronizing with 117's neural link… complete. Preparations for enemy engagement are ready. Looks like I get to try first-hand how to fend properly against these knifes instead of being ambushed again."

"It isn't exactly a textbook ambush," 117 remarked. "This is just bullying."

"Meh… two of us versus all of them."

"Yes," 117 smiled. "That's what makes it fair."

The first splatterbug appeared ten meters away and let out a whooping cry which sounded like the signal to attack. Instantly, several of them closed in and began to rush the two amborgs.

"Are you going to ask them to surrender?" 5 asked in a serious tone.

"Not this time," 117 replied, "I am not responsible if anyone dies. We just need to fight them off to grab my grandfather's attention. If we live, then we can listen to him."

"And if we die?"

"Take as many as you can with you."

A few of the splatterbugs ran in slowly firing weapons at the pair in the center but this barely made 117 or 5 flinch. Letting out their crazy war-cries, the ones with knives charged in and when they were close enough, they made their moves. 5 swung his leg like a bat and knocked several gang members flying or out cold. 117 began shooting what was left of the ammunition inside the rifle. 117 fired five shots which resulted in five kills before the rifle jammed. He hit the release and then ripped the magazine out and tossed the rifle into the air. Quickly he caught and threw the clip off at another gangster and then caught the empty rifle. Imitating 5, 117 also began to swing it like a bat and swatted at anyone who came to close.

As the two amborgs continued to battle against what seemed to be an endless swarm, there soon began to be some signs of trouble. 5's leg was holding up with all the brute force but 117's rifle was falling apart with every blow. 5 instantly passed a signal to 117 and he acknowledged by throwing the rifle over the back of his shoulder. 5 caught it easily and passed him his leg in exchange. 5 took the rifle, ripped off the barrel and threw it away into someone's face. He lifted the rest of the rifle up over his head with his right arm and brought it down to the ground, smashing it in half. One half flew up into the air from the amount of force he used. With his left arm, 5 grasped the piece and threw it towards three enemies who were unfortunate enough to stand in front of each other. The first was hit in the chest by the rifle piece and flew backwards. Like dominoes, the three of them flew back and landed on the street hard. 5 then caught the other half of the rifle and threw it in the opposite direction which yielded similar results.

117 saw a splatter-bug with a knife approaching and threw the leg over his head again which was caught perfectly by 5. This allowed 117 to properly face the charging knife-wielder with his arms. When the splatterbug was close enough, 117 blocked, grabbed the knife with his left hand, hit the splatter bug in the head repeatedly with the other hand and kicked him away. 117 now wielded a perfectly good knife and focused on his next target.

After a few more bouts and clashes with the dwindling ranks of the gang members, 117 and 5 both looked around after it was all over. Their time logs indicated it had been thirty six minutes since the battle started but it did feel like an exhausting eternity. Dead or unconscious splatter-bugs were all over the place. All the bodies littered the ground and the two amborgs instantly returned to a passive state, except for 5 who was still staggering on one leg.

"How many was that?" 5 looked around as he held onto his leg.

"I counted seventy-three," 117 said. He was beginning to feel tired from both his injuries and the long fight. "Hang on a moment."

117 threw his knife into the distance and someone screamed.

"Correction. Seventy four."

"Yeah I have the same count. An amazing number of splatter-bugs," 5 noted, "You think we killed off all of their people?"

"Highly improbable," 117 said as he scanned the area again. "It is strange that they pressed their attack when they had no hope. Why bother attacking when this is the result?"

"When you give powerful weapons to highly motivated people, then retreat is no longer an option."

117 whirled around which made 5 fall to the ground.

"Hey!" He cried as 117 faced the newcomer. Immediately recognizing the voice he began to feel angry.

"You!" He pointed at his grandfather who stood a few meters away.

"Here's the thing David," The old man smiled, "When you give free-to-play players the right equipment to take down the boss, it doesn't matter how many times they are defeated, they will keep coming and keep fighting until you are dead and they reap the rewards of the loot that is dropped. Who knows what might have happened if I turned a blind eye on you and you lost your lives too quickly when it was too late?"

"How was stabbing me your best way of informing me of the danger?" 117 asked in an aggressive tone. He didn't need to speak with his mouth but he knew the signal in his head was heard by whatever equipment the man had. "You could have just said so."

"Well I figured," His grandpa said, "I doubt you would have believed me if I came forward in the first place. By the time you figured out the truth in those… calculations, I probably wouldn't have been so optimistic. You needed to face the reality of it. I wanted you to feel scared. You became angry and motivated to seek out the truth. It could have gone differently but yes I did believe this was the best way. I left you alive didn't I? The enemy would have shown less mercy. I know I would have."

117, still suspicious, glared at the hooded man and tried to comprehend what he had just said.

"Maybe I believe you," He said. "But you better answer my questions and get to the point now."

"Done," The old man smirked. "But lower your fists ok? I come in peace. It's not worth getting beat up again."

"Yeah. Don't mind me, I'll just lie here and die slowly in the next twenty-four decades."

117 instantly turned around and helped 5 get back on his feet. 5 motioned for 117 to let him move on his own and hopped after him.

"Whoa there," The old man took a careful look at 5, "I see you got knifed. Definitely an LTO. How did that happen?"

"We can probably stick with I was one of the amborgs who found out too late," 5 said cheekily. "A lucky hit from an ambush."

"All right boy," 117's grandfather said after pondering a few moments. "It's time you learned about what's happening underground. There are many weapons that are being spread around to all the gangs not just here but everywhere. I don't know who it is which means they have a heavily secured network. With the amborgs to help us however, we may be able to save L.A. and possibly the whole country from total chaos and destruction. We won't be able to stop the initial thing from happening. It's already too late but we can still do what we can to build a dam before the flood arrives. Now let's get moving."

117 pulled 5's arm around his shoulder again.

"You take point," He said to the old man.

The old man laughed.

"Still don't trust me?" He smirked.

"Negative."

"Well you'll have to starting now," The old man sighed. "Come on. I know a place where we can shelter down in. You also might want to tell Mandy to stay on the line and hold off on the next bathroom break. I really would rather not repeat any important information."

"How do you know her name?" 117 asked suspiciously and stopped suddenly. Even 5 looked from him to his grandfather with a look of concern.

"I have ways," The hooded man turned and looked at the two of them with a smirk, "By the way, I don't think you knew about this but that Lieutenant Palmer? That charming man? That was Mandy's fiancée you just saved. Thought you should know in case she was ever going to tell you. But it looks like that blank expression on your quiet and obvious face tells me that you didn't know."

117 blinked. He didn't recall showing any indication of changing the expression on his face. But this old man was reading him just like a children's book.

"How do you know this?" He asked while 5 remained silent. "The lieutenant referred to that lady in the photo as Ellie."

"Why didn't you just do facial recognition on the photo when you looked at it?"

"I was being polite," 117 replied casually. "It's not usually our business to do facial recognition scans on personal property of civilians or military personnel."

"But you have high access to records at A.I. Industries," 117's grandpa asked with a hopeful look. "You would have seen that her full name is Mandy Elizabeth Walker."

"Ok seriously…"

From the back of 117's head Mandy was beginning to freak out.

"I don't care if he says he's your grandpa David," She said. "But he's starting to scare the living daylights out of me…"

117 didn't reply. His grandfather stared back at him but eventually his smile faded.

"Let me guess," he said stroking his beard, "You haven't bothered to even look at your own technician's file."

"To do so would breach a basic level of privacy and trust," 117 responded harshly. "We are programmed…"

"I get it," The old man sighed, "You kids have an ethics programming. Man that just sucks the fun out of everything."

At that moment, many other figures appeared out of nowhere and surrounded the trio. They weren't splatter-bugs but they all wore similar clothing that 117's grandfather was wearing. Still, he kept a close eye on them. He didn't want to let down his guard again like the last time.

"David, you wanted answers, and you're going to get them," His grandfather explained as the large party began to move as a group up the street and into an alleyway. "In return, I need your help along with Kendrick and the other amborgs. Let me introduce you to my own security group. We're not as strong or fast as you kids but we get the job done at the end of the day."

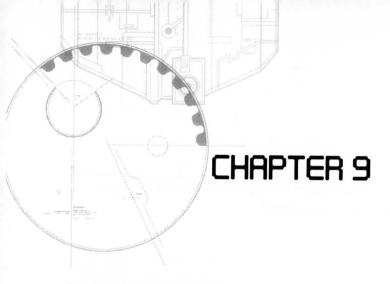

CHAPTER 9

Los Angeles "Underground"

"Los Angeles, Underground" 117's grandfather said, "I'll be honest with you David. I really did set up a base under the city just so I could say cool stuff like, 'welcome to the underground.' Heh he."

117 sat across from his grandfather and didn't move. They had settled deep under the city in a massive tunnel which must have been constructed and abandoned decades ago. Now it seemed to be home to a group that had completely managed to be hidden off the radar from the amborgs. 117's grandfather sat on a comfy lawn chair and waved a hand at the ceiling.

"This place is one of many all over the world," He said, "Built during the third world war in case of nuclear fallout. At first it was only for VIPs but then it became the right thing to make it suitable in case we had to make long term arrangements. The population could stay here and flourish for decades while all the destruction and turmoil all raged far above. But obviously, that wasn't the case. The war ended. Everyone celebrated and then eventually, the only ones who knew about these secret caches were the street rats that worked up the courage to wander this deep underground in this man-made labyrinth. So I've been doing the same thing just like Dr. Kendrick has been doing. Taking all the poor bastards of the world and enjoying my itsy bitsy nations of control to maintain security around the world."

117 stared silently. Although he was listening, he had made the decision to only listen. The instant he had set foot into this hidden

fortress, he had lost contact with Mandy. 5 also had experienced the same thing. The signal back to A.I. Industries was faint but impossible to transmit back to the surface. Not paying attention to 117's silence, the old man continued with his story.

"Your dad didn't like what I was getting in to but believe me, I didn't have a choice," He said sighing. "The police and the military weren't doing well enough. At the time, after the end of the war, so many bad doors led to such a terrible time for everyone. I had my fair share of fighting with my brethren in politics and on the street so I felt obligated to take matters into my own hands and try to make things better by putting more of myself into it. But obviously, it involved skirting around rules and corners so it made us look like black market dealers. When you and Serina were children, your dad told me to stay away to keep you kids away from what we did. I still think it's ironic how he disapproved but he still supported me. Err... indirectly that is... He convinced Dr. Kendrick of yours to provide us with experimental equipment. So that's why you can communicate with us without a nearby bracelet. I have a device similar to parts in your CPU that can link and relay messages. This thing in my ear that looks like a hearing aid? It's actually what locks onto your signal and plays what you're saying at the back of your mind when you want to speak to me. It's probably all old stuff to you kids but we've been able to hold our own at everything we've faced. God, I miss him. Your dad was a great man... I loved him. I just never got the chance to say it that often to him. The thing is, we weren't against each other. Our whole family was just passionate and devoted to doing what we all thought was right for the world we lived on. Your dad and I just... we didn't have the same ideologies and we just worked on completely different methods to achieving peace."

117 blinked and looked down at the floor. He had never expected to hear this sort of story about his father. Then again, he was beginning to realize how much he could barely remember. He immediately began to feel ashamed for not trying to figure this out sooner. After some quick thinking, he then sent a signal to his grandfather's equipment.

"Well, my number of questions have now minimized," He said, "But there is the issue of familial trust."

His grandfather stared and then began to chuckle. After a few moments, he stopped, looked at 117 in the eye and grinned.

"You got to let that go David. Ha ha."

117 pointed a finger behind his back and indicated the exact spot where the knife wound was.

"You stabbed me in the back," 117 said angrily.

"Hey, humor an old man would ya?" The old man chuckled. "Would you rather I just show you the weapon and tell you it could kill you? That's the easy and the longer way of doing things. I prefer to be more direct, it's usually the fastest way to get the point across. And as a bonus, that's how we met. So it can be a good memory. Isn't that sweet?"

117 looked around in confusion but then stopped and looked back at his grandfather. He was determined not to take his eyes off at all.

"I do not understand... I detect nothing in the vicinity affiliated with or that contains any sugar..."

"Boy, when this is over, you got to learn how to properly have a chat..."

A couple of people ran by behind but 117 ignored them, he stared at his newly discovered relative with a very serious look. His grandfather sighed and then pulled a cigarette from his pocket.

"Ok kid," He said taking the cigarette and pointing it at 117, "Don't be so wound up. Wound up... Hehe get it? Because you're like a wind-up toy."

There was another bout of silence as 117 didn't respond to the joke. His grandfather sighed again and lit the cigarette and held it to his mouth.

"Nothing?" He asked raising an eyebrow. "Ok come on, I admit that that was a bad joke from someone my age but we're family. I mean I am entitled to say stupid things with relatives of... a certain modern nature. We should be getting to know each other and talking about... familial bonding? Or something like that."

117 raised an eyebrow but still did not make a sound. It was almost like talking to a dog. The old man scratched the back of his head, thinking about what to think of next for a casual ice-breaker.

"I might as well be talking to myself..." He muttered as he put the cigarette into an ashtray next to him, "Would you at least blink? You can do the whole, 'I'm watching you,' thing all you want but at least say something. Say something that's not aggressive so that it doesn't feel like we're going to bust each other to pieces. Seriously, I'm being completely honest when I say that you're creeping me out..."

Another pause. Then...

"Creeping you out was not my intention."

117's response was fast and quiet but it caused his grandfather to yell (FINALLY!!). 117 sighed and then put on a smirk.

"I was calculating all the possible ways your head could explode," He said.

"If you weren't a computer, boy," His grandfather stared into the amborg's eyes and grinned, "I'd say you were *almost* like your dad whenever we got into a fight. Seriously, you may be an amborg but what is it with you and exploding heads? Your dad was like that as well whenever someone ticked him off. Must run deep in the family apparently."

"Have I... broken a nerve? Grandfather?"

"It's touched a nerve, son, and... my name is Mark, David. I probably should have told you that," He replied when 117 unclenched his fists and relaxed a little. "If you don't feel like calling me old man or grandpa," He said grabbing a screwdriver. "Then I hope we can have a fresh start at least with knowing each other's names."

117 nodded.

"Mark," He repeated. "Grandpa Mark. Old man Mark. I'm not sure that name actually suits you."

"You could always use my last name," His grandfather shrugged. He was tuning his equipment with the screwdriver as he said this. "Actually, it's our last names. I mean it hasn't been ruled out."

"That would be releasing classified information," 117 explained with concern. "Our last names may inflict further harm on those closest to us. I believe our first names make our business more personal. In that scenario, Mark sounds better. But our last names ensure our legacy is still alive."

"I can take care of myself thank you very much," The old man chuckled. "But you're probably right. No one needs to know our family name. You keep your number as your last name but I'm glad you all haven't thrown away your heritage."

"We are not all machines."

"Heh. That's an understatement. By the way, when are your buddies about to get here?"

Mark put down the screwdriver and 117 returned his gaze.

"When did you realize I activated my homing device?" 117 turned to look over his shoulder. At a table several feet away, some of his grandfather's followers were reattaching 5's leg. 5 looked over at 117 and gave a thumbs-up indicating that he was ok.

"The homing device is installed in your wrist," Grandpa sat up straighter and pointed at his own wrist, "It's activated in a very complicated sequence with your fingers that only the amborgs know. I know how to observe your behavior so I could immediately tell you were activating it when we came in since this place masks a lot of communications signals."

117 stood up and approached Mark carefully.

"How do you have all of this information?" He asked curiously. "For a normal human, it should be restricted."

"Remember David, I am not bound completely by the law," His grandfather said informatively and he pointed at the ceiling. "This place is supposed to be abandoned but you think I'm going to follow that rule? It's a nice place. I live here. Boom. Simple as that. I hate to sound condescending but even an amborg with sophisticated calculations constantly running through your mind should be able to work out the fact that I have a good feed of information."

"You have many contacts then?"

Mark chuckled.

"That's an understatement," He said. "The police forces in almost half the states are giving us info. I have people all over the world and I even have some people at A.I. industries looking after Kendrick. You'd be surprised at the people that hate him."

"Police?" 117's head tilted to the side, "Are you possibly referring to…"

"Captain Bradley is an informant only," His grandfather cut him off, "She also doesn't really approve of me but she considers me an ally from past encounters. She operates as the face of the LAPD with my support. She told me about you when she first met you and I knew I had to see you at that point. You should have seen her reaction when I explained my plan of how to meet you. Almost flipped."

"She was against you meeting me?" 117 asked. It was a little hard to believe that Captain Bradley had gone to bat for him. "Captain Bradley? We are referring to the same one are we?"

"I know she really doesn't seem the type," Mark sighed in agreement, "But she went along with it when I came forward with all the Intel I had. Big softie for you kids actually. When we found out someone made weapons specifically to kill or harm the amborgs, that's not something we overlook, someone means to do serious business. If this sort of thing was kept out of reach from behind the scenes of the local police and even your common criminal organizations, then it's been perfectly concealed from A.I. Industries. So Captain Bradley helped stage the whole thing… well. She had no idea about the stabbing part. She's still pissed I almost endangered your life."

"You believe that someone is planning to fight the amborgs?" 117 asked but his grandfather shrugged.

"I'm one of the best information brokers in the underworld," Mark said bluntly. "If I don't know the identity or even the complex details of this… plot, then I'm telling you to be careful David. But I have feeling it's already begun if common criminals are getting blades in mass quantities. It's like someone's arming their troops for something big. These small street battles across the country aren't the big issue anymore. It's camouflaging something that even the U.S. military isn't planning on ignoring. You saw how bad it was with Lieutenant Palmer earlier. Forget about the times in the past when the police needed military reinforcements to suppress common riots. The battle that happened today was actual war. Or at least a skirmish that kicked off something big. We have to be ready now."

This was surprising to hear even to 117. He had predicted the possibility that one day, a threat would emerge but this was sooner than he originally thought. He thought about the amborgs and their methods on handling situations like what had happened earlier. Were they even capable of preparing for a war? It wasn't what they were built for though.

"Even with all of this and our help," 117 said pointing at Mark's arms. "The equipment my father provided isn't enough? This could potentially be too much to handle for several of us."

Grandpa Mark pulled back his sleeve and revealed a type of metal brace on his arm. 117 stared at the device. It looked old and had a crude design which he had never seen before. The brace had a few attachments which were embedded within the arm itself.

"This was experimental equipment originally designed for the local police," He said rolling up both sleeves, "It was before Kendrick made a breakthrough with LTO plating and fusion. Back then, augmentation through implants and cybernetic equipment that you could slip on and off was the latest fashion. At first these braces were already too much to handle for me but I got used to it. The only thing I'm concerned of is dying of old age without finishing this fight. Trust me, you kids all have a higher chance of making it to the end than I do."

"If you bested me," 117 said reassuringly, "Then your chances are the same as mine based on what you have described to me. Perhaps you could purchase security drones and just relax through the whole thing when it happens. Retire while you still can at your age."

"Funding for robotic drones was and still is expensive these days," Mark replied. He did smile at 117's idea though and leaned back as if a sudden wave of exhaustion washed all over his body. "Retirement is not for me I'm afraid though," He muttered grimly, "Not now. I'd rather have one margarita in the end instead of constantly laying around getting one for the rest of my life. Getting good things handed to me instead of earning it myself in this time is just not right for me. Only the rich can afford vacations, proper security programs and drones. No. As long as there still people living off the streets, I'll keep working full-time for them. Those margaritas can wait. Someday, David. You will understand those moments when you've truly succeeded. They happen rarely but when they do, appreciate it."

"One day," 117 said with a small smile. "I will be able to trust you. One day, I will understand fully that you are possibly the last family I have apart from my brothers and sisters. One day, we will share that margarita together... Grandpa."

"I thought you kids didn't drink," Mark chuckled. He looked up at 117 with a wide smile.

"If I am going to still be human," 117 shrugged. "Perhaps, I should partake in a few bad habits to boost my social skills."

"Sounds good to me son."

"There is still something I don't get..." 117 said thinking about what was said earlier. "What is your relationship to Captain Bradley?"

"We go way back," Mark pressed a button on his right arm brace and a holographic photo shone brightly in the air from the projector. It showed a young man and woman in very formal clothing.

"See?" Mark said cheerfully, "I took her to prom!"

117 stared in wide-eyed at the holographic photo. If he had only heard it, he wouldn't have believed it. As he examined the couple more closely, he realized however unlikely it was, his grandfather was telling the truth.

"How long ago was this...?" 117 asked feeling very unnerved and slightly disturbed at seeing such a young looking Captain Bradley in a single shoulder-strapped dress.

"She was prom queen," Mark replied winking. "It's been years now... give or take quite a few decades I think. With anti-aging technology, she sure doesn't look so old so it's hard to remember. Senile is definitely not in her vocabulary. Bless her heart. She still has a nice figure but I do wish I was crowned King. There would have been a lot more satisfaction."

Mark shut off the projector and then looked around. He leaned to the left and looked behind 117.

"By the way, David, you mind calling off your girlfriend before she kills one of my guys?"

There was yell from behind which caused 117 to whirl around. 5 had disappeared from the table and 117 saw him falling to the ground. In the midst of the commotion, 117 spotted 43 in locked combat with the people who had been reattaching 5's leg. She had appeared from nowhere and somehow entered the area while avoiding detection. While he admired her skill, 117 leaped forward and began to stop her when all of a sudden, complete pandemonium ensued. Before he had the chance to send a communication to 43's CPU, several of his grandfather's hooded fighters began to engage her. Ignoring 5's calls to stand-down, 43 stood her ground and took on everyone who charged.

Making instant calculations, 117 moved into the fray. 43 was handling nine of the vigilantes quite perfectly. The problem however, was that more people were going up against her, which either would result in 43 being overpowered or crippling a significant number of Mark's personnel. As he struggled to move closer, a few of the hooded figures were being sent flying past him.

She might tear them apart actually, 117 thought in an agitated tone. Must stop her now!

117 hopped over one of them who had just been sent sliding across the floor. He only had a few seconds to examine if that person was alright when another vigilante flew towards him causing him to duck down. Sidestepping another person and moving forward, 117 eventually found himself caught in the whirlwind of people. Finally, 117 dodged the fifth person and saw his opportunity. He charged power to his legs and leaped forward with his arms outstretched, pinning 43 against the wall.

"Stop! They are not our enemy!" 117 linked up as he grabbed and held onto both of her arms.

"They took 5's leg off!" She protested angrily, "What was I supposed to do?! Let them?! I had to do something!!"

"They were reattaching it!" 5 shouted as he joined the conversation. "Man that was surprising..."

All the vigilantes instantly calmed down and stopped. The fighting ceased and everyone backed off.

"He was in no real danger," 117 said reassuringly.

43 shook her arms out of 117's grasp, looked around and bowed her head sheepishly. She coughed and cleared her throat in an attempt to hide her embarrassment.

"Well, sometimes… jumping to conclusions makes things more interesting," She muttered.

5 walked up to the pair of them. His leg, fully reattached, looked stiff and was causing him to limp. He massaged the upper thigh and sighed.

"Yeah," 5 reported casually. "It was all a misunderstanding. No harm no foul. Almost… I'm just going to sit over there and wait for my leg to reconnect. Give you lovebirds some time."

"Yeah David!" Grandpa Mark yelled from the background, "Plant a big one on her! Let her know you're ok!"

Upon hearing these words, 43 blushed and began to turn a deep shade of red. Suddenly, a faint beeping noise came out of all three amborg's wrists.

"Whoa… A temperature spike," 5 said observingly, "I don't think I've ever seen you this embarrassed before 43."

"Well that might have been a steam vent I passed earlier when I made my way here," She said calmly as she turned her head away promptly. "My skin sensors are probably malfunctioning in this environment. We should get back so I can get it checked."

Without another word, she stalked off before anyone could reply. 5 turned to 117 and smiled. He held up his hand and 117 looked. 5's heat sensor wasn't even on from what he could scan. Now he realized what had happened.

"That wasn't nice 5," 117 said angrily. "She was in distress."

"Oh well, it was payback for knocking me onto the ground," 5 shrugged. "Stop looking at me like that, I am still entitled to some fun in my condition. Besides, malfunction in the environment. Heh. I've heard worse excuses. I wonder what she was so defensive about."

"You know perfectly what it was," 117 said looking at where 43 had disappeared to. "Was that level of peer pressure necessary?"

"Don't even deny it 117. I am speaking directly at one of the causes of her supposed malfunction."

"Sarcasm detected," 117 looked firmly away from 5 and intentionally rolled his eyes, "My proper response would be to tell you to shut up."

"Ahem."

Both of them turned to face 117's grandpa who was holding something in his hands. He put it in 117's hands and both amborgs bent closer to have a better look. It was a small circular device with an orange button in the center. It didn't look special at all until he flipped it over and saw a name written on the underside.

"Is that my father's name?" 117 inspected it clearly for a second time, "That is his name."

"Yes it is, David," The old man said happily, "He invented that before he died. It serves as a beacon. It's always linked to my brace so if you click it, I'll know. I told him if he needed help, just press that button and I'd get the message. It may look like an ordinary button, but once you press it, my brace can locate from where you last activated it and I can follow your trail. Why don't you tinker with that and give me a call soon. It's the least I can do for you if you ever get in trouble with someone other than me."

117 clicked the button once and suddenly, his grandfather's arm brace beeped. A light shone from the wrist and his grandfather tapped his arm brace.

"I should put that on mute from now on," he muttered. "It'd be bad if you needed my help and it went off in a bad time."

"Is this supposed to be some sort of method to slip past my suspicions?" 117 raised his eyebrow. "Giving gifts from my deceased parents could be another trick."

His grandfather looked back at 117 and shook his head in a disgruntled manner. He looked as if he had just been in an emotional wreck.

"David," He said, "It's not about trying to deceive you. That belonged to your father. You should take it now. That's all there is to it. You don't need to be so suspicious of me anymore. Remember when we talked about margaritas and Captain Bradley being prom queen? Those are the things I want to talk to you about. I want to see you happy and secure about your surroundings. I understand it will be a long road but I want to help you."

"Sorry grandfather," 117 nodded. "That was out of line."

"If I'm going to be honest," Mark replied with a sigh. "Your father would definitely feel the exact same way. Now I think it's time you went home now. Remember David, there's going to be changes the more you fight out in the world. Stay on guard."

"Loosely translated," 5 whispered to 117. "I think that just means don't speak to strangers."

"Exactly 5," Mark chuckled.

117 looked down at the button in his hand and pocketed it. Making sure it was secure, he nodded to his grandfather again.

"Thank you grandpa," He replied. "I will consider your help and look to you as an ally in the future. Thank you for having us as your guests."

"My pleasure."

* * *

5 and 117 made their way through the tunnel that 43 had went through. The route they took up to the surface was a different one but 117's grandfather said it was the fastest way to get back to where they had initially parked. As they turned the twelfth corner, they saw the exit and sunlight was pouring through. 43 stood waiting for them at the end. They both met up with her and together they emerged from the entrance near one of the market districts of the city. It was roughly miles from where 5 and 117 safely evacuated Lieutenant Palmer. The three of them made their way towards the urban districts where they had parked their drop-pods. A lot of people turned and stared at the three amborgs walking casually down the street but they ignored them. They all just wanted to be home.

"Do you think it will happen soon? The threat he was warning about?" 5 asked after a few minutes of silence. "I think he made it sound pretty anti-climactic though. Where is the excitement at that point?"

"Our sole occupation is the welfare and maintenance of a proper civil population," 43 recited off the top of her head. "That was one of our original protocols when we became cybernetically augmented. The world is in such bad shape and has suffered for so long that if something bad happens, it is very common and we do not believe it to be such a serious thing. Perhaps his warning was meant to tell us to be alert and not lose focus. We have been on so many operations that it is very easy to be bored."

"Grandpa Mark does not want us off-guard," 117 said. "Perhaps that is why he beat me. I was under the impression that I could handle myself that night. But then it became an unexpected turn of events and I didn't know what to do. He was saying the amborgs are getting too attached with ourselves. We need to consistently adapt and become better or we will be badly hurt."

"I can agree to that," 5 said thoughtfully. "I might even add some secret weapons to my leg while we are discussing the future."

As the trio of amborgs wandered back out into the open and were in a good place for reception, they decided it was time to call home. Everyone soon reestablished contact with their technicians. Mandy's frantic voice suddenly spoke into 117's head.

"David? Are you there? I thought you guys were goners," She asked nervously, "How did you end up in the market district?"

"We traveled through some tunnels," 117 raised a finger and tapped his head to clear the signal, "It seems that tech support is unavailable in the Underground."

"So it seems. I'm just glad, you're all ok. Now get back to A.I. Industries, Kendrick's orders," Mandy replied really quickly, "We're sending your drop-pods a little closer to you."

"Thank you Mandy," 117 looked up to the sky, "You will not believe what I have learned."

"Save it for later David," Mandy impatiently but she stopped and continued in a calm and caring tone, "By the way, thanks for saving my fiancée. It means a lot to me. Really it does."

"It was the right thing to do Ellie," 117 continued on as 43 and 5 both waved to him to go faster. There was a clatter in the background of 117's head and he heard Mandy speak again. This time she sounded flustered.

"David, please don't call me that. EVER. Only my fiancée gets to call me that."

"If you say so Mandy."

"Come on boys," 43 interrupted. She lifted a finger and pointed, "Our ride home is that way. Dr. Kendrick wants a report from both of you so we can make sense of what's been happening."

"Is it possible to get all of us together?" 5 asked while a few bystanders gave them some curious stares as they walked past, "Last I heard, I thought we were all over the place."

"You can thank 117 for that when he told Kendrick to bring everyone back," 43 smiled, "We're having a big amborg family reunion."

"Wow…" 5's eyes widened. "What did I miss exactly?"

"Was it wrong?' 117 inquired, ignoring 5's question. "What would have happened if a call-back hadn't been initiated?"

"I don't know," 43 said with a shrug, "You and 5 are the only ones so far to receive this much damage. Speaking of which, you might want to check up on that leg 5. You are still limping."

"Oh great," 5 said with uncertainty, "I hope it'll just be a regular scan."

"Ah no," 43 said sheepishly, "They need to take your leg off again to run diagnostics."

5 put up his hands, shrugged and walked ahead of them.

"Well, what else have I got to lose?" He asked before ending his communication link.

Leaving 43 and 117 to hang back, 117 felt that it was time to reopen another conversation with 43. Unfortunately, that wasn't the case. As soon as 5 was out of earshot, she immediately turned and punched him in the face. He straightened up in complete bewilderment. She hadn't used a lot of force but it was enough to cause him to stagger to the ground.

"What was that for?!" He asked defensively but was cut off instantly when she suddenly embraced him tightly.

Baffled, 117 awkwardly brought his arms up and patted her on the back three times. To finish, he added a simple, "there, there," to lift her spirits. If 5's heat scanner was going to pick something up, this would definitely have been one of those moments.

"Don't go running off like that again," She said as she burrowed her head into his shoulder, "The homing beacon you sent made me worried and when I ran in and saw 5 with those people holding his leg, I thought you had..."

Understanding the situation immediately, 117 held her shoulders, mimicked her movement and embraced her tightly.

"It's all right now 43, I'm fine. Now shall we go home?"

She let go of him and smiled.

"Sounds good to me."

As they walked after 5, 117 massaged the place where she had punched him.

"But was punching me really necessary?" 117 asked wincing a little. He could still feel the pain. 43 turned and thought for a minute.

"That was an imitation actually," She admitted. "999 does it to 917 whenever he does something stupid like that and worries her. I asked myself what she would do if you wanted to talk to me again in private."

"43," 117 said with an annoyed look. "When has it ever been wise to imitate 999's behavior? What was the name that we decided on for her?"

"The lone wolf of A.I. Industries," 43 said with a dramatic flair. "But you knew that already right?"

"Yes," He said. "I was making sure you knew that. It was a confirmation."

"You don't have to worry 117," 43 snickered. "999 and I are equal in terms of being bad-asses. But if we were both paired side by side, I am one of the nicer ones."

"Considering that 917 is the only one capable of communicating with her," 117 recalled thinking of their brother and sister amborgs. "A very odd pair. I do not know how he gets along with a girl so reserved."

"We can finish this when we go home," 43 said as they both saw 5 standing in front of their drop-pods. "There has been enough excitement for one day."

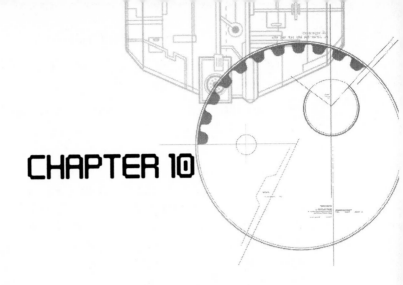

CHAPTER 10

Christmas Day

Time passed rather quickly ever since 117 spoke with his grandfather. In that gap, he never forgot about it and was constantly on guard. After he submitted his report to Dr. Kendrick and the other amborgs, new protocols had been updated to help ease the tension and uneasiness that had developed. Even though it was the winter holiday, 117 still wanted to maintain a sense of security and constant vigilance. He was on his way to the big Christmas party to hopefully find time to relax for the first time in weeks. As he turned a corner, he felt a small twinge in his back. He massaged it briefly and checked his bio-scans. The scar from the knife wound in his back would always be there to serve as a reminder of his first defeat. He was only allowed to take off the bandages a week ago so he wasn't surprised it was acting up in small ways.

117 continued down the hall but slowed his pace to monitor his back. As he did so, he ended up walking by Number 8 and 9's quarters. All of a sudden, an explosion came from inside 8's quarters stopping him in his tracks. Out of habit, 117 leaped to the wall furthest away from where the blast came from and hunched down. Instantly, the door across from 8's quarters opened and 13 sped out of his room. He sped-walk by, ignoring 117's defensive stance and pretended as if nothing was going on.

"I don't want to be here to see what happens this time," He said irritably and disappeared fast around the corner. "I believe

I will drop in on the Christmas party a few minutes early. Merry Christmas and see you later 117."

"See-you-there-13," 117 replied, stunned at how fast 13 was gone. He wasn't sure if 13 had even heard.

117 barely had time to turn his head when suddenly, the door to 8's room burst open. He saw Stuart 8 run outside, head on fire, and attempting to put it out. Without even linking up with him, 117 ran to the emergency panel and grabbed the fire extinguisher (which had been voted by several amborgs to remain there on a consistent basis) and began putting him out instantly. The extinguishing agent covered 8 in white foam, immediately putting out the flames. While he wasn't too severely damaged, he gave a look of utmost fury. At that same moment, Christy 9 came out of her room and instantly took a photo with a large grin on her face.

"Annnndd... Merry Christmas to you 8!" She said cheerfully, "I was planning to take a picture of him on fire but this works too!"

8 wasn't amused at all.

"9! A flamer grenade?! I just finished cleaning up for the Christmas party!" He shouted. Somehow 117 was included in the group chat when he shouted this.

117 placed the extinguisher back in the holder and radioed the custodian as the two of them began to throw insults. This time however, there were very few insults which was a first.

"Always worrying for nothing. You won't be late," 9 said reassuringly in a teasing manner which 117 was sure she had spent months practicing on, "If you start now, you can clean up in at least a minute and thirty second window and still be in time for the party."

"You mean you could have made me late?"

"I chose not to," 9 winked, "Consider that a gift from my precious thoughts of you during this lovely yuletide."

With a grin, she went back inside her quarters and the door shut. A loud click indicated to the two amborgs that she had safely locked herself inside.

117 looked at 8 who was staring angrily at her door. 8 almost looked like he was about to yell but couldn't seem to find the right

words. He looked to 117 for help but all 117 could do was give him a smile of sympathy.

"Don't look at me," 117 said sternly, "You two cannot seem to stop pulling pranks on each other so it's your own responsibility to bear. Now go and get cleaned. We have a party to attend and Dr. Kendrick wants all of us there looking our best."

Stunned, 8 looked almost as if he was about to argue but then thought better and nodded. He turned around and went back inside his quarters without another word. 117 checked both 8 and 9's quarters for a few seconds and nodded when he was sure there wasn't going to be any more imminent trouble. He was amazed how he had commanded such authority just now to a first group amborg. He would have to make a note of how to do that again later.

Just then, a clatter brought his attention behind him. 117 turned and saw the janitor come around the corner. 117 instantly walked forward to help but stopped when the old man waved his arm.

"Ah 117, I may look old but I'm still capable of doing the job. It's great to see you though!" The janitor said cheerfully wielding his mop and clenching his bucket of tools, "So what's the story? What happened between 8 and 9 this time?"

"Flamer grenade," 117 explained as he pointed at the remains of the mess. "There are some remnants of the extinguishing agent in the hallway. Are you certain I cannot assist in anyway?"

The janitor brushed away 117's hand again which had automatically extended for the mop. The short old man clung onto his tools stubbornly and chuckled.

"Hey, I'm not as old as you think. Remember, I can get the job done no matter how big it is," He smiled, "A flamer grenade? Well it's a good thing you guys are indestructible."

"That is not entirely accurate," 117 smiled. "But your praise is appreciated. I do have time to help if you do change your mind."

"I'm fine David 117," The old man smirked and began mopping the floor, "Go and find that 43 and make something of yourselves. Get some action. Merry Christmas! And remember, you've been working hard. Whatever you face, just know that a lot of us believe in you kid. That wound in your back will always be there but anyone who attacks you like that cannot destroy one thing."

"What is that?"

"The courage in your heart and the will to fight."

The man smiled and went back to cleaning. To this, 117 didn't have a response. Instead, he walked away down the hall and went in the opposite direction away from where the party was held. He soon found himself outside one of the small research labs which was a small library database as well. Instead of browsing the shelves, he went straight to the front desk. There was only one librarian on duty who acknowledged 117 briefly but then turned his attention back to what he was reading.

"David 117," he said without looking up, "It's a surprise to see you on this particular occasion. Isn't the party starting soon?"

"Yes," he replied, "But I have twelve minutes to spare. Interesting. Everyone is so concerned about the time when amborgs are always never late. Aside from that, what I have to talk about won't be long."

"Of course. What can I help you with?" He asked as he lowered his book and looked up.

"That janitor, Stan," 117 asked politely, "Does he have family?"

"Yes, I believe he has a wife and two children. This is a peculiar inquiry 117 which I don't think can be found in the library. Why do you ask?"

"Like you, I do not believe anyone should be working on this day," 117 explained. He thought of Stan cleaning the long and empty hallways and then said, "Can you call them from their residence and ask them to come over to the party? Once you have done so, you should bring yourself as well along with anyone else you know of attempting to be alone."

"Thanks 117," The librarian smiled. "Some people prefer to be alone though. Me for example, I'd rather sit here and read a book instead of dealing with other people. And I hope you'll respect my privacy and not ask why."

"I understand," 117 said politely, "I just felt that you did not have to be alone so I included you in an invitation. I was hopeful you could spend time having fun."

The man behind the desk chuckled as he flipped through the pages attempting to locate where he had stopped.

"Well 117," He replied, "I appreciate you thinking of me. It's usually a lot more than what most humans would do in general. Besides... I'm already having fun. Now go to the party without me. I'll see what I can do about Stan's family. I don't think they had too many plans this winter since his poor wife has been having medical issues. They should have nothing stopping them from coming but be aware that they may not want to."

"Understood. Thank you for your help."

117 turned to leave but was stopped when the librarian called to him again.

"Wait a moment," He said, "117, you could have checked the database for that information... why did you stop in here other than invite me to the party?"

"Oh pardon me," 117 admitted with twinge of embarrassment. "I have been busy that I almost forgot about the other reason of why I came. It was meant to... kill two birds with one stone. But I believe I should tell you that one of the research managers is planning to crush you."

"Crush me?" The man replied in bewilderment. "Someone wants to beat me up later?"

"That is not what I believe to be the intention," 117 replied. "Instead of violence, they expressed that they wanted to express an interest in you."

"Oh..." The librarian chuckled. "It's they have a crush on me 117. Not they want to crush me."

"Oh. My mistake."

The man shook his head laughing and sat back down. Picking his book up again, he waved to 117.

"Now get out of here already," He said smiling, "You keeping track of the time?"

To get to the gym, 117 decided to take a walk down the hall of commemoration. It was a bit of a long way but he felt that the party could get started without him for a few minutes. When he reached the photo of his parents, 117 sat down and watched as the photo began to play its short video loop. As his parents danced happily in the holo-picture, 117 smiled. He thought very briefly about his parents being able to reach out to him but instantly shut out the idea. Brooding over something that might have been was meant for another time. Once his parents stopped dancing and the hologram shut off, 117 stood up and placed a hand on the photo again and opened his mouth. He took a breath and spoke the following words.

"Merry...zzt...'cough' Christzzt...mas," He managed to get out, "I... love...you."

And he stood up, took one last look down the hall and walked on to the gym.

117 then passed a window and looked outside. There was clear white snow falling on the grounds. He could see the defense drones standing guard at the entrances and pacing the fences as they usually did. 117 imagined children and their families playing in the snow outside. In place of the fence and defense drones, there were tables and people were having fun celebrating outside. No violence, no paranoia, just a place to finally have no worries or fears. Then, he realized he was playing memories from his summer database. Strange, he thought as he rubbed his eyes and checked his eyesight. He had mistakenly added the images outside which was very peculiar. He needed to get his eyes checked at his next diagnostics test.

The party had just begun when 117 stepped inside the gym which had been completely redecorated to a ballroom setting. There was a dance floor, buffet and the DJ drones were even decorated for the evening. All the security didn't have weapons which pleased 117. Almost every employee plus the tough-looking guards had their families there and all of them were taking in the moments with their loved ones. The kids were definitely the ones running around with the most excitement. Looking around, 117 saw that the female amborgs had all decided to dress up for the party and were wearing custom-made gowns and dresses. All the male amborgs (From their human education) were all making small gestures and nervously pulling at the neck of their clothes at the sight of all their female compatriots. Several of the male amborgs were in suits and tuxedos which made 117 feel underdressed but he didn't feel too bad when he saw that many of them were just wearing their amborg jackets. When they weren't dirty or covered with mud stains, they did look very formal.

117 noticed Mr. Ramirez with his daughter Thalia. Both came up to 117 and shook his hand and Thalia topped it off with a hug. 8 and 9 had shown up without any damage by the look of it and were on their best behavior. (Dr. Kendrick was eyeing both of them from a distance very closely.) To get his mind off of observing the whole place, someone walked up behind and linked up.

"Cutting it a bit close 117. What's on your mind?"

"Nothing much Leonard 1," 117 turned and shook 1's hand. He hadn't seen the first amborg in a long time and was beginning to feel very overwhelmed to be speaking to the very first person to successfully become an amborg. Nevertheless he continued the small talk, "I see that you are also late."

"Well, I was notifying the janitor Stan to attend the party with me," 1 explained and began eyeing 8 and 9 who were both drinking punch at the buffet. 3 was keeping a steady eye on them and 7 appeared to be holding a type of rifle which 117 hadn't seen before. "I reminded him that it was unfitting to be working on a holiday and that he should be here. But from what I found out, it seems like you already beat me to the punch. Well done."

"I assumed that he was motivated to work hard to continue providing for his family despite it being Christmas," 117 hypothesized. "His wife having medical issues and his children in the middle of their grade school and high school education must be taking a toll. After all, someone with that amount of dedication and loyalty probably would like to stay away from others enjoying their fun together with their own families."

"Interesting 117," 1 nodded in agreement, "Why do I have a... feeling that you are withholding information?"

"It is a surprise," 117 smiled and held up a finger to his lips, "You will know when you see it."

"Very well," 1 acknowledged, "Then I won't question the matter further. I trust your surprise will be enlightening. Merry Christmas David 117."

"To you as well, Leonard 1," 117 replied and 1 walked off into the crowd.

For the next few minutes 117 amused himself around the four amborg chef team at the buffet table. Things were going smoothly until 8 and 9 were at it again. The two of them had decided to start a punch battle which 117 could only assume resulted from a private argument. The situation become worse when some children decided to join in. As several cups of punch was flung all over the place, many adults became worried and all looked on anxiously. Amborgs and children did not make a good combination even when it was a non-hostile situation. Finally, 3 took action.

She grabbed the rifle from 7's hands and fired one shot at the ceiling. A red light sparked from the weapon like a flare but when it reached the top of the ceiling, it burst and split into multiple red lights and sparkles flew all over the place. It dissipated just a few meters above everyone's heads but it didn't hit anyone. The children all cheered and begged for more while the amborgs all stared curiously. Even 8 and 9 stopped mid-fight to look.

"ALL RIGHT!" 3's voice rang out in the heads of all the amborgs in the vicinity causing them all to cringe. Several adults came up to the kids and ushered them away as the amborgs all listened to 3. "THIS thing here is something research developed! Actually, I invented it and they let me keep the prototype. The safety has been applied so it is harmless but if it was not on, then those sparks would have been seriously painful. I call it the POP gun! And that was the first setting out of twenty! Who wants to see setting two?"

The children, completely oblivious to the loud scolding the amborgs had just been exposed to, continued to cheer and ask for more of 3's fireworks even despite the fact that most of the parents were dragging or carrying them away from the buffet table. All the surrounding adults relaxed and things went back to normal. 8 and 9 ceased their little fight and went back to behaving politely. The twins, 92 and 93 followed them around and stuck close to them to ensure nothing else happened. 117 then turned to 3 and requested a drink.

"Those two!" She huffed as 117 watched her make a mixture, "I made punch to be consumed, not to be thrown around! This stuff is perfectly organic from everything here and they want to use it as ammunition."

She bent down and picked out a glass and began making a mixture as 117 spoke cheerfully.

"It is all right Missy 3," he said reassuringly, "They probably make this party much livelier anyway."

"Only if they were not so keen to prank each other... Here you go, a new recipe for you," 3 announced as she put a glass in 117's hand. It was fizzing quite loudly which looked oddly familiar. Forgetting to scan it, 117 drank it anyway. Just like the night when he had been backstabbed, he turned his head sharply, pulled a face and steam erupted from his ears. 3 was smiling and pretending not to laugh.

"You got this recipe from Giuseppe!" 117 coughed and a smoke ring came out.

"Well what do you expect 117?" 3 shrugged, "I had to find something you...liked. Or rather, something close. But this was something you were familiar with at least so now I can make your special cocktail."

Before he could say anything, the music had changed and the mood of the atmosphere seemed to quiet down. 117 turned around and to him, it looked as if a wave a relief had taken the crowd. Everyone was moving out of the dance floor for the people in the center. Missy 3 glanced dreamily at the center of the floor as a very old traditional dance began to play.

"A slow dance!" 3 exclaimed clapping her hands excitedly. "Oh I must participate! Where is 7?"

117 was still trying to clear his throat of her drink mixture when she ran off to find a partner. Looks like the buffet is self-serving, 117 thought as he burped more smoke out.

He looked at the center and saw some amborgs pairing up and dancing around the circle. It was only after seeing some of the problems a couple of them were having did he realize one specific detail he had put off. 117 did not know how to dance. Getting an idea, he decided to begin searching for someone he knew would be able to help him. In less than ten seconds, he had found Mandy in the arms of Lieutenant Palmer. He made his way over to where they had decided to keep their dance isolated from the circle.

"There you are David," she said happily when he approached. The two of them stopped dancing to face him. Lieutenant Palmer extended his hand out which 117 took with a smile.

"What I have to ask won't be long, Lieutenant," 117 said politely, "May I...cut in?"

"Why not? I'll go get some drinks," Palmer looked to Mandy and she nodded. He then walked away towards the buffet table. 117 then placed his left hand on Mandy's hip and held her other hand with his right.

"Query," He looked at Mandy who was wearing a business jacket and regular work skirt. The standard clothes he always saw her wear. "You have not dressed for the occasion Mandy?"

She shook her head as they slowly began to step but after two, they didn't move at all.

"Didn't have the time," She sighed lifting her shoulders, "All that matters to me is that Palmer is here. Besides, I don't think a gown is my kind of dress. I'll have to try one on after we save the world. Aside from that, I didn't know you danced David."

"To be quite honest, I can't," 117 responded sheepishly, "I was hoping you could teach me."

"For starters David, we should probably move again."

"Oh... That would be a wise solution," He replied and began to lead.

Unfortunately, it wasn't a good start. As they clumsily moved across the floor, he stepped on Mandy's feet several times after only fifteen seconds. Instantly, she stopped him before the bones in her feet continued to suffer. She probably could have withstood the pain a lot longer had it been with a regular human but an amborg practically weighed twice as much.

"Ok David," She winced and hunched over at the pain from her feet, "I don't understand. You do so well in your regular classes. What went wrong?"

"I am unable to mimic your movement unless I stare at your foot movement," He said casually. "Remember in class, we always danced with each other or practice drones. It is taking me some time to register you as a new dance partner."

Mandy took another breath and thought of a solution.

"Ok, this time," She said, "Look at my feet and I will lead this time. Providing the feeling in my feet ever come back."

Then they started to dance again. This time, there were no mistakes at all. Despite 117's gaze at the floor and the fact that Mandy almost looked as if she was steering a refrigerator on two feet, the two of them managed to get the hang of dancing. After the song ended however, Mandy had managed to work up quite a sweat.

"Ok David," She panted. The dance had left her slightly winded from leading around the floor. "Now you lead."

"Lead where Mandy?" 117 asked with a puzzled look on his face while Mandy took a couple of breaths and then they began to dance again but slowly. She looked as if she had just finished an intensive aerobics session.

"Do you see how I'm forcing you to move in certain directions?" She asked. "Did you notice when I led you in a turn? Here, let me show you at this column."

She led him near a column and promptly turned so the two of them could avoid dancing into it. 117 observed the movement and nodded.

"Ah I understand now," He said. "I was looking at your foot movement during that sequence and I believe I have it."

Unconvinced by this reaction, Mandy decided to test him.

"David look up."

He shifted his gaze from the floor straight up to the ceiling which caused Mandy to shake her head and laugh.

"No David, look at me," She shook her head. "Look at your partner's eyes. The person you're dancing with remember?"

Not saying anything, 117 looked. His CPU processor identified Mandy's eyes as one hundred percent normal and completely identical the last time he saw them. But he decided not to bring it up sensing that something else might go wrong. As he began to properly lead, she exhaled and relaxed as he took over. He led them smoothly and without error once around the floor back to where they started and that's when Mandy smiled brightly.

"Now that's how you take someone for a dance."

After the song ended, the two of them left the dance floor and went to go find Palmer. The two of them found him at the beverage table where he was trying to resolve an issue with number 13. The doctor amborg, Vanessa 6 stood by him trying to run a scan against his protests. Apparently Palmer had mistakenly picked up a drink specially made for Number 22 and was spitting out whatever it was that was mixed into the glass. 13 quickly held up a pail under Palmer's mouth which he pushed away gently.

"Hey honey are you ok?" Mandy said as she patted his back (117 also began running a scan too). He straightened up and put the glass down on the table which 13 picked up, sniffed it and poured it out.

"Oh yeah sure," He said cheerfully as he pulled a handkerchief from his pocket and coughed into it. "I was just enjoying drinks with 13. There was a bit of a mix up but I keep telling the ever so persistent 6 that I'm ok. No seriously I am. Can I have a drink without motor oil mixed into it please?"

"Motor oil?" Mandy gave a look of shock. "I thought you guys established safety protocols. Separate amborg cocktails from the regular human ones so this doesn't happen."

117 held up his hand in front of Palmer's throat and began scanning. 13 gave an apologetic smile and ducked under the table to find something to cleanse Palmer's throat. He stood back up and tossed a vial to 6 who caught it easily.

"Take this now," She instructed. "Even though most of it was thrown up, it was still a custom drink for Sarah 22. That blend of motor oil was slightly toxic but necessary for some of her cybernetics. We need to make sure you get it out of your system completely so this is a neutralizing agent."

"He is in no danger," 117 said reassuringly as he lowered his arm, "Luckily the Lieutenant managed to eject the vile contents of the drink out of his mouth. Well done sir in your vomiting."

"Thanks? Can you guys stop with the scanning please? Thanks," The Lieutenant straightened up, swallowed the contents of the vial and Mandy helped him to the nearest sink. As they walked away, 117 turned to 13 who looked after the two humans with concern.

"What did that drink contain?"

"Oh it was nothing serious," 13 replied even though he looked really nervous. "22 has a previous history of allergies to certain spices. Remember that one time she had an allergic reaction and kept telling us about her performance issues? Turns out the allergic reaction had a couple of bad side effects with a couple of her processors and she hasn't been feeling well. I was only trying to synthesize something she would be able to consume normally and you know how she likes motor oil."

"If she was still human," 6 added, "That allergic reaction could have very well hospitalized her for a long period of time. 22 has been taking a prescription ever since but that could have harmed the lieutenant permanently. I would very much like to avoid check-ups tonight. This is not the right kind of outfit to do a medical screening in... So many people have been staring."

6 put her equipment back in her bag and walked away. 117 turned back to 13 who chuckled nervously. There was only one problem that remained.

"13," 117 said, "You say that the mixture was intended for 22. But where is she? If she was here, this mix-up with Lieutenant Palmer might have been avoided."

13 looked around.

"Well actually," He said, "I was hoping she would stop by soon. I felt bad for her condition so I wanted to give her something to drink. I am not one of the servers though so I cannot leave this station. That was reserved for her."

117 eyed 13 very suspiciously and a grin slowly emerged. 13 stared back with a look of concern.

"What is it? Is something wrong?" He asked nervously.

"Nothing 13," 117 said as he reached forward and gave 13 a pat on the shoulder. "Perhaps you could make another one. Maybe 22 will still stop by."

"Maybe," 13 said grabbing some bottles. "Thanks 117."

117 turned and walked away from the table. Oddly enough, he found 22 sitting alone at a table relaxing. The seat that she was sitting in was far enough to conceal her from where 13 was working. No wonder she hadn't seen the mix-up earlier. She looked up when she noticed 117.

"Hello 117, are you alone as well? Well actually, that sounded a little harsh. At least 43 will be here in a bit," She sighed sadly as she looked at the dance floor. She had decided to wear an emerald colored dress for the party which matched with several of the decorations and lights.

"For the moment, I am. But 22," 117 leaned forward and said, "If you are finding yourself in need of a partner, I believe the solution can be found sixty-eight degrees to the left."

She turned to look in the directions he had given her. Both of them saw 13 at the drinks station who was having a bit of trouble. He had made a mistake with a concoction and it had exploded which was attracting the attention of several people. The small explosion had left his face pitch black and he had probably one of the biggest frowns of disappointment that 117 had ever seen. 22's facial expression turned into a sympathetic smile. As she stood up, 117 handed a handkerchief to her which she accepted silently. She nodded thankfully and walked towards 13. He wasn't able to see the end result when someone spoke behind him.

"You seem to be having fun helping almost everyone. How about you help me for a bit?"

117 turned and someone fell into his open arms.

"Merry Christmas 43, I have been searching for you all evening," 117 said smiling. "How may I be of service?"

"How about being my date this holiday?" She asked. "All evening you say? That is a bunch of bull. The night is still young after all."

He stepped back to take a look at her dress. It was light green, with a single strap over her left shoulder. There was a cut-out above her thigh so a bit of her leg was revealed. She twirled around showing her bare upper back and smiled.

"You think this looks bad on me?" She asked clasping onto his hands once she finished twirling.

"Of course not. In fact, you are the most beautiful thing I have ever seen," 117 bowed his head and she curtsied in response.

"Well then, I guess you should tell me what I missed and what you've been up to," She said as she linked her arm around his outstretched elbow. "I just spoke to 6, what was all that about Lieutenant Palmer consuming 22's motor oil?"

The two of them walked around the entire room and chatted about what had happened in her absence. 8 and 9 almost causing trouble, 13's crush on 22, and 3's new weapon. It felt like a lot had happened in such a short time but there was still much of the party still waiting.

"Wow," 43 nodded, "That might be a lot more activity and entertainment than our last deployment. All of us under one party house getting into a lot of mischief and deploying our own methods of what is perceived as fun."

"Affirmative, by now there should be two things by my calculations that should be occurring at this time," 117 looked around and scanned the crowds, "Oh there he is. Look 43."

Both of them turned to see the gym entrance open and two people entered. Theo 917 was leading Stan into the gym. He was still in his work suit but someone had given him a tie to wear and he looked utterly confused as to what was happening. Dr. Kendrick greeted him warmly and led him in without question.

"How sweet!" 43 said happily as they watched Stan effortlessly do a fist bump with 917. "I have never seen Stan at any of the parties we hold."

"Wait till you see the next phase of my plan," 117 leaned in closed and lowered his volume to a whisper. Both continued to watch as the door opened a second time and an elderly woman pushed by a young woman on a wheelchair and a little boy entered the gym. Stan had also turned to look at the arrivals and instantly, a smile lit up his face. Without a moment's notice, they saw him embracing all of them. 43 turned to 117.

"Is that his family?" She said in awe, "How heart-warming."

"All it took was a phone call," 117 said casually. "Imagine that."

"You called for them to be sent here?" 43 held her hands to her heart, "117, that is very considerate. On Christmas too. Oh it is sweet to see Stan and his family. What a wonderful gift."

When that part of the plan was finished and Stan's family was fully immersed in the party, 117 took 43 by the hands and led her to the edge of the dance floor and began leading her around. They danced past Mr. Ramirez who had Thalia sitting on his shoulders swaying left and right to the music. Dr. Kendrick was also nearby making several people laugh while the amborgs nearby just stood silently contemplating his jokes. As they continued on, they saw 917 and Alice 999 in close proximity having a conversation.

"Is 999 actually participating in the festivities?" 43 asked with an impressed look on her face. 117 turned them around to get a brief glimpse which was all he needed to see what 43 had observed. "This is probably the only time I have ever seen her open up more than usual. Too bad she is not wearing a dress though. I am actually a little curious to see how she would look."

"43, I did not know you liked judging people on their outward appearance," 117 said in an amazed tone as he spun her around. "It is not polite."

"I was not saying she was unattractive," 43 exclaimed, "I feel that with her, it takes many steps in order for her to step out of a comfort zone. For instance, this is the first time I have ever seen her let her own hair down. It is my wish and I am hoping that someday before I die, I will see her put on something that distinguishes her natural beauty. After all, after the world is at peace, we might be out of a job and may actually have time for vacations. Something that a lot of people work for."

"Well that is why she is known as a lone wolf," Said 117. "She is almost as deadly as you and it takes a lot of patience to really know her. Despite her rough looking exterior, 917 always has had the ability to see things in people and everything else that not everyone would mostly see. His relationship with 999 seems to be perfectly balanced. Very interesting. Her hair down does seem to make her more approachable and less intimidating."

"Do you think their relationship is similar to like ours?" 43 asked as 117 dipped her.

"Possibly," 117 replied. "You are more outspoken though. We are both together now. As everyone constantly says, we aren't all the same. I like to think that we aren't better than them but we have our own special relationship that no one can match. Precisely because it's unique only to the two of us."

As they continued to dance, 43 suddenly remembered and asked 117 another question.

"So what was the second thing you had planned?"

117 stopped and looked curiously at her while holding his hands tightly around her waist.

"I was hoping you would ask that question but I have experienced a high level of anxiety in preparing the right response."

"Really? You 117?" 43 raised an eyebrow, "Why would you of all people be full of anxiety?"

The stopped their dance and walked side by side to one of the steel pillars near the outside of the dance floor. 43 inched a bit closer to 117's side.

"You should never have to be anxious around me," 43 said empathetically, "I mean. We are at that stage where we can always tell each other what is on our minds... right?"

"Of course," 117 replied quickly, "It isn't that complicated at all. I am very anxious about what is next because I still need to give you my gift. I spent a majority of my afternoon making preparations for it. So please 43. Would you close your eyes?"

As she closed her eyes, 117 reached into his pocket and pulled out a box. As he did this, there was a loud 'chink' and he looked up wondering what it was. Someone had fired a dart which had sunk into the pillar a few feet above their heads. Dangling from it, 117 noticed that there was mistletoe attached. He scanned the angle and looked for the point of origin based on its trajectory. In the distance, he saw 297, 35 and 57 waving. The trio of amborgs all grinned and gave him the thumbs-up.

"Oh why not?" 117 muttered inside his head. 43's eyes were still closed so he needed to move fast.

He put the box in his left hand and with his right, he cradled her cheek in the palm of his hand and leaned in to kiss her. As their lips met, he pressed firmly against her. Although it wasn't how he originally planned it out, it had to do for now. Feeling unsure of if this was the right way, 117 felt like pulling back until 43 put her arms around his neck and properly returned the kiss. They broke off after a few seconds and pulled away slowly but were still in a heavy embrace.

"Very nice move with the mistletoe dart," She remarked as she glanced upwards. "Now why don't you tell me what's in the box?"

Not hesitating at all, 117 opened the box, to reveal a silver chain. 43 gasped as she picked it up and held it. From her expression, he knew all the work he had put into it had paid off.

"This for me? David 117, it is beautiful! Where did you find this?"

"I made it myself," He explained as he slipped the chain over her wrist and secured it. "Now you know what I was in the middle of accomplishing during my spare time. It is made of material from where we lived before we came here to A.I. Industries. It is durable and can shine even with the faintest light so remember to conceal it in stealth missions. Now you may carry a piece of our home here where we currently live and wherever we go."

"Oh... if I had known, I would have gotten you something equally as good,"" She looked crestfallen but 117 held her hand tightly. "I mean I did get you something but yours has more sentimentality..."

A waiter walked casually behind 43 who reached a hand behind. The waiter dropped something into her hand and then walked off. She held up her present for 117 to see. It was a mini glass figurine of two swans entwined around each other.

"It is also custom made," She said as he took the glass figurine from her. "I always loved how swans moved so I made this based off of a pair I once saw when I was deployed to their natural habitat."

117 looked at the swans and he placed them inside the box that had previously contained his gift to her.

"There, it is safe with me and I shall treasure this," He said pocketing the box. "It will not be as if I was going to carry it with me into combat."

"Of course not," 43 chuckled. "I do not believe those swans are built for it."

She hugged him again and they continued to slowly dance in their place of solitude. Until 43 broke the silence.

"117," She said, "I wanted to tell you something and I hope that... tonight is the first of many. We have known each other for a long time and along with everyone here at A.I. Industries, we often refer to each other as brother and sister. But in our time here, I have noticed a few of the amborgs pursuing deeper relationships with each other and even with normal humans. Some of them do it as experiments for social activity credit but every now and then, true legitimate feeling arise from all of the parameters. So I wanted to tell you that even though we have survived together and worked together for so long, I wanted to tell you that I do not wish to be your sister anymore. Instead I want to be more than that and I wanted to tell you... I love you. Without any complications or detailed analysis, this is the truth that I want you to know."

"Well, I believe the proper response..." 117 replied taking a breath. "Without complications or the most simplest of calculations. I love you as well. Even after our emotions were changed when we became amborgs, I know that deep down, this was what I always wanted. You have become strong, independent and the most attractive woman I have had the privilege of growing up with. I know that without you, things would be very different."

The two of them smiled and gazed into each other's eyes. They shared another small kiss when suddenly, the music stopped and they heard Dr. Kendrick's voice ring over the speaker. They both looked and saw Dr. Kendrick standing on the stage where the DJ was.

"Attention amborgs, ladies and gentlemen and children of all ages," He spoke loudly, "I wanted to thank everyone for putting their efforts into this night and it's been a pleasure working with all of you. Thank you all for coming tonight! Christy 8. Stuart 9. That's enough pranks for the evening."

The crowd all applauded and Dr. Kendrick waved and gave a little bow but looked in the back and gave a hard stare. From the back 8 and 9 both stood side by side and didn't move. Several people in the crowd raised a glass and took a swig as he continued with his speech.

"Now I have several announcements before we continue the rest of the evening," He said. "The first is a minor one but I believe that it should be declared to the world! My head of medical staff here and my personal friend, Dr. Wildman would like to introduce a new addition to his staff!"

Dr. Wildman was shorter than Dr. Kendrick by a few inches but the two of them looked like biological siblings. The only difference in their white lab coats was that Dr. Wildman was sporting the Red Cross on his chest. Dr. Kendrick handed the microphone over to him and he spoke quite enthusiastically.

"Yes, thank you John," He said smiling. "Well, it was meant to be a surprise but we apparently had an incident at the bar which showed off this person's unique skills at work. Yesterday, I filed the paperwork and it is my great privilege to welcome one of the amborgs onto the medical staff. She has shown great interest and dedication into the health and welfare of humans as well as her siblings among the amborgs. Vanessa 6, this is my Christmas present to you. I welcome you as part of my staff and I hope you will continue to learn everything there is to know about caring for others and the treatment of the most powerful and vicious plagues out on the battlefields that we cannot see with our naked eyes. If our world ever reaches a point of peace, I hope you will consider this as your trade for a long time."

Everyone in the audience cheered and applauded as Dr. Wildman raised his arm and waved at 6 who looked very surprised but was also looking very happy. Many amborgs and people were congratulating her. With that announcement finished, Dr. Wildman handed the microphone back to Dr. Kendrick and walked off stage. He personally went up to 6 and gave her a hug.

"Congratulations 6," Dr. Kendrick smiled, "We are all proud of you as well as the other amborgs. Thank you Dr. Wildman. I think she's blushing. She's very surprised well done. Now then, for the next present I have."

One of the research scientists went up on stage and handed him something on a tray. Dr. Kendrick thanked the man and he grabbed one of the devices and held it up for everyone to see. It looked like one of the standard issue bracelets that everyone wore for the amborgs to communicate with.

"I would like to apologize to the inconveniences and the problems that almost all of the amborgs had to face in the field," Dr. Kendrick said, "It was a fool's idea to send the amborgs into the field where the only people they could get their voice out was through police, soldiers, or emergency personnel when their voice could have been used for many more that needed it. Countless lives, both innocent and the enemy could have been saved if the amborgs had their voices. The standard issue bracelets are easy to manufacture but based on all the combat my children face, they aren't durable and many incidents have left the amborgs making difficult choices. They can't offer the enemy a chance to surrender because they sound like they're in pain every time their mouths open. Many of them have actually developed the ability to speak again but how long will it be until they fully use their voices again? Well until then, I offer the amborgs this."

He held up the bracelet for everyone to see high above his head.

"These are new bracelets forged from the hard working minds of my research staff," Dr. Kendrick said proudly, "Made to withstand the worst conditions known to man and completely built to suit the needs of the amborgs. No more will you need to link up with other people that have bracelets. Now you will carry your own that will always transmit your voices. It is my wish that you accept these with my apologies. They did not come when you needed them the most and I'm sorry it took so many wrongs to make this a right."

"Hear hear!" Someone shouted in the crowd. "Let the amborgs speak again!"

Everyone applauded and cheered. All the amborgs looked at Dr. Kendrick excitedly. They did not hold any angst against him at all. Amongst themselves, they didn't show any hate at all because they already had forgave their creator and respected him a lot more.

"Finally! Research has provided us with new stuff!" 297 called out from a nearby bracelet. "About time!"

"Thank you 297! Your impatience definitely contributed to the progress of your new toys."

Everyone laughed and 297 gave Dr. Kendrick a thumbs up who placed the bracelet back on the tray. He then spoke into the microphone again.

"They have been specially designed, after careful inspection of the results from several operations, for the amborgs so they have the means to properly communicate when there is no outlet. So to speak, every amborg now has their own personal speaker. These bracelets are much more different than the standard ones the military and police have. Capable of withstanding intense heat, braving deep-freeze scenarios, transmit with other bracelets from at least ten kilometers away, and very hard to destroy. I hope that you will use these bracelets to the best of their ability. Learn how to wear and continue to do the right thing with them. Also to keep with the Christmas spirit, they come in nice wrapped presents."

Dr. Kendrick took a glass of water and chugged it. When he caught his breath, he continued.

"That is also not the only news I have tonight as well. You are all aware that volunteers for the third group have been selected. Well the deadline for their formal appearance was supposed to be in three days but that was a rumor I asked my staff to spread. They really came online after a purposefully falsified scheduling of augmentation two days ago and they have done magnificently in the testing centers. Which is why I give to you on Christmas day, the third group of amborgs! This time, all of the volunteers have survived the procedures and before my last announcement, I hope that we never lose anyone else who risked their lives for this stage of evolution."

The door to the gym opened and thirty amborgs walked into the gym all displaying nervous but looks of intense curiosity.

"Funny," 43 muttered to 117 privately, "If the crowd was not paying attention to them right now, they look a lot more inconspicuous in terms of human behavior than we did when our systems were installed and put online."

"Dr. Kendrick must be perfecting the augmentation," 117 remarked.

The third group amborgs were all quiet as everyone staring displayed loud noises of awe and wonder. A few of them applauded.

They appeared to be very young to the older amborgs even though every amborg's physique did not change after the enhancement procedure. Even 117 felt a little old watching the young amborgs despite his eighteen year old appearance. Dr. Kendrick then cleared his throat and spoke again.

"This will be my last announcement before we allow the party to commence again. Due to recent events, based off of several reports and evidence gathered, there will be new protocols implemented effective immediately," He said informatively. "It would appear that the circumstances have made it unsafe for the amborgs to go out into the field alone. We will continue performing our duties where we are needed and when we are needed but we will not allow us to be cornered as if there are packs of wolves waiting to hunt. Amborgs of the first and second group, when deployed, will be accompanied by at least one, or more amborgs. Teams will be formed and we will do everything together. Our enemies have weapons that have completely changed our perspective of the playing field and we will do everything we can to level the ground. Third group amborgs, I have brought you here to meet your brothers and sisters. Mingle, have fun, bond with each other, and protect each other. Assemble your teams, coordinate with each team member, and work together. Merry Christmas. Thank you and have a wonderful evening."

"Play on my friends," He shouted to the bot DJs and they began playing more music.

As the music restarted, the crowd dispersed. All the amborgs began making their way towards the third group. None of them had any idea where to go. Every other employee and their family members moved out of the way for the amborgs to mingle as they all went back to what they were doing before the announcements.

"117, that announcement has me thinking."

43 inched closer to 117 as they moved with the rest of the amborgs towards the Third group's gathering place.

"Is it about being in a team together?" 117 asked as they slid past some security officers. "Because you already know what the answer is if you ask."

"No of course," 43 said, "My point is that we will be probably mentoring the kids. They look so innocent, young and defenseless. I wanted to ask that no matter what happens, we find a way for us never to be split apart again. I never want to fight with you again."

"Were you referring to our relationship?" 117 asked with concern. "I thought we had a very nice start for about eighteen minutes and thirty six seconds. Is it at an end already?"

"No 117," 43 said as she kissed him again which made his uneasiness vanish instantly. "I just wanted to apologize for my behavior after you came back from your grandfather until now. I was upset and angry because I thought you had needlessly risked your life but that was selfish of me. You were doing that while thinking of our needs and the greater good. I hated it when all we would do was just greet each other briefly, pass in the halls without acknowledging each other, and improvise new strategies for the future without so much as... a decent conversation in between. Your reports and advising to Dr. Kendrick in the last month is made up of seventy two percent of what he has presented to us tonight on Christmas. Don't be modest. Understand that I am not accusing you of negligence. In fact, you have done the complete opposite for all of us. But I missed you and I know that in the time we spent not interacting with each other, I have become one of those girls that couldn't stand it. I want you in a non-obsessive manner where we can always be happy. I want to fight with you instead of against you covertly. Yes I am flattered that we will be in a team from now on. But the additional request I have is, let us work together no matter the circumstances. I don't want us to be broken apart."

"Then I will never neglect you again," 117 replied, "As a typical male, even cybernetic, I am sorry that we have not had the time. I never knew you were in distress. I did miss you as the whole industry evolved. I will never allow that to happen again. We will face everything together. I promise."

She smiled and pecked him on the cheek. Looking into her eyes, 117 knew that that was what she had wanted to hear after what felt like an eternity. From that point on, he would never stop appreciating her and never turn her away.

"Come on," She urged him towards the other amborgs. "Shall we meet the third group?"

As the two of them began to mingle with the third group, the veteran amborg's presence made them back away out of fear but soon, as the conversations began, they were able to relax and were welcomed warmly. Immediately, the First and Second group were both amazed and felt sympathetic for their personal acts of courage and sacrifice prior to being found by Dr. Kendrick. The backgrounds before they became cybernetic were roughly similar to several of the older amborgs. Teams began to form almost instantly.

53, 54, and 55 were triplets surviving on the streets as beggars living off of whatever food they could acquire. They had the rare misfortune of accidently trying to steal Dr. Kendrick's lunch when he was attempting to go incognito in New York. The twins 92 and 93 instantly warmed up to the three very quickly.

345 was an orphan from the slums of San Francisco. She had developed a passion for math in elementary school and had been a prodigy that was unmatched before losing her parents. As a result, she was sent to a decaying orphanage where the owners believed her to look old enough and sold her to a brothel to make ends meet. Luckily, police had shut down the establishment and rescued her and other young children from their enslavement. 999, despite her hard stare, had come from a similar predicament and began to listen to 345 immediately.

922 had been hit by a high-speeding truck and was found by one of Dr. Kendrick's scouts in a hospital in Chicago in poor hospital conditions. The staff mysteriously had no information on his family which prompted a deeper investigation. Soon, Dr. Kendrick found out he was orphaned and had been living on the streets for eight long years since his father had died when he was nine. 922 had been deemed crippled and unable to make a full recovery because of his injuries which made Kendrick offer him the chance every other amborg candidate had also been offered. 1 and 5 both were in deep conversation with 922. 5 had a hand on his leg as 922 popped off the prosthetic hand from his own wrist and held it up for the two First group amborgs to see.

The amborgs were all bonding so quickly that it almost looked like there weren't any more to talk to. 117 and 43 both were about to consider dropping in on another conversation when two specific amborgs caught his eye. He pointed over to where they were standing and 43 silently followed. Both of them weaved through the crowd and walked up to the isolated pair, a boy and a girl, that were both very nervous and holding each other's hands very tightly. A couple to couple conversation was probably a way to ease the tension, 43 transmitted to 117 privately.

"Designation?" 117 asked the two of them as he sent out a communication. "What are your names and numbers?"

It was the girl who spoke first.

"My designation is Carol 466," She said as they linked up to 117 and 43. "It is the short version of my full name Carolina."

"Carolina?" 43 asked curiously with a smile on her face, "Are you North or South?"

466 returned her smile with a curious and puzzled look. Obviously, she was making an attempt to understand 43's question but before she could answer, the male amborg interrupted.

"The one and only."

117, 43 and 466 looked at the boy who looked sheepishly towards the ground. 466 blushed slightly and attempted to hide her smile. 43 looked to 117 and back to both of the two of them.

"Well that was unexpected," 117 chuckled. Both the boy and 466 continued to look away from each other but were bright red. "Blunt. But an honest answer. What is your name?"

"Dominic 501," The boy replied in 117's mind. He cleared his throat and extending a hand which 117 shook. "My nickname is Donut."

It was his last sentence that made 43 sputter. Or rather, she didn't actually make any noise, she just made the movement and the sputtering noise went off in all of their heads.

"Forgive me, I couldn't help but laugh a little," She coughed and spoke in their heads clearly. "You are kidding? Right?"

501's silence indicated otherwise which made 43 nod in understanding but she couldn't help continuing to smile.

"Well," 117 said pausing awkwardly. "Would you be interested in telling us why you are named after a dessert like food?"

"Yes," 43 added as she forced herself not to smile and tried to be serious, "Dom would probably be a much better nickname. I think a lot of Fast & Furious fans, the ones that you save and that still watch the franchise will find that name much more appealing."

"It never stuck," 501 admitted which was pretty much all he said as he turned to look at 466 who shrugged.

"Really?" 43 asked with a surprised look. "I have a strange feeling..."

"Which is her way of saying she has a hard time believing that is the whole truth," 117 pointed out.

"Exactly," 43 nodded as she continued with her curious analysis. "Are you really telling the truth?"

"What he means to say is," 466 interrupted, "It is a very long story. He was being serious about it not sticking. I knew him since grade school and there was a... incident that branded him for life."

"Well hopefully you become comfortable to the point where you would like to share that... incident with us," 117 nodded reassuringly. "But everyone else will probably be very curious now that the subject has been brought up."

"But we asked first so remember to tell us about it first," 43 added.

"Will do," 501 smiled meekly. "Would you like me to get you something?"

At that point, 466 nudged him and he shut up instantly.

"501," She muttered. "Abruptly changing the subject like that was hardly considered subtle. I thought we agreed we were not going to suck up pathetically to our elders."

"That wasn't pathetic at all!" 43 exclaimed. "We are definitely not elders. Please do not put yourself down. We would all like to be friends and nothing said in the next portions of the conversation will be considered stupid."

"Actually prior to arriving at the party, we established proper protocols on how to behave socially to members of the First or Second Group," 501 explained. "Among our last minute subjects in the third category of our sub-listing, we have many alternatives for small talk. For example, we had descriptions of the weather all the way to brown-nosing."

"Which he decided to act upon prematurely ahead of our original plans," 466 sighed as she gave them an innocent look. "We don't want to scare you off. Everyone says that 501 talks too much and that I'm awkward and shy."

"Truth," A third group amborg said as they passed by. 43 laughed a little.

"Trust me, it takes a lot to scare us off," She said. "Don't worry about sucking up or anything like that at all. We will not... bite. I just feel that I am staring at a clone of 117 from when we first started as amborgs. Overthinking everything and always adding unnecessary topics to the conversation was his thing for a while."

"Um hey?" 117 looked at 43 with a questioning look. "I'm standing right here."

"Now he doesn't do it so much," 43 added instantly. "Anyway, if you two would like to consider helping us form our team, we would love to work with you in the future."

501 and 466 looked at each other and then slowly, their eyes lit up and they revealed very small but genuine smiles. They looked as if it was the best news they had heard in their lives.

"That settles it," 117 smiled. "I look forward to working with you two."

"Even though all the amborg groups will be working together like one family," 43 said as she hugged 117's arm tightly. "I really do believe that you two are the amborgs that we will bond with the most."

"I think that statement is correct 43." He stood in front of the two third group amborgs and sized them up really quickly, "I assume that there is no possible way to separate the two of you?"

"Oh no," 466 piped up, "Not really at the least. I have to be around to make sure he shuts up at the right moments. He is an eccentric individual."

"Plus she is gorgeous."

501 had spoken without thinking which made the other three amborgs stare.

"I mean," He stammered, "Yeah, I appreciate her a lot. No I mean..."

43 held up her hand and he stopped. To add to his silence, 466 nudged him a lot harder than the last time and gave him a look of embarrassment.

"Alright you two," She said, "Stick with me and 117, and you shall be fine. And before you ask, I did not tell you to glue yourselves to us. Classic example of how 117 used to interpret what everyone told him to do. Stay and enjoy the party. Learn to relax."

As 43 and 117 walked away from the pair, 117 held her hand.

"Oh come on," He said, "I am getting better at not being so literal."

"Yes you are," She remarked in a joking manner, "Still... interesting couple. They only remind me of us in a small way. They might even be stranger too."

"Indeed," 117 glanced over his shoulder, "It was like seeing... us again. Did we use to be like that?"

"Not entirely 117."

"I hope we do not regret this."

43 leaned away, pulling on his arm. The two of them were moving towards the dance floor and 117 knew exactly what she had in mind for the rest of the party.

"There is nothing to regret," She said, "Come on 117, I think we should make use of the rest of the evening. Shall we dance? And maybe later, a night cap? I will make your favorite cocktail."

"Does everyone know about that now?"

43 laughed and the two of them returned to the center of the floor with everyone else. The two of them danced the rest of the evening and spent the rest of the holiday with each other. As did several other amborgs. Even if all of them were silent most of the time, they did enjoy the party more than anyone human could possibly imagine.

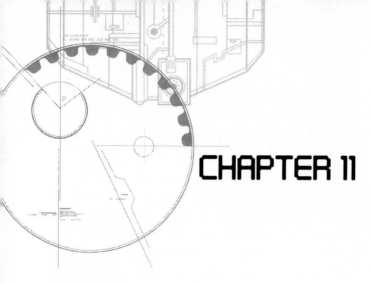

CHAPTER 11

2128 January
Suspected Drug Factory, Chicago

"117! 117! Help! I require immediate assistance!"

"If you wait one more second Donut, I can provide you with all the assistance you need. For now though, please shut up!"

501 was backed against a wall, surrounded by ten thugs, all were brandishing LTO knifes. Just before they all had the chance to close in, 117 dropped down from a nearby cargo crate and landed on one of the thugs. He ran forward and stood next to the hunched amborg, grabbed him by the back of the neck and lifted him so he straightened up. The two of them then readied themselves as the other nine assailants walked forward.

"Thank you 117," 501 muttered gratefully back to 117's mind as 117 let go of him and he straightened up. "I am sorry if I have begun babbling again... it is not happening intentionally."

"Doesn't he ever stop?" Mandy groaned as she spoke in the back of 117's mind.

117 shrugged and immediately grabbed 501's left arm. Not replying to Mandy, he lifted the third group amborg up off his feet and swung him at the bad guys.

"What are you doing 117?!" He exclaimed as 117 swung him outward and his feet smacked into a few of the men trying to get in close. "Hey! Look out!"

501 had only struck four of them in the attack. Five were left standing staring awkwardly at what 117 had done. Carrying him by the waist, 501 looked around helplessly as he was carried on his side while 117 continued to think of other battle strategies.

"117!" He cried, "Please put me down! I can take care of the last five guys."

"My thoughts exactly!" 117 smirked, "Not a bad idea Donut. Get ready to land."

"Land where? Wha… hey wait!"

501's protests were cut off as 117 threw 501 with tremendous force so that he flew and body slammed the remaining thugs. Even though they were all knocked down, 501 still had a lot of momentum and continued to fly several feet across the room. Instead of landing on his feet, 501 ended up doing a somersault and rolled into a pile of crates.

"For an amborg," 117 said as he ran over to where 501 was feebly recovering from the impact. As he approached, he punched another gangster who tried to jump attack him. "You have strange responses to hostile situations."

"That's not all either," Mandy added in the back of 117's mind. "Have you ever seen such a sheepish amborg? His tech's probably getting a massive headache like I am."

"Who has the worst headache?" 117 replied privately. "The amborg or the technician?"

"Very funny David."

117 leaned forward and grabbed 501's hand, pulling him up.

"My system performance drops when I am in hostile situations!" 501 muttered as he regained his foothold. "I wonder how 466 is doing. I cannot refrain from talking too fast in situations like this without her guidance and words of pulchritudinous perfection."

Rolling his eyes, 117 punched 501 in the ribs casually. 501 bent forward as if he was vomiting. He straightened back up, blinked and then looked back at 117 with a completely normal and calm stature. His panicky state was completely gone in an instant.

"Thanks 117," He nodded in relief, "I needed that."

501 took two steps to the left and noticed a small emergency wall panel. Ripping it open, he pulled out the fire extinguisher inside and threw it at another gangster who had just appeared around the corner. A loud clang knocked the enemy unconscious. He turned to look back at 117 with a small smile on his face.

"My... pleasure," 117 said eyeing the person hit by the extinguisher. "Was that really you who just used the word 'pulchritudinous' in a sentence?"

501 looked around and briefly scanned the area.

"I believe I was the only one in the vicinity capable of talking," 501 said nodding casually. "Yes I did."

"I think everyone listening to this conversation is jumping straight for a dictionary right now," 117 muttered.

"What do you mean?"

117 lifted his right foot, put it down inside a rusty pail on the floor. He flicked his leg upwards and sent the bucket flying into another incoming assailant. A loud gong indicated he had hit the target perfectly.

"You know how our technicians are always watching our movements and actions?" 117 said as the two of them began walking towards another doorway. "Sometimes Mandy says I say things that could be considered out of this dimension. She refers to them as fourth wall jokes. Except I never really know when or how I use them exactly."

"Perhaps I should give it a try some time," 501 said.

The two of them entered another room and stood back to back. Many of the human enemies they kept encountering as they went deeper in the facility were dwindling. They were beginning to encounter a lot of drones. As tall as regular humans and designed solely for combat, the two of them began to fight them off.

"This is a lot of stolen tech!" 501 called out as he ripped a drone's arm off. "They must have their own personal drone army!"

"Hopefully after... this," 117 replied crushing a drone's neck with his fingers, "We will be able to find out who is responsible for smuggling so much hardware."

"Hard to believe that we got here because the military got a tip-off from this location right?"

117 paused briefly. As the fight ended, 501 looked around to make sure there wasn't anything else moving. 117 looked at 501, determined to avoid revealing information about his grandfather. He wasn't sure that 501's maturity could handle the truth.

"Yes," 117 replied slowly. "Hard? Possibly. But sometimes tip-offs are very helpful. Come on. We need to rendezvous with the girls as soon as possible."

"You got it big brother."

Checking his map on his HUD, 117 checked for 43 and 466's locators. They were on the other side of the complex and they needed to cut through an open courtyard. The rest of the amborgs that was deployed with them were converging on the center of the complex while squads of soldiers cleared the outer structures. They had little time.

501 and 117 proceeded out into the courtyard and spotted the entrance they needed to go through. However they stopped and saw a group of soldiers under fire several yards from the entrance.

"Those soldiers will not be able to reach the main entrance to support us in their current situation," 117 looked at where the shooters were and identified four enemy riflemen, "Stay here 501, I will be back after I clear the way."

501 nodded as 117 got a running start and jumped up to the second floor. He quickly scanned the room he jumped into and climbed through the window as silently as possible. The noise from the gunmen masked the sound of his landing. When the coast was clear, 117 moved to the door and opened it slowly. Peeping through the small gap down the hall, he could see the four gunners opening fire down into the courtyard from the windows. As quietly as he could 117 snuck out and began to creep up on them when his bracelet lit up.

"117," 501's voice said loudly, "I have a question."

117's opened his wide in horror. The four gunmen stopped shooting, turned and stared as 501's voice kept coming through.

"Oh wait," He said, "Forget that I had a question, the gunmen have stopped firing on the soldiers. Did you take them out yet?"

Not answering the question, 117 looked right into the eyes of the first gunman who looked very confused. Chuckling slightly, 117 smiled showing his teeth and then brought a fist forward. He punched the first gunman who flew into the second and third. As the three of them fell over unconscious, the fourth took one look at his fallen pals, dropped his gun and scurried away.

"Well..." Mandy chuckled nervously, "That went well. We really need to get 501 to learn about proper battle protocol. I'll have a few words with his technician."

"At least you aren't required to work with him," 117 said with a sigh.

He climbed out one of the windows and dropped back into the courtyard. 501 ran up to 117 followed by the soldiers who looked relieved to be out of danger. As the soldiers formed up and began to prepare for entry to the ground floor, 117 took 501 aside.

"501," He said on a private channel. "If you had a question to ask, why did you send it on an open frequency to my bracelet when it could have been in private? You gave away my position!"

"Oh so that was why they stopped shooting," 501 chuckled nervously. "Well at least you got them. Right?"

"How did you pass combat training? You're a hazard in the field. No offense."

"None taken. Whatever failures I make in the field I make up for in diplomacy, tact and analysis for problem solving certain scenarios," 501 shrugged.

"That doesn't make me feel better," 117 replied rolling his eyes.

As they made their way inside. 501 and 117 both became escorts to the small squad of soldiers and they were following the shortest possible route. Pretty soon, they found themselves taking cover and crouching behind some concrete slabs in an open room. A perfect place for an ambush, 117 thought, if they weren't careful, someone could potentially kill them the instant they peeked up. They crawled behind some crates and were extremely quiet until...

"117, why are we sneaking around?" 501 asked curiously out of 117's bracelet. He had whispered it this time but the squad immediately hunched down indicating it was still too loud. Luckily, no one else made a sound. Ignoring them, 501 lowered the volume and continued, "I thought we had the advantage?"

If it weren't for the fact that they all had to be quiet, 117 almost was about to do exactly what it looked like the soldier behind 501 was about to do. Instead, he counted to four, resisted the urge to yell and then gave 501 a look of disbelief.

"501," 117 whispered. He was too preoccupied to switch to a private channel so he broadcasted it on 501's bracelet at the lowest volume. "Including the two of us and the soldiers we have accompanying us, we number only seven. We cannot afford to be detected. Especially since, forgive me for being blunt, they aren't exactly bulletproof. A firefight right now is the last thing we need."

"How bad could the situation possibly be?" 501 asked innocently as he stuck his head up for a look.

A loud bang rang out through the entire room as 501 fell to the floor with a bullet mark in his head. Despite all the intense and shocked looks on all the soldiers, 117 looked on in utter amusement trying very hard not to burst out laughing.

"Situation updated... Sniper," he noted which made all the soldiers crouch even lower.

One of them, a staff sergeant, crawled over to 117.

"Ok..." He breathed in a concerned tone. "Aside from your buddy taking one in the head, we kinda need to get to the main complex of the warehouse with as little setbacks as possible, set some charges, and blow this place up. We got a job to finish and we'd rather not die today."

"I beg your pardon?" 501 interrupted as he sat up and sat against the concrete slab, "Why are you trying to commit suicide?"

"What?"

The sergeant stared and looked to 117 who was rolling his eyes again.

"Look pal," He whispered when 117 didn't respond. "I don't know where you got that idea but there is absolutely no suicide involved in this plan whatsoever!"

"Yes there is!" 501 argued, "When you say to set charges, you obviously are referring to explosives but then you said as a final instruction, you plan to blow the complex up WITH you and your comrades. Therefore, I conclude you are committing suicide and the intended genocide of your men."

The sergeant stared at 501 with a look of enormous disbelief. 117 placed a hand to his forehead and shook his head. In the back of his head, he heard a faint slap. Mandy also had done a face-palm.

As the argument continued, 117 grabbed a pistol from one of the soldiers, stood up, took aim and fired twice into the distance. There was a yell which made everyone stop arguing immediately. Everyone peeped over the concrete slab and looked to where 117 had shot. The sergeant looked and then signaled when he realized it was clear.

"Is your amborg buddy here for real?" He said, signaling the rest of the squad to move up. 117 returned the pistol back to the soldier he borrowed it from.

"Unfortunately," He replied casually, "I work with this guy on a consistent basis. A literal answer would be yes, he is for real. He is also fairly new in this line of work and he listens to specifics. To correct, be specific and just roll with it. No guarantees at all though if he will grow out of it."

The man in uniform pondered for a second. He was almost about to ask 117 what that had all meant. Instead, he turned to 501 and placed a hand on the third group amborg's shoulder.

"Look," The sergeant said as each man in his squad turned to him for the next set of orders, "There is not going to be a suicide. Not on my watch. We will set the explosives and then leave. Then we blow the place up. The men and women under my command as well as my brothers or sisters in arms are brave and I am proud to be fighting alongside such individuals. I will never allow them to die like that. I will keep them safe because it's my responsibility. Just like it's yours to help us finish the job and go home."

501 nodded in understanding. He smiled and then looked to 117 for instructions. Just like the way the soldiers were looking at the sergeant.

"You didn't necessarily need to say all of that," 117 said smiling and nodding admiringly. "But your soldiers will follow you now for as long as they live. Come on Donut. It isn't polite to keep ladies waiting."

As the two of them left the squad, 117 heard the soldiers beginning to chatter amongst themselves.

"Hey sarge," One of them said, "Thanks."

After they had split up from the squad, 117 and 501 were in another corridor attempting to hack a door.

"All I'm saying 117, if the situation wants to get better, I should do it!"

"No."

"I know my performance has not been perfect but I think you should give me the opportunity to try it sometime."

"No."

"But I really think it will work. If you would just let me..."

"NO!"

117 pulled the outside cover of a security panel off the wall when he said no the third time. The security door was significantly hard to hack which was interesting. A warehouse of this caliber shouldn't have this type of security, he thought, as he examined the subroutines and tried to figure out the password. While he was doing this, 501 was keeping a lookout but also passing the time brainstorming ideas.

"Aww, why not?" He asked while examining a grenade he had picked up from a previous fight two corridors back, "Grenade juggling would be a great game! We could teach it to everyone! We toss a bunch of grenades at each other, but then someone throws a live one and whoever catches and gets blown up by it, loses or gets out!"

"No!" 117 repeated again, "The last time we gave you a grenade, you blew up the entire supply of practice dummies! Please do not turn this into a Mario Party game... Amborgs may be capable of withstanding certain blast levels of that caliber but even we would agree to normal human standards of not attempting to be idiots because we can."

"Well it could still be my choice," 501 muttered, "Just a thought."

501 sighed and threw the grenade down the hall. It bounced off the end and disappeared around the corner. Seconds later, there was a loud explosion at the end of the hall. 117 stopped hacking and stared at 501 quietly with an angry look.

"Sorry," 501 bit his lip and sagged his shoulders. "I think I will just keep watch for real now."

117 sighed. He thought about saying something but words couldn't describe how he was feeling. Instead of getting angry, he decided to go back to decrypting the code on the lock.

"Ok then," 501 reached a hand out towards the open panel, "Can I at least help with the lock?"

"No wait!"

117's response came too late. 501 accidentally stuck his hand into the power control box and was instantly electrocuted. His head was smoking as he withdrew his hand after all the power had been dispelled into his systems. Inspecting the damage, 117 stood up and looked him over but 501 meekly held up a thumbs-up. At that moment the access panel turned green and the door opened.

"I didn't need help," 117 sighed as he chuckled at 501's new look. "But that was nicely done."

"At least I managed to get a compliment out of you this mission," 501 coughed. "Even if I suck at doing things right, I still get things done. I think I will take point."

"Sheesh," Mandy said, "Where did they find that guy?"

"I doubt it's the time to be stereotypical but I bet it's from someplace special," 117 remarked as he followed 501.

The two of them walked down the middle of a rather large hallway when the door at the other end opened up. There was a series of loud thuds as something enormous stomped in through the entrance. 501 and 117 both stared wide-eyed at what appeared to be the largest and biggest robot anyone had ever conceived before. It looked heavy and armed to the teeth.

"Resist and you will be put down," The robot announced in a deep menacing voice. "Amborgs, prepare to be crushed."

"Whoa..." 501 exclaimed as he observed and tried to scan the giant, "How come we don't have something like that? Because that thing is cool... except it wants to kill us."

"The better question Donut," 117 interrupted, "...is WHY they have something like that. Mandy? Please tell me you have begun analyzing the... thing bot?"

"I'm on it David," She said urgently as the two amborgs stood their ground. The robot was marching straight for them, "Give me all the data you got and I'll scan for any weaknesses. But you have to at least distract it for a few minutes. This isn't anything I've ever seen before."

"Unknown hostile," 117 remarked, "This is a problem."

"ARGH!"

One of the arms on the robot had lunged forward grabbing 501 by the legs. He was picked up helplessly and then swung around in many directions. The other arm extended and pointed straight at 117. He saw what looked like a barrel extend from the end and began to whine and light up. Thinking quickly, 117 diverted energy to his leg joints and braced for the incoming attack.

The robot shot a fireball from its arm as 501 continued to be flung all over like a ragdoll. 117 immediately jumped out of the way as the fire stuck the wall next to him. He scanned the temperature of the impact point and examined the velocity. He did manage to dodge it, but he could feel the heat burrowing through his jacket. Hot and fast, he thought, not a good combination.

"Mandy," 117 panted as he leaped forward and avoided another fireball. "Please speed up the scan!"

"Going as fast as I can!" Mandy replied. "501's technician says try getting behind it. It will probably have a blind spot from the back!"

"I copy!"

117 charged for the robot's legs. It disengaged its fireball shooter and a giant blade swung out. As 117 slid under the giant chassis, the robot swung its arm and he felt the blade slam a few inches

behind. Getting back on his feet, he turned quickly to see that there was a blind spot. The robot was having a hard time turning around and had decided to go back to swinging 501 around again. He needed to free the young amborg quickly.

117 jumped onto the robot's back and punched into the left shoulder socket. This made it respond by throwing 501 down the hall and both arms shot upward in an attempt to grab 117. 117 clung onto the joints and dodged the robot's massive fingers as it clawed helplessly like someone trying to get rid of an itch.

There was too much armor on the upper shoulder region, 117 looked up and down the shoulder joint he had just punched. Since he was up there, perhaps he could take out the head. Pulling himself upwards, 117 wrapped his right arm around the neck of the robot and swung so he was face to face with the red colored visor. Not wasting another moment, 117 lifted his other arm and punched the head as hard as he could. A couple of groaning electrical noises came from the robot but it still didn't seem to do much damage.

Suddenly, a loud clang from below made 117 glance down. 501 had gotten up and confidently punched the robot in its leg but his smile faded when the robot retaliated. It kicked 501 and sent him bouncing off the walls in the hallway like a pinball. 117 tried to line up another punch but the one of the giant arms pressed its fingers around the back of his neck and 117 was pulled away from its face. Reaching up and grasping the robot's fingers, 117 attempted to free himself but the giant was already ahead of him. 117 suddenly felt himself flying backwards and landed onto the ground. He tried to regain his senses but he felt himself roll into something heavy and it fell on top of him. Struggling to figure out what was going on, he realized it was 501 who had fallen on him. As the two of them tried to untangle themselves quickly, the robot stepped towards them preparing to fire another fireball.

"What do we do now?!" 501 asked as the two of them scrambled to their feet and dodged another flame.

"Well the dilemma is if we are unable to defeat it now," 117 explained, "I really believe it will be worse if it reaches the others."

"Hey 117," 501 panted. "You want to try throwing me again?"

"Are you sure?"

"Hey, I'm willing to do it this time."

Without another word, 117 thought for second and then agreed. What could go wrong, he wondered as 501 lifted an arm and he grasped it tightly with both hands. He lifted 501 up, mustered all the strength he could and threw him straight at the giant behemoth.

"SUPERMAAANN!!" 501 cried out triumphantly.

It looked like it was about to work. But the robot instantly side-stepped out of the way and allowed 501 to fly past.

"How does something that huge move so fast but can't turn around?!" Mandy exclaimed in shock as 117 stared wide-eyed at where 501 flew. 501 practically planted himself into the plating. Seconds later, he fell to the floor with a painful thud.

"Maybe we should try that again," He said weakly to 117. "It might work."

117 stared. The robot seemed to be calculating which of the two it should go after. After a few seconds, it turned around slowly and faced 501 and began to close in. 117 quickly scanned the back of what he was seeing and then Mandy cried out gleefully.

"THERE!" She shouted in 117's head. "Right there in the waistline on the left. There's a small gap in his lower back. If you pry it open, I detect a propane tank of some sorts underneath! Ignite it!"

117 sprinted toward his target. The instant he was close enough, the robot whipped around and smacked 117 into the wall. Feeling shaken up, 117 lay on his side and saw the robot turn to face 501 again who was struggling to get back up. The robot instantly began to charge its weapon again. Seeing this, 117 got up and ran again. He leaped up and grabbed onto the robot's back. This caused it to be confused and it fired its weapon prematurely. The fireball flew and barely missed 501's head who was still in a daze but had managed to duck down out of the line of fire. Hanging on for dear life, 117 grabbed and snapped off a piece of metal from part of the armor and began hacking at the location Mandy indicated. The hole he made revealed a small red nozzle which he knocked off immediately. Propane gas began to leak out with a hiss. With the piece of metal, 117 scraped it along the inside causing sparks to form. Releasing his grip, 117 kicked and pushed himself away.

He flew back a few inches when the propane gas ignited causing the entire back of the robot to explode. The blast sent 117 flying and he felt the flames hit him right in the chest. 117 landed on his back and rolled into a crouch and looked at the robot. A bunch of systems powered down and it dropped on its knees. 117 stood up, walked next to it, placed a hand on the back of its head and pushed it forward. The robot fell into the floor with a giant clang. 501 got up on his feet and blinked rapidly.

"Man," 501 sighed as he got up on his feet. "What kind of stuff are we dealing with?"

"Maybe this… thing can tell us," 117 said as he reached for the head and yanked it off. "See what you can salvage and transmit the data to the technicians. Maybe we can figure out who built this."

"Are you alright?" 501 asked curiously as he examined the burnt out tank. "You did take a lot of damage."

"I'm fine," 117 nodded to acknowledge 501. He turned over the head and attempted to find a serial number or anything leading to the manufacturer. "You should probably thank your technician. Their support is what keeps us alive."

"You're welcome boys. Not that 501's tech did much help anyway," Mandy replied smugly from the back of his head, "I think he pissed himself…"

"What was that?" 501 asked curiously.

117 turned to look at him again.

"Basically, you should consider speaking with your technician about regulating his urinary movement so he can avoid procuring accidents during high-intensity emotional situations."

"Oh ok," 501 nodded and gave a small smile.

"David," Mandy groaned, "We still need to work on your language just a bit more. I can't get that image out of my head now…"

"I rephrased what I was originally going to say to something more professional," 117 replied, "I believe I deserve points for not dialing it down to something primitive and even gross."

"I don't think I even want to ask what the unprofessional version was," She said with a shudder in her voice.

"Would you like to hear…?"

"NO!"

She had shouted so loud that 117 cringed causing 501 to flinch. When 117 motioned that everything was fine, 501 then went back to work.

"She is really a nice person," 501 admitted, "But she is scary at times."

117 said nothing, nodded in agreement, stepped over the wreckage and they continued to scan the robot. 501 also participated in the scanning. It truly was a remarkable piece of engineering. What was mysterious was what they found next.

"117," 501 said worried, "I am checking all known databases and there is no design specifications or even blueprints for a robot of this nature."

"I am also seeing the same results," 117 said looking for any clues on the limbs, "Your statement confirms it. Mandy, I am not finding any original plans or designs. I have checked and cross-referenced with all known robotics labs, industries, corporations, and manufacturers worldwide but I may be malfunctioning slightly because I am not finding any known matches."

"No David, you aren't," Mandy replied in confusion, "I am seeing the same thing. Hyperion Tech, Universal Inc., Russian, Chinese, European Worldwide Care... I am even digging up T.A.R.D.E.C. databases which might be the wrong thing to do but nothing. This robot's plans... They're either hard to trace, non-existent or maybe they weren't even drafted."

"Maybe we are looking at it wrong."

117 turned to 501 and motioned for him to explain.

"You remember in the Iron Man movie with Robert Downey Jr.?" 501 asked, "When he was stuck in the cave, the terrorists couldn't see the plans for his Mark one suit because he separated it onto multiple sheets. Only by pressing the sheets down on top of each other firmly could you actually see the full blueprints. Maybe in this case, we could be looking at the wrong image."

"It is a fully operational robot with no blueprints Donut," 117 replied. "What do you mean by the wrong image?"

"What if it we looked at it backwards? Here at our feet is a live scale version of the nonexistent blueprint but we check to see if any of the parts were made by any known corporations."

"I think I know what he means David," Mandy replied. "Maybe it's like how special vehicles are made. Not all of the parts of a tank were manufactured in one place. Factories usually try to build complex devices and the parts in same places these days. But there are plenty of minor sub division companies that do send parts to be built together to make new stuff in a separate construction facility. Maybe there is a part in this giant metal hunk we could link to something."

"So perhaps a match will come up if we scan individual parts," 117 finished. "Hopefully this thing was not built from scratch. Now we can see who is responsible for building this."

And with that, they quickly scanned each individual part of the robot. From every circuit down to the last screw. Suddenly, a green light rang out in the databases. Multiple lights in fact as Mandy gave a cry of triumphant joy.

"Eureka!" Mandy exclaimed. "We got something!"

Suddenly, she became silent as 117 waited to hear her discovery. Then she began speaking again in a very disappointed tone.

"The good news is we are onto something," She said grimly, "The bad news is that it might be a lot more complicated than we thought. I am getting matches for several components from specific companies but that's the problem."

She forwarded the data to 117's forehead and he examined it in his HUD.

"I have a ton of matches," She explained as she sifted and cleared up the cluster so he could see clearly. "The parts in the joints, the legs, weapons, electric systems, tactical, plating... It's all custom. It's like Batman ordered these parts conspicuously to secretly build a murder-bot."

"This robot was not built by one but multiple manufacturers," 501 said in awe. "Or at least, that statement is almost true."

"Good observation 501," 117 said, "It is not a complete dead end. This robot, although we cannot find a blueprint, actually has used parts from several robotic installations. Look here, the leg design and the parts forming the feet. It is based off Chinese and Italian technology. The plating and structure supporting the neck. I now recognize that from what the Russians and Germans have made for certain vehicle suspensions. And these weapons... they are Hyperion Tech. The computer and power storage components from... various car companies."

"It looks like I'm going to have to make a lot of phone calls," Mandy sighed. "If we can't find a blueprint but all these parts were brought together to make... this robot, then we might be in big trouble. At least we can get a few steps closer contacting these companies."

"They also might not even know these parts were used like this," 117 remarked. "Most companies do not care what their materials are used for, as long as someone with money comes along and can afford the right price. For instance, Hyperion Tech is not a weapons manufacturer. But their tech has been modified and weaponized. Something or someone is setting up for something. We best be cautious. Whoever built this has taken so many technologies, so many techniques, styles and designs to create a machine of war."

"I wonder though," 501 said. "If that is what is about to happen."

"Either way," 117 explained, "We should inform the right authorities about it. Perhaps the military can learn about what they could be facing."

"117. Come take a look over here," 501 said holding up the arm. "My technician found it in the scans. Look behind the elbow."

117 walked over and examined the part that 501 was indicating. There was a barcode and an identification number printed in dark ink. The font size was pretty small which was most likely why they had never seen it during the fight until now.

"I see the numbers 00034," He muttered as 501 nodded.

"Yes," 501 said, "This could possibly not be the only one."

"If we can find the source of where this robot is being mass produced," 117 thought, "We could probably avoid a giant bloodbath. I would hate to fight against an army of these even with all the amborgs at our side."

"A robot out of the prototype phase and possibly a lot more like it," 501 shuddered. "How do we deal with this?"

"If we can shut them down now," 117 stated, "We can prevent something horrible. If we fail, then we get better. We may be the only ones capable of defending against something so powerful. At that point, we need to hold the line and not give up."

"Ok David," Mandy spoke when the two of them abandoned the wreckage and left the hallway. "I'm going to start making some calls and try to get some information. You good if I go dark for a while?"

"Not a problem Mandy," 117 replied.

As they stepped through, 501 nervously looked back to see if the robot really was dead. When it remained limp, he followed 117 and allowed the door to close shut. As an extra precaution, he broke the lock just to be safe.

* * *

In another part of the warehouse, a similar incident had just occurred. 466 was stumbling after 43 who looked exhausted. Both of them were covered in ice and soaked. They looked as if they had come out of the freezer.

"What on earth was that?" 466 panted as she slumped against the wall. 43 looked back and examined her right arm which was encased in a block of ice.

"Unknown," she said checking to make sure the coast was clear. "A new defense drone of some kind. It was fun attempting to destroy it but that was bigger than anything I have ever seen."

466 nodded as she tried to help hack 43's arm out of the ice. When it wasn't working, she tried exhaling on it.

"Right!" 466 noted as she stood back up after 43 told her to stop, "It tried to freeze the floor in an attempt to keep us unbalanced but we then used that to our advantage."

43 nodded as she smacked her hand into the wall in an attempt to free her arm. The ice stuck on as frozen as ever. It was definitely

not ordinary ice, which was certain. It had been quite a strange day for them. She rested and then thought of what they did.

"Yes, then I ducked behind it, jammed its arm joints so it froze itself in the head. Then we were able to break it easily after you crushed the neck."

"Can I request that we do not do that again?" 466 stretched and began tapping the ice on 43's arm.

"Stop that," 43 said impatiently as two of them began walking to their next objective, "I do not think I can guarantee a way to avoid another attack like that. There might be more."

They heard a muffled explosion from another part of the facility where the battle was taking place. Although it was quiet and distant, 43 gave 466 a reassuring look which prompted the third group amborg to change the subject.

"I wonder how poor Donut is handling without me," 466 sighed as the two of them trudged slowly through another hall. It was almost as if it was built like a weird maze.

43 chuckled.

"I know 117," She said dubiously. "He will take care of 501...err Donut to the best of his ability. Even though I know that sometimes, he dislikes the company."

"I apologize, 501 talks WAY too much," 466 looked behind her, "It is understandable that 117 would be irritated. I mean, he gets into accidents, constantly gives away locations of allies, and gets shot in the head a lot. Not to mention, he questions logic in orders, acts a bit strange for an amborg, and also..."

43 held up a hand and placed it over 466's mouth. Even though she hadn't actually been speaking with her real voice, the action did tell her to instantly stop talking. 43's bracelet stopped shining and 466 listened attentively.

"Carolina, I really like you," 43 said smiling. "You do not talk as much as... Donut but you are also very descriptive even to the simplest questions. To be honest, 117 and I really do enjoy the company of you two. But to put it bluntly, you two just... try too hard.

466 looked down at the floor and then back at 43.

"Do you really enjoy our company?" She asked feeling flattered.

"Yes... and sometimes no," 43 responded casually, "Trust me. 117 and I laugh about all the crazy things you have done but you two do the funniest things just at the wrong time."

"Well I only met 501 a few years before Dr. Kendrick found us so I only know a bit about his childhood," 466 said. "I was always someone far too outspoken and always wondering what dreams I could accomplish. Now I am an amborg and I doubt many of my past friends are alive to see what I am doing now."

"You make them proud," 43 replied compassionately. "But that was probably too much information again. Save that for when we are not in the field."

"43. I was wondering something. Are you still feeling angry about the time I shot a sniper round into your..."

43 with her arm of ice held it up to indicate silence and 466 stopped.

"Let's not discuss that 466," 43 blushed, "I want you to promise me you will not disclose that information to anyone. It still stings since it was an incendiary bullet."

466 nodded and 43 lowered her hand. They continued to walk down the hall when the door next to them slid open and 117 and 501 came through from the other side. The sight of seeing each other amazed the four of them. 501 and 117 were covered in soot and there were burn marks all over them. Whereas the girls contradicted this with all of the ice.

"You know," 466 leaned over whispered on a separate channel with 43, "501 has a bullet wound to his head. I think it would be very appropriate to add your bullet incident for humorous effect."

"More like an embarrassing effect," 43 replied giving 466 a look. "Connection open."

117 looked at the block of ice on 43's arm with a tired but surprised look.

"What happened to you two?" He asked curiously.

"Some giant robot with freezing weapons," 43 replied hammering her frozen arm into the wall. Some of the ice was chipped off but she was still annoyed at how it still clung. "Nothing we have ever seen before. What about you two? Did you fall into a furnace?"

"Not exactly," 117 replied.

"A giant walking furnace is probably the accurate description," 501 said chuckling. 117 nodded in agreement as he dusted the soot off his jacket.

"Giant robot never seen before," 117 explained. "That is the shorter version."

"Ooh," 501 said excitedly, "Can I give the long version?"

"Oh… that really is not necessary," 43 mumbled but it was too late.

"We started with the initial drop on the outskirts of the facility. I got lost and felt into the mud right after we left our deployment pods. 117 washed it off by throwing bucket of water on me. We split up to secure checkpoints for army troops. After securing mine, I was surrounding by a group of thugs where my nerves began to affect my system performance…"

43 began to slouch against the wall with a dazed look while 117 was suppressing a smile. 466 was the only one listening with pure empathy. The report continued as 501 didn't pay attention to the look on 43's face.

"…After 117 threw me, we defeated the thugs and then moved on. I gave away 117's position later as he was attempting to take on some gunmen. Later I was shot in the head by a sniper rifle at high velocity which I really enjoyed. And we just fought a really large defense drone who shot fireballs at us. He was very mean… Oh and I was electrocuted trying to open a door."

43 sighed and examined the damage on 117 instead.

"Well it looks as if you suffered most of the flame damage," She said. "Was this robot similar to this?"

She transmitted an image from her head to her bracelet and the projector lit up revealing a holographic image of the same robot that 117 and 501 had fought earlier.

"Exactly," 117 nodded, "Except ours was a fire based weapon systems. Whereas yours appeared to be the exact opposite."

"I know right?" 43 sighed as 501 continued describing his story to 466. "I mean seriously, someone is trying to make Pokémon out of giant robots. That is either the coolest or the strangest thing I have ever heard of."

"Well," 117 smiled, "On the bright side, I was able to melt the ice off."

"Wait what?"

43 looked down at her arm and found that 117 had melted the block of ice to where she could see the outline of her sleeve perfectly.

"How did you do that?" She said with a surprised but impressed look. "When did you do that?"

"I did battle a fire bot earlier," 117 shrugged, "I still am feeling pretty heated from that encounter so I figured I needed time to cool off. 501 provided a good distraction."

"You need to provide a new way with words," 43 chuckled, "Because what you did does not make sense."

"We are amborgs," 117 pointed out. "Does anything we do make sense?"

"True. You did throw 501 at a lot of stuff today."

The two of them turned to face the other amborgs. 501 had just finished wrapping things up in his "report" and they looked ready to continue.

"And that wraps up everything up till now," he said facing 43 and 117 with 466.

"Well then," 117 said to the three of them. "We should keep moving now."

The four of them finally made it to the center of the facility and met up with the other amborg teams. Some soldiers were trying to set some explosives with a group of engineers precisely on schedule.

"Look, more amborgs!" Someone shouted. Quickly, 297 and 3 appeared and walked up to the four arrivals with optimistic looks.

"Charges are in place," 3 said enthusiastically, "Other amborg teams are now mopping up the rest of the facility. We can wrap this up and be home in time for me to practice a new recipe. Also we encountered some giant sized robots so that will make an interesting report."

"Very well," 117 acknowledged, "501, 466, go to these coordinates and help with the demolitions."

The two third group amborgs nodded and instantly went to the coordinates that he had indicated. 297 smirked as they left.

"So how was it? Did 501 cause more problems again?"

117 gave 297 a light nudge on his shoulder. The two of them smirked and then went the opposite directions.

"When we get back I will tell you," 117 said.

43 and 117 walked into the center to move towards the center hub. Several engineers along with their squadrons were coordinating the procedures. Most of them were trying to download as much data off the computers before destroying the place. After they checked the progression of the set-up, 43 and 117 set up a private channel to have a conversation. They roughly had a few minutes before they were ready to evacuate. One of the engineers handed 117 a data-pad.

"Here," He said quickly before turning to dig through the computers again. "This is most of what we could steal off the computers. We gave 297 and 3 all that we first got when we came in here and this is a bit more that we found."

"Thank you soldier," 117 nodded and immediately began to scan the data. He then conversed privately with 43.

"Manifests, shipping and inventory lists. Wait," She said looking over the recovered information. "A lot of it must have been corrupted or destroyed when we infiltrated the place. But still, all of it is generic information about the company that owned this place before it was abandoned. Several years before our time."

"I was just about to comment about that," 117 examined the room. "No robotic laboratory-grade equipment, drugs or evidence that there was a gang hiding here."

Based on what 117 could discern from the abandoned room, he was sure he was right. There didn't seem to be any indication that there had been anyone living here as the briefing reports had indicated. They had brought at least four teams of amborgs based on the Intel but still it was a very small goal to fight for. Based on the opposition, it was clearly indicating the signs of a set-up.

"You know," 43 said turning around and looking towards the entrance, "I get the feeling we should get out of here fast. This place is too abandoned for any kind of operations for a criminal gang or mass production of those robots. Someone wanted us here."

"Agreed," 117 said, "297, 3. We need a status report from the troops. Inform the other teams to be cautious. We need to evacuate now. 501 and 466, report to our positions now. Time to head home."

"Ok 117," 501 replied over the channel. "This place is pretty creepy anyway."

"I hear you Donut," 117 replied. "43. Do you want to do one quick patrol around the room before we go? We might find something we missed."

117 had his back turned to her. When she didn't reply, he turned around. She was standing ahead of him just a few feet from him but was motionless.

"43?" He said starting to feel concerned.

Slowly, 43 turned around and then 117 saw what was keeping her from speaking. Embedded in her chest was a knife. It was a unique shade of silver which was what gave it away. An LTO knife. 43 looked at 117 with a dazed look.

"I got careless," She stammered in a private communication.

The transmission from 43 instantly cut off though after those words. She lifted her hand and tried to reach for 117 but she began to fall forward. He stepped forward and caught her. He quickly flipped her over and was too shocked to say anything. For a moment, he wanted to pull the knife out but was too afraid of hurting her by mistake. 43 looked up at him with vacant eyes. She was in a lot of pain but he was helpless.

117 lost all sense of what happened in the next few seconds. Everyone turned and fixed their eyes on their position and then a commotion started. The surrounding soldiers instantly raised

their rifles and became alert while at the same time, all amborgs turned and looked in 117 and 43's direction.

"43?" He spoke quietly into her head.

He did not receive any response. She opened her mouth and was desperately trying to inhale but just from looking at her, 117 knew that it was difficult. He immediately switched to his bracelet. When there was still no response, he tried speaking with his real voice but she hung motionless in his arms, gazing at the ceiling and barely showing any life signs.

117 could hear 297 shouting orders in the background. Both he and 3 picked up objects and throwing them towards the ceiling. The soldiers were also concentrating their fire at the same location on the balcony above. 117 looked up where all the fire was being directed and saw a figure in black armor standing on a balcony. The helmet he was wearing masked his face completely and his armor was deflecting the bullets that were plastering him. The figure directed its gaze at 117 and the two of them looked at each other for a minute before he disappeared out of view. It was him. He was the cause of all of this.

"117!"

117 heard 297 calling out to him but as he looked up, he saw 297 also fall to the ground clutching his shoulder. There was another LTO knife stuck in the back of his shoulder. Thrown from somewhere above. All of sudden, 117 remembered hearing his grandfather's warnings.

"43," He whispered desperately with his real voice. "No... Stay. Reconnect amborg 43. You have fallen out of contact. Please respond."

He could hear Mandy calling out to him in the back of his head but he had no strength to reply.

"This is amborg 3 declaring an emergency!" 3 commanded in the background. "Two amborgs down! Notify 6! We have amborgs down! Returning home with medical emergencies! Sending reports!"

The next few moments were agony and 117 had very vague memories of them even happening. He didn't let go of 43. Not in the recovery unit back to A.I. industries and when he walked and carried her to medical. Everyone was ready to receive her but 117 did not let them. He ran and carried her into the medical bay and none of the medical staff, not even Dr. Wildman could convince him. Finally, 117 remembered 6 blocking him and offering him two options. To either leave 43 in capable hands or be put behind bars. At some point, Dr. Kendrick also was there and convinced 117 to let her go and he could trust his word. They removed and carried 43 to the emergency room. However, none of the doctors or medical personnel on hand had ever operated on an amborg before so Dr. Kendrick and some specialists as well as 6 joined the team in the operation. His instructions to 117 was to stay put and await orders.

Outside the medical bay, 117 stood. Silently waiting as Mandy tried to talk to him. Although he was listening, his entire focus was on the person who had attacked the amborg he loved. And for the first time in his life, 117 felt something different flow through his circuits. Massive amounts of energy was flowing rapidly to every part of his limbs and directly through his CPU to his mind. Immediately, 117 looked at his hands and came to one conclusion. He was angry. For the first time in his life, he was remembering and acting out on an emotion he hadn't felt in years. Was it anger though? His CPU was not able to calculate it. In fact, the flow of energy had shorted out his regular programming. What is happening? He asked himself as Mandy attempted to grab his attention. She was being very persistent and unwilling to turn away from helping.

Suddenly, the sign above the medical bay flashed except it wasn't a very common alert. In fact, 117 had only heard about this specific alert in their briefings. Dr. Kendrick had activated a very rare protocol. It was the first time he ever made this type of alert and every amborg was witnessing it everywhere. As if by magic, every amborg, in the field or back at home all stopped and felt the alert ringing on their CPUs. An amborg was in critical condition.

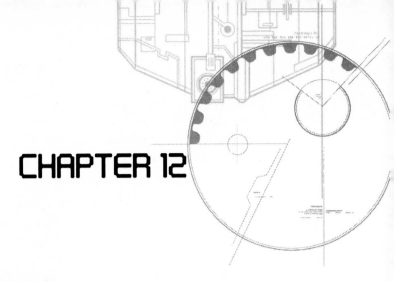

CHAPTER 12

Twelve hours later, Medical Bay

"Say that again?"

"Dr. Kendrick, as far as I know, we have her stabilized. We compared her life signs to Vanessa 6 and for a human, she should be waking up. But for reasons we can't explain, she won't. The combination of cybernetic implants and human biology are clashing so we can only hope for the faintest possibility that she'll even wake up. I'm sorry John, we weren't prepared for something like this. If we were, maybe 43 had a chance. But not even 6 knew what to do. It's almost like she's developed a fear of feeling unhelpful. And if my head assistant, a medical amborg, is feeling like that. It's even more serious. Something happened when the blade pierced her neural connections in the upper abdomen. We repaired the physical damage but a neurology test showed her systems are slowly failing."

"I SAW THE TEST!"

117 heard Dr. Kendrick yell but didn't say anything or even react beyond shifting slightly in his chair. For a moment, there was silence. Then 117 heard Dr. Wildman speak again.

"I'm sorry John," He said with a deep breath. "I'm SORRY!"

The two men both shouted so loud that it rang through the entire bay. Almost no one else, if they were in the vicinity dared to make a sound.

"From a doctor to another," Dr. Wildman breathed, "From a friend to a friend. I'm sorry it got like this. Serina 43 has time left. But with every passing day down to each hour. She will die. All we can do is monitor and pray. I know it's hard to hear one of your daughters being in this situation but you can't lose it now. If you do, your other children will be orphans again. They look up to you and will falter even more if you give up."

"At least we have reason to look into scenarios like this more," Dr. Kendrick muttered. "Sorry I yelled. I just couldn't believe that the equipment I designed for these children was failing. As a scientist, it's hard to hear that kind of truth. As the adopted father for the amborgs, I can't bury them in the ground. Not when they chose willingly to fight for a better tomorrow."

"That's the thing," Dr. Wildman spoke up. "That's why they volunteered. You promised them a better life and they knew the risks. They accepted death long before an incident like this happened. They accepted before you lost the first child during augmentation. They were already on the path to death when you pulled them back and gave them a choice."

"Unfortunately," Dr. Kendrick replied, "That is slightly problematic now that every amborg now has refused a deployment. They're afraid. Collectively, I've never seen them act this way before."

"Remember everyone who criticized us when the amborgs first showed up in the field? Many people said it was good that they didn't have feelings. Then there were all these shrinks and psychics who claimed that the amborgs had ghosts bursting with rage inside trying to get the feelings out. For the first time since I saw them, I don't see bytes of calculations trying to figure out human emotions anymore. They're feeling pain and its helping them create patterns of thinking that don't logically make sense. They're knowing how to be human. I feel as if I can talk to them now and help them."

"The emotional barrier was never a forced option," Dr. Kendrick said, "It was inhibited which was an odd side effect. The older amborgs are resilient. They've kept order for a long time but I'm afraid psychologically for the young ones. To be honest, I have no idea what I can do."

"Talk to 117," Dr. Wildman said. "I think he needs you now."

"Thank you Gene," Dr. Kendrick sighed. "Go get some rest. You earned it."

117 heard footsteps receding which indicated Dr. Wildman had returned to his office. Suddenly he heard footsteps approaching the curtain surrounding 43's bed.

"117?"

Dr. Kendrick entered without waiting for an answer. 117 barely moved as he felt Dr. Kendrick grab a seat next to him. The two of them watched and kept vigil over 43 who was resting in the hospital bed.

"David," He replied as he removed his spectacles. "What are you feeling right now?"

"I don't know," 117 whispered using his real voice. The pain in his throat began to build so he switched back to his bracelet. "I heard everything. I have no idea what to feel but… these feeling are flowing through my mind. It is not painful. It is… anger. Negative feelings. But nothing to direct it to."

"I know," Dr. Kendrick said grasping 117's shoulder. "It is a buildup of very strong emotions. But don't let it become a mental breakdown David. You've always been strong. I'm sorry though that this had to happen. I can't imagine what it's like for you. You two were happy and it's been your right to feel like this now that someone has stepped in so to speak. But as painful as it is for me to say this, you can't stay here brooding over her. Unless you haven't been doing that and that's fine. It was actually 297 and 6 who felt really nervous about confronting you about this. I had to say 'confronting.' That was definitely not supposed to be aggressive at all… Some father I am."

"Why would someone do this?"

117's question made Dr. Kendrick stop talking. After a brief moment, there was a pause. They listened to the monitor next to 43's head beep continuously until Dr. Kendrick spoke up again.

"I don't know 117," He sighed. "Did I ever tell you about my wife?"

"I had no idea you were married," 117 replied.

"Oh good!" Dr. Kendrick exclaimed. He chuckled out of relief before continuing. "Well, at least I know there are some classified files you kids have chosen not to look into. Anyway…"

Dr. Kendrick pulled out a photo from his pocket. It revealed a beautiful woman with glasses. 117 wasn't sure if it was sheer irony but she was wearing a lab coat that looked just like the one Dr. Kendrick wore.

"I was devastated when they told me I was going to lose her," He said, "Although it was decades ago, I still remember. No matter how long my anti-aging treatment lasts for me. She was an astronomer, one of the brightest scientists I ever met who constantly dreamed of soaring into outer space for mankind. Very pretty too. She could make me feel capable of anything."

Dr. Kendrick took a deep breath as 117 listened attentively. He held the photo of his wife in his hand and looked at her smile.

"I was supposed to meet her for dinner," He explained. "But at the time, my research just piled on and I chose that over her that night. She must have gotten tired of waiting that evening so she drove home by herself. I got home very late to a ringing phone and they told me about the accident. I broke David. I thought I lost everything. Until I found an anniversary message from her. Then, I picked myself up and now look where we are. I am a father to all of you and if she had been alive, she'd probably be able to provide better comfort than I can."

"I lost my father."

Dr. Kendrick turned to face 117.

"I lost my father and my mother," 117 said thinking of his family and the one he had currently. "I didn't know who he was until I realized my grandfather was still alive. He is my real family and maybe someday, we can be a real family. But for now, you have cared for me enough for me to say you are my father. Surrogate or not, through you, you have granted me another real family and it will always get bigger over time. Through you, you can also tell me about my past family too because under all the circumstances and the reality of it. I am here now because of family. I just… I want to bring that man to justice. 43 deserves that. But I have no clue how to start."

"Well it sounds like you already started," Dr. Kendrick replied. "Think about what 43 would do if she wasn't in that bed. I'm sure that she'd be right back at it. Seriously, you boys and girls are the bravest things and the best creations of my life. Screw anyone who criticizes you for your beliefs, sexual orientations, physiques, intelligence, or status. You are the next step for humanity and you will figure this out."

"Then I should be with the other amborgs," 117 replied after thinking for a few seconds. "We should not let the fear of death stop us from helping the people who need us. The avengers never quit whenever they lost a comrade. They endured and kept fighting."

117 got up and thought about the next move. He bid a quick farewell to Dr. Kendrick and asked for any updates about 43's status while he was gone. As he walked towards the entrance of the medical bay, he passed 297 who was wearing a bandage over his shoulder.

"117," 297 said with a surprised look. He hadn't expected to see 117 already up and about, "Are you alright?"

"I believe so," 117 said examining 297's wound. "Is your shoulder ok?"

"Forget my shoulder," 297 said waving a hand. "It will recover. But what about you and 43? I overheard the doctor's argument."

"I know," 117 nodded grimly. "Now is not the time though to be worried about her. We can deal with that after we catch the man responsible. This incident has left me with a lot of feelings and emotions that I would like resolved. Are you willing to get out there again 297?"

"To hell with my wounds," 297 nodded. With his other arm, 297 placed his arm firmly on 117's shoulder. "I want to keep fighting too. This man may have hurt me. But he hurt you more. I won't allow my own brother and sister to suffer. 43 meant a lot to the Second Group. It would make me feel worse if I was left out of this fight."

"As soon as your arm gets better," 117 said, "I think it is time we prepared more for the upcoming fight. How is your aim?"

297 smirked and brought up a holographic image of a sniper rifle on his bracelet.

"Best in the Second Group," He said.

"Well, I hope you plan on hunting because we will need that."

The two of them left the medical bay together. Eventually they reached a path that went two ways. 297 stated he needed to stop by the armory. 117 walked the other way. He needed to address the amborgs.

The other eighty seven amborgs were gathered together in the gym. All of them were in groups and all standing together nervously. Either they were silently communicating with their minds or it was the most awkward gathering ever since no one was actually saying anything out loud. Then 117 entered the gym. All the amborgs slowly straightened up and instantly looked in his direction. Pretty soon, they all silently surrounded him. Number 5 walked up to 117.

"If you are not at 43's side," He said, "I guess you have something to say."

"Yes," 117 nodded. "I feel it is time to take action."

"Good luck telling the rest of them that," 5 replied. "They are all scared about what is out there now. The floor is yours now."

Number 28 walked up and placed her hand sympathetically on his shoulder.

"We heard that 43 was in critical condition. Is everything alright?" She said. But before 117 could reply, they were interrupted by several more questions from the large crowd.

"Can she be saved?" Another amborg from the Second group piped up. "What is happening?"

"She has gone under an emergency operation," A Third group amborg near 117 replied. "What do you think?!"

"QUIET!" 117 called out using his real voice.

The crowd fell silent as 117 felt his throat burn. It didn't hurt as much as before anymore which was good. Now that he had their attention, he needed to tell the truth.

They all stared with burning curiosity. 117 certainly had expected some sort of interrogation but he had not imagined all the other amborgs to be in such a panic. He instantly switched to his bracelet. Before he could continue, 6 transmitted a private message to him.

"117," She said, "Speaking as the doctor in our family, I always knew someday, I would have to work on healing one of you when it was serious enough. But 43 is unconscious under life support. It is your choice to disclose her condition and diagnosis but I was unable to help even though the same implants and cybernetics are built in me. That is a serious blow morally to my skills in training to be the best doctor in the world. I am speaking modestly of course."

"I know," 117 replied. "I was not ready to hear the truth. But instead of moping around, we can do better. Will you stand with me?"

"You forget 117," 6 smiled softly. "Healing is my specialty. I believe there is no disease that is incurable. I will change the field of medicine worldwide. Believe me, I will always be at everyone's side when they call for me and I will not stop until Serina 43 gets back up."

"Wonderful," 117 sighed with relief. "Time to convince the rest of them."

"Not really," 6 replied. "The First Group is ready to follow you. Technically half the Second Group and all the Third Group are the ones who need your reassurance right now. You may not know it, but you actually have already become quite the leader in this."

117 looked at the third group amborg who had spoken shortly before he had asked for silence.

"Are you going to hide yourself and hope that the enemy will go away?" He asked and the third group amborg instantly looked down and didn't say another word.

"117," 3 spoke up for everyone to hear, "You saw what happened to 43. Anyone of us could be the next one lying in the medical center. Fatally wounded or even dead. That is enough to scare all of us. We are with you all the way. But that warehouse job was some of the third group's first assignment in the field. Someone in thick evil armor, pardon the cliché, demonstrated to the younger amborgs that we can be knifed."

"Tell them why we should follow you."

1 turned up behind 117 and gave 117 a nudge.

"Remember," 1 explained, "We are ready and at your disposal. Deep down, we all want to bring this man to justice. But we lack your motivation."

117 faced the crowd of cybernetically enhanced teens who were all waiting. There were a few that already looked like they were good to go. In the mix however, 117 saw 466 surrounded by a few Third group amborgs who looked nervous. They had every right, especially since 466 only had fought with 43 for a short time. 117 chose his words carefully, thought about what to say and finally, he sent a message to all of them. He needed everyone's help.

"What happened to 43 does not mean we should cower in fear," 117 said. "Fear is a natural thing for humans and us as well. We may have forgotten that but almost all of us are beginning to remember what it feels like. I know that the fear of death is upon us. We are not invincible as we thought. It was our mistake to believe that there was no way anyone could find the means to harm us. But I am not going to sit here and wait for 43 to wake up and see us acting like cowards. Come on! We can withstand anything. Except for LTO blades, minus a nuclear explosion or you know, any kind of weapons of mass destruction."

"But 117," Someone from the Second Group said. "No one is running around with W.M.D. This is close and personal. Our sister 43 is in the medical bay. How do we finish this and bring that guy to justice if every criminal has a knife up their sleeve."

"What is the one thing those criminals have felt since we became a hindrance on their plans?" 117 asked all of them. "They hate us. They hate us because we stumbled onto their world and said it wasn't right. They have every motivation to dislike us because we are ruining their lifestyles, their profits, their desires to kill. They are motivated to kill us, they have the tools and they have been continuing to battle us no matter how many times we send them behind bars. We do not hate them equally in return though. Why is that? Because personally, we keep fighting to save the lives of all we encounter. Even on the worst missions, we kept fighting because we provided help to those who needed it. My motivation and feelings have been changing sporadically. But I know that now, I do not want 43 to wake up to me moping around. We signed up for this and staked our lives out for this danger. If we hide now, who will save the people that are still being hurt out there? We have the ability and the responsibility to do the right thing. Each one of us has our own agenda and our own goals. I can respect each and every one of you. All I am asking if you will step up and get better. If they evolve to try and defeat us, then two can play at this game. The man who wounded 43 is mine but we will get better and be prepared to be stronger."

"I will follow that."

Everyone turned to watch 297 walking into the gym with a sniper rifle. It was the same one that 117 had seen him display on his bracelet back in the medical bay.

"We learn our weaknesses to the fullest extent and we work to try and avoid situations like this in the future," 297 stated. "Start from the basics. Rework our CQC. We can work together to find a way to prevent things like this from happening again. 43 would want us to get back out there and continue fighting even with all the risks that we're now facing. After all, I fight better from a distance."

"Yet you are also equally terrifying if someone gets close," 5 joked.

117 looked back at the crowd. 1, 3, 5, 6, 297 and the entire First Group were moving to stand next to him. 35 and 57 looked at other Second Group amborgs and pushed them into the massive line. This left 917 and 999 who was trying to convince the Third Group.

"I may be a lone wolf," 999 said without batting a smile. "But even I get pissed when someone hurts someone I know and they run. We are trained to hunt those who incite injustice. I think it might be time to get back out there."

501 and 466 both stepped forward. They stood in the middle between the amborgs surrounding 117 and the Third Group still contemplating.

"I will follow 117," 501 stated bravely. "I only know him a little but I do not want to sit here. I want to do something and he gives me orders. So I will await my command."

"I lost my partner," 466 said. "43 was and still is awesome. I want to be just as awesome like her."

She turned to face the remaining amborgs.

"Look to the amborgs standing across from you," 466 said gesturing to all of them. "Look to the person on your left. Look to the volunteer on your right. We all will die eventually. All that matters is what we do until then. If you can accept that, then step forward. If you are brave enough to understand that we still have a job to do, that we and a lot of other people risked their lives for what we have then we should stand together. If we give up, their memories will be shamed and they will have died for nothing."

The Third Group looked at 466. Everyone pondered for a moment and then they all began to come to an agreement. 917 looked at 117 with a grin.

"I think that says it all," He said giving 117 a thumbs up. Even 999 gave a slight nod of acknowledgement. "What's the plan boss?"

"I think we need to refresh everything," 117 said. "We should convert the gym to something appropriate for advanced forms of training."

Like clockwork, everyone dispersed and began to make adjustments. Several Third Group amborgs were led by 1 and they began to set up stations all over the gym.

3 went to the cafeteria with the amborg chefs.

"We can't think on empty stomachs," She said, "I'll get take out."

999 and 917 along with some of the Second Group left for the armory after 117 finished speaking.

"Perhaps it's time we considered fighting our enemies on common ground," She said. "Shall we get some swords 917?"

"You know me too well," 917 chuckled.

"Alright!" 6 called to anyone listening. "We need to set up a medical station here. I will be talking about set-up under pressure, teaching refresher courses of basic first aid until professionals arrive to assist, and how to handle people carefully. When I finish, you will know how to help others or I will poison your food."

297 had somehow procured a table and placed his rifle on the stand with a clatter.

"Ok everyone," He said, "Weapons training is in this corner of the gym. We need a shooting range, sparring area, and a lot of training drones or dummies. Everyone needs to get acquainted with as many weapons as possible and select their favorites for the field. Like 117 said, we have always gone into the field practically unarmed. While that doesn't make sense, we change that protocol completely. Now, if we are preparing for a bigger threat. Then we need to act like war is coming. Come to me if you want to face it sooner than anyone else."

117 stood with 5 in the center of the gym. He couldn't believe how fast they had all suddenly found courage. Minutes before, they waited in fear. Now they were beginning to step up beyond what they were built for.

"Did you imagine it would be like this?" 5 asked.

"Not really," 117 replied. "I think we're just winging it."

"What if this guy never resurfaces? What if he attacked 43, just for kicks? Like just an ordinary crook would do?"

"I refuse to believe that Johnny," 117 replied. "Otherwise, that man's story would have no fulfillment to this plot. This act of aggression. This man reminds me of one specific type of killer. A hunter. It is not over. All we can do unfortunately is wait for the next attack."

"I know. All we can do is get better," 5 said nodding. "It's not the best plan but at least it's better than standing around being afraid with everyone else. Oh. It looks like Mandy needs to talk to you."

117 turned to see Mandy running forward with a data-pad in her arm. She had a big smile on her face. 117 was very happy to see her.

"Finally out of the medical bay?" She asked. "Sorry don't answer that. Look David, I was just down there and I brought flowers for 43. But I have all the information from all those companies from the giant robot you took down so I'm very excited. Well I mean it's a bit dull but at least we can sort through this."

"I would love to Mandy," 117 replied. "I am sorry, I was having a moment of weakness."

"And I'm glad you're not letting it stop you," She said patting his cheek softly. "If something happened to Palmer, it would probably be the other way around and our positions would be flipped. No matter what happens, I'm proud of you."

"Thank you for being my technician," 117 said. "Shall we look at the data and you tell me what you have been able to dig up?"

"Alright well," Mandy activated the data-pad and a bunch of company logos showed up along with several logs. "I managed to contact all of the companies that had something or little to contribute to designing our large friend. According to all of what I gathered, they've been conducting business transactions over the last couple of years with someone who has been paying all the bills. It may have been the man who put 43... 'Ahem' anyway, if anyone is designing a giant war machine, it's this mysterious man. He has money, illegal or legally acquired, doesn't matter. I've received a lot of shipping manifests and records. These parts from all these companies were sent from all over the world to the U.S. Get this, it was all legally done too. These companies just had a wealthy customer buy their parts without knowing what the real purpose was for. Right now the police have warned them about these machines and we have sent proof that their parts are used. They've stopped all known shipments to this dealer but based on all the shipments already sent, it might not be good enough."

"Obviously," 117 noted. "Anyone who comes up with the money, they usually don't ask too many questions. The companies you contacted have been completely in the dark about this?"

"So far," Mandy shrugged, "They all claim they had no idea about designs for this robot. They just all thought it was a high paying client hobbyist so they didn't question it. Business people... they suck. Even if we checked all the rich people around the world, it's still a lot in the upper class to investigate. It could be anyone."

"Well it is a start," 117 replied. "If these companies have stopped shipments to the U.S. then all we have to worry about is figuring what kind of threat we've managed to stop and what remains for us to clean up."

"Well, let's go do some more digging."

* * *
** ** **

Present Day, Classroom 312

"What did you think Sarah?"

Sarah looked up from the screen. She grabbed a tissue from Mandy's desk and wiped her eyes.

"Forgive me," She said as Mandy stared. "It was very shocking to see something like that to happen to one of my predecessors. The records do inform us of Serina 43's death but we never really knew about what led up to that. The full details were always a blur."

"I didn't think it'd make you cry," Mandy chuckled slightly as she handed the whole box to Sarah. "That's probably the first time I've ever seen an amborg break out in tears in a very long time."

"A moment of weakness," Sarah repeated from the video. "Most humans go through those types of phases for a long time. Amborgs can get over things within minutes. But it doesn't feel right."

"Oh? Why do you say that?"

"When people move on from issues that should be addressed, like when 117 motivated them to get over their fears and courage, sometimes it increases the chances of forgetting the real issues. When you have friends who insult or make you feel bad, some people tell you to get over it and just do whatever to forget it. It always feel like they're avoiding the real issues."

"True," Mandy nodded, "But you need to know that almost every human are idiots. Not everyone knows how to really comfort one another when you need it. They just default to the best setting they think will get rid of everything and hope it solves itself without it interfering with their life. Kind of like how Dr. Kendrick tried talking 117 when he was looking after 43. He didn't know how to talk about it when 117 needed it. He didn't know how to discuss his wife even though the experience was roughly similar in many ways."

"That makes sense," Sarah said. "This story is enlightening and also very realistic on emotions."

"Not all stories are happy," Mandy replied. "But 117 didn't give up. He almost did for about ten minutes but he was motivated. We can be weak at times. It will happen to us and it changes us in a very important way. Has nothing to do with if you're evolved or the poorest person on earth. It's just how it can motivate us. Even the bad guys too."

"I'd like to keep watching please," Sarah said clutching the box of tissues.

"Well we do have all evening," Mandy sighed. "Whatever it takes to make you understand my big point at the end of this. Computer, begin playing again."

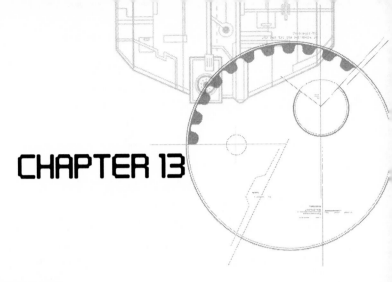

CHAPTER 13

2128, A.I. Industries Gymnasium
Five days later

✱✱ ✱✱ ✱✱

"Well done, 66. But unfortunately, your reflex probabilities have deteriorated by seven percent."

"It's not my fault! 73 and 61 surrounded me from both sides! Dealing with common enemies is simple enough. But two amborgs is a real challenge."

Keith 66 sat up on the mats with a very angry look. He had just been the victim of being ganged up by two other amborgs who practically wiped the floor with him. Literally and metaphorically.

"No one is saying anyone is at fault," Kat 4 replied. She extended a hand out and 66 grabbed it. "We need to teach you how to deal with multiple opponents at a time. Your fighting style has been primarily centered on taking down one person at a time. Your next session is with three amborgs. The equivalent to at least eighteen bad guys. This should make you fight better."

"Aww, my joints!"

Keith 66 got up reluctantly and walked over to the custom charging station. His next fight wouldn't be for at least twenty minutes so he spent the most of it trying to enjoy the charge. One of the technicians had set it up in the gym since many of the amborgs' activities were confined there most of the time. While the energy flowed to his reserves, he looked over at a group of second and third group amborgs who were performing some experiments with a rather excited technician.

"Now everyone, pay attention," The technician was explaining, "Research just developed these gizmos and they are fun as hell to use. Physics will pay tribute to this over the centuries!"

He threw a red orb toward some cones. A red light expanded and then with a blinding flash, the cones disappeared. The technician laughed gleefully causing all the amborgs to stare in astonishment. He stopped laughing when no one else did and casually cleared his throat.

"Sorry," He said a little off-put at the quiet reception. Raising his glove, the orb he threw came back and instantly landed in the padded material. He removed it with his other hand, and threw it again to some other part of the gym. Another blinding flash caused everyone to stop. Instead of empty space, the cones were back which caused a couple of third group amborgs to jump. The amborgs observing the experiment were amazed and very impressed.

"Wow this is really amazing," Derrick 274 from the second group spoke up, "Interesting. You have developed technology to miniaturize inanimate objects for convenient travel. A very efficient method for shipping supplies for instance."

"YES!" The technician chuckled but his smile faded as a couple amborgs began examining them, "Well... that's one thing you can do with them. You can also use them for combat purposes too. A bunch of us at the lab loved figuring out how to use them like grenades. As an added feature, you can link through to it with your CPU and you can set the option to either transport, disintegrate (for opening doors or walls) or explode. Obviously, it won't stay intact with the last two options but the more stuff you keep locked up during transport mode, it actually would theoretically survive the explosion if by accident you used it in combat. I wouldn't keep your valuables in it though. You could even capture and store a person inside one of these devices too."

Everyone's smile faded. The technician also stopped chuckling and saw all of them staring nervously at the orb. Everyone wanted to ask the question but they were afraid of what the answer might be.

"Well. Not to sound a little doubtful," Jon 125 spoke up. "But… is it safe to capture humans with these?"

"Well we have tested it on various animals and it's actually pretty safe," The technician nodded, "They all come back. We actually never made it to human trials when all of this happened. So, I would not advise it. But results would help on the less fortunate. Sorry, I shouldn't say stuff like that. The right thing is always the moral way to science. Not our natural curiosities."

"May we try one?" One of the amborgs asked.

"I don't see why not," The technician said, "Just try not to throw it near someone. HEY WAIT!"

It was too late. 274 had half-heard the conversation and already thrown one of the orbs without actually looking where he threw it. It landed next to 297. Everyone's eyes widened as the orb activated and with a great flash, 297 disappeared from where he stood. Ryan 35, who had been talking with 297 moments before stopped and whirled around looking for him. He looked helplessly at 274's group but they all stared back silently unable to describe what had just happened.

274 was rooted to the spot.

"Oh no," He said quietly.

The technician also was in a state of panic. But without expressing it, he struggled to remain as calm as possible. Using the glove in his hand, he summoned the orb which rolled away from 35 and shot straight into his hand. He quickly dropped the orb to the ground, allowed it to roll away so it wasn't near anyone and activated it.

There was another bright flash but unfortunately, the part of the gym he had rolled it to remained the same. 297 was nowhere in sight.

"Sir?" 125 said. "Where is 297?"

"How odd," The technician replied nervously. "Well like I said, we never made it to human trials so it obviously might be different if we captured one but based on all the organic data we've amassed so far, he should be fine. This first test is getting worse with every second."

The technician patiently checked his watch and looked around.

"Alright, I'll take a closer look at the orb to see if it's defective," He said, "The worst case scenario is he's just trapped in there at a small scale."

"AAAAAHHH!!!"

They all looked up and 297 fell from the ceiling and landed on the ground with a gigantic thud. Everyone in the vicinity scattered at the sudden impact. 35 ran over to 297 and immediately began to scan him. He gave a thumbs-up to indicate that 297 was ok. 297 was helped back to his feet and he seemed to be alright but slightly disorientated and shaken up.

"There he is!" The tech said smiling again. The group all got up and ran over to where 297 was pulling himself onto his feet with support from 35.

"What did you feel 297?" The tech asked. "Or... How do you feel? Are you alright?"

"I do not know," He stammered. He quickly shook his head and instantly calmed down, "For a minute there, everyone disappeared and I was in someplace. A giant sphere of some sorts. All alone and trapped. Then another moment, I saw a blinding flash of light and then I felt myself being sent flying upwards and the next thing I knew, I was up in ceiling supports above and then I lost my grip while I was trying to regain my senses."

"That's interesting," The technician said giving 297 a pat on the shoulder. "In an instance, the orb actually propelled you upwards into the ceiling. All in the blink and flash of an eye. This will definitely be good for research."

The technician then ran off leaving 297 with 274 and 125. The other amborgs all sighed and relaxed. 125 quickly picked up and threw away the orb next to 297's feet and pointed at 274 without a moment's notice.

"He did it," 125 said immediately. Instead of protesting against his amborg sibling, 274 looked quickly at where 125 had thrown the orb.

"125," He said panicking, "You should pick that up before..."

Another bright flash interrupted him. 125, 274 and 297 both turned and stared in the direction of the flash.

"Uh oh..." 297 looked, "Who was standing there?! I saw someone disappear!"

"Umm, I think Dr. Kendrick," 125 replied in shock, "If I remember correctly."

There wasn't any more reason for what came next. Instantly, someone was already yelling what the three amborgs were scrambling to do.

"QUICK! BRING HIM BACK!"

On the other side of the gym, similar chaos was also brewing. 335 was being carried out of the gym after a bad accident with one of their upgrades. Amborgs from the third group were shocked. 999, Louis 777, and 56 of the second group were trying to keep the younger amborgs calm.

"What happened to 335?!" One of them panicked. "Is she ok?!"

"We cannot lie to them 9 cubed," 56 joked. "Our only option is to tell the truth."

"I agree," 777 nodded, "335 should be fine but I believe it has hindered the third group's ability to cope considering that did not go well."

999 pondered for a minute. How did I get stuck with the cybernetic upgrades? She thought angrily. Despite her feelings, she nodded in agreement to the other two amborgs.

"Now it is all right," She said, "335 is in good condition. It was just an accident."

Before she could continue, several artificial intelligence units sparked and appeared next to the amborgs. Ten of them glowed out of the walls and floated chattering amongst themselves. They were very angry at each other.

"Well didn't go well..." An A.I. named Taylor shrugged, "Who was supposed to integrate with 335's CPU again?"

All of the other AI's shrugged and glanced around. Taylor groaned and turned a shade of yellow.

"Great," He said when none of them responded, "An advanced group of artificial intelligence created by one of the smartest men on earth and we can't even remember who was supposed to pair up with one amborg."

"Don't be concerned Taylor," 777 said reassuringly, "It was an accident."

"Why do we have to learn to integrate with an amborg anyway?" Taylor placed his hands on his holographic hips. He changed to a bright green color as he added, "It's never been attempted before even if we can actually be transported in your CPUs."

"Dr. Kendrick believes that if certain AI's pair up with an amborg, then the calculation output, performance issues and systems should increase by a large percentage. What we are attempting is to find compatible AI's for each amborg. It reminds me of a twenty first century game that humans used to play. I have found the gameplay to be quite amusing. Ever heard of the game Halo?"

"We don't play videogames," Taylor said bluntly and all the other AIs nodded in agreement. 777 sighed.

"The reason I mention Halo is because," 777 sighed. "The A.I. paired with Master Chief is Cortana. She was flash-cloned from the mind of Dr. Halsey. Also she was allowed to choose which Spartan she wanted to pair with. She chose the most compatible which was the Master Chief. We believe that A.I.s from A.I. Industries, whether they were made from scratch or based off real personalities, will permanently increase our performance for future encounters. We could also transport A.I.s in our CPUs to other systems or computers on future deployments. You know, just like in Halo. You guys coop yourselves up here all the time, don't you want to go on an adventure?"

"Well putting that aside," 999 stepped in, "We should not get off-topic. It would have been easier to integrate if you were all paying attention. But now we are minus one amborg for a bit of time thanks to all of you trying to help."

"Well when you ask us to do something never been done before, something is bound to go wrong," Taylor replied quietly. There was an obvious sense of guilt in his voice which the amborgs heard instantly.

"That would be because all ten of you tried to upload into her CPU at the same time," 56 noted while scratching his head, "Her hard drive was not able to cope. Consider yourselves lucky she did not go insane with eleven people trying to gain control of her brain."

"Yeah, it was a good thing she fainted from all the pressure," 777 chuckled but quickly stopped when he saw 999 glaring at him.

"Alright enough!" She said. She wanted to get back to work and try to finish this before dinner, "We need to focus. The third group amborgs are anxious and we need to get this done. Artificial Intelligences, you will pair up with an amborg. ONE A.I. to ONE amborg. Let's avoid another accident. Practice makes perfect."

"Right," Taylor nodded and the other A.I.s began floating around to the waiting amborgs, "OVERTIME!"

On the other side of the gym. Near 6's medical station, Dr. Kendrick was seated on a crate with 501. He had just been cleared by 6 for work provided he take it easy. After all, not a lot of people could really recover from being unwillingly snatched and shrunk inside a small handheld prison.

"Are you sure you are alright Doctor?" 501 asked nervously as Dr. Kendrick was outfitting a new gadget on his arm, "I feel nervous about accepting this new equipment after your latest predicament. Are you sure your mind is functioning normally?"

"Pfft, I'm fine Donut!" Dr. Kendrick chuckled lazily which made 501 extremely nervous, "It's not every day you get teleported into a compressed sphere of a miniature baseball and then instantly back to reality. I'm great!"

He let out a loud maniacal laugh which was all 501 needed to be afraid. Even with the lie detector built inside his system, 501 knew Dr. Kendrick was still slightly disorientated and not telling the full truth.

"Ok 501," Dr. Kendrick took a few breaths and focused. He blinked a few times before speaking again. "This arm bracelet when used, emits an electronic charge which should disable... well anything really. That's the idea but I designed it to zap a lot of stuff."

Upon hearing this, 501 lifted his arm and activated it. There was a loud zapping noise followed by a loud yell.

"OW!"

They watched as 466 jumped up in pain. When she was back on her feet, she began massaging her lower back. There was an electrical burn mark right where the electricity had struck.

"Uhh, Donut, I didn't tell you to fire it," Dr. Kendrick stared. The electricity had snapped him back to his senses. Now alert, he stared nervously from 501 to 466.

"It was an accident," Said 501 with an even terrified look on his face, "Umm sorry 466, I did not intend to shoot you in the butt."

Both of them averted their eyes as 466 massaged where the electricity had actually struck. It wasn't until a few seconds later that she marched right over and belted 501 in the face. While they had looked away, she had taken the opportunity to sneak up and exact revenge.

"OW!" 501 cried, "I believe I said I was sorry!"

"You IDIOT!" She yelled blushing furiously.

* * *

In the halls of another corridor, a team of first group amborgs were casually enjoying a leisurely stroll before another one of their assigned training sessions. Clint 11, Danielle 12, Tiana 19, and Jennifer 24 were walking down towards the medical center to ask for some supplies for the gym that 6 had asked for. Since she hadn't actually specified a time of delivery, they were taking their time to enjoy a brief break. They also had considered visiting 43 to continue relaxing away from the intensive workouts. As they rounded the final corner, they all saw the entrance to the medical facility. But just before they could enter, a few security guards ran up and prepared to draw their weapons. Concerned, they walked up to the guards.

"What is wrong?" 11 inquired.

One of the security guards shrugged.

"We received a security alert," He explained. "Miss Mandy called for us. We don't know what's wrong."

The four amborgs, puzzled, leaned closer to the door along with the guards. As quietly as possible, they tried to listen for any disturbances. At first, everything seemed fine until there was an almighty crash that made them back away slowly.

The guards all jumped back in terror whereas the amborgs slightly flinched. Their weapons were instantly drawn and they stood staring nervously at the door. All four amborgs looked at each other, quickly set a layout plan and readied themselves. 19 signaled for the guards to split up and flank the doors. As they did so, another crash happened behind the door. This time, there were voices accompanying the loud noises of destruction. Amidst the chaos inside, the amborgs recognized 117's voice.

"43 stop!" He shouted from behind the door. "Mandy! Are you alright?!"

"I'm fine David!" A second voice sounded from inside, "Please get your girlfriend to calm down!"

"Let. Me. OUT!!" Someone screamed followed by another crash.

Outside, everyone stared at each other in confusion. Something was definitely not right.

"That sounded like 43," One of the confused guards said looking at everyone else.

The four amborgs looked at each other again and modified the tactical plan to a newer version. They shifted to the front and had the guards move back.

"Obviously it was," 19 nodded in response. "Guards, you may want to step back slightly. Let us try to get a bearing of what is happening inside."

As the guards backed further away from the door, 24 and 11 walked up to the door. They both reached out their hands and placed them on the door without opening it. It had gone silent but there were vibrations all over the door frame which meant there was still hostile movement on the other side. From the noise alone, it sounded like a Tasmanian devil had been unleashed inside to match the destruction of a miniature earthquake. Suddenly, another crash occurred shaking the door. Both 24 and 11 withdrew their hands while 12 and 19 stood on each side of the entrance. The guards backed away some more. Something had slammed into the door. The voices inside continued to shout.

"Mandy no! Get over here!" They heard 117 shout, "Pick up that hospital mattress and just hide behind it!"

"Oh right!" They heard her reply, "A mattress is supposed to protect me from a super enhanced cybernetic girl!"

"Desperate times! 43, please stand down! It's me David 117!"

"I'll stand down! Right after you agree to LET ME OUT!"

"That's going to be difficult 43. Oh no…"

Outside, there was barely anytime to make out 117's faltering voice when another loud crash shook the hallway. The door, being struck by the latest blow, bent outwards from the impact. The guards looked like they were about to panic. All of the amborgs instantly readied a defensive stance and put on serious looks. 43 by the sound of it had turned hostile.

"Security detail, retreat to a safe area," 19 ordered, "This is definitely not your fight."

"Yeah, I get the message," The security guard nodded, "Come guys. MOVE!"

All of the security guards sprinted down the hall as another blow slammed into the door. The four amborgs coordinated together and took a step back away from the door.

"Right," 11 scoffed. "Not their fight. But what about us?"

"I really would not like to hear the answer to that," 12 said.

"Well what is the plan?" 11 asked nervously. "19?"

"How should I know?" She shrugged nervously, "117 seems to be handling it well."

"43, umm…honey. I know you're angry but please let me explain! Calm down. Hey! Put me down this instant! I… Uh-oh."

There was a loud muffled boom and a thud.

"Or not," 19 said nervously as the team shifted around, "Ok we will attempt to hold her here. First we need to wait for her next move."

Seconds later, there was another giant crash as the door bent outwards even further. Amazingly, the door was holding on fairly well but not for long based on their scan of the structural integrity.

"I calculate... with sarcasm," 12 noted, "Her next move is, fight her way through the door and us. Is anyone else noting how bad a position we might be in?"

A few more thuds, crashes and loud metal grinding noises occurred as the structure of the door weakened piece by piece. The team's morale slowly began to diminish slowly. They had fought against 43 before in training but in this state, she was practically unpredictable.

"It's ok!" Said 24 as optimistically as possible. The atmosphere of the team was starting to get to her, "Think of this as an ambush scenario!"

"Are you kidding?" 19 chuckled nervously. "This is 43. The best fighter out of all of us. Even 999 admits that she can't beat her one on one."

"Well, it was nice knowing you guys," 11 sighed..

"You aren't planning on running away are you 11?" The girls turned to stare at him.

"Of course not," He said, "If we ran now, then others less fortunate would be fighting 43. Impossible odds and death at the hands of an attractive woman. Not exactly my first way to die but why not?"

The door was surprisingly a lot stronger than they originally thought as three more blows struck it with tremendous force. It became quiet for a few seconds and then with another almighty crash, the door flew out of its frame and towards the four of them. All of them ducked and avoided it easily but looked up at the silhouette standing in the entryway. 43, all dressed in her regular clothing was cracking her neck and was planting a fist into her other hand.

"Ok," She snarled, "Who's first?"

"Umm, perhaps," 19 gulped, "Now would be the appropriate time to signal a full facility alert."

"Status update," 12 said slowly, "We're dead."

* * *

Alarms instantly rang out across the entire facility. Everyone in the library stopped and listened. Every drone was instantly placed on high alert. Everyone in the cafeteria stopped what they were doing. Thalia, from her room, went from enjoying a silent imaginary tea party to a loud noise almost rupturing her eardrums. Even Stan stopped waxing to floor when one of the amborgs began screaming through the hallways. The voice over the P.A. was yelling the full details for everyone on site that were able to listen.

"Alarm! Alarm! Second group amborg on the loose! Extreme security measures required! Battle conditions on site! Amborg 43 is hostile! Medical bay reports minor injuries and one amborg casualty."

Dr. Kendrick and most of his staff ran quickly to where the fight was supposedly now taking place. They ran inside the observation room on the second floor of a warehouse gazed inside and saw the sea of cargo containers and supplies.

"Where are they? What the hell is going on?" Dr. Kendrick muttered in a concerned tone.

He needed to find out what was going on for such a large alert. An entrance down below suddenly flew open and 11, 12, 19, and 24 ran through into the warehouse. Dr. Kendrick and his technicians stared as the four amborgs displayed looks of terror across their faces. One of the technicians quickly patched the receiver and soon they were hearing the conversation down below.

"RETREAT! RUN!" 11 was yelling as their voices came through the speaker. 19 and 24 were both running side by side, trying to pass one another. "I don't want to die!"

"Where is she?!" 12 yelled in confusion glancing quickly all around them. "Help us!"

"There they are," Kendrick watched as the amborg team of four stopped to catch their breaths. He quickly pressed a button and spoke into the communication terminal, "I need all amborgs combat ready. Those of you close by please report to warehouse one dash sixteen alpha. I need an A.I. to report to my position now!"

He then switched buttons and spoke into the warehouse.

"It's alright kids," He said reassuringly. "Just stay calm and we'll have help for you."

"Please hurry Dr. Kendrick!" The amborgs below cried as they scrambled through all of the different aisles.

No sooner did they yell this, the door reopened again and Dr. Kendrick saw 43 dash inside. Even though the amborgs had hidden themselves in another part of the facility, she was obviously hunting for them. Oh boy, Dr. Kendrick quickly wiped the sweat off his brow, it's a game of cat and mouse. He quickly switched the communications back to the general broadcast.

"Whoever gets this message," Kendrick gaped through the glass, looking for the first group amborgs. He quickly added frantically, "You might want to speed up on getting here fast otherwise we're going to lose four more amborgs. Double time it now! Where's my A.I.?!"

* * *
** ** **

"I guess we are putting our new skills to the test," 5 said as he ran out of the gym with 1, 3, and 4. They were also joined by Ziggy 2 at an intersection and the first five amborgs made their way to the warehouse. They greeted each other without stopping and ran for the coordinates. As they ran, several other amborgs stayed behind to coordinate tactics. 297 rallied a few amborgs, A.I.s and drones.

"Everyone listen up!" 297 said picking up his rifle. He looked at it, thought about the present situation and changed his mind. Fighting 43 with the best rifle they had was probably going to kill her.

"A.I.s and security will lead all regular staff and civilians to safe areas away from the warehouse," He said quickly grabbing a few handguns, ""Once everyone is accounted for, AIs, lock the entryways so 43 will not be able to get to our personnel. All other amborgs converge to warehouse one dash sixteen alpha. Any questions?"

He paused briefly to let someone speak up but no one responded.

"Alright then," He said pulling the slide back on the pistol. "Move out!"

"297," One of the A.I.s called out. "We are only going to stop 43 right?"

"We will do everything we can," 297 replied. "That is all I can say for now. Based on the report though, she is definitely being uncooperative."

"Well," The A.I. flashed blue. "Please make sure she doesn't get killed. This isn't normal. Even if we've never experienced this type of incident before."

"Alright," 297 said as they left the gym. "I will keep that in mind and inform the others."

Meanwhile, 11, 12, 19 and 24 were all standing in a diamond formation among a few crates and other supplies. Each one of them faced in one of four directions but 43 had disappeared. Now they were completely on the defensive.

"Can any of you locate her?" 24 looked around but was unable to detect their sister. She transmitted with the others privately, "She has disappeared! I don't see any sign of an approach. Anyone hear anything?"

"Absolutely nothing," 11 said nervously glancing around, "But I think we should try to ACK!"

An arm shot out from a nearby crate and grabbed 11 by the scruff of his jacket collar. It pulled him in and his head hit the crate hard. And then the entire side panel of the crate flew towards the rest of them. The three of them dodged easily but 11 was pushed into the wall opposite with the panel squashing him against another crate.

"OW!" He groaned weakly, "I found her."

43 lunged from the crate and punched 12 in the face. She blocked 19's attack, kicked her in the stomach and sent her rolling away. 12 and 24 regrouped and tried to coordinate but 43 blocked their attacks easily and rapidly hit each of them and knocked them to the ground. 11 crawled out from behind the panel.

"We need better firepower," He groaned as he ran towards some boxes. He leaped on top and ran to where he could be seen from the observation post. Seeing Dr. Kendrick inside the observation room, he waved frantically.

"Doctor!" He shouted through the communications in the observation room. "Help us! What can we use in here?!"

"Technically everything Clint! Stay calm!" Dr. Kendrick's voice spoke on a private channel. "This warehouse has roughly a lot of things that could be used to your advantage! But just be careful. 297 just told me that we should try to capture 43. I'm sending you the shipping logs and inventory lists now. But you need to watch for the hazardous materials, if the fighting gets out of hand, we could lose the whole warehouse!"

"Don't kill 43 and all of us at the same time," 11 sighed as he brought up the first inventory page. "Sounds simple enough."

He quickly ran to another crate. Making sure he was well within hearing distance of the ensuing brawl, he began digging through the box to look for a weapon. 11 was digging through a crate when a door slid open and 297 ran in. The two of them linked up and he included 297 into his conversation.

"11! What's the situation? What are you doing?" 297 looked in the box with him and grabbed an oddly shaped survival knife. "Huh. The file says discontinued for poor durability design."

"Focus 297! You really need to ask about the situation?" 11 asked and dug deeper into the box. "We might need to go to a different box if this stuff is all discontinued. I am acquiring a better... hello there. Hey here's something."

He pulled out a hand-held weapon with multiple cylinders around the barrel which caused 297 to step back and wield his knife defensively.

"11," 297 said very slowly, "Do you know how to properly wield that weapon? Do you even know what it is?"

"Yes," He replied quietly, "Well that statement is partially accurate. I ran simulations with it but I have never used it in all perceptions of reality. It was a discontinued prototype but I know how it works."

"Are you sure 11?" 297 said sternly.

297 lowered the knife but did not take his eye off of the weapon. Before anyone could say anything else, there was a loud crash and 19 flew by. The two amborgs briefly caught her look of fear as she whizzed past.

"HELP!" She screamed as she landed into a pile of crates.

11 looked 297 in the eye. Without another word, he activated the weapon. The cylinders lit up and a loud whining sound indicated it was charging.

"Unless you need more reason," He said as the cylinders turned a bright blue, "I'm damn sure."

The two of them ran out and quickly came up with a small plan. 11 jumped and climbed upwards to gain a better vantage point and 297 kept to the grounds. The two of them maneuvered their way towards the sounds of the fighting. 297 turned a corner and saw them. He quickly signaled 11 and they began to act out their plan.

12, 19 and 24 were all losing drastically. In the seconds after Kendrick had issued an emergency distress. They were holding out as long as they possibly could. Unfortunately, only a fraction of amborgs from each group had responded to the call for reinforcements and they wouldn't arrive for another few minutes. In the midst of the fighting, 43 had shoved a crate over 12's head causing her to stumble around trying to get it off. Picking herself out of some crates she had been thrown into, 19 tried to come up from behind but was grabbed and flipped over 43's shoulder, falling into the ground. As 19 was spread across the floor, 43 punched her right in the stomach, forcing the floor to collapse and causing her to be shoved straight into the ground. In response, 24 began to run around in a circle causing 43 to mirror her. As the two of them circled each other in a rapid whirlwind, 24 stopped running at the last second, stepped inwards and rapidly tried to reach out a hand to grab 19. 43 continued to zoom around, failing to notice his sudden stop but soon she realized what 24 was doing. 43 slowed to a stop and began to charge at the two amborgs. But before she could, a voice shouted from behind.

"Hey sis!!"

43 ducked as a weird looking knife flew over her head. She stood up, turned and looked at her new opponent which turned out to be 297. 24 immediately went back to pulling 19 out of the ground. 297 stood alone and pulled out another knife.

"Your behavior is unacceptable 43," He said sternly, "Cease hostilities now. I will not repeat this."

"Of course not," 43 smiled as she instantly began walking toward him, "Bringing a knife to a fist-fight 297? Tisk tisk."

She didn't realize that 297 was acting as bait. He glanced over her shoulder quickly and saw 11 moving into position on top of a stack of cargo containers. He had to keep her focus on him. 43 raised her fists as she walked closer to 297, who also readied a defensive stance. But before anyone could make a move, a crate fell from one of the ceiling cranes. It landed with a loud crash and separated 297 from 43.

"Yes! I saved 297!"

297 looked up at the crane controls and his eyes widened in horror. 501 was waving from behind the controls.

"Hey 297! Did it work? Did I get her?"

"Idiot!" 297 said angrily on a private channel. "The container had completely blocked him from 43 and he had no way of knowing which direction she could be coming from. "You are interfering in the middle of a plan 501!"

"Oh really? Sorry!"

"297! She saw me!"

297 climbed over the crate and looked down the other side. When the crate had separated him from 43's line of sight, she had turned around and checked the surrounding area which unfortunately blew 11's cover. 297 was about to drop down on top of 43 when 11 quickly aimed and fired his weapon.

"Fire in the hole!" He cried as the weapon discharged and shot its payload.

A blue light shot out of the first barrel and it rotated to load the next one. 43 side stepped the beam easily and looked at where it struck. The plating in the floor had heated up and turned bright blue and orange. Seconds later, it disintegrated. All that was left was a burning hole in the ground which left the watching crowd staring silently.

"Hey 11!" 297 said, "It might be a good idea to stop using that."

It was 43 however who had the worst reaction.

"You tried to disintegrate me?!" She said with a look of disgust. "Eat this buster!"

She rolled over to the side, picked up a piece of broken metal and threw it at 11. It went so fast that 11 barely had time to dodge. As he stumbled to maintain his balance, he accidentally pulled the trigger again and it fired again. The beam struck a metal pillar and split into multiple beams bouncing everywhere. Everywhere the beams hit, holes were melting into various surfaces. Luckily, no one was hit.

"Oh crap!" 11 cried out as he fell on his bottom. "Sorry!"

As 11 struggled to get up, 43 sprinted and leapt up to him with lightning speed. Just as he was getting up, she grabbed the cylinder weapon, turned him around and centered him. She kicked him and sent him falling towards the ground. He landed next to 24 and 19.

43 then brought the weapon down over her knee, smashed it and threw the pieces at 297 who jumped off the crate and fell to the floor. As he straightened up, 43 ran over and stood within inches from his face.

"I hate it when you do that," 297 sighed.

"My specialty," 43 said angrily.

297 tried to fight her but in a second, 43 disarmed him, kneed him in the stomach and threw him over to the pile of amborgs struggling to get back up. 24 had succeeded in pulling 19 out of the ground. Both of them quickly helped get the crate off of 12. The three of them then crawled and slunk their way to meet up with 297 and 11.

"What do we do now?" 12 asked as she massaged her neck.

All of them stood and watched where 43 stood. She didn't attack or throw anything else from where she was positioned. Instead she just watched all of them waiting for the next challenger. Suddenly another voice from behind answered 12's question.

"How about an upgrade?"

A mix of amborgs instantly arrived into the field. 1, 3, 5, 35, 57, 125, 274, 777 and 999 instantly dropped in. All of them were carrying weapons and readying defensive positions. 11, 12, 19, 24, and 297 instantly joined their ranks. The five of them were massaging their joints in relief. 43 stared at all of them and readied herself.

"Not that I sound nervous or anything," 19 said with a nervous smile. "But how come there aren't any more of you?"

"Well the others are either securing the civilians, still on the way, or otherwise preoccupied," 1 replied. "After all, eighty nine amborgs versus one is a little unfair don't you think?"

"Are you kidding?" 297 protested. "It's already fourteen versus one and it can't get any more fair enough for 43."

"Just so you know," 43 taunted. "Fifty amborgs, that's probably my maximum but I can settle for all of you for now."

"Yeah," 5 muttered, "We're dead."

"Some reinforcements," 24 sighed. "You guys are most welcome but we're supposed to be trying to capture her."

"How often do we get to fight our little sister for real?" 3 asked nervously.

"What does it matter?" 999 said. "I do enjoy a challenge."

11 stared at 999 with a look of horror.

"That doesn't sound really helpful," he said.

3 stepped forward and charged her pop gun. The rest of them all looked at her as she bravely stepped in front of the group.

"Alright everyone," She explained. "In short, we drew the short straws. So basically, that means we keep 43 in here while every other amborg locks down every possible way out."

"Anyone need weapons?" 274 distributed arms amongst them.

He had certainly grabbed a strange assortment of weapons anyone had ever seen. 43 actually stared at all of them as if she was watching the worst circus in the world.

"You guys look like a time machine blew up and turned you into the weirdest looking D&D party," She said.

She couldn't be more right. 1 was holding a vintage flame thrower in his arms. 5 and 999 both had short range grenade launchers. 274 held some of the transport cubes from earlier and 125 stepped away, arming a five foot, eight barrel shot-gun. 777 had somehow picked up a baseball bat in the middle of the warehouse. 57 picked up an electric saw. Finally, 35 drew a tomahawk. ("Where did you even get that?" 5 said staring.)

Without another moment to spare, the four other amborgs grabbed the last few weapons the party had brought.

"Seriously?" 11 said in disbelief pulling a sword from 5's shoulder bag, "Where did you acquire a rapier?"

"I borrowed it from Kendrick's office," 5 said casually, "I had 13 hack his office."

"Hey! Now that is a collectible!"

All of them, including 43, turned and looked at the observation post. Kendrick was staring wide-eyed at all of them in shock. Everyone looked amongst each other and all shrugged their shoulders.

"I will acquire another one for you doctor," 5 said innocently with a sheepish grin on his face. "How hard could it be to replicate one of these?"

"Johnny, that's not the point!" Dr. Kendrick shouted, "Oh never mind."

"Cool, is this new from research?" 19 picked up what looked like a lightsaber. Unfortunately, when she pressed the button, a long wire extended out of it and electricity began crackle from it. She wielded the electric whip carefully. "I didn't think they made these anymore. Shocking!"

"Hey watch it!" 125 yelled as the wire curled next to his feet.

"I call dibs on the magnum!" 12 said excitedly as she pulled back on the chamber of a very dusty weapon. This left 24 with the last item.

"Seriously?" She said feeling disappointed, "An arrow? What can I do with this??"

"Come on 24," 1 replied, "You're holding the world's deadliest bumper sticker right there in your hand. Just remember not to stick it somewhere it shouldn't go. Otherwise Dr. Kendrick will kill us if 43 doesn't."

"Everyone lock and load!" 5 shouted, "We have incoming and she looks a little too happy!"

"Oh yeah sure,' Said 3, "All we have to do is take on the only amborg who could probably kill all of us instantly. And may I also point out she is kind of having a rage moment? What could go wrong?"

Before anyone could reply however, 43 charged.

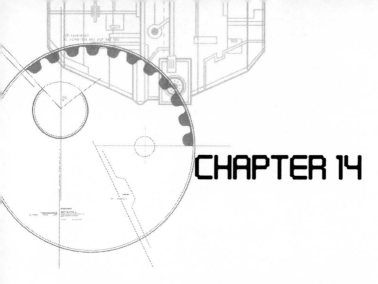

CHAPTER 14

Ten minutes earlier, Amborg Industries North Entrance

"Halt. You are entering a restricted area. You must turn back and leave."

"Leave? After all the trouble poor old me took to get here?"

117's grandfather Mark stood outside the gates with a few of his henchmen. He was under the impression that 117 had sent for him but the guards, which turned out to be a bunch of talkative security drones, had him completely stonewalled.

"Running scan on pronounced visitors," The security drone stated as it looked Mark and his guards up and down. You are currently equipped with anatomical equipment which should safely allow you to proceed in the opposite direction. Some pieces of this equipment could also be considered as weapons. Please leave now before a hostile situation occurs. Please have a nice day."

"Well I have other things to do," Mark replied casually. "Now if you would please step aside. There's stuff that needs doing that your little circuit board can't even begin to fathom."

"Sir, we may be drones," The guard replied in a deep monotone. "It is true we do not have emotions but we can still understand insults. With that manner of disrespect, we politely ask that you leave now."

"Boy are you a sensitive little..."

Mark stopped and immediately held his tongue. This was getting nowhere. The drone looked at him curiously but didn't question it. Starting to get impatient, he looked over the shoulder of the security drone, attempting to look for someone human. He had expected a trip inside Amborg Industries to be an easy one but he couldn't help but feel that 117 had called him here as a prank instead of an emergency.

"My apologies sir," The drone said again, "No matter how many times you request access, you do not appear to be hostile but I still cannot permit you access to the complex. As I said before, you have no clearance and your visit is unscheduled which is unauthorized. Therefore you and your party must leave."

The old man groaned and thought of what to say next. But then he noticed something odd. True, A.I. industries used drones to watch the entrances but as he looked around, he couldn't help but notice one specific thing. The security gate was missing one detail which he could have sworn was different in the past.

"Say, I do think that this could be resolved if I spoke to someone high up," He said. "It doesn't have to be Kendrick but maybe the guard running this gate? Where are the guards?"

"Your query is unclear," The drone replied and indicated with a small gesture to the rest of the drones, "As you can see, the guards are at their post."

"No you dumb drone," Grandpa Mark snapped, "The human guards. Doesn't Kendrick have human guards out here? The ones who KNOW how to talk to visitors? He's got to have someone biological on guard instead of all robots."

"All of the HUMAN guards are not at their posts because of a critical situation. I also find that last statement to be prejudiced," The drone replied casually.

"Oh yeah? Critical? Wait, what do you mean prejudiced?" Grandpa leaned forward but immediately understood what the drone was saying. He quickly waved his hands and shook them defensively, "Ok, I admit I might have overreacted on that last statement. I got nothing against robots or drones."

Except when they're being a pain, he thought silently to himself, then I can just pummel them. But the drones didn't need to know that. The last thing he needed was a confrontation on one of the front doorsteps of a very popular location.

"Look," He said as friendly as he could possibly muster in his tone of voice. "I said I was sorry for the bigotry but I'm still in a bit of a rush. Now what are the human guards doing?"

"That information is classified," The drone said in its very dull tone.

"Classified?" Grandpa repeated mockingly in the same tone. He then replied with, "Well I guess they must be helping contain a psychopathic A.I. on a rampage or supervising the amborg training?"

"No," The drone said enthusiastically, "They are attempting to suppress amborg 43 in the warehouse...oops. I have said too much."

The drone shook its head, brought its hand up and slapped itself. Grandpa Mark looked on triumphantly at the drone's mistake.

"HA!" He laughed, "A little trickery and deceit and you drones can't help yourself. Now why don't you tell me why 43 is being... suppressed you say? That's... interesting. What does that even mean??"

"That is classified," The drone repeated again which routed it back to square one. Starting to feel a bit annoyed, the old man took a step forward and looked the drone right in the eye. Or rather, the red light coming from the lens in its forehead.

"Really? You're really going to go through this again?" Grandpa sighed and thought for a moment, "Ok... Well what if I told you a family member of mine is in there? I'm visiting them?"

There was a brief pause as the drone analyzed the question and then spoke back to him.

"State your name and your relative's name please. If they verify your identity and allow it, you may pass," The drone held up an arm without even questioning the query. On it, there was a screen, which lit up. With its other hand, the drone began typing on the keypad rapidly.

"Uhh, my name is... Mark and the relative I am looking for... is... David," Grandpa Mark said casually. Well, our last name is kind of dull, he thought. But I want to see what we get.

The drone scanned the pad and then looked back up. There was short pause and then the pad made a loud noise. A recording of a bell sounded out which ended the search.

"Unfortunately based on your limited answers," The security drone said blatantly, "I have found a few records cross-referenced to those specific names."

"Oh... yay," Said Grandpa as he rolled his eyes. "Give me the short answers."

"There are four Davids' on site in these records," The drone said as it looked through the files. The screen brought up a face to each of the names the robot listed out, "David Peterson in Engineering. David Beckam in Research. David Rakalpulco in Security. David Tortellini in armor division..."

"Tortellini??"

One of the vigilantes accompanying 117's grandfather snickered but shut up immediately when the old man turned and glared at him.

"Sorry," He replied as Mark turned to face the drone again.

"What about my grandson David?" He hadn't seen 117's face on the drone's search and that meant one thing. He was going to get sent away if he didn't get to the bottom of this. "Why wasn't he a part of the list?"

The drone looked back at the pad. And then it looked at Grandpa Mark again as if it hadn't made a mistake. After another moment of silence, the drone began typing again.

"If your relative is not among these records, your statement about visiting a relative can only be concluded as a lie," The drone said bluntly.

"I did make it up on the spot if that didn't tip you off you dumb drone," The old man muttered.

"However, if you believe that you are being wronged and you do have a relative. I shall search again. This time, let me factor...

grandson... into the mix. Estimating age of visiting relative and rechecking records."

Grandpa Mark tapped his foot as the robot looked over the pad again for the next couple of seconds.

"The records show..." The robot looked back up, "...Nothing."

"WHAT?!" Grandpa Mark snatched the drone's arm and skimmed through the data listing, "How could there be nothing?"

"I am sorry sir," The drone replied innocently as it took the pad back, "I cannot find any indication that you are related or for that matter affiliated to any of the known Davids' in A.I. company records."

"Grr," Mark sighed. "I didn't want to resort to this specifically because it was supposed to be a secret. But he needs me so I will do it. Try searching for him under Test subjects?"

"Searching...test subject? ...In A.I. company records?" The drone looked back down at the pad and shook its head, "I am sorry, there are still no records."

"How specific do you want me to get?! This is a big secret that I'm really trying not to hint at!" Grandpa shook his head in disbelief. If this went on, he would probably suffer a heart attack if it wasn't for his implants keeping him healthy. Finally, he sighed and admitted defeat.

"Try the Amborgs. David?" Mark groaned. "117 of the Second Group?"

"Searching..." The drone looked down and did another search. "One result matches with the parameters of the query. There is in fact a David among the amborgs. Most commonly referred and designated as David 117."

"GOOD! That's the one," Mark sighed with relief as he clapped his hands cheerfully, "Now let me in."

"I cannot allow that sir."

"WHAT NOW?!!!"

"All amborgs do not have relatives," The defense drone stated rather firmly. "Dr. Kendrick specifically selects orphans who have no family. Therefore, your statement that you are a relative is invalid. Which also adds on to my previous observation that you were lying."

Grandpa Mark groaned and paced back and forth in frustration. He took a few breaths and calmed down. Happy thoughts, he thought as he looked the drone in the eye. I promised David no violence, he thought as he considered his next question carefully. I'm trying to be a nice grandpa.

"Ok ok," He said, "Umm, why don't you call Kendrick and have him vouch for me? My son used to work for him. He knows me. Or... He knows of me."

"If you refuse to give me your full name," The drone replied, "It's hard to verify your identity."

"Discretion is pretty damn important to me," Mark snapped. "Can't you just pull up a directory and let me scroll through the names? It won't take too long. I could even write my son's name and show it to you if I want to avoid telling or sharing it out loud. Even as a machine, you should know the meaning of protecting the family name literally."

"I am sorry sir," The drone said, "The situation is understandable but we do have security measures. As for someone vouching for you, Doctor Kendrick's safety protocol dictates I cannot allow him outside to... prove your identity. The statistical likelihood that a kidnapping attempt is a possibility with someone of your specific caliber."

"Wow," Mark sighed. "You are probably one of the most paranoid and annoying security guards I've ever encountered..."

"I get that a lot," The drone replied casually.

"What do you mean you don't let him outside?" Mark asked skeptically. "How the hell does he go to select new amborgs then?"

"Oh..." The drone looked down and brought a finger up, "Err... A moment please."

"No," Mark said shaking his hand. "There isn't going to be another moment. Have you ever heard of something called Google?"

The robot nodded as the old man slowly placed his hand on its shoulder.

"Yeah the thing is Robot," He said inquisitively and as obnoxiously possible. "I think Google is smarter and faster than you are."

"That statement is false sir," The robot challenged confidently, "Besides, google is my main source to look at images of the gorgeous T-910 model. Those things are built within suitable parameters. Very attractive."

Taken aback, Mark blinked at what he had just heard. Did the A.I. industries security drone just state emotional interests in another object? What kind of human lessons were they teaching these drones? Ignoring this, Mark thought up a way to use this to his advantage.

"I got bad news for you defense drone," He said cheekily to the drone, "The T-910 is a toy. It is not a real robot."

He had put a lot of emphasis on the last sentence and waited for a response. The robot waited four seconds and then began warbling undiscernible noises.

"What? Impossible," It began to sputter. "All of my calculations of meeting one... I had hoped to meet the robot of my dreams and seek out an evolved lifestyle. Impossible. This cannot be true... NOOOOOOOOOOOOOOO!!"

The drone turned and walked back towards the complex. Another drone stared but turned and walked up to address the hooded figures who were looking on in utter amusement. The second drone greeted them as Mark groaned again.

"How many of you do I have to mentally break to get inside the damn building?" He asked sarcastically.

"I could not help overhearing your conversation with number zero eight seven five," The new drone said courteously. "Is it true the T-Nine One Zero is just a toy?"

"That was only partially true," Mark replied. "Its processors aren't up to date with drones built like yourself. At most, you could say it's the human equivalent of a very bad children's aide or G.P.S. Your buddy zero eight seven five has really bad taste."

"He dreams a lot sir," The drone replied.

"Tell him I know the owners and the designers for the T-Nine One Zero," Mark replied. "I'll put in a word to have one custom made and shipped. He could use the companionship."

"Very well sir," The drone replied, "But there is only one problem that remains. Which I am duty bound in my programming to uphold."

"What's that?" The smile faded from Mark's face.

"I still cannot let you in without authorization."

"God damn it."

The other hooded colleagues chuckled and burst out laughing.

"Well looks like we're stuck here," One spoke to the other. The other one looked back, "At this rate, we'll be the ones to die of old age until we get in."

* * *
** ** **

Warehouse one dash sixteen alpha
Status: Forty Eight percent destroyed

"Ok 3 you cut around, 297 will watch your flanks. 5 and I will attempt to distract her from the front."

"Understood 1. That is until Donut finds us first."

"Hey guys! What are you doing over there?"

"Uh-oh..."

The four amborgs all flinched at hearing 501 calling them. Not only did this screw up their plan, they had just enough time to look up. By the time they did, it was already too late. 43 dropped in the center of their huddle and the battle resumed. She kicked 5 and 1 swiftly in the chests. As they went flying off, she dodged a shot fired from Missy's pop gun and slammed 297 into the floor. Then, she grabbed him by the legs and used him as a bat to knock 3 away. Mid swing, she had released her grasp on 297 and he was also sent crashing into the wall.

235

"Ok if 43 is not going to be the one that kills us," 5 groaned as he picked himself off the ground, "I want to at least kill 501 before I die. He is definitely team killing us."

1 had gotten tangled in a net from being kicked. While he fumbled around trying get himself out, he saw 43 battling with 297. Just then a crate appeared overhead. 501 had maneuvered the crane just above where the duel was taking place.

"I wonder why 501's antics remind me of someone. This is worse than Red versus Blue. 501," 1 called, "Switch to a private channel. No! Do not respond to this message. Instead, I need you to release the hooks holding up the crate above 297. Can you understand at least that much?"

Without a word, 501 looked down from the operating room of the crane and back at 1. He nodded and held a thumbs-up. The crate was instantly released from the crane and fell with speed. Noticing this, 297 jumped out of the way. Staying put, 43 looked up and the crate fell right on top of her.

"Did it work?" 297 asked as he straightened up to look. Just in time to see the crate fly towards him, "Nope. It didn't work."

A gigantic crash sounded in the vicinity as the few amborgs who could still see watched as 297 disappeared as the heavy cargo crate hit him head on. Several meters out of 43's reach, 11 was frantically trying to help 12, 19, and 24. Another crate had been shoved over 12's head again and 19, from her position on top of a crate sitting behind 12 was trying to yank it off. 24 was examining the remains of her rifle.

"Well," She said as she threw one half of it behind her. "This situation could not get worse could it?"

She threw the other piece to 11 who caught it and frowned as 12 stood still shaking her crated head from side to side. Just then a radio transmission came in.

"Any amborg currently not engaged in combat, please respond. This is 917. Anyone out there?"

"Theo!" 11 lifted his head and put his palm on the side of his face at the transmission. "We actually aren't fighting right now but we are stuck in the warehouse with a lunatic sister on the loose. What's up with you?"

"Nothing much 11," 917 responded, "I was hoping for good news but all I have to report is quite the opposite. 92 and 93 are helping me try to free 117 but that is where good news and bad news fit in."

"What is wrong?" 24 walked closer to the group and joined the group conversation, "Go ahead 917."

"Well," 917 hesitated, "117 is buried about twelve feet and four inches into high steel and concrete which we can thank 43 for. It's like she dug a cave... The twins are trying to excavate and dig him out with the help of 335 who is feeling a lot better from the A.I. party from the gym. It is also very dusty and we are running out of power so the excavation work is slow thanks to the hard training we have been doing."

"Thanks 917, I have a vague image," 11 replied as he listened quietly. The fighting had moved and was far off in another section of the warehouse so they were safe for now. "What is the good news?"

"That was the good news 11," 917 responded nervously, "117 seems to be trying to tell us something but 43 did something to him so his system is rebooting. He cannot talk but is trying to with his voice and the roof of this place is making us uneasy. But you must warn whoever is fighting 43 now to cease their attack."

"What?! You want us to stop fighting?!" 12 yelled. Her voice came from her bracelet since her head was still stuck inside the crate. 24 snapped at her to keep still as 19 kept pulling.

"Sorry, I phrased that wrong. You should try to avoid killing 43 by accident. From what we were able to interpret from 117," 917 continued, "Something is terribly wrong with 43's circuitry. Her after surgery repairs are uh... activating some side effects."

"Wait how could 117 tell you if he is rebooting his own system?" 11 looked at the rest of them in confusion.

"He spoke out-loud 11! I already explained that!" 917 shouted impatiently through the transmission.

Suddenly, there was a loud crash in the background of the transmission. At the same time, there was a loud rumbling noise that soon followed which presumably came from the medical center. The amborgs in the warehouse recognized the faint voices of the twins and 335 from their incomprehensive screaming in 917's transmission. They were in serious trouble by the sound of it.

"Ok you two," 335's voice replaced 917's in the transmission. "I need you to hit these two points while I hit this point here. Ready? Now! This should get him out."

"Hey!" 917 yelled. "Be careful! Watch out for the..."

Three simultaneous thuds came out of 11's bracelet. Suddenly, another loud crash occurred. As 11 listened closely, he heard 917 exclaiming in surprise and then more noises clustered the transmission as all of them let out even more screams.

"...Or not," Said 335 faintly after the yelling had all subsided. "Listen we need to get support beams in here. Where was that maintenance worker? We need some more engineers here!"

"We got to get all human personnel out!" 92's voice shouted. "It's too dangerous! 93, grab that guy! He got hit by the rubble! Get the medics!"

"Unfortunately," 93 spoke. "43 knocked out the entire medical staff..."

"At least she didn't kill anyone," 335 replied reassuringly.

11 stared at his bracelet with a worried look. Suddenly, 917's voice spoke again.

"We will continue to try and get 117 out," He said. "Chances are, 43 will listen to him. But for now, hold her as best you can. There is a suspected chance that she may be killed if one of us succeeds in damaging her upon retaliation."

"You kidding?" 19 cut into the transmission, "She buried 117 twelve feet in the wall! Her own boyfriend! How are we supposed to avoid fighting her? Ask politely?!"

"Well we got to try something," 917 replied, "Uh-oh... I need to act as a make-shift support beam. 335 just took a piece of the ceiling to the head. As if her head has gone through enough trauma."

As the transmission ended, 11 made a new call. He desperately tried to make contact with 1. Luckily the warehouse signal was clearer than the environment from the medical facility.

"1 did you hear that conversation by any chance?"

"Yes," 1's voice responded as loud crash occurred in the distance. "See if you can get over here. I believe 917 is right. Something is happening and it doesn't look good. For now, we keep 43 occupied until 117 arrives."

"Understood," 11 replied.

"HEY!" 12 said angrily. "Help me get this crate off my head before you guys run off!!"

Simultaneously, 11, 19 and 24 punched different parts of the crate. It split apart and 12 was freed. Unfortunately, the impacts from the three of them had caused giant vibrations which made her dizzy.

"Thank... you," She replied lazily. The impact had shorted her sensory cognition so she practically knelt down to the ground.

"You are welcome," 11 nodded patiently. "Stay here 12. When you get the strength, see if you can find the other amborgs who are already beaten and lying around. It's a maze in here thanks to all this destruction."

"11," 1's voice spoke again. "Can you guys hurry up? 43 just pulled out the... arrow? 24! I thought you had it!"

"I don't," 24 said as she fumbled in her pockets again, "I seem to have... misplaced it. Or... 43 must have taken it when she beat me, 11, 12, and 19 earlier."

"That... is apparent," 1 responded.

* * *

1 was not happy at all. He stared as 43 walked slowly to a nearby crate and lifted the arrow. 43 stuck the blank arrow to the side of the crate she picked and stepped back. The arrow was pointed perfectly in alignment to her left which happened to be the exact path 1 was standing in.

The arrow lit up and instantly, the crate lifted off the ground and flew towards 1 who ran and slid on his knees under the giant projectile. The crate crashed against the wall and stuck to the side of the warehouse wall. As 1 straightened up, 43 moved directly in front of him and the two of them began sparring.

** ** **

"Yikes. Not the arrow," Dr. Kendrick exclaimed as he watched from the observation room, "An elegant but also really annoying weapon."

As he said this, the arrow stopped shining brightly and the crate fell off the side of the warehouse wall and straight to the floor.

"Wow Doctor," One of the assistants complimented as Kendrick wiped the sweat off his forehead. "Designing a tool which can change an object's gravity. What happens if you put the arrow on an object and it's pointed up?"

"What do you mean?" Kendrick was only partially paying attention as a few crates flew by the window.

"You know... UP?" The technician repeated. "At the sky? Towards the moon? Outer space? It is capable of propelling something that far right?"

"Oh UP," Dr. Kendrick said still looking out the window. "No chance of that happening. It only lasts for a few minutes. Just like what happened to the crate. It automatically shuts down so in the events something shoots upward, it comes back down. That's the idea at least. I mean, do you know how much power it takes for something's gravity to change? Not the most energy efficient. I'd also rather avoid contributing personally to the space program."

"Does that include people?" The technician asked curiously. A crate flew up and hit the observation room window causing all of them to duck down and cower.

"People?" Dr. Kendrick pushed his glasses back up his nose.

"Yes has anyone ever been stuck with an arrow?" The technician nodded.

"Yeah... uhh. Let's just say that it's been tried and not a lot resulted from it," Dr. Kendrick stood up. "Unless you got protection, don't do it. Right? Get it?"

"I got the joke Doctor. So nothing happened?" The technician asked questioningly.

"Keep thinking that kid," Dr. Kendrick said chuckling nervously placed a hand on the tech's shoulder.

*⁎ *⁎ *⁎

"That is it 43! No more arrow for you!"

"Who's going to stop me?" 43 smirked. "You?"

"At this rate," 1 replied as he used the last of his strength to prevent from being thrown over. "I believe that might actually be a possibility."

Both of them were grasping each other's arms tightly and trying to maneuver their legs around the deadlock so they could kick each other. Sensing a small opening in her defense, 1 then made his move and hit her right on the head with an enormous head butt. 43 released her grip, staggered back and fell into a crouch, disoriented.

"Serina 43, stop! Control yourself," 1 commanded, "You're slowing down. That isn't good and we both know it. Stop now and we can fix the issue."

"Save it lead for brains!" She spat.

"Our brains are lead technically. From a certain point of view," 1 said casually.

This caused her to leap at him in anger but before she reached him a blinding light lit up the area and she fell to the ground. Blue bands of energy were holding her in place. 1 turned to look at the new arrival.

"Let me handle this now."

117 brushed some gravel off his shoulder. 917, 92, 93, and 335 were on each of his side. Two on the left and two on the right with 117 in the center. 1 nodded and ran off to look for any other wounded amborgs. The energy bands holding 43 shattered as she freed herself.

"No big deal," She scoffed. Getting back to her feet, she lifted her arms but as she did so, her arms began to tremble a little. "I can… take on all of you."

"No," 117 said, "You're very weak. Surely now, you've realized you haven't recovered. You need to stop now so we can help you heal."

"Right," She brushed off that comment with a snarl, "Never knew you to be manipulative."

"No," He repeated, "If I was lying, then you wouldn't have been caught by the energy rings. Your performance is degrading rapidly 43. This adrenaline induced rage is a side effect of your recovery. Release 274 and 125 from the experimental orbs and stand down."

At these words 43 became even angrier. But before she could make another move, she suddenly dropped to her knees and put her hands to her head.

"AAH!" She cried out of her bracelet, "Please make it stop! Help me!"

The rest of them quickly surrounded her. 117 scooped her into his arms. 917 reached in her pockets, pulled out a transport orb and tossed it away from them. The orb flashed and seconds later, 274 and 125 dropped to the ground with two loud thuds.

"Ugh," 125 spoke out of his bracelet, "That was not fun."

274 nodded in agreement but didn't say a word. Both of them stood up and leaned against a crate. Evidently, they looked really sick. The orbs were bad news for whoever was caught in the entrapment zone. But still pretty handy.

117 looked at 43 who was still in pain. Her screaming had stopped and she was groaning softly. All of a sudden, her hand reached up and made contact with the side of 117's head. 117 instantly felt something surge inside of him. All of the other amborgs stared.

"What happened?" 917 said with a concerned look.

✷ ✷ ✷

43 found herself in front of a door. She didn't recall seeing that door recently. A wooden door with hinges and a door-knob. How primitive, she thought as she looked behind her. The other amborgs were nowhere in sight which was surprising. She could have sworn they were all surrounding her moments ago.

I got to find someone, she thought as she turned to look at the wooden door. Where is everyone? I have to before I lose control of myself entirely.

Quickly she grasped the handle and opened the door. She hadn't seen or felt a door like this since she was very young. It was very old compared to how gates or doorways were built in the present. The only kind you'd find in very well-kept locations or in rundown lower class slums.

Inside, she found a room filled with standard furniture from the twenty-first century. There were also toys on the floor, sprawled across a blanket in the middle of the living room. She stepped and placed her feet carefully around them without stepping on them as if she had stumbled onto a child's minefield. Looking up, she saw a glass door that led to a patio. A beam of sunlight was pouring in and she almost felt tempted to try and step outside. However, it didn't feel right. Instead, she extended her hand to feel the glass. It was smooth and very cold but it felt very unnatural than what she knew about how real modern glass was made. It was that moment she realized it was because she wasn't analyzing everything like she usually did. Were her cybernetics not functioning?

"Hi there."

43 retracted her hand and whirled around to see a familiar face.

"David?" She said but then brought a hand up to her mouth.

She had spoken with her real voice without realizing it. She looked at her left wrist and realized her bracelet was gone. The figure at the table smiled and stood up. 43 instantly lowered her arm and decided to speak again but the shock from her earlier question stopped her.

"Who are you?" 117 asked politely with a warm smile when she chose not to say anything. He was also speaking from his mouth which looked so different and strange than how he normally spoke.

"You don't know me?" 43 asked.

"I'm afraid not."

"Then... Where are we?"

"It's my home," 117 replied. "Or if you want specifics, it's a very deep level of cyberspace that very few can actually get into."

"Cyberspace?" 43 asked. "But this place looks so real. I mean, it looks familiar to me. Why?"

"Maybe a reference will help for context," 117 chuckled. "Ever seen the matrix movie?"

43 gave him a look of content.

"Ok, I guess that was a little too soon," David chuckled when 43 didn't respond. "Well, you could say this place manifested after you arrived. I know where it is since it's from 117's memories. I'm a little surprised you don't. It created itself when it detected your presence."

"But..." Serina looked around, "Earlier, I was surrounded by you and everyone else. They were beating the crap out of me."

"If you like," David smiled. "I could send a message to myself. You'd have to wait awhile though. Messages to David 117's brain travel very slowly with all the clusters of data running through his neurons and CPU. We are after all inside the very heart of his... cyber mind."

"You're just an image of him?" Serina asked. "Before we became amborgs?"

"Yes and no," David replied. "But I'm not him entirely. I am his center."

"His what?"

"Center," David repeated, "I'm a caretaker. Well to be exact, the A.I. of his Central Processing Unit. An image that manifested to make sure this place continues to run. Even I don't understand myself but Dr. Kendrick literally is the smartest man on the planet. Without knowing it, this world became a reality at the microscopic level and I came online years ago when the David 117 you knew became an amborg. My purpose is to make sure his system doesn't die."

"But how did I get in here? Did I leave my body?" 43 said nervously. She lifted her hands and turned them over. "This feels so real but I know it's not. If I believe what you're telling me."

"I believe you did something impossible," David said, "You mistakenly and unknowingly initiated a data transfer into this memory unit. Somehow, this room manifested itself to accept you and here you are. If I had to guess, your original body, when it made contact with 117 in the scene you just described, ejected you, the caretaker of your own CPU over to here by accident."

"You don't get out much?"

"No."

43 smirked slightly.

"You're awfully smart for someone supposedly cooped up in cyberspace," She said taking a step back.

"We're smarter than we think if you find the time. That goes for everyone in general," 117 replied cheerfully. "Unfortunately, there isn't enough power here to let the two of us have more time to chat. The system can't support a foreign caretaker and it already knows you're here."

"What?" 43 turned to look in his face. "What do you mean? I got distracted by the fact that I'm in cyberspace. I remember being in the hospital but then something came over me. Can you help me?"

"Hmm, well that's the issue," 117 replied. "I'd like to listen more but this place can't hold data for two amborg caretakers. The foreign program system is coming and you won't survive the purge if you don't leave in a few minutes."

"Foreign program," Serina muttered as she thought carefully. "When I woke up from the hospital bed, I felt angry. As if something had taken a hold of me. Does that mean anything to you?"

"Hmm," 117 pondered. "From what I know about you, you're in a lot of pain and you're trying to get rid of it. Sounds like your cybernetics are battling with your human side. It's almost like your body is battling it out trying to fix the problem but tearing it down at the same time."

"I think I kinda get it," 43 sighed. "I think you just explained to me what they've all been saying already. I'm dying."

"That's too bad," 117 frowned. "You seem like a really nice person. So young too to experience that type of feeling."

"Hopefully I can make the most of it before it's over."

117 smiled.

"At least you're optimistic," He said. "Sorry. I really would like you to stay but trouble is coming."

117 walked to the door and motioned for her to follow.

"Even if this message might not reach 117," 43 said as she went to the door. "Will you tell him that I love him very much?"

"I can do that," 117 nodded. "If you promise to tell him this. Because as a caretaker, I get to see floods of information that passes through. Tell him that life is tough but know that there is a deeper being inside of all of us, be it science or spiritual that holds onto our humanity. He just needs to stop and dig deep every once in a while."

"It might take me a while to have that thought come up in my mind," 43 muttered.

"Oh well," 117 shrugged. "It was worth a shot. But I'm glad I was able to share that with someone else at least."

"Does 117 know I'm here?" 43 asked. "With you?"

"I doubt it," 117 said pulling the door handle. "In cyberspace, things happen faster than you can imagine. It will only be an instant's notice and they'll all think nothing happened when you go back to your body."

As the door opened and a small breeze began to blow 43 towards the exit, she asked one last question before being swept off.

"Hey! Is this real? Not some weird cyber prank?"

"It never was!" David said as he remained rooted to the spot. "A prank I mean! That depends on what you believe! I can't tell you what to believe in. That's always been yours and every person's right!"

*** *** ***

"What happened?" 917 said with a concerned look.

117 had just collapsed and bent over but he remained on his feet. Crouching, he grasped onto 43 who had fainted. Her hand was still clinging onto his head which he shrugged off.

"I'm running a scan," 335 said as she quickly held up a hand and slowly swept it across in front of the two amborgs, "Her vitals are alright but her CPU is losing power for some reason. Oh. Wait a minute, energy levels are returning to normal. He is waking up. Are you alright 117?"

"I am fine," 117 shrugged as he shook his head to get his bearings, "I don't seem to feel different. 43 is unconscious but somehow, I saw what was on her mind. Or... I caught a brief glimpse of what she was thinking of."

"What was it?" 917 asked as some medical officers ran in and assisted by taking 43 out of 117's arms. They lifted her onto a hover-bed and pushed her out of the warehouse.

"That man..." 117 spoke up, "The man who shot her. She was fighting through us to get out and find him."

"Strange," 335 put her hand up to her chin, 'She seems to be losing control of herself. Her condition is worsening even though she has come out of her coma. I can understand why she'd be very motivated to exact vengeance but we cannot allow her to destroy a whole warehouse again to just let her. This behavior is of utter hatred."

"Then you have one solution," a voice said.

All of them turned to see Grandpa Mark walking up with a few vigilantes. He pulled his hood back and put on a grim face.

"You have to find that man and stop him," The old man said bluntly causing all of them to stare at each other in confusion. Seeing the looks on their faces, Mark quickly added, "43's sole objective is to hunt down the one person who hurt her and put her through this much pain. He'll have to be found quickly too. 43 doesn't look like she'll last any longer. By taking that piece out of the equation, that will be better news for her if she decides to burst out of her restraints again. Right?"

"Will she go back to normal? Once we accomplish the task?" 117 inquired. His grandfather held up his arms and shook his head.

"I wouldn't know," Mark replied. "Hopefully it calms her down and makes her mental state return to normal..."

He turned to see all the damage in the warehouse. Several of the wounded amborgs were being helped or stumbling towards the exit.

"… because I really doubt you all could handle something like this again."

"We will at least be able to adapt," 917 sighed. "But as you say, 43 has the same line of thinking as all of us so her adaptation will most likely counter everything we do. Either way, if she wakes, we're screwed."

"Hold the phone," 335 interrupted. "Is this your grandfather 117?"

Before 117 could answer, they were interrupted by Dr. Kendrick who walked up to the amborgs and surveyed the damage. He was sweating but looking relieved that the fighting had subsided.

"Is everyone alright?" He asked to which everyone grimly nodded.

All the amborgs spoke simultaneously and uttered their confirmation. Many of the ones who could still lift a finger even gave a thumbs up.

Dr. Kendrick then turned to acknowledge Grandpa Mark who waved casually.

"Kendrick!" Mark said in what appeared to be a strained voice. "Umm. It's been a while."

"Well I never thought I'd say this but I'm actually glad to see you for once," Dr. Kendrick nodded gratefully.

The two men shook hands but there was something creating tension. 117 then remembered that the link between his grandfather and Dr. Kendrick was himself and his own father. That had to complicate things a lot.

"By the way," Kendrick looked and stared at Mark's group of hooded freelancers, "How did you get in? I thought the defense drones would have annoyed you to death. I'm impressed you even made it in here."

"Ah. About that," Grandpa Mark withdrew his hand and pulled a piece of metal from his pockets, "You might want to fix this guy up. I kind of ripped his main processor off."

"Well that's one way to do it,' Dr. Kendrick took the head piece with a look of extreme bewilderment. "The poor thing won't be able to talk for a while after I reinstall this."

"Yeah. At least it will be less annoying. You can bill me for that later. Anyway, it would appear I was called here for no reason now."

"That isn't true," 117 immediately interrupted, "There is a good reason why I called you here but then 43 went on a rampage. I was basically going to ask what sort of intelligence you have about 43's attacker. Also if possible, it would be beneficial if we could investigate his whereabouts together."

"Oh...I see. Well," Mark said meekly. "I guess I could check my files. Perhaps another place to talk would be better."

As everyone walked towards the warehouse entrance to recuperate, 117 couldn't help but shake his head a bit. Something had made him feel dizzy for some reason. 1 walked up and patted his shoulder.

"Is something wrong?" 1 asked as they stepped into the hall. "Are you sure you're ok?"

"No," 117 replied, "At least... I don't think so. I feel different... Like something warm flowed through my body reminding me of something from a long time ago. But now it's gone."

"Strange," 1 did a scan on 117, "I don't see anything wrong or out of place."

"My self-diagnostic is saying the same thing," 117 nodded, "But more importantly, I think I need to check on Mandy."

Both of them continued on down the hall with the rest of the beaten and worn-out amborgs. Several of them looked as if they would fall apart at any moment. Until they would encounter the person who had attacked 43, things would have to go back to the way it was for the time being. It was a long road ahead and they needed to work on what was to come.

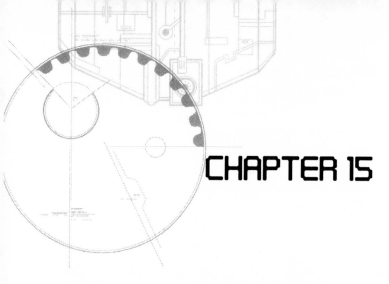

CHAPTER 15

2128 February, Three Weeks Later, Harlem Neoteric district, New York

"Come on Tashoneh! Give it back!"

"You have to catch me first Rick!"

Tashoneh ran as fast as he could away from his friends. Despite how young and small he was, he had learned how to move around very fast in the streets. He crawled through a small hole in a fence that he knew Rick and the others were too big to fit through. As he clambered away snickering, he heard the rattling of the chainmail fence behind him. He turned his head and saw Rick trying to climb over the fence. His other friend Abigail was watching with a fearful look.

"Come back Tashoneh!" She called. "Don't run so far!"

"I'll get him Abigail," Rick said angrily as he made it to the top of the fence.

"No wait! Don't leave me!"

"It isn't funny anymore Tashoneh!" Rick called as he climbed over the fence and dropped to the ground. Abigail also scrambled up the fence as quickly as she could. "Come back here now!"

"Follow me!" Tashoneh cried as he kept running. Pretty soon he heard the pattering footsteps that indicated that Rick and Abigail were catching up. Tashoneh instantly ran around a corner and towards the warehouse sitting across the street. Suddenly he heard Rick cry out.

"NO Tashoneh! That place isn't safe!"

"It's fine Rick!" Tashoneh called back. "I've been here hundreds of times!"

Tashoneh looked back at Rick who was staring wide-eyed right back at him. He ignored the older boy's warnings and dove through a tiny hole in the side of the building. When he straightened up, he froze. A group of people were sitting in the middle of the room and they all turned to stare. Before Tashoneh could gather his thoughts or back out, he felt a shove from behind as Rick scrambled in after him.

"Tashoneh!" Rick whispered urgently when he saw the other people in the warehouse, "Bad people... We have to run! It's dangerous!"

"Yeah," Tashoneh stammered as the people began moving towards them. "Let's... oof!"

The two boys had backed into Abigail who had also followed them inside.

"What are you two doing?" She asked but then saw the crowd moving towards them. "Uh-oh."

The three of them huddled together and tried to back out slowly but the adults were faster and instantly had them surrounded. The hole they had crawled in was blocked by one of them and they had nowhere to go. Suddenly, loud thuds began to shake the ground as the kids looked around the stranger's legs to see what was coming their way.

Giant robots were walking their way which made the kids freeze with fear. These bots were massive to their eyes and with red lights gazing menacingly at them. They had never seen this type of robot before.

"What's the matter kids? Lost?" One of the figures laughed. "Come over here! We got... lots of... mmm... nice things for you."

The three kids stood their ground. One of the robots made a loud whining noise and they saw its arms glowing brightly. As it rose, they heard loud joints and circuits whirring loudly as it stomped closer and closer. They cowered to the ground in fear as the floor shook with loud tremors and the mini-quakes made them jump up and down higher as the robots drew nearer.

"Come on boys!" The same man shouted. They saw him draw a knife. Several others also pulled out a wide variety of weapons, "This robot isn't mean. He just wants to...play! We'll just send your bodies back to your parents. An accident on your play-date."

All three of them clung to each other. They closed their eyes as they all pressed their heads together and prepared for the worst. A loud crashing noise then caused them to open their eyes curiously as they saw the adults all looking up and away.

All of them and the robots diverted their attention to the roof and began to yell.

"It's the amborgs!" One of them cried.

The children all watched silently as the people surrounding them were charging towards the center of the warehouse. Several figures had dropped from the ceiling along with some broken glass. They all stared wide-eyed at their rescuers.

"WHOA!" Tashoneh exclaimed as he, Rick and Abigail stood. "It's them!"

Instead of crawling out the hole, the kids of them scurried to the side and hid behind one of the large pillars. Loud noises kept them hidden as they peeped out to witness the unfolding action.

"Awesome!" Rick yelled.

"They're so cool!" Abigail cried, completely forgetting about being scared.

The next thing they knew, things were being thrown around the room. Loud crashes and screams were being thrown into the mix. After the dust had cleared, the children saw the giant robot swinging at who was left standing. Five tall new strangers weaved in and out of the robots reach until finally, two of them leapt into the air and landed on its back. The other three began attacking the legs with speeds so fast, the kids didn't dare to blink. The other giant robot seemed to be having problems aiming at its buddy and was avoiding any further combat.

After another two minutes, the first massive bot let out a massive groan and fell to the floor. The five figures, without even hesitating moved towards the second bot and it too began to swing wildly at them. They all circled and repeated their routine and it followed the same fate. They all moved aside as the other robot crashed to the ground.

When the dust had settled, the five figures surrounded the pile of dead robots for a few seconds and began to look around, making a quick sweep of the area. One of them noticed the three children though as they looked around.

"What on earth are you kids doing here?!"

The children all stared. They hadn't seen any of their mouths move yet, one of the girl's voices had spoken from somewhere else.

"Just like the stories!" Rick whispered. "They really don't talk like us!"

A girl had walked over to the pillar they were still hiding behind and put her hands on her hips.

"I asked you kids a question," She said sternly. This time, the kids saw golden bracelet on her wrist flashing. Her voice was being projected from the weird looking band. The three kids looked up at her right in the eye.

"We were just playing," Tashoneh replied. "We came in here by accident."

"Next time," The female amborg replied. "Be more careful when you're away from home or your parents. You'll be safe."

"We will," Rick said. "You really are like the stories our parents taught about us."

"Strong and fast," Tashoneh added.

"Taller than normal people," Abigail added admiringly.

The amborg gazed at them sternly. Compliments did nothing to change her expression.

"Thanks for the observation," She replied. "We are tall, strong and fast."

"Pretty and badass too," Abigail added rather enthusiastically.

"No cursing or swearing until you are older," The amborg snapped. "Flattery will not adjust my feelings."

"Are you an angel?" Rick asked rather suddenly.

The amborg stopped for a moment but then knelt down. She tilted her head and gazed at Rick with a questioning stare.

"No I'm not," She answered after a moment. "But... what made you ask such a thing?"

"You're beautiful," Rick said, "My mom said that angels look just like us when they want to but you can almost tell they're not human because they look special. They talk differently but almost like the way we do. They live among us all the time and when we're in trouble, they'll come down or reveal themselves to save us before it's too late."

The female amborg sighed and then smiled slightly.

"To be accurate," She said pointing towards the hole. "I'm not really what you would think of at first glance. Now go home already and be safe from here. Don't allow anyone to take you and put you where you are not supposed to be."

The three kids all said a quick goodbye and ran off. As they all disappeared one by one through the hole. Abigail looked back at the amborg and gave a big wave.

"Thank you number 999!"

999 gave the little girl a wave as she watched them disappear. When they were gone, she stood up. Some footsteps drew closer as she turned to see 917 walking up.

"They called you an angel," Said 917, "Interesting choice to describe people like us. Ever thought of yourself as a celestial being every now and then?"

"Very amusing 917," 999 snapped. "Being compared to a being of such great power is ridiculous."

"So why did you admit to being one to the kids?" 917 asked.

"We may not be celestial," 999 replied. "But are you really going to tell a child that something they believe in doesn't exist? I was merely playing along."

"Maybe," 917 smirked. "But there is one thing you can't deny. It must feel great giving children like those three hope in these times. Your character may not be full of empathy all the time, but you aren't a completely cold lone wolf."

"I am not a complete human when it comes to my abilities," 999 said.

"We have many things that normal humans don't have," 917 pondered. "But remember what 117 said? We are still human. Just at a very advanced level."

"I wonder though..." 999 looked at the two boys running away, "If we can even go back to our basic humanity especially when children call us angels."

"Is that why you were taken aback? You speak as if both human and amborg are bad things."

917 gazed at the hole where the kids had left.

"Remember we are not completely the same," He said. "But we have a base to look back to. Something we can fall back on in the events we don't know who we are. We have evolved but there is nothing that says we can't go back to our human ways."

"Well said 917," 999's technician rang in through both their heads, "It isn't easy Alice 999 but deep down, you're the same as me. Physically you're different but on the inside, we have the same organs. Mandy says that everyone still retains their humanity even when all else fails."

"I have the feeling you two have been channeling 117's spirit," 999 said rolling her eyes.

"Well," 917 shrugged. "I do have a one-seven in my number. Maybe that might be one part of it."

999 looked down at the ground and back at 917 who nodded. He knew that she wanted to laugh at his joke even though it was a little stupid. Instead, she brought her fist down onto the side of her thigh and bit her lip. Without another word, the two of them rejoined the other three amborgs in their team.

"That was not funny," She said.

"Right," 917 winked as he put an arm around her shoulder. "Hmm...Angel."

917 switched the conversation to a private channel so only the two of them could speak.

"I like that name," He said. "That should be your call-sign or as humans reference it as... Your nickname."

"Alice Angel 999," She replied on the same frequency and shrugged. "It sounds really contradicting to my character."

"No," 917 said. "Try saying it without your number. Alice Angel sounds better. Besides, you do closely resemble an angel."

"Is this an attempt at flattery 917?"

"It might be," He smirked, "You should dress as an angel for Halloween. See how that goes."

"I would rather be a dark one," She sighed angrily. "Thanks for giving me reason to hate you for the rest of the day."

"Love you too you crazy sister," 917 took his arm off her shoulder.

"Oh shut up."

She turned her head away from his gaze but she smiled to herself quickly as the other amborgs were doing scans of the wreckage.

"You really don't want to push your luck there," 999 huffed.

"You know Alice," Her technician spoke up, "It's always ok for a lone wolf to accept some compliments."

"I would rather chew on steel," 999 replied stubbornly, "Besides, as much as I like the name, it doesn't change what kind of person I am."

As she finished the private conversation with her technician, 917 disengaged their own conversation and opened up to everyone else. As they began rummaging through the various electronics, 917 sent out a message.

"117? Do you read us? This is team six," He said as he tapped his head.

"Confirmed 917, have you cleared the objective?" 117 responded immediately.

"Affirmative," 917 looked around the area. 999 gave a thumbs up and he nodded in confirmation. "Area is clear but it looks as if there is no sign of what we were looking for. Seriously, every hint we get on this guy, he must be a step ahead of us. He is a very formidable opponent. According to what we discovered in the robots' databanks, this was not the only hideout here in New York. We need to alert the army. There are several of these bad bots hidden all over the city according to what we salvaged. We cannot fight so many without backup."

"Understood 917."

"Hey 117," 917 said. "We need to come up with a new plan. These giant robots were originally our clues to finding this man. But we should not spend all of our time responding to these things every time they make an appearance. The more we do that, we risk more innocent lives to these murder bots."

"Unfortunately, it's all we can do for the moment," 117 replied. "But you're right. To stop the threat, we need to go straight for the source. We will brainstorm new plans as soon as possible. Take your group south while I alert the military. And then rendezvous at the following coordinates."

"Coordinates received."

As soon as 917 said this, a nearby wall in the side of the warehouse blew outwards. From another room, another pair of giant robots stomped inside.

"Umm 117?" 917 looked up at the two behemoths and could have sworn he could hear them growling. "There will be a small delay."

"How long?"

917 watched as 999 and the other three amborgs were already leaping at the new opponents.

"Give us about two minutes and thirty four seconds," 917 calculated as he knelt forward and instantly surged towards the fight.

*** *** ***

"No rush is necessary, 917," 117 replied as he heard an explosion behind him.

A small storage building's door blew outward and a jeep drove out. It swerved and then began gunning straight for 117. Behind it, a pair of the giant behemoth robots marched out and began walking in the opposite direction. The jeep drove right into 117 and before he knew it, he was clinging onto the hood. Barely feeling anything from the impact, he stared at the driver with a very neutral expression.

"I have found a distraction," 117 muttered as he shut off the transmission.

He climbed up onto the hood and put both hands onto the front of the window. This caused the driver to speed up in a panic which caused 117 to lean even further towards the driver. He curled up his hands into a fist and punched straight through the window. He reached through the shattered glass and grabbed the driver by the clothes on his neck. With ease, 117 pulled the driver towards him but then instantly pushed him back into his seat. The driver hit his head against the headrest and was instantly knocked out from the force.

117 held on tightly as the car began to swerve slightly. The driver's foot was still on the gas which was making the jeep rocket down the street. Gaining a foothold, 117 climbed on top of the hood and leaped in the air. The car sped out under him. As 117 landed into the ground, he leaned forward and slid backwards against the rough pavement. He heard a tremendous crash and glanced behind him. The jeep had driven and stopped into a brick wall. Seconds later, a bit of the wall above, fell over and crushed the vehicle flat.

117 dusted himself off and walked on. There were loud booms echoing across the streets of the district. He recognized the noise and the patterns immediately. More of those robots had been unleashed and were stomping around.

"Well that went well," Mandy spoke through his head. "You ok David?"

117 reached up and tapped his head. There was little damage to his vitals and he seemed to be alright.

"Of course Mandy. I am in perfect condition."

"Nobody is perfect David," Mandy chuckled, "Not even an amborg."

"Is this another scenario where my argument is invalid no matter how much evidence I put...on the table?"

"Yes David," She sighed. "I'm always right and you're just too stubborn to admit it."

"To be fair," 117 replied. "It is not stubbornness. I choose not to continue arguing because you would dislike the amount of information I prepare for my arguments."

"Mmhmm sure," Mandy chuckled. "Do you want to know where your next objective is or not?"

"Yes Mandy," 117 smiled. "Where exactly did I end up?"

"That jeep carried you pretty far from your team," Mandy replied in 117's head. "If you want, you can proceed to the objective alone or rendezvous with 297, 57, and the twins. They're pretty close to you. Oh and 466 and 501 are with them as well."

"I believe that I shall proceed alone, it will be quicker," 117 responded immediately.

"You know that you're never going to get used to him if you avoid him right?" Mandy replied in a very resentful tone.

"I never specified I was avoiding him," 117 replied casually.

"Ok then enlighten me," Mandy replied. "Don't you want to spend a bit more quality time with Donut?"

"Now is not good for quality time," 117 replied with a very irritated sigh. "There is no time all of a sudden so I will make up for it by going to the objective alone."

"You're being a donkey you know that right?"

"Be careful with that kind of language Mandy," 117 said warningly. "There could be children watching. Slander about the human anatomy is unnecessary especially with a metaphor to a live creature. They have feelings too."

*　*　*

Five blocks away, 3 was looking down at 501 who was sprawled across the pavement. The twins and 297 were making chuckling motions. 501 instantly got up and massaged his head. A metal fragment from a bullet fell to the ground.

"Seriously Donut," 3 said sympathetically, "Can you please attempt a single mission without taking damage from a bullet straight to your skull? Seriously, 6 has given up and just trained us to keep an eye on you whenever you get injured."

"Hmm, that is a difficult query to answer 3," 297 interrupted, "At this rate, when you include factors from previous assignments and missions while also taking into consideration his desperation for charging into open combat and his need for portraying his masculinity for 466, I calculate that he is incapable of simple requests of that small magnitude."

The twins grinned at these calculations and shook violently with fits of silent laughter. 466 glared at them but 3 was also struggling not to be mad as she bit back a smile as well. 501 stood up and removed the bullet piece in his forehead and flicked it off into the distance.

"You guys suck," 501 frowned sheepishly.

Ever since his first accident with the sniper from the Chicago deployment, it had started a trend which didn't seem to want to end. No matter how hard he tried.

"Hmm, nice distance 501," 92 remarked as he looked off into the distance. "Trying to imitate 117. Not bad."

"That is also correct," 3 said beginning to smile, "Despite your problems with enemy sniper fire, he is also beginning to learn how to take on multiple opponents more efficiently. It's not a problem now is it?"

She put a lot of emphasis into her last question as she stared at the others sternly. That shut the twins up instantly. 297 patted 501 on the shoulder respectfully.

"Well we can proceed safely now since Donut is ok," He complimented. "We should move now."

"So let us continue on to the objective," 466 pointed down the sidewalk. "We have heavy enemy signals directly ahead. We need to stop them from wreaking havoc."

Everyone nodded in agreement but then 501 shot up and got to his feet.

"Sure! I will go first!" He said confidently.

Ignoring the shocked and protests of the team, he walked ahead. Seconds later, a shot rang out and he fell to the ground again. 466 glared at 297 who held up his hands quickly.

"Did you hear any indication that I gave orders for him to take point?" He said innocently. "Because that time was his own fault."

"We did not say anything that time," The twins said in synchronization, "Do we get points for that?"

This resulted in 466 and 3 turning to each other, whispering on a private channel, nodding, and punching 92 and 93 while 297 crawled over to 501 and slapped him awake.

What a day, he thought as he grabbed the bullet fragments and brushed them out of 501's hair.

* * *
** ** **

"How many of the giant robots have we fought?"

"I lost track after six 917. Even that is making me sore. Physically and mentally."

917 and 999 were sitting on a couch in a living room of an apartment complex. Separated from their team and feeling like they had just put down a swarm of elephants. One of the giant robots they fought was crackling and sizzling at their feet. Its head had been pulled from its neck socket and destroyed. Both of them were covered in plaster and dust. They sat quietly and were watching the view from the large hole in the wall that they had been thrown through.

"You look good with dusty hair," 917 said to lighten the mood. He instantly shut up at the look 999 gave him.

Instead of replying to him, she turned to look over her shoulder and lit her bracelet up.

"We are terribly sorry about the damage and we would like to advise that medical teams will be dispatched to ensure no one is injured," She explained. "Please forgive us for crashing through your wall and interrupting dinner."

The family that she was talking too were all cowering up against the wall behind an overturned dinner table. The father who was shaking in fear, nodded to acknowledge her but made no sound. The children, instead of fear, were staring at the amborgs with looks of intense curiosity. They were far too young to understand what had just happened.

"Yes and we promise also, no more additional surprises," 917 nodded encouragingly. "We will take care of all the damage expenses."

"Yeah," 999 sighed. "Since Dr. Kendrick is rich beyond belief."

"You think if we ask," 917 pondered. "Do you think he would build Iron Man suits for all of us?"

"I think the bigger question," 999 said irritably, "Is how come he is so rich and he hasn't become Batman?"

"Look at you!" 917 chuckled. "The Angel's first nerd joke!"

All of a sudden, the giant behemoth's head lit up and spoke. Since it was no longer properly attached to the rest of its body, it was unable to actually strike any of them. It was making a lot of effort to make noise though which caused the wife of the family to shriek in fear.

"Must... kill... amborgs," The head of the machine sputtered with its dying voice.

917 and 999 groaned, both of them turned to stare at each other, nodded and stomped on the robot's head instantly crushing it. It gave a loud warbling noise which gradually died out. Then they sat back comfortably in the sofa, and looked at the family again.

"We promise," 917 said reassuringly and as confidently as he could, "No more surprises."

"I told you we should have just crushed its head," 999 snapped. "No. You just wanted to take it home for analysis."

"Ok I was wrong alright?"

Immediately after 917 finished talking, the front door burst inwards and 117 flew into the living room. He landed right next to the sofa with a thud which made 917 and 999 turn around casually. From the dining room, the family hid behind the table and only their eyes could be seen as their home underwent another sudden rampage. They turned to look at 117 and then at the hole where the front door had just been.

They looked and saw a behemoth standing outside snarling. 117 without saying a word, turned, looked at 917 and 999 sitting on the couch and at the crushed robot at their feet, nodded, and then charged out the front door. 999 looked at the family a third time.

"I believe that in making another promise of no surprises," She paused, "I believe I will have... how you say... jinxed the situation. To avoid that, we promise to pay for the damages, your family will be compensated and... Please excuse us. We will execute an action you did not have the courage to say out loud. WE will leave quickly."

917 and 999 both got up and charged after 117. Who had apparently tackled the giant robot and disappeared out of sight. The family all stared at the damage and didn't dare to move. The wife pulled on her husband's sleeve and breathed silently.

"Remember when you always talked about moving?" She breathed as the amborgs all clattered and crashed out of their home. "I changed my mind, let's go to Africa. At least there isn't a lot of bad things over there and the amborgs don't normally visit that region."

"There could also be crime over there too honey," The husband stuttered. "It could also be just as bad as it is here."

"I know sweetheart..." She said clinging onto his arm, "I just don't know if I can take this anymore. Big metal robots crashing through our apartment! Seven to eight foot tall teenagers covered in plaster and dust sitting comfortably on our furniture! Our front door getting knocked over not by bullets, cars, garbage dumpsters or gangsters... but a amborg with another one of those big… things standing in the hallway!!"

"Well..." He replied, "At least we didn't die... Despite how convenient that really sounds."

Their children, ignoring the tension, were having the times of their lives. Although they had stayed silent, now they were causing a tiny uproar to which their parents didn't even bother to address.

"WOW!" They cheered. "MOMMY! DADDY! AMBORGS! CAN WE BE LIKE THEM!?"

*
** ** **

Outside, 917, 999, and 117 were sitting on the wreckage of the crushed robot. All of them showed signs of fatigue even though they weren't actually tired at all. As a matter a fact, their energy levels were peaking at around seventy percent. As the sun set in the distance, many street lights began to turn on. They had been out a full day.

"Well here is a positive speculation," 917 spoke as he stared at the orange light disappearing behind a building, "At least we gain more experience and we are definitely defeating them in less time. But that does not make up for our sore joints."

Both 999 and 117 stared but then they thought for a minute and then nodded in agreement. As 117 stood up and began walking away, 999 spoke up.

"117," She said, "This has gone on for practically the whole day... Sections of New York has been attacked. I have two ideas. One, we call those big robots behemoths since they are big pieces of annoying scrap. Two, we need to change tactics. Have we really accomplished anything with those things running around under the control of common gangs? We have brought nothing but destruction and have little to show for the innocent lives we have laid waste to."

"She is right 117," 917 massaged his shoulder. "It has been a very long and difficult day. We know why you are motivated but the fact is, we wish you would try not to be so conservative. Can we at least rest a few seconds if you will not say anything about your plans?"

Still walking, 117 linked up to 999 and 917. He replied in a calm and casual tone.

"43 does not have the luxury of seconds," He said solemnly.

This made 917 and 999 get up immediately. As they followed him, Mandy then buzzed in on the communication.

"What's got you so motivated David?"

117 checked all the data the amborg teams had all compiled. Several of them had reported that they had successfully extracted

data chips from a few of the behemoths. It wasn't a lot but it was a start at least.

"We are catching up to him," 117 said as he grabbed a data-chip from his own pocket and was tossing it up and down. "This will hopefully lead us to the final boss."

"Really?" 999 shook her head as they walked down the silent street. A few people were sticking their heads out to check to see if the coast was clear but they all ducked back inside their home when they saw the amborg trio. "First he guilt-trips us with his sickly girlfriend as a motivational kicker and now he is quoting video-game puns? I really hope we have a plan."

"You cannot expect everyone to have everything done, written and laid out in presentation format. I do have a plan," 117 protested, "Not all of one that is… but I have part of one. Formulating a whole plan takes too long as an amborg. It used to be we would consider too many options at a time and then it would be too late. I am basing this whole search on my own instincts. Just ask me later and I will have a better answer to your queries. Hopefully."

"So I guess we are winging it," Said 917 observantly, "I was getting tired of running around with rules and procedures anyway. Shall we just go do battle against the crazy assassin and figure it out as we go? Great plan."

"Nice sarcasm."

"Thanks."

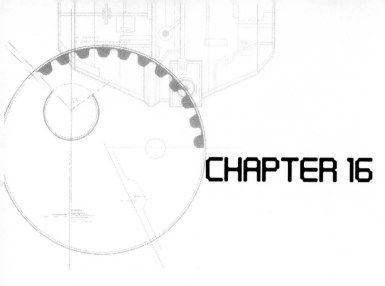

CHAPTER 16

2135, Amborg Industries

"Amborg Johnny 5. Please assist with clean up. The custodians and security request that you clean after yourself."

The voice over the intercom cut through the story like a dagger as 5 gave a sigh and stood up. He looked at his mud-stained clothes and nodded towards the P.A. speaker. Brad gave small sigh of disappointment.

"Aww, must I report for cleaning?" He asked cheekily. He winked at Brad who stared curiously as 5 purposely said aloud, "I am currently in the midst of retelling a pretty good story."

"NOW number 5," The person over the P.A. said with an annoyed tone immediately in response to his question. "You trailed mud in six corridors. Do not give Stan any more work. Move it."

"Ok ok. I got it 2," 5 called out randomly. Chuckling, he turned to bid a quick farewell to the two humans. "Excuse me Doctor. Pleasure to have met you Brad. Enjoy the rest of the story."

He walked away and left the gym. After he vanished out of sight, Dr. Kendrick suggested a lunch break before getting back to the story. Both he and Brad left the gym and paced the corridors, making their way to the cafeteria. As they went, a thought suddenly crossed Brad's mind.

"I have a question Doctor," He said as they walked past a corner.

"Hmm?"

Kendrick lit a cigarette but it was instantly put out when a nozzle extended out from the side of the wall. The hole sent out a burst of wind which immediately blew it out. An A.I. that was passing by shook his head sternly at Kendrick and zoomed away. Looking at the unlit cigarette, he put it inside a case with a sigh and placed it inside his coat pocket.

"Drat!" He snapped his fingers but at the same time, he couldn't help but chuckle a little. "I can't seem to smoke anywhere anymore. If it isn't the amborgs telling me it's bad for my health, it's the A.I.'s hacking into the fire suppression systems just to extinguish my flames. Ha."

"Right sir," Brad chuckled, "They do look up to you. Naturally, it's not surprising they keep a close eye on your health. They serve and protect everyone."

"That they do," Dr. Kendrick nodded in agreement. "What was your question?"

"If we currently live in an era of peace," Brad started but chose his words carefully. "Why is it that you still look for potential children to be amborgs? Is it still necessary in these times?"

"Very necessary," Dr. Kendrick nodded. "Peace in this time is mostly assured but for a very especially select few individuals, they need help. These lucky souls are taken in by me to become next generation amborgs. But as the times are becoming more stable, you are correct in questioning if the amborgs are necessary. The end of the story will probably surprise you. Perhaps it might be better to find someone else to assist in the depiction."

"Perhaps we can find Mandy?" Brad asked. "It feels like she and 117 are the ones who had the most involvement."

"Someone say my name?"

Both of them turned and saw Mandy approaching from an intersecting corridor. By now, she must have already been 117's technician for many years. Brad looked and realized that she looked just the way that 117 had described her earlier to a tee. She wore her usual outfit and carried a file of reports which she had just finished writing during regular work hours. Despite her look of exhaustion however, she carried a small smile on her face which gave a look of confidence and motivation to finish the day.

"You look tired Ms. Mandy," Dr. Kendrick noted bluntly.

"At least I look younger than you Doctor," she rolled her eyes with a curt smile. "Is this the graduating student I heard would be visiting with you?"

"Yes," Dr. Kendrick patted Brad on the shoulder and nudged him forward a bit. "Brad, this is David 117's technician, whom you have heard a lot about. Mandy, this is a potential person who will be seeing us shortly after his schooling is finished."

"A pleasure," Brad's hand reached forward and her free hand grasped it.

"Glad to meet you," she smiled. "Have you made plans for college?"

"I've been accepted to seventeen already," Brad replied quickly.

"Seventeen?" Mandy's eyes widened. "I probably don't have to ask how many applications you've filled out. I can tell you have great skills. You another one of those eccentric geniuses or something that makes normal people look bad?"

Brad grinned and shrugged modestly. To hear that from a very famous A.I. industries employee was enough to make the blood rush to his head.

"It's an honor to hear that from someone who also is famous in the academic community," He said, "I heard you went to school really young as well."

"Went to college at sixteen," Mandy said casually, "And then graduated in two years. I was accepted at A.I. industries after... a good deal of interviews."

"More like a ludicrous amount," Dr. Kendrick added with a smirk on his face, "I had gotten word that someone had sent in over a hundred job applications here and I took it upon myself to find out personally who was so insistent on working here."

"Impressive," Said Brad, "I guess you are a really devoted person. To your studies, to the amborgs and your husband."

"What?"

Brad's smile also faded. He looked to Dr. Kendrick and then back to Mandy who also stared. Her smile faded and was replaced by a look of absolute confusion.

"Aren't you married?" Brad asked. "I thought Dr. Kendrick made a mistake when he referred to you as Ms. instead of Mrs."

"OH, that's not entirely accurate," Mandy nodded. Understanding immediately what was going on, she chuckled. "I'm not married yet. Ha. I'm still engaged to my fiancée. Our work just keeps us apart from each other for long periods of time but we both give each other something lovable to think about. It sounds stupid but it works. Just take my word for it."

"How long has the engagement been in place?" Brad asked curiously. He immediately thought of what had been revealed in the story so far. "Must have been a long time. In the story, you were already engaged and that was a while ago."

Mandy held up her hand to show the ring on her finger. But as she did so, she also extended and retracted her fingers and quickly counted.

"Close to 7 years now," She said, "But we plan on setting up a time and place soon... again. Just so long as it isn't destroyed by the time our wedding takes place... again."

"Isn't it the sixth time now that something has happened to cancel your wedding Mandy?" Dr. Kendrick thought for a moment and was thinking hard.

"Fifth," She corrected chuckling nervously. Coughing slightly, she straightened the files she carried and her other had brushed some hair behind her ear, "The last time when the amborgs tried to plan the wedding? That doesn't count... I mean. It was nice that they finally felt it necessary to assume command after the previous failures but I have said time and time again that amborgs planning my wedding is not my dream of getting hitched."

"That gives me an idea," Dr. Kendrick said, "Why don't you join us Mandy. I'm sure you could help fill in and finish the story that I've been telling Brad. There are a lot more points of view that need to be fully explained that I alone are mostly not qualified for."

"Why wouldn't you be qualified?" Brad asked curiously.

"He means," Mandy interrupted teasingly. "People who are technicians are usually the ones that go over footage that the amborgs see. He doesn't have the time to watch every byte of data so that's what the technicians are for. In a way, I was there."

"Exactly," Dr. Kendrick nodded. "She'll literally have seen through the eyes of 117 of the rest of the story. We could definitely use your help Mandy."

"Me? I have to file these reports," Mandy held up the folder. Several unorganized pages were hanging out of it in a crooked manner. "I'm not sure whether I'll have time for storytelling. But uh… What story are we talking about? Since we're on the subject."

"117 and the events leading up to the Domino Incident. Now forget the reports," He replied as he took them out of her hands. "I'll take care of them myself later."

"Like you did last time?" Mandy asked as her hands went after the folders that Dr. Kendrick was purposely moving away from her. "And they ended up in the garbage?"

"I'll put them in my top priority cabinet," Dr. Kendrick replied. "Besides, the A.I.s store all of this information away after they're filed by hand."

"If you say so doctor," Mandy sighed and began to follow them further down the hall, "Can we stop by the cafeteria and get dinner at least? I really need food."

"It's that late already? Really? Oh. Well we were on our way to have dinner anyway," Dr. Kendrick nodded in consent. He gestured down the hall and the three of them continued down the hall, "Brad, let's go grab today's meal. You should definitely try 3's spaghetti. She taught it to many people before she left."

"All right doctor," Brad nodded excitedly and checked the time. "I won't have to be home for a few more hours."

"That doesn't matter," Mandy replied. She did a small arching motion with her arms. "With the new shuttles, we'll have you home in under ten minutes."

They made their way to the cafeteria. There wasn't a lot of activity but many people were already enjoying their dinner. Dr. Kendrick pointed out the librarian that 117 had asked for help during the Christmas party. He also introduced Brad to some of the defense drones that had participated in the fight against 43 when she had come out of her coma. Brad was amazed how sentient they were and afraid to talk about her. Some amborgs were also taking time to have food as well but they ate silently which was quite normal for the entire staff. Obviously, they were communicating quietly amongst themselves. Kendrick, Brad and Mandy walked up to the counter where one of the chefs was scooping food onto plates.

"Good evening Dr. Kendrick," They all beamed when they saw Dr. Kendrick.

Instantly, three trays were fetched and plates with food were distributed out before they even had the chance to open their mouths. Brad stared in awe and immediately enjoyed the succulent smell that the noodles spread with sauce was giving out. The aroma was so captivating, he felt as if he was about collapse.

"Is this the student that 117 and 5 have been marveling about?" One of the chefs asked.

Brad sheepishly rubbed his foot across the floor and bowed his head as he picked up his tray. One of the chefs gave him a cup of water.

"Has everyone been talking about me?" Brad blushed again, "Oh I'm not really that interesting."

"On the contrary," The chef smiled as they all began to walk away towards a table. "We rarely have visitors as young as you. But with the peace that's been hanging around, it's a comfort to see the next generation developing a sense of curiosity to learn. Every time someone important arrives, we make it our business to make you feel welcome. Plus, the amborgs know everything."

The chefs bowed their heads as the three of them made their way to a table and found one occupied by none other than George Ramirez. The A.I. Industries representative looked up from his newspaper, swallowed his bite, and acknowledged the trio.

"Dr. Kendrick!" He exclaimed, setting his paper down on the table, and stood to shake Kendrick's hand. "Nice to see you sir and Ms. Mandy as well. I assume this is the student that is such a fan of your work."

"It's good to see you too George. May we join you?" Dr. Kendrick set his tray on the table and took George's hand. When he consented, he pulled a seat for Mandy and motioned to Brad and they all sat.

"Of course Doctor," Mr. Ramirez smiled, "It's always a pleasure to share a meal with you."

"How's your daughter Thalia doing George?" Mandy asked. Mr. Ramirez laughed and smiled warmly.

"Thalia wants to spend all of her vacation days here to see you and the amborgs," He replied. He set aside the newspaper and picked up more noodles with his fork. "But boarding school is practically the only obstacle keeping her where she is."

"A sweet person such as herself could never stay away from here," Dr. Kendrick said. Give my warmest regards to her. Let me know when she flies back and I will pay for it."

"I will sir but it's your money," Mr. Ramirez sat back down looking guilty but Dr. Kendrick shook his hand at him.

"George, we are eating and sharing a lovely meal together. Call me John! You're practically family among us," He said cheerfully. "Thalia always had a home here anyway. What's the point of being rich if I don't give some of it away?"

"I'm afraid I hold you with the highest and utmost respect sir. Despite the number of years I have worked for you, it will still take time for me to be comfortable with talking to you on a first-name basis," George grinned sheepishly and looked down at his plate. "But you have been a good friend to me. Still, I could never put myself at an equal level to you."

"After all these years? I'm not a tyrant placing power over all of you. Oh well, I guess it was worth a shot," Kendrick sighed as he scooped some food in his mouth. Everyone laughed when he put on an evil face and then went back to eating. "Anyway, I was wondering if you would also help as well. Your input along with Mandy's would greatly help me finish the story Brad's been hearing about."

"I'd love to," Mr. Ramirez nodded as he returned to his food, "What would you like to know? Which story?"

"Domino Incident. Brad? Do you have any questions for the A.I. Industries representative?" Dr. Kendrick shifted his attention to Brad who looked up with his mouth full. "Ask away."

"Oh," Brad quickly swallowed. When his mouth was clear he spoke, "Is it difficult to maintain good relations with businesses?"

"It's my job to make sure that relations are always good," George replied calmly. "Dr. Kendrick got most of his funds from his own family fortune. Because the fortune is so huge, threats from any contributing businesses are pointless. Any business Dr. Kendrick allies with is practically like giving away free gasoline. He is actually respected fairly well in both politicians' and business professional's eyes. We just have to look good in the eyes of the business world and make sure it doesn't look like we're doing a ton of secretive things. There were times that some businesses thought that we were plotting secret evil genius plans. The government actually thought Kendrick was staging a coup on the country. Or didn't they once say you had aligned with terrorists, Doctor?"

"You're kidding!" Brad's mouth dropped and his eyes widened.

"Oh yes," Dr. Kendrick smiled, "The president was worried that I had taken matters into my own hands. So to avoid being the weird Batman sort of freak everyone was thinking I had become, I introduced the president to a few of the amborgs and let him tour the facility. I went as far as to give him full access to my technology but with high security clearances and heavy regulations to make sure nothing goes wrong. Avoiding all the gruesome details, the government almost felt that I had a power just like what happened during the Dominoe Incident."

"Plotting to stage a coup," Brad said amazingly as Mandy chuckled quietly, "How could anyone believe that Dr. Kendrick would want to overthrow the government? That's unthinkable."

"Well," Mandy said waving her fork towards the ceiling. "Knowing Dr. Kendrick and how secretive he was before he began the actual designing of the amborg schematics? I'd definitely be suspicious about what he was doing a couple of decades ago. He would probably run this world better than some people."

"That's also possible. But I can assure you, I don't want to do that," Dr. Kendrick said quickly when they all stared at him with suspicious looks, "It is what happened during the Domino incident. No one thought it could be done, but a one man war did happen during that time. And the amborgs, my children barely saved this country from being destroyed. And I think it's about time we got to that part of the story. Ready Brad?"

"Yes please," Brad wiped his forehead. The food was actually very warm and causing him to sweat. "The Domino Incident was one of our most tragic times many years ago. I'd be greatly interested in knowing your perspective instead of what the textbooks say these days."

"Alright then. Mandy? George? Feel free to join in whenever you feel like I'm telling it wrong."

Mandy raised an eyebrow. She grabbed her cup of water and took a few gulps. Grabbing another bite, she leaned forward.

"From what I know of you doctor," Mandy said bluntly, "You probably have been misinterpreting everything."

"Very funny," Dr. Kendrick shook his head. "Now then. Shortly after the battle of New York. The next few months became a dark passing in the history of the world."

*
**   *
**   *
**

Independence Hall, Pennsylvania
2128, 22 July, 3:32 PM
Three months after Battle of New York.

"This is the East Coast Broadcasting System and we are reporting with a breaking update on the situation which has now been ravaging the country for the past two days. We are now going to switch to one of our reporters live to the situation just outside Independence Hall where our very own Ashley Jenkins is there with the report. Ashley, tell us what's going on down there."

"John," Ashley spoke into the camera as a sudden pop caused her to flinch. Brushing it off, she spoke as calmly as possible. "I am reporting live at the intersection between fifth and sixth-street with Independence hall right behind me. The area down the road has turned into a massive battleground as gangs from all over the area have launched a massive attack. Local law enforcement has been close to eradicated or wounded and we are facing a similar situation to the Battle of New York some months ago. Other locations such as Chicago, Los Angeles, Seattle, Houston, Miami and several other large cities have also fallen under attack from a string of explosions in key locations. And the army is facing enemy numbers which seem to have come from the dark. There has been virtually no warning of this sudden attack across the country and we are slowly being overwhelmed with so many cities calling desperately for help from the amborgs but they are spread too thin. It isn't clear if they will arrive. All of our military and defensive assets have been stretched to the bone. We have also just received word that the United Nations has begun an assessment of the situation in an emergency meeting shortly a few hours ago."

An explosion sounded nearby making the young reporter nervous. She grasped the microphone tightly almost causing it to break. Startled, she turned towards the sounds of the battle and cringed as another explosion and a few screams joined the mix just nearby. Many people were running away from the chaos in a desperate attempt to flee. With them, police officers and soldiers were escorting them to safety. One of them, very worn out and tired, ran up to the news crew.

"We have a new situation!" The officer yelled as the camera man directed the video recorder at him. Jenkins watched in horror and listened. "We got to get out of here fast! Find someplace safe!"

"Where are we going?!" Ashley Jenkins yelled as an explosion tore down a building nearby. "We can't just leave Independence hall! I thought this place was supposed to be the safe zone. We were assured that we'd be away from the fighting!"

"Obviously not!" The officer yelled as he looked over his shoulder. "Listen! We got to get out of here now! Otherwise you will be..."

He was cut off as an explosion detonated directly behind him. All of them fell to the ground from the force of the shock wave. Ashley felt the heat in the air as she was pushed to the ground. At first, things seemed to be fuzzy. She blinked a couple of times and saw the officer lying on the ground unconscious in front of her. She turned her head to see her camera-man on the ground as well. The camera was tilted upward and the lens was bent and cracked. With everything coming back into focus, she heard a voice coming from the police officer's radio while the two men stirred feebly.

"Come in!" The radio crackled. "If anyone can read, pull back! All units still at Independence hall need to evac now! Enemy forces are overrunning defensive positions."

The radio buzzed and crackled. Ashley crawled over and picked up the radio and pressed the receiver and yelled into it.

"Hello?!" She cried as the radio sparked. The explosion had damaged bits and pieces of the receiver. "This is Ashley Jenkins with E.C.B.S.! Please, you have to send help!"

"Calm down Ms. Jenkins," The same voice said calmly on the other end. The crackle of the radio was starting to get louder, "Take a deep breath and let me know what is happening. Are you with a member of my police force?"

"He's unconscious!" Ashley yelled desperately and felt fear flow through her whole body. "My camera-man... I think he's still alive but they're both on the ground! Please send us help. I can hear the shooting getting louder!"

"Alright calm down!" The voice replied, "I need you to stay calm. I'm right here, do not stop talking understand? Reinforcements will move in and take over the area surrounding Independence hall. I don't know who was it that ordered the retreat but we are not allowing the enemy to take over our historical monument. We have confirmed amborg assistance."

"Please hurry!!" Ashley looked up and saw something that scared her. A massive giant like robot was marching towards Independence hall followed by a large mob. The robot growled and scanned the area. It spotted Ashley and marched closer. The crowd behind it was whooping and firing off their guns into the air. She couldn't move a muscle. Was this the end?

"Independence hall targeted," A loud robotic voice sounded from the giant. "Destroying U.S. monument. We shall crush the enemy's morale."

Ashley saw the robot lift its arm and a bright red light began to emanate from it. It was pointed directly at the building and she was right in its path. Realizing her situation, she instantly lifted the radio right to her mouth and breathed.

"Please tell my family... I love them very much."

The mob behind the robot had begun to walk in front and were jeering and yelling with joy. Ashley looked at them and then held up the radio receiver.

"Uh. Ms. Jenkins," The officer over the radio said. "That's not really necessary."

"...And tell them that I'm sorry that I was caught up in this," She said ignoring the man's replies. "I'm Ashley Jenkins. Oh crap. Signing off."

She instantly shut her eyes but then didn't wait to see what happened next. Instead, she heard loud noises occur in the surrounding area. Explosions occurred, heat was discharged all over the place, massive thuds and crashes rang in the air. However, the pain she thought was coming didn't seem to make it to her. She had expected a fiery inferno but she felt completely fine. Also, many people were screaming all around her which was surprising. Hadn't there been a large mob cheering earlier? She immediately opened her eyes and stared in amazement.

A large figure had dropped in front of her and the stunned officer blocking whatever attacks had been thrown at them. She casually glanced behind her and saw that Independence hall was still standing. She blinked and turned to look at her savior in utter confusion. A number was glowing brightly on the jacket of the person who had stepped in. She recognized the color immediately.

"Are you alright Ms. Jenkins?"

The voice was also robotic but not as angry as the giant. It sounded young and full of empathy. Every word that came out was in synch to the lights flashing from the amborg's bracelet. Without saying a word, she meekly nodded.

"Very good," The figure in front of her replied. "Stay very still and don't move. We'll take care of this."

"We?" She stammered still dumbstruck from all of the chaos. The figure turned its head and glanced at her briefly, smiled and nodded in response. "We."

Suddenly, she felt the atmosphere go quiet. Something had changed and Ashley heard footsteps approach from behind. She turned and saw a massive crowd approaching. They didn't appear to be army or police. In fact, they seemed to be incredibly young to her eyes even though the records stated they were older. Cybernetic teenagers, but extremely taller than the average human. The amborgs had arrived in full force evidently. They didn't wear any armor but regular clothing and she saw that they had different numbers on their chests and were carrying a wide variety of weapons. All of them had very serious, solemn looks on their faces. One of them tripped and fell over and was helped up to his feet by a girl. Ashley had seen them before and heard of their accomplishments but had never seen so many of them at a single time. Getting an idea, she leaned over and picked up the camera. Her camera man was still alive but in no position to help. Ashley immediately checked to see that it was still operating and she pointed it at the large crowd that had arrived.

"This is Ashley Jenkins reporting... If you can see this, I am in the middle of something incredible," She said breathlessly into the microphone. "I have just been saved by Dr. Kendrick's amborgs. They are here in such a large group. I don't think I've seen this before. They have successfully arrived and they are entering the defensive. This has to be a miracle."

She pointed the camera at the one she felt was the leader of the group and hoped that everyone watching was seeing what she was seeing. Not only was it an exclusive, but it was probably the most incredible scene she had ever seen before in all of her years as a reporter.

David 117 stepped forward and was flanked by all members of the first, second, and third group. Except for one. All eighty nine of them were marching forward except Donut who fell for the umpteenth time.

"Objective secured," 117 broadcasted to the group, "We are now engaging the enemy. Press forward!"

"Stay safe," Mandy's voice ran through his head. "Find the bastard who shot 43. Make him pay for everything he's done."

He leaped forward and charged. However, instead of running at a slow pace, he increased his powers and practically zoomed down the street to meet the enemy who were also charging. Although they were moving at a very insignificant speed, they all looked prepared to take on the more upgraded amborgs. 117 wasn't the only one who had jumped to a higher energy level. Several more members of the amborgs, thanks to their recent training, also had increased their speed and ran alongside 117 pace by pace.

The radio in Ms. Jenkins hands crackled again and another voice sounded out.

"Attention all army and police personnel," He said, "We will now be forming a perimeter around the area of Independence hall. A triage center will be formed. Do not attempt to engage alongside with the amborg group."

*
**   *
**   *
**

"Hold on a moment."

Sarah paused the video and looked at Mandy with a confused look.

"The story seems to have jumped a segment," She said. "There should be something that led up to the final battle of Pennsylvania."

"Calm down Sarah," Mandy chuckled. "You interrupted the story at exactly the same time I did. Let me just keep playing."

Sarah nodded apologetically and then returned her attention back to the screen as Mandy hit the play button again.

*
**   *
**   *
**

2135

"WAIT! Stop, stop, stop."

Everyone turned to look at Mandy was shaking her head disapprovingly. Dr. Kendrick, whose mouth still hung open, closed it and stared with a little sign of angst. It was not every day that he would be interrupted in the middle of a story.

"What's wrong?" He asked. Mr. Ramirez and Brad also looked at Mandy in confusion. "Have I left out something already?"

Well, you can't just start right there at that point of the story," Mandy said stubbornly, "People actually want to know about the important stuff in between the story otherwise, what's the point?

Oh hey, build up the plot with so much drama and then... it ended here. Really exciting."

"I felt that going straight to the final part of the incident would be better than actually going through all the details," Dr. Kendrick muttered as he shrugged. Mandy shook her head.

"No doctor," She said, "Knowing is half the battle remember? Come on, I think the best part took place before Pennsylvania. Little spoiler for you Brad. Everything finished in Pennsylvania but that wasn't the only place to be affected by the Domino Incident. We need to go specifically to the places they went to. And before all of you groan in frustration, I'm just going to say that it was only three places before Pennsylvania where the amborgs concentrated. Feel better now? It's not about the way it ended. It's about what the amborgs had to do to make their decisions that brought them to that final battle."

Dr. Kendrick looked at Mandy and then at Brad. She stared him in the eye and tilted her head. He knew what this meant. One head twitch from Mandy usually meant that she was right. Sighing, he nodded and looked at Brad. Mr. Ramirez coughed and made an excruciating attempt to not look amused.

"Alright then," Kendrick said feeling Mandy's triumphant eyes bearing down on him. "Since Mandy was so kind to remind me, let's do a little flashback of the... hehe... flashback. The best place to do that would be... Before the whole Incident began. Just before in fact."

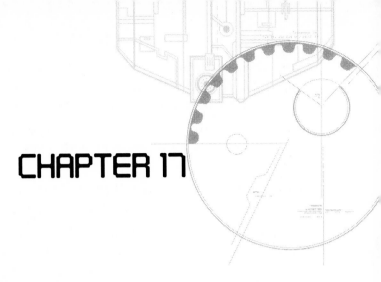

CHAPTER 17

117 placed a data-pad on the table. A three-dimensional holo-screen lit up and a descending cascade of numbers began to fill the screen. To the naked eye, it didn't look like much but 117 did not take his eyes off the cascading waterfall of lit numbers. He was searching for a pattern, clues, a hint, in order to figure out where the assassin, as everyone decided to call him, was hiding. Somewhere in this complexly built code was the key to figuring it out.

Dr. Kendrick was staring at the pad and running some calculations in his portable arm keypad. After a few minutes of silence, 117 straightened up and sat in a chair and buried his face in his hands.

"Don't give up David."

Mandy showed up with some cups of coffee for the three of them. Dr. Kendrick, grabbing one cup, thanked her graciously before returning back to his arm-pad. 117 lifted his head and downed his in one gulp instantly. She placed her hand on his shoulder. She had constantly reminded him not to overdo it but she let it slide this one time.

"Not even amborgs can solve everything instantaneously," she remarked casually as 117 nodded reluctantly.

"We must be patient and eventually, the answer will be discovered," He finished confidently. This caused Mandy to stare. She didn't think he would use that kind of answer.

"You remembered..." Taken aback, she set the coffee tray on a nearby counter and returned to his side. "I guess you really do pay attention."

"I always am," 117 replied. "I remember everything."

Mandy kept her hand on his shoulder without a word. Dr. Kendrick turned and looked at the two of them with a calm look. He too did not say anything. Instead, he removed his glasses, turned his back to the table, and sat on the edge of it. The room became silent. It became so eerie that the only sounds that pierced the silence were the numbers on the hologram. They continued to flow downwards on the screen like raindrops.

"117, there is a time," Dr. Kendrick spoke when they came to another standstill, "When a small break is necessary. I didn't build you so that you were condemned to work infinitely."

"But we are no closer to finding this man," 117 muttered. He slowly inhaled and then let it out of his mouth like he had been educated to do. "We are... back at the first square."

"No we are not," Dr. Kendrick walked up to 117 and pointed a finger at the amborg's forehead. "It was you who brought back this data from New York. You came up with the training that brought the amborgs back up to their highest readiness levels. You were the one who went to your grandfather for help and his sources in New York informed us that something big was about to happen. Because of your instinct, we managed to save New York from being completely decimated which resulted from you revealing the existence of the hidden giant robots. You probably saved many lives with this strategy before it was too late."

117 listened to these words and sat up straighter. He processed what the doctor had said and nodded after a brief moment. He was right, they were definitely not behind.

"Thank you doctor," 117 said as he stood up. He walked back over to the screen. "We mustn't stop... I didn't spend the last few weeks hacking this data to give up now."

117 stood up and went back to the table and began to type rapidly into the keys. Dr. Kendrick stood to his left and looked over the numbers while Mandy took a place on his right side. She casually looked at Dr. Kendrick who winked back at her. Then they quickly went back to the screen.

"So… Why are you so fired up?" She said looking at his face. It wasn't 117 she was looking at directly. The face that she saw was suddenly distant, determined, and clouded with tension.

"Asides from the Doctor's motivational words?" He said glancing at her, "Well, I will do anything for 43… She still hasn't opened her eyes. Not since her temper tantrum."

Dr. Kendrick looked at 117 who continued to talk out of his bracelet. By now practically every person at amborg industries already knew why 117 and the amborgs were in this state. It had never been done before but one of their own had been put out of commission.

"She will not wake up," 117 isolated some numbers and highlighted them on the screen. "Dr. Wildman even stated that she might never awaken again. Forever. I will move the nearest mountain just to have her see me again. But at the same time, there is no sense in sitting there being upset when the needs of people, citizens, parents, families, soldiers, children… and humans come first. I can never be prepared to lose 43 but I will steel myself with every memory I have of her because her condition has caused my motivation to drastically increase in a positive way. I am planning to direct all of my negativity towards him."

117 clenched the edge of the table and the sound of metal filled the room as his fingers dug into the steel frame. Several of the lab technicians stared with concern.

"He needs to understand," 117 said angrily as his energy levels rose. "He crossed the line. It ends when I defeat him and make him pay for taking what I cherished most. The line has been drawn, and it will not be crossed. I will face him again. And I will make sure this injustice does not go unsolved."

No one said anything for the next few minutes. Every second was then devoted to decoding the data-pad. Every now and then a technician would say a few words to Kendrick but the situation remained the same. The encrypted data was stumping many of them. Pretty soon, it was only Dr. Kendrick and 117 keeping the optimism in the decoding. Finally, 117 lifted his hand and spoke out-loud.

"I have it," He said softly as his throat burned.

"You did?" Dr. Kendrick looked the data over again but unfortunately, he had not found whatever it was that 117 had found. "I don't understand."

"As I looked at the wave of numbers that appeared," 117 said bringing up the numbers he had originally highlighted. "I attempted to decode and locate a single key number in the data, a recurring code for example, but we could not," 117 shifted his hands and began to rapidly type into the keypad. "This is a very intensive encryption which we assumed based on this assassin's methodology. Is it a set of map coordinates, plans, or various reports? Unfortunately, because we assumed that it was a heavy encryption of this particular content, we accidently overlooked one thing."

"What's that David?" Mandy looked at the data and blinked a few times. Obviously, this made no sense at all to her. She eagerly awaited expectantly to hear what he was talking about.

"I found in this data... a single reoccurring number which came up," His hands moved like lightning on the keypad that it caused Mandy to feel dizzy. She had forgotten how fast they could move even when they were stationary. "The reason the decryption took so long was because our search filter decided not to focus on how simple it really was. As a result, we did not realize what this file actually was."

"Is it a code?" Mandy tilted her head as 117 brought up a number and highlighted it.

"No," He smirked, "Or rather, it partially resembles one. But what if the number was not an encryption code? What if it was played as..."

"...A video file," Dr. Kendrick finished opening his eyes in astonishment. 117 nodded in acknowledgement.

"Fascinating," Kendrick removed his spectacles, "A very old common thing of the past. It was right there in front of us and we missed it. This adversary knows the oldest tricks in the book. All this modern technology managing to hide such an old-fashioned trick of the past."

"Disguising a video file code was quite common decades ago and obviously not something a hacker would search for at first glance," 117 pressed the keypad a few more times and hit the enter key and the numbers on the screen disappeared. "As Sherlock Holmes once said, eliminate all other factors, and the one which remains must be the truth. The Sign of Four, chapter one, page ninety-two. Eighteen ninety."

"I got it David. I know who Holmes is," Mandy bit back a smile. That was the 117 she was used to hearing, "So we've been overestimating this guy? Is that why we've been having such a hard time finding him?"

Mandy looked at the screen curiously but Kendrick shook his head. There was definitely truth in what she said but he was still skeptical.

"In a way..." He said pushing his glasses up his nose. "With this example, we have overestimated our enemy and failed to notice the video file but that doesn't mean we should automatically assume that should change our methods instantly in the upcoming battle."

The video feed on the screen shifted and began to play the video. The numbers opened up and continued to scroll downwards on the left and right leaving a dark space in the center column for them to see. Finally the file lit up and played its message.

"Hello Dr. Kendrick and to your little amborg pets, I bid a giant welcome. For you have discovered my little challenge."

"Oh great," Mandy sighed. "What is it with villains and the word 'challenge'?"

"Are we hunting Jango Fett?" Dr. Kendrick asked.

It was the T-shaped visor on the helmet that 117 remembered seeing on the ledge. The assassin, still covered in his armored suit stood in a dark background where the light illuminated only his head and shoulders. 117 felt his fists clench as the video kept playing.

"I thought that it'd be appropriate to provide you with the means to find me in this test," The assassin spoke in a very casual but taunting tone, "I do hope there was no trouble finding my video file. Everything is so new that... I just got bored of the societal norm. So a little bit of old-fashioned trickery. Since you obviously spotted it, then I say... good job for you. Unfortunately, it doesn't get easier."

The message continued as they saw man move around in his chair. He began to lift his arms and make gestures with his hands as if talking wasn't passing the message along.

"John Kendrick. The ideal genius inventor. You go on and on flaunting those tall unsociable orphans and one day it dawned on me that they haven't received a proper er... more formal challenge of their so-called abilities. Call it a game or whatever you want."

Mandy glanced nervously at 117 and Kendrick who were both listening attentively and focused solely on the screen. Dr. Kendrick had raised an eyebrow. Being directly addressed by the enemy had hit a mark. The assassin then pointed a finger at the screen.

"Your...children as you call them," He said putting lots of emphasis on 'children,' "They are weak! Vulnerable! Robots that you force to do your bidding!! Since you have idolized and given them gifts that make them superhuman, I offer a challenge! Which began when I placed that knife deep inside that girl's chest! I have proven that they are not as strong as everyone thinks."

117 clenched his fist. He was using 43 as a symbol for this message.

"He's mine," 117 snarled. Dr. Kendrick held his hand up to signal for silence.

"Has the poor thing died yet? I only wanted to see how emotional her brothers and sisters would get when they saw that they could be hurt. Pretty little thing... All of the amborgs are so cold and in such a struggle to find their own basic humanity. It shouldn't be too hard for them to ignore the death of one of their own. After all, they don't have voices to cry out in anguish."

"You wanted to give us a challenge," 117 spoke in a very casual and cool tone as the message continued, "Proceed quickly before I destroy the screen."

"Am I boring you? I didn't think so. The challenge is speed, endurance, and strength. I have smuggled bombs in certain sections of each building, each town, each city, and each location across the United States. Oh don't worry, the first ones won't be anywhere near enough to kill any civilians. I'm being conveniently nice so listen up. The initial explosions will just be large enough to get them running. To leave their homes. To evacuate. Run around in the open streets like one massive turkey shoot for my robots and gang members across this country who've sworn allegiance to me. It's not easy keeping criminals, gang members, and drug-addicts in line so I honestly don't know what they'll do. Don't blame me if they go off on their own little rampage. That's the idea since the chaos will force everyone into disarray. Therefore, your jobs will be to simply try and stop me."

"He's declaring an all-out war..." Mandy gasped. "That's crazy!"

"Oh but I believe I won't be attacking all of them simultaneously... Is that even more convenient enough? This is the best part. No... I am going to start with location after location. Unless you manage to make your decisions carefully, unless you want to prevent nation-wide destruction, then like a string of dominoes, all of the cities, all of your armies and your homes will burn. And that is when you'll lose. Time is running out. If it will make it easy, I'll even provide a head start for where the first attack will take place. Make it to this place before the second riddle is destroyed and you will find the next large domino. Remember though, you can try but I guarantee you will not be able to save everyone. My forces are already in position. Now it's time for you to set up your own pieces. Ask yourself this, how far are you willing to risk innocent lives? Just to find me? If in the end, you manage to make it to the finish, I will wait for your judgment but fail to find me, and you won't see me or catch me again unless I want you to. Are you ready for it?"

None of them spoke a word. Mandy was still trying to comprehend all she had just heard. She silently got out her phone and instinctively began to send a message to Palmer. But what would she say? 117 and Dr. Kendrick were looking slightly stunned. It really was a war. Before anyone in the room could comprehend, the man in the video spoke the first riddle.

"Although this historical father figure was famous here, he was born in Virginia. The Eagle landed in the long conflict after the challenge from thirty-five with this bit of trivia.

In a twist, the last dancer of Communism sought refuge in the land of the free. The place where hearts first found the ability to be taken to people unfortunate as thee."

"Got it."

Mandy and Kendrick stared at 117. He stared back and shrugged. They hated how quickly amborgs could solve riddles. The masked man leaned towards the camera.

"If you go there, you could probably save one city from about eighty percent of the damage... but don't forget there are bombs everywhere too. Ha. Try not to stick around. If you succeed in thwarting me there, you will be met with even worse opposition in the next locations where I've hidden the other clues and puzzle pieces. You might also be able to find the deadlines for when I detonate. They will all be made clear in due time. There are three waves of explosives. When you solve the first riddle and stop me in the first location, I detonate the second wave at a time I specify. So you'd better get to this place fast if you want to figure it out. During the bombings of the second wave, my forces will then make their move and launch the attack of a lifetime. The second riddle will divert you to the place where the heaviest of the attacks will be concentrated in. And finally, in the third wave, it will be up to you amborgs to try and figure out where I am in the middle of the chaos. Decisions will be made, but I wonder how long you will last at that point. Fortunately for you, I want to be found, otherwise this challenge is moot. This place will put you out of your way a bit but it will test how fast you can make it there before my army kills thousands. After you reach the first location, keep in mind of this next one."

"Why doesn't he just bomb everything at once?" Dr. Kendrick murmured. "To a man of his skill and resources, it would probably be the best solution if his intention is to make us look bad in his victory."

They all pondered silently as the second riddle was recited.

"If it was blackjack, then 21 would be the game to force an opponent's surrender. It is the number of sisters tied and affiliated to this beauty also a neighbor to ice and water.

This large sound houses the entrance and exit to new horizons enabling travelers to proceed to and fro. The beacon at 605 can be the safest in view but also the dangerous when wrongly going below."

Mandy and Kendrick both looked at 117. Evidently, he had already solved it. He thought for a few seconds and nodded immediately without even blinking.

"Seriously," Mandy whispered to Dr. Kendrick. "I think they may be TOO good."

"I heard that," 117 did not even peel his eyes away from the screen. The message played on.

"Be warned, your numbers are limited and you cannot save everyone. Once you finish the first challenge and move to the second, you'd better hightail to the next objective otherwise you will be known as failures who couldn't ensure humanity's safety. While you take the time to collect your thoughts and plan your defensive strategy, I will also be throwing in a couple more obstacles. These three riddles aren't the only thing I offer in this challenge. Choose not to avoid them however and there will be consequences. Just know that I'm always a step ahead. And now, here is my final riddle assuming you still have the time and strength to keep up and move on."

"You remember by simple reenactment, and waste countless moments ogling the first animals displayed, technology arose from keys after free world's victory, despite its nickname, its title was taken away.

He is a falsely named follower but provided a well-known creation in the wood to provide art and harmony, a seamstress sits quietly and watches light created, as the toll sounds true and stands in tranquility."

For the third time, Mandy and Dr. Kendrick along with a group of technicians stared at 117. For the next few seconds, he thought hard but then looked at them all in turn and shook his head. Taken aback, Mandy stared suspiciously and then joined everyone else's gaze back to the screen. Where the assassin spoke again.

"I know how fast your amborg minds work. I am assuming, the amborg, whoever is with you Kendrick has already solved all three riddles. It should be a cinch."

Dr. Kendrick looked back at 117 who shook his head again and held up three fingers. As they went back to the message, the assassin waved his hand in farewell.

"Well then, I look forward to when you reach the finish line. Oh. One last thing," The assassin help up his gloved index finger. "If you're wondering what's my reason for doing all this? Would you believe me if I told you, just because I can? Yes? No? You better hope your children are up for the task Kendrick because if they slip up, they may accidentally cause the rest of the dominoes to fall. As they said during the Cold War, prevent a domino incident. Have fun because the games have begun. You have a matter of hours to reach the first location. Finish the challenges of the first riddle in that time, you will only partially be done. Once that time is up, I will detonate and the second riddle comes to play. Have fun."

The screen instantly stopped and the video message ended. Dr. Kendrick immediately turned to a technician and everyone scrambled around. 117 immediately left the room and sped down the hall, followed by Mandy and Kendrick.

"Where are you going? David? What's the first location?" Mandy panted as she sprinted breathlessly down the hall after him.

"There is no time!" He said quickly. They rounded a corner and she slipped. Kendrick immediately reached out a hand and pulled her up. The fall caused the two of them to drop behind a bit. They sprinted through the corridor looking at 117's figure disappearing rapidly at the other end and saw him disappear through a door. As they ran, the hallways lit up and lights began traveling alongside and shot through the same door.

"Dr. Kendrick to the whole facility!" Kendrick lifted his arm and spoke into his bracelet. "Full alert. Prepare for amborg deployment! All employees and everyone able to walk and think, prepare for my instructions."

At these words, the alarm sounded off into the hall.

"Boy, I'm getting to that age where I can't keep up anymore!" Dr. Kendrick chuckled as the hallways instantly were bathed in a crimson light. Mandy rolled her eyes. "We're here!" She yelled as they reached the door and ran inside.

"Entering Amborg Deployment Pod Facility," The A.I. voice sounded out as the doors slid open.

All the other amborgs were checking their pods and taking their seats inside each of them. Multiple teams of security guards were assisting with loading every pod to their maximum storage capacity. Clearly they were already prepared to rush out at any moment. Thanks to multiple drills and training maneuvers, they were all ready to go within a few minutes. The AIs were running diagnostics and looking over the last launch procedures while Dr. Kendrick's scientists were pushing carts full of supplies around to each of the pods and checking each Amborg's vitals.

"Whatever you need in the field, take it now! R&D is working on new tech and has given you all that we can use in the field, any other supplies needed will be air-dropped upon request," One of the guards called while gesturing to the cart next to him like a salesman. An amborg picked a rifle from the stash as another shook his head and headed straight to his pod instead without anything.

"I'll stick with this thanks," 3 nodded as she clutched her pop gun. The guard nodded pushed the cart ahead to another section of the hangar.

While Mandy proceeded straight to 117's pod, Dr. Kendrick jogged to 501 and 466 who were both lying on the floor. Electricity was sparking around the two of them and the surrounding guards were stepping away cautiously. He realized that 501 had activated his electrical wrist bracer again.

"Sorry!" 501 apologized frantically as he picked himself up. 466 grabbed his extended hand and he pulled her up. "I didn't mean to discharge the bracelet again!"

"We really need to design a safety for that," 466 made a sighing gesture, grabbed a belt of knifes, got up and walked away to her pod. Dr. Kendrick held 501's arm and examined the wrist bracer as she muttered, "What foreseeable use could we have for that in future situations?"

"Look Dominic," Dr. Kendrick sighed as he tapped a button. The weapon hummed loudly and then there was silence. "This is the power setting. I purposely memorized where the hidden buttons are and you can too if you bother to read the instruction manual. So the enemy won't know how to work it, you can easily connect your CPU's signal to even familiarize with it if you don't feel like reading. See? You had this at maximum. Are you trying to vaporize yourself?"

Dr. Kendrick sighed as 501 blushed sheepishly at the discovery.

"At least you only hit yourself and 466," 501 stood with help from Dr. Kendrick and he looked the third group amborg briefly. "Otherwise you would have probably electrocuted and fried a normal person's brain."

The surrounding guards all looked at each other nervously backed even further away. 501 gulped and nodded vigorously.

"I didn't mean there would necessarily be permanent damage," Dr. Kendrick scowled at the guards. "Although death is one of the most likely scenarios," he muttered when they were out of earshot.

He hit another button on the bracer and Dr. Kendrick nodded to 501.

"Take really good care son," He said. "You're very eager to do battle and always try to impress the others. Be sure to slow down and keep a mindful eye. Keep asking yourself if you're doing alright before you leap without looking. Now did you remember what I did to raise and lower the setting?"

501 stopped and pondered for two seconds and then nodded very slowly. Dr. Kendrick smiled.

"Yes."

"That is what will make you win by default," Dr. Kendrick replied softly. "You along with everyone else are the bridge between robotics and humans. We don't know what this man wants but we do know he is a danger to us and worse to innocent people. So come home safely. Save the world. Never give up."

"Are we soldiers?" 501 asked curiously.

"You weren't meant to be," Dr. Kendrick replied. "That I know for sure. I only gave you all a choice. To live a different life. Most people on the internet and the public just assume I give you lucky few a better life. No I always need to specify it's only a different life where you get the chance to make yourselves better. Soldier or not, you all voluntarily risked your lives. For science or for your lives, you are all special."

"When I get home," 501 smiled. "Maybe opening a candy shop might be a good start. If I wanted to do something for fun."

"Get in your pod," Dr. Kendrick chuckled, "Relax. Come home when you're done and then you can tell me more. Wear your seatbelt."

"Is that an order?"

"Not really," Dr. Kendrick said tilting his head. "It's a request as your adopted father. Your real parents would probably come back from the dead to haunt me if I allowed you to die."

"Considering who my parents were," 501 sighed, "They probably wouldn't."

"I wouldn't say that 501," Dr. Kendrick said. "I know that they would be proud of you."

"Then where are they?"

That was a question that Dr. Kendrick couldn't answer.

Number 274 and 125 were both sitting comfortably in their pods. They had been waiting for the order to ship out so they had camped with a few other amborgs in the deployment bay. They had just finished their seventieth round of Egyptian rat-screw when they heard Dr. Kendrick give the order only moments ago. Both of them sat quietly until 125 broke the silence.

"Hey 274," He said casually as he checked his systems. The instruments and dials were all glowing in the green areas. As his fuel levels slowly rose he stored his cards inside one of the storage compartments. If he kept shuffling, he'd wear out the deck before it would even be put in play. "You think this is going to be a big one?" He asked twirling his forefingers clockwise.

"Probably," 274 shrugged as he nervously checked his harness for the sixth time. "You remember that one class when they taught us feelings of agitation, restlessness, tension, anxiety, and apprehension?"

"Of course I remember," 125 leaned his head forward and looked at 274, "I think I failed that class or... The instructor said I nailed it but I did not have a hammer and a nail at that time. Ha ha."

"Well. I believe I feel... nervous," 274 looked and checked his own equipment. It had all been stashed in the storage unit of the pod. "It feels strange," He said as he secured the compartment. "Especially since the last time I have a memory of it is long before I became an amborg."

"Well it is common and an interesting feeling to discover considering we do not particularly have them."

125 leaned back and looked at the ceiling of his pod.

"Maybe this might be something important to think about," He pondered.

A few feet away, 117 had strapped himself into his pod. Mandy was checking on him. She still was demanding an answer to what it was that the video had told 117. Especially since the reason she was so annoyed was because 117 had already shared the video to all the amborgs while she had followed him to the deployment bay. In that short time, the amborgs were all in synch and ready to head to the first location after collectively deciphering the riddles.

"Mandy, I advise that you go to your position now and establish communication with me once we are airborne," The instructions were given very quickly but she stayed put.

As he picked up a knife and drew it from the sheath, she remembered the day they first met. How innocent and lonely he was when he had stood in line with the other amborgs. Now he was practically a warrior, heading off to battle and all grown up. All of the amborgs had come so far. Especially 117.

"Your grandfather would be proud," She blurted out.

"That is a reasonable but unnecessary assumption," 117 said looking up at Mandy. "He has already shown evidence of empathy but I have never heard him admit it out-loud." He began pressing buttons on his left hand side. "I would rather know what my parents think of me now. What would they say?"

"Don't think about it in the moment," Mandy sighed. She had forgotten entirely about the riddles. "Wherever they are in spirit. You can tell me again how it isn't possible to know what the deceased are thinking. But I'll say it anyway. They believe in you just like I do. Because if you continue to live, even without your cybernetics, that's the way to keep going at it every day."

117 thought for a moment. As the pods hissed in the backgrounds, he put the knife away.

"I will consider that," He said softly.

"Good," Mandy said smirking. "Because if all else fails, just know that I'm right in everything I say. Then you'll be fine. Now will you please tell me the answers to the riddles?"

"Get off the pad and to your station and I will agree to your terms," 117 replied.

"Clear A.D.P. zones! Launch in two minutes!"

The P.A. announced the order throughout the entire bay. Everyone was scrambling away from the pods and leaving through the exits. The engines on all of the pods except for 43's activated and began to roar loudly. Mandy glanced at 117 and nodded. A loud buzzer began to sound off which prompted her to leave quickly.

He smiled back and closed the pod door. From inside, the systems hummed louder and power was directed into the console. 117 closed his eyes and took a deep breath. It didn't do anything except trigger his oxygen intake sensors. Ignoring this, he shut off his sensors and breathed again. He felt air rush past his nostrils and found the sensation intriguing. As he switched the sensors back on, he inputted coordinates into the navigation unit.

"This is amborg 117," He spoke out-loud and multiple screens appeared on his window revealing all of the other amborgs within their pods, "We will be dropping into the first city now. I am uploading the message sent by the assassin to your pods for viewing should you want to watch it as an inflight movie. Watch it, memorize it, and be prepared to travel across the country lightly. We will undoubtedly be facing intensive battle later on in the day or possibly the days after today. Prepare for a long fight, I do not believe this will be a quick and decisive battle like the ones we have previously faced before in our lives. We are dropping into the blind but have courage. Stay together..."

From his screen, 297, 5, 57, and 917 all smirked. Smiling with confidence, several of the amborgs were listening intently. None of them had a worried look anymore. They were all ready. Everyone else began to acknowledge 117's speech. All of them were in agreement.

"I find this speech to be very inspirational. Eight out of ten."

"Really? Only an eight?"

From his screen, Number 1 bowed his head to 117 while 2 shook his head. Then he looked up with a smirk. 117 nodded at the screen with a small smile. A loud roar sounded outside as the giant hatch in the hangar's roof opened up above. "Well, it was not entirely perfect," 1 snickered while 117 looked up the top viewport at the sky.

"Mandy are you there?" 117 transmitted from his head.

"In position David," she responded. "What do you need?"

117 thought for a minute and pulled Grandpa's button from his pocket. In order to fight, he thought, then they would need help sooner rather than later. From whoever was available and could ally with them. But was that wise? To bring together everyone all at once or save a few for the reserves? This man has everything pitting against us, 117 thought. Then we will have to bring all we have to match him.

"Mandy," He said pressing the button. He instantly came up with a message, thought hard and transmitted it into the button hoping his grandfather would receive it, "How is your fiancee?"

"Tom?" Her puzzled tone rang through his head. "He's fine. His troops and every base in the country have been on standby since the battle of New York. Do I need to ask why?"

"I do not know if you did but send a transmission to him and have him piggyback it to all known law enforcement and army personnel." 117 hit a button and the pod began to rumble. "Full alert status. Major attack imminent. We need everyone who can fight at the ready."

"Understood David 117," Mandy spoke calmly, "Good luck."

"Thanks," 117 replied. "I think it is now the proper time to tell you where we are all going."

With that, the pods launched and flew off into the sky. They cleared the landing bay and emptied it out completely with trails of smoke. Once they reached a certain altitude, they adjusted and then flew off horizontally. If anyone had chosen to look up at the sky at just the right moments, they would have seen lights flying overhead at speeds they could not even begin to imagine.

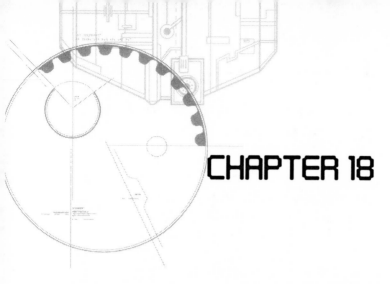

CHAPTER 18

Two hours later, Center-point Energy Plaza Building, Forty Seventh floor

A loud crash filled the room of the empty floor. The door flew off the hinges quite easily and 917 sprinted into the room alone. He briefly looked to the right and to the left. His scanner was beeping rapidly and his HUD was fixed on one point.

Activating proximity sensor, he thought. Turning on the spot, he moved down the aisle way.

"This is 917," He said. "The room seems to be blocking my sensors. I am getting close to the signal and it's in here but I have a really bad feeling about this."

"What do you mean?" His technician asked.

"Like we're running out of time."

He found a set of garbage cans where there was trash on the floor near one of them. Suspecting that was his target even though he could barely detect the readings, 917 jogged over. He dug his hands into a garbage can and shuffled his hands through all of the disposed trash.

"Someone would have definitely have had to scatter this mess in order to hide a…"

917's hands felt something solid. Grasping it, he gently pulled it out and laid it on the floor.

"…bomb," He finished. "Really nasty looking device."

The instant he pulled it out of the garbage can, his sensor instantly found and locked onto the device again. Was it the garbage can or something in the room? There was something that had prevented him from detecting the bomb but there was too much to do.

"Quick," 917 said to his technician. "Scan the garbage can! And see if this floor underwent any changes within the past year! I need to dismantle this thing as soon as possible. Initial observations show there is no timer indicating any form of a countdown. Not a typical explosive."

"917," His technician replied. "I can get you the building's construction records easily. But you got to scan that garbage can as best as you can!"

With his right hand, 917 grabbed the bomb and tried to open it. With his left hand, he placed it on the garbage can.

"Tactile contact confirmed," He said. "Analyzing."

"917 come in."

117's voice added to the transmission.

"This is 917," He examined the device carefully and looked for a way to deactivate it with his right hand. When he was done with his hand analysis of the garbage can, his left hand whipped back to the bomb, "I have found the last bomb signature at the top floor. Attempting to disarm now."

"Understood 917," 117 said. Although it was the last bomb the detected minutes ago, he sounded very frantic. "But why the delay? Did you have any problems?"

"There were some complications evacuating the building," 917 opened a compartment and stared inside so his tech could see as well. Wires and switches were organized in a very chaotic assembly. Typical, he thought grudgingly. "Humans do not really exceed at evacuating when there is a threat until after it has happened. It is an odd observation in several books, movies and real time events. The building is clear though. But something in this room was masking my sensors which prevented me from locating the bomb. Had to search manually."

"Does it have a timer?"

"Nope."

"Then we are on at least on the same track," 117 sighed. "Only a fraction of the explosives that were big enough had a countdown but we have no way of identifying whether the smaller ones will detonate simultaneously or at random times."

There was a loud beep from the canister that 917 held in his hand. A light was now shining bright red as a loud tone began to ring out. Suddenly, it began to beep rapidly and louder.

"917?" 117's concerned voice sounded through 917's head. "Respond, is everything ok? What is your status?"

"I am afraid my answer will not be met with approval," 917 said angrily. "Objective failed."

"917!"

⁎ ⁎ ⁎

Down below, 117 was desperately trying to hear what 917 was saying. But then, there was a loud rumbling close by. 117 immediately ran to the window and looked out. At first there was nothing until bits of debris dropped past the window. Tiny flames and furniture dropped like fireflies. 117 looked up and saw an entire floor of the center-point building blown out. He looked down into the street and scanned for a body but saw nothing resembling 917. Looking back up towards the fiery inferno, he desperately tried to resume communications. Using his eyes and readjusting them, he tried to zoom in. A series of sounds and beeps sounded through his head notified him that other amborgs were also listening in.

"917!!" 117 shouted as he punched the window and it cracked on impact. "Can you hear me?!"

"I hear you!" A voice shouted back in 117's head. "Stop shouting!"

117 continued to gaze at the smoke coming from the blown floor.

"Where are you 917?" 117 asked. "Are you alright?"

"Just hanging here," 917 replied. "If you look at the figure hanging from a bunch of steel beams trying to climb back to the building floor, it is probably me!"

117 continued to focus in on the blast area and scanned with his infrared vision. He could see a lot better now through the haze but was still unable to locate 917.

"Can you spot him Mandy?"

Mandy spoke into his head.

"His technician has got his location... I'm pinpointing the source of his transmission," She muttered rapidly. "Confirmed! Scan and visualize these coordinates!"

Enhancing his scope, 117 zoomed his eyeballs in and saw that 917 was clearly alright. Despite the force of the explosion, 917 looked as if he had just swept through a chimney. His clothes were still intact but severely burned out and he looked as if he was about to fall any moment.

"I have multiple burns and damage all over," 917 reported. "Easily fixed but I need help getting back to the ground first."

"Climb back on to the floor 917!" 117 instructed. 917's head turned and stared in his direction.

"I would really like to 117!" He communicated back, "But the instant I move, this beam will fall apart and down I go!! Actually, that might be the only alternative I got. See if you can get someone nearby to catch me!"

"How are we supposed to do that?"

"Oh figure something out!" 917 said desperately. "We can do things that we were not originally built to do! I would really like to avoid face planting and burying myself into the road from this height!"

117 stared up at 917 as all the other amborgs listening to the transmission began to mumble to themselves. Their immediate responses had flooded his whole head and he had to mute them in order to hear himself think. It felt like a whole gossiping ring had initiated among them as everyone pitched in ideas on what to do. Several suggested leaving him there until another amborg could climb up there. Others suggesting building a net with their

bodies in a last minute team effort. Words spread like wildfire in their heads. In this case, Terabytes. 117 looked up at 917 who let go of one of his hands and tried to reach for the ledge. 917 tried extending his hand but instantly pulled back and grasped onto the beam again as it began to slowly inch downwards.

"Oh boy," 917 muttered in 117's head. "If anyone is close by, I would appreciate it if you guys would get ready to catch me... now!"

117 looked up and flinched in horror. The beam finally gave way and 917 began to plummet down towards the ground. He quickly tried to punch the glass again and it only cracked.

"Hurricane proof glass?" 117 analyzed the cracked surface as he grasped a nearby chair. "Who installs this material in the middle of Texas?"

As he smashed through the window, he leaped down onto the next roof of the building next door. But 917 had seconds and he knew he wouldn't be able to reach him.

"If he gets stuck in the ground, we lose time getting 917 out," 117 thought to himself, "And if we leave 917 behind, we lose one amborg. If we lose amborgs at each location, we will not be able to finish this. It is only the first hurdle."

As gravity did its work, 117 continued to run across the roofs to try and make it to 917 but he was too far.

"All amborgs standby," 1 suddenly responded. "I have him!"

117 saw a figure appear and collide with 917 during the middle of the fall. The two amborgs changed course and flew into the side of the building. The two amborgs both attempted to grasp onto the building but there wasn't anything to clamp onto. It did help slow them down and they continued towards the concrete ground at a safer speed. Both of them bounced off the wall and dropped into the pavement with a thud. Seeing that they were alright, 117 jumped into the street and ran over to them. 1 was lifting himself to his feet and pulling 917 to an upright position as 117 ran up.

"I am in your debt 1," 917 acknowledged while he tested his head rotation and tilted to the left. "I would have very much hated it if I embedded and memorialized myself."

As the three amborgs stood up straight, there were a few explosions in the distance.

"We didn't get them all?!" 1 said with a shocked look.

"Their signatures must have been camouflaged just like the one up there!" 917 said. "Our satellite tracking must not be powerful enough!"

"At this rate," 117 said with concern. "More people will be caught unexpectedly. We will need to expand our search parameters and move quickly!"

"All amborgs to the rally point," 1 said. "Return to the drop-pods for an emergency briefing!"

"We will have to make it quick," 117 said as the three of them began to run. "Mandy, coordinate with all the other technicians. Warn the military that there are bombs that are undetectable by our best scanners!"

"Right 117," Mandy replied.

"It would also be best to order the military not to send civilians down designated evacuation routes. Sweep the areas of where civilians would normally gather during an attack or terrorist situation. It is most likely that the designated safe zone locations are not safe anymore."

"Good point 917," 117 nodded. "But that may cause even more problems."

"Have military commanders change fixed safe zone points," 1 said. "Each commanding officer of the region's battle group should have extensive knowledge of the territory surrounding or on their bases. Civilians will most likely have to be flown out or escorted from the cities to military installations if the urban areas are declared unsafe. Their security is going to have a field day..."

"But it's all we can do," 117 replied. "We have the best technology and we cannot even find a small percentage of the explosives. If the military rejects this strategy, then millions of people will still be in danger. The whole country is now a minefield."

"Talk about playing on legendary difficulty," 917 muttered.

Minutes later, the amborgs were back at the drop-pods. The explosions had stopped and it appeared that Houston was safe.

117 was standing with a map in the center of the massive circle of cybernetic teens.

"Alright, we have managed to complete part of the compilation of riddles," He said. "The military forces at Lackland AFB have secured the area and the rest of the state reports minimal casualties. We have air support now and were successful in disrupting a majority of the explosives. Now we must focus on assisting the location in the second riddle and leave the area and hope it stays defended. And if we correctly assume there is a schedule, we need to move quickly otherwise the rest of the cities will fall."

"Maybe the main ones," 3 inquired. "But what about the small towns and surrounding regions? We cannot abandon those people as well. Their priorities rank equal to those of the bigger cities."

"The fact is 3," 999 replied. "We don't have the resources or sufficient manpower for those regions. We can request for the military to divert Special Forces squads to evacuate. Chances of combat in the small towns and neighborhoods will probably be slim."

"But what happens when we pull the Special Forces away from the regular battalions?" 92 asked. "We will be running into the major cities with recruits straight out of boot camp!"

"For one thing, that should give them the drive they need to fight and defend their home country," 1 responded motioning for 92 to take it down a notch. "Calm down 92. The last thing we need to be doing is arguing amongst ourselves. Keep going Angel."

"If combat spreads to the small towns," 999 explained. "They can take care of the situation. They are the best and statistically could take on most of the amborgs in a firefight. They should have no foreseeable issues because as small teams, they are trained to be cut off from support for long durations of time. As for the regular military and reserve forces in the larger cities, they will have to make do. Whatever city we end up in will have the benefits of our leadership and assistance. But if there is one thing the military is capable of, it is uniformity under pressure. Regardless of if you are specially trained or a fresh conscript."

"The military can handle themselves," 5 nodded in agreement. "They may not exactly train for a world war scenario in their own home country but that is the advantage we have. If we think of it in football terms, we have the home team advantage."

"For how long though I wonder," 117 said with concern. "I don't think the military thought of dealing with masses of giant robots and adrenaline stimmed gangs of criminals as a most likely scenario for military conflict."

"According to military guidelines," 501 said informatively. "That sort of scenario is right below nation-wide cyber-attack."

"Dang," 466 snapped her fingers. "According to a military poll, that section is one of the least read sections in the battle manuals at boot camp. Human thinking is strange."

"Where are you two getting that from?" 117 and everyone turned to stare at the two third group amborgs. "Are you hacking into the military networks?"

"Uhh… no," 501 said quickly with a meek smile.

"Anyway," 117 continued as he highlighted a few bright orange dots on the map. Their location lit up in green. "This is an update of the explosions we just heard. After the bomb that 917 discovered detonated, there have been many reports from law enforcement and military forces across the country."

A few of the amborgs smiles faded and everyone shifted nervously but kept their attention focused on him. 117 looked around grimly at all of them.

"Local law enforcement and regular military forces have declared a nationwide all-out emergency," 117 said. "Local crime and multiple gangs are attacking in and swiftly attempting to eliminate our foothold in our own territory. Many people have evacuated but we are receiving incoming casualties. Martial law has been declared."

"So it really is an all-out war?" One of the 3rd group amborgs asked and 117 nodded.

"An insurgence would probably be the better word," He replied. "What matters now is the next location. Everyone set your coordinates for Seattle."

"Why there I wonder?" 1 asked as he played the riddle again on his own personal channel. "I have no doubts about the answer being right but it feels too remote."

"Maybe it is a challenge to test our endurance," 297 pondered thoughtfully. "Normally when we deploy into the field, it is just to one place only. If I might infer an assumption, we may possibly be circumnavigating across the entire United States."

297 lifted a finger and pointed at the map. First he highlighted where they were located and zoomed the map out so it showed the entire country. A bright green light lit up in Houston Texas with tiny red dots. Several other red lights began to pop across the whole map.

"By sending us here, from our successful deduction of the first riddle," He said, "We have just passed the challenge of speed... barely. Evacuating a large city is exceptionally difficult even under at least a couple of hours. 917's explosion demonstrated that this challenge has risks. This person wants us to potentially fail."

"If he has developed the means to camouflage his weapons," 917 replied. "It only proves we also have a disadvantage."

"Well then we just need to play by his rules," 3 said as she took control of the map and swiped it to the right and zoomed in on Seattle. As they spoke, more red dots began to blink. "Sending us all over the place in order to see if we can fill the proper constraints. We should not forget that the assassin mentions in the video that there will be additional challenges for us at each location. How come there is no such challenge here? Unless we stumbled into a trap."

"It is probably just previews," 5 said. "Paving the way towards opening night. The big question is, do we separate ourselves to all the other cities being attacked or do we concentrate on Seattle? He is forcing us to choose between saving a city full of people or spreading out across the country to save all of them. And... I am counting how many of us there are right now. There hilariously isn't enough of us if we do split up."

117 zoomed the map back out and looked at all the red dots on the major populated cities. 5 was correct. The situation possibly could be better if each amborg separated and went to each of

the dots on the map. However, they had only eighty nine of them and there were over hundreds of dots signaling the calls for help from many people. Plus, they had to assume that there were giant behemoth bots roaming around. Definitely not something an amborg wants to face alone, he thought. Thinking quickly, 117 made his decision.

"To your pods!" He ordered, "All of us will fly to Seattle. We will notify the National Guard troops in that area to concentrate their efforts in other areas close by while we try to find clues. We will provide a full defense of the city simultaneously. Anything that may be a hidden challenge. And also, we will regrettably have to send word to any forces across the nation that an immediate amborg response is not possible."

Everyone acknowledged these orders and scrambled to their pods. A few of them were instantly lifting off and shooting into the distance. 117 climbed into his pod and shut the door. Mandy appeared on the screen looking really exhausted. 117 pushed a button and activated the thrusters and his pod roared to life.

"What's wrong Mandy?" He asked as his pod lifted off and began soaring into the air.

"It doesn't look good David," She replied. "After the Battle of New York, the military and police forces pulled every reserve member they had to active duty. But even with all of that mobilization, we are amazingly outnumbered. High levels of violence and damage are surfacing everywhere and it's flooding all the networks. It's total chaos."

"And in the midst of the crisis," 117 replied. "This man remains hidden as the country falls apart."

"Pretty much the dark ages gone violent," Mandy added. "Police and Military are getting tons of calls for help and in turn, they keep calling us for amborg support. We had to get the A.I.s to help us sift through all the chatter."

"What about the explosives we encountered?"

"Based on the analysis of the ones you were able to disarm," Mandy replied. "They have a very basic design and it is quite simple. However, the way they are cloaked from sensors is difficult. The ones that have detonated are all in random areas and there is little to help us theorize where they are all hidden. We're trying our best to see if there are any common patterns to the layout."

"We also have to assume the rules are not set as well," 117 inferred. "He gave us three riddles. Three locations. But who knows what else there is we may miss. He could be misleading us along the way."

"Don't say that," She warned over the system, "If you let him get in your head or any of the others, you will play right into his hands. It's what he wants to see and show to the public. The failure of the amborgs. I wonder... but that might be his goal. He wants to be able to prove to the world that amborgs can't save everyone. He wants to shatter everyone's belief in you. Don't make yourself vulnerable."

"I will try," 117 sighed. "Stand by Mandy. We are approaching Seattle airspace."

Suddenly, he had an idea. They would have to do it sooner or later so he figured now would be a good time to change their way of thinking.

"This is 117 to all amborgs," He said. "Do not land in one landing zone together in the same spot. We are now going to initiate team protocols. First group amborgs take point and rally your teams. Pick your landing zones and deploy all across the city."

As everyone began confirming and acknowledging the change in protocol, 117 felt his pod rumble and he checked the map. He was thankful for the speeds the deployment pods could reach. With a sudden crash and a thud, the pod landed into the ground. When all become quiet, 117 unstrapped himself. At the same time the door flew open and he leaped out instantly. Gunfire and loud cries rang out the instant he stepped out. Bullets flew by as 117 looked around. There were flames in parts of the city. He walked forward to find a proper vantage point.

We were too late, he thought, the city is under siege. He looked over into the urban district of Seattle and briefly scanned the surrounding area when he received a communication.

"117, this is 18."

"Yes 18? I hear you."

"The twins and I have found something," 18 replied. "We picked a landing zone near some heavy enemy activity and we stumbled upon something we think might be important. Well… 92 stumbled actually. His pod was hit by anti-air fire and it deflected his landing pattern into a warehouse. From what he says, it looks like he fell into what might be considered the enemy command center here in Seattle."

"Understood," 117 nodded, "I am proceeding to your destination. Cover that area in a two block radius with the twins and I will notify the second group to move in."

Before he could finish, he was distracted as a police car exploded to his right. A police officer, weaponless was fighting hand to hand with a couple of gangsters. As 117 ran forward to assist, another amborg leaped in and pulled the gangsters away from the officer. Within seconds, the officer thanked the amborg and went to help a little boy who had hidden behind a dumpster. 117 turned the other way and ran down the street. That is one more that we have rescued, he thought, millions more in need of support.

"Amborg 117 to all amborgs," He transmitted, "The third group will focus on Search and Rescue for civilians and assist local law enforcement in this area. The second group will rally to these coordinates and eliminate any threats but you will only engage in SAR as a secondary objective and create a perimeter. Coordinate with amborg Kiden 18 for details surrounding her approximate location. I want five volunteers to return to their pods and circle the skies and maintain full readiness to fly to the next locations but only on my order. Acknowledge."

Eighty eight short beeps all sounded off in his head. It was slightly painful to listen to the high-pitched noises but 117 smiled gratefully and was glad to hear every one of them acknowledging the commands and sprinted faster.

* * *
** ** **

Downtown Los Angeles: At the same moment

Excessive casualties sustained. Amborg deployment requested. Request delayed until further notice. Assistance unavailable.

"Hey, tell my brother that he'll be fine."

"Don't talk Lewis."

Lewis coughed as he laid in the asphalt. Harrison was sitting next to him exhausted and covered in asphalt. Lewis was bleeding from his stomach but Harrison had placed whatever cloth he could grab hold of and was putting pressure on the wound. Both of them were armed in full police combat gear but they had been practically overwhelmed immediately after learning of a massive assault that had been reported by the military. Harrison had pulled Lewis away from the battle and they found refuge near some abandoned cars.

"I don't think I'll make it through this one," Lewis stared at Harrison and coughed again. His eyelids began to droop as Harrison looked back at his partner with disgust.

"Don't say that touchy feely bullshit kid," He spat out as he wiped the sweat from his forehead, "You're going to make it and you're going to go home in one piece. You are not pulling this on me. I don't even think you're dying."

"No good sir, I feel sleepy."

"Hey, we're partners..." Harrison grasped Lewis' hand tightly, "If you're going to die. It's going be me that'll kill you, you ungrateful little... kid."

All of a sudden, Lewis closed his eyes and went limp. Harrison immediately stopped talking and gaped. Everything in the background, the screams, the shots, and the explosions didn't register anymore. It all became hollow as Harrison gazed at the body in front of him and was at a loss for words. Just then, footsteps attracted his attention. The lone officer looked up into the eyes of a gangster who was grinning mischievously back.

"Do you fear death cop?" He said mockingly as he pointed a gun directly at Harrison's face who was on the verge of tears. Harrison gritted his teeth, held back his feelings and stared determinedly at the bandit standing above him.

"You can't intimidate me. I've always been prepared to die," He spat. Harrison seethed with fury as a teardrop fell from his eye, "Stop mocking me and do it you cheap coward."

"Well now," The gangster showed Harrison a gold toothy smile. "You got some tough attitude there. I think…"

A loud bang interrupted the man and Harrison ducked his head forward. He looked up again and saw his assailant lying flat on his chest. His back was riddled with shrapnel from a shotgun. A very powerful one too. Harrison looked up and saw Chief Bradley standing a few feet behind.

"No one takes cheap shots at my officers. Not on my watch," She snarled. "Especially when they're down."

"Captain Bradley," Harrison said quietly. He felt relieved but at the same time, reverted back to his state of grief as he turned his attention back to Lewis. "He got hit when we moved into the checkpoint. We were falling back to another defensive position but the line left him stranded too far in the front. Got picked off."

Bradley walked over and examined Lewis as well. She laid her gun down and took a deep breath.

"LEWIS!" She bellowed. Her sudden outburst caused Harrison to jump. The noise instantly stopped his tears from flowing. "IF YOU DON'T GET UP THIS INSTANT AND DEFEND THIS CITY WITH THE REST OF MY OFFICERS, I WILL PERSONALLY CRAWL THROUGH THE DEPTHS OF HELL AND KILL YOU MYSELF FOR LEAVING US TO DEAL WITH THIS!!"

Harrison stared at the chief in shock and then down at Lewis' limp body. Nothing happened. Chief Bradley sighed in frustration, inhaled and yelled again.

"SO WAKE UP ALREADY!"

There was a yelp as Lewis shot straight up. Harrison stared wide-eyed at what he saw. It wasn't a second too soon though that his wounded partner's hand shot to his stomach.

"Agh," Lewis groaned as he clenched his stomach. "Why does it feel like someone rear ended me."

"What the…" Harrison gasped. He was completely shocked at what had transpired. "It's a… miracle?"

Bradley scoffed with mere satisfaction as Lewis looked around dazedly. He looked up at Harrison with a scared look.

"Harrison…" He said shakily, "I had the worst nightmare! I was in a bright place, there was a light and then an angel appeared. When I saw her face, it was…Bradley. The angel punched me and sent me falling back to earth… What does it mean?"

Lewis turned his head hopefully but then saw Bradley. He went pale and flinched. He was attempting to crawl away in fear but Harrison kept him still.

"It wasn't a dream," Bradley muttered under her breath. "It means you better cut the crap and get your gun out."

Lewis stared at Harrison.

"It wasn't a dream?" He asked.

"No. I'm just glad you haven't gone yet."

Rolling her eyes, Chief Bradley grabbed her shotgun and clambered back to her feet.

"Angel my boot," She muttered as she marched down the street while the two of them stayed behind.

As she walked to an overturned car, she stopped suddenly and listened. The battle was far away but it wasn't what she had heard. She instantly pointed her shotgun at a second floor window on her right and pulled the trigger.

At first, nothing happened, until seconds later, the window crashed outward as a body fell out of the side of the building. The dead splatter-bug dropped onto the overturned car and fell over onto the ground. Right at Bradley's feet. She pointed the gun at the body and fired again.

"Cheap shots," She sniffed. "They never quit."

"Still as sharp and as sexy as ever."

Without turning around, Bradley stood up straighter and gripped the shotgun tightly. It was the voice she recognized that prompted her to boil with fury.

"You don't want to sneak up on me Mark," She spoke in a forced but calm voice. She pointed the barrel at the dead body, "Otherwise you'll end up like my new friend."

She turned and pivoted on the spot. Pointing the barrel right at 117's grandfather.

"You did always go through new friends really fast," He remarked as he approached slowly with caution. Holding his hands up, he stopped when she pulled the pump-action mechanism back. He remembered the last time he had seen her and already knew what to expect. "I thought I'd drop in to see how you were."

"You sure picked a crazy time to check up on me," She said gesturing at all the destruction around the abandoned street.

She instantly pulled the trigger right as Mark swatted the shotgun barrel away to the right from his face. The blast caused Bradley's arms to ride up at which point, he grasped the tightly onto the gun.

"Before you try that again," He said as the two of them struggled to gain control over the firearm. "There is something you should know."

Bradley brought up her feet and kicked him in the rib. Still maintaining his grip on her shotgun, he keeled forward.

"I see you're wearing your custom steel boots again," He coughed.

He stood back upright and with the help of his arm implants, he pulled Bradley toward him and kissed her right on the mouth. They locked lips for a few seconds but then she instantly stepped back, letting go of the shotgun.

"You sure pick the weirdest times," She snapped as she brought up the back of her hand and wiped her mouth. "Old geezer."

"You're not that far off either," Mark chuckled. "I'm only older by a few years."

"Now ain't the time!" Bradley said holding her hand outwards. She motioned for him to hand over her shotgun back. "I've got a city to defend!"

She turned her head to listen to the surrounding explosions nearby.

"It's never the time for us isn't it?" Mark said with a bit of a whine in his voice. He cocked the gun and placed it firmly in her hand. She then whirled around and took aim but didn't see any targets.

"Well let me see and double check real quick," She said sassily. "The city I swore to uphold and defend as its guardian is currently on fire, being bombed and overrun by people with no decency, respect or honor towards the innocent. I definitely without a doubt think it ISN'T THE TIME!"

"Well what a coincidence!" Mark replied as he pulled his head more over his head as if it had slipped back too far. "That's what I'm here to help you with."

"It's never been this bad before," Bradley said as the two of them began walking slowly down the street. "I had to bring in so many officers off reserve duty. Where the heck is your tin-head grandson? This is one time I'll appreciate his help."

"Last I heard? Off saving the country," Mark replied bluntly, "He sent me here specifically to help him monitor West Coast activities for the man responsible. He also divided my vigilantes all over the place to have eyes and ears everywhere. He really is starting to grow into a natural-born leader and the latest update that the military is keeping from you which he feels obligated to share is that someone has declared an all-out war against the nation."

"Well would it kill him to send some of his buddies here? We're dying out here."

"He's in the middle of something important," Mark shook his head, "If he comes here, it risks doom upon all of us."

"What kind of mission is this?"

"A rescue of society as we know it."

Mark stroked his beard and stood next to her while she contemplated the information he had just given.

"Sounds tough," She muttered. She only could feel a part of what that was like. She was already the head of tons of officers. Most were wounded, injured, missing, or dead.

"You know, it does make me think of…" Mark laughed, "David's behavior reminds me of you when you were on your first real assignment. You put six thugs in the hospital with your bare hands right?"

"I haven't thought about that in years but I do remember how good it felt to kick their sorry asses," Bradley remembered how young she had been and smiled softly. "I hope your grandson is as motivated like I was my first big assignment. If the fate of this country is in his hands, then the whole world is too. No room for failure in this case."

"Absolutely right," Mark replied. "No room at all."

"Well then. In that case, would you like a head-start?" She asked as she jogged ahead. "I'm probably going to get more of them if you fall behind."

"Damn," Mark smirked as he chased after her. "What a woman."

* * *
** ** **

Back in Seattle.

"It is a message written in pencil. How primitive. This guy must really hate us or has a prejudice against modern stencils."

18 showed 117 the paper she held in her hands.

"It looks like a bunch of nonsense," He said. "At first glance to human eyes. Did you read it?"

"I just finished deciphering it actually."

18 held up a piece of paper and scanned it without blinking. Then pointed her finger at the wall. Instantly, her finger lit up like a flashlight. 117, and the rest of 18's team all turned and looked at where the light was projecting. Her finger converted into a mini-projector and displayed the words on the wall.

"I am currently running through all of the words that were written... in pencil," 18 rolled her eyes, the words on the make-shift screen began to disappear and a few of them remained highlighted on the wall. "Most of them," She explained as 14 and 15 glanced towards the roof, "...are complete poetic nonsense but I managed to locate some words with hidden meaning. Feel free to clarify."

The remaining words left on the wall were highlighted for 117 to see. He slowly recited them aloud.

"The youth are a hindrance and must be dealt with...," He read, "Learning shall be destroyed...The Next Generation will die and I will make it so."

"He did not just use star trek as a reference!" 18 muttered angrily. She was one of the few Trekkies among the amborgs. "Even Patrick Stewart would probably hate this guy."

Just then a noise sounded from above and a figure dropped in from the ceiling but none of them moved to retaliate. Amborg 17 straightened up and joined the group.

"Area is clear," She reported, "The enemy presence in Seattle has dropped to fifteen percent. Washington Battle group is ready to send us reinforcements if necessary."

"Tell them to send whatever troops they can spare south to Oregon and California," 117 replied. "Get word to Camp Pendleton. Once the fighting is finished on the West Coast, we can send them east."

"You got it 117."

"Thanks Kathy," 18 said without taking her eyes off the wall. Out of the corner of her eyes, she saw 17 nod and walk a few feet away. 14 and 15 also walked out of the circle and began patrolling the interior. The warehouse was pretty empty and there were a few crates but none of them could see any actual threats.

117 continued reading as 18 continued to flash the message portions on the wall. Several sentences were added after the reference to Star Trek.

"Your soldiers are young and capable," She recited to 117, "Without weapons however, they are vulnerable and waiting to be slaughtered like sheep... Keeping your pets in one location is a mistake... With minimal protection, things are bound to go wrong especially when they won't see me coming."

117 looked at 18 who looked mortified. It didn't take long. The two of them instantly realized what the message was talking about.

"That monster..." she said, "All of those young innocent children. Students. He wants to destroy the best of everything."

"Even the best school in the country," 117 said.

Immediately, 117 immediately sent out a transmission. 14, 15, and 17 rejoined them and 117 led them all out in a rapid pace. The group charged down the street swiftly but began splitting up. Like a pair of monkeys, 14 and 15 went left and climbed a building with lightning speed and disappeared out of sight. 17 nodded to 18 and ducked down an alley to their right.

"All amborgs return to your pods now! We have found a critical obstacle and we are diverting from the original plan!" He ordered as he and 18 ran down another intersection within seconds, "All of you already in your pods, launch and head to the following coordinates I am transmitting! Change mission priorities."

"But 117," 501 responded over the channel, "We have not been able to secure the city. I see a group of people crying for help."

"Do what you can!" 117 replied urgently, "But get to your pod and launch as soon as possible. The police and armed forces here should maintain the situation since we have cleared out a majority of the area but we need to leave now!"

"Understood 117," 501 confirmed the orders, "But there have been problems opening the door to my pod. It has not been functioning properly since we left."

"Try kicking it," 117 leapt over an overturned car and 18 followed suit. "We need to rally now."

"Thanks," 501 said cheerfully, "It worked."

"18," 117 turned to look at her, "Ready a full tactical defensive plan. We are dropping directly into a potential combat zone."

"After today?" 18 shrugged as they stopped at a traffic signal, "One more drop into the flames doesn't seem so intimidating."

"Good luck 18," 117 nodded to her.

"Same to you 117," She said as she sprinted in the opposite direction and the link broke.

"This is 117," David ran over a hedge and headed back towards where he parked his pod, "I am transmitting the full message left by the assassin. And the new target he has included to our list of priorities. Mandy?"

"I got it David," Mandy spoke through the comm channel, "Transmitting recordings to all amborgs. They see what you saw now. David, is it true what his target is?"

"Yes indeed Mandy," 117 punched through a brick wall and instantly found the area where he had landed. "It is a place where I believe you know very well."

"Tom was heading there before Texas," Mandy said. "He had the idea of initiating campus wide evacuation and sending security forces."

"Mandy," 117 said as he slid under a truck. "Get me in touch with Palmer. Whether or not he is authorized, he needs to warn the commanding officers and the regular staff."

"Copy that David," Mandy replied, "I'm getting him for you now and trying to send a communique, priority one. Attack on the Academy imminent. We need to send as many troops as we can."

"Negative Mandy," 117 replied. "There will be panic if we send troops in. Even if it is not a possibility, we may end up leading our army into an ambush. We need to defend the entrances to the grounds save as many people as we can. Tell Palmer to try and get the school's staff on alert. We need as many ships in the air to get the student population out. The Academy is not as large as a city so the amborgs can equally disperse into the area."

"Got it David," Mandy panted as he heard her typing rapidly in the back of his head. "But based on how bad it is, the casualty estimate isn't good."

"Don't worry about the estimates," 117 said as he reached his pod. "Divert all our satellite capabilities to the Academy. Is there any enemy activity?"

"None," Mandy replied. "But they could be hiding their signatures."

"Then we need to hurry," 117 said. "We only have a few hours if I had to make my best guess."

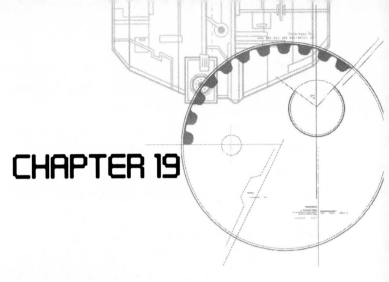

CHAPTER 19

Location: East of Miles City, Montana.
West of Bismarck, North Dakota.
North of Rapid City, South Dakota. South of Canada.

The Academy. A couple of hours prior to Texas & Seattle bombings.

** ** **

"Hey Audrey!"

College sophomore Audrey Wright turned around at the sound of her older brother Thomas' praising tone. She was on her way back to her dorm room from a simulation exercise but for her brother, she definitely wasn't going to get away. He waved a paper at her.

"Did you see the results of your simulation?" He said staring wide eyed with a big grin on his face.

"Of course," She replied. "Why?"

"Why she says," Thomas sighed. "You got the highest score! That's higher than mine when I was a sophomore!"

"It's not a big deal," She shrugged. "You could have done it just like me."

"Nah," Thomas said. "My brain isn't wired for your kind of multi-tasking. You do know that the officers stationed here will want to see you about this right?"

"I've already seen so many officers now that I don't want to even think about it," She said grimly.

"Hey."

Thomas grabbed Audrey by the arm as she turned to leave and held her back.

"I was only trying to tell you that you're doing a great job," Thomas said as the smile faded from his face. "That you're moving on fairly well and I'm glad you're putting your skills to work."

"I don't want anyone seeing me like mom and dad," Audrey sighed as she shook loose from his grip. "Everyone keeps coming up to me to try and say stuff but they don't know what to say. I don't want to talk to anyone and I don't care about education at the moment."

"What do you want?" Thomas asked. "I seriously doubt you want to be held back a year. Considering your grades are the best in your class."

"I'm only a good student because it'll help me leave here faster," Audrey said. "I'll be stuck here getting so much unwanted attention if I decided to go a different direction. I just know that now, I don't want anyone to tell me stuff. I want time to myself."

"You're in the biggest school in the country," Thomas sighed. "You know that might be difficult considering our lineage."

Seeing that he wasn't having an effect on her, Thomas smiled warmly and held up his arms in surrender.

"Alright," He sighed. "I'll let it go this time. I was just really excited to see that you actually did something above and beyond. It almost seemed like you were you again when you first started coming to school here. Mom and Dad would be proud of you."

"Why am I the big deal here?" Audrey asked. "They're proud of you too. Those test results just prove my point. All everyone sees is my mom when I try to excel nowadays and when they talk to me, it hurts."

"I know what you mean," Thomas said as he turned to walk away. "I'm your brother remember? But it's been seven months already and even with the way we've adjusted, we got to go on. This sheet of paper only shows me that you still got the motivation to finish what you started."

As he walked away, Audrey returned to her room. She sat down at her computer and swiped the screen to turn it on. As it booted up, she looked at a portrait of her parents next to the console. Both of them had worn their military uniforms when the picture had been taken. The more she gazed at the photo, she thought for a moment what Thomas had said.

"It's hard moving on," Audrey muttered as she grabbed the picture. "I mean, school is fine but... I feel like it is weird living up to such a strong legacy. And everyone trying to talk with me just makes it feel awkward and sad. When I was kid, I thought this would make me happy. But right now, I'm not sure this is what I want to do anymore... Mom? Dad? What should I do?"

"Is there a problem Cadet Wright? Perhaps a phone call home will help instead of talking to an inanimate photo."

Her computer, now fully activated, lit up and instantly began to talk on its own. Unfazed, she smiled.

"Hi Carter," She replied happily. Her computer flashed its lights and revealed a blank screen with a yellow line across the center. The lines pulsed and created waves as her computer began to speak.

"Talking to ourselves," The electronic voice spoke. "Is that the new social norm these days?"

"It's an old social norm which people have always done for centuries," Audrey replied as she pulled a notebook from a drawer and began flipping through the pages. "Especially when people are troubled which I don't really know how to describe. How are you today?"

Carter flashed his screen and it changed to a bright blue.

"Oh the usual," He said in a casual drone, "Daily weather is fine, the dust in your room is minimal, and my hard-drive is starting to brighten up with all of my software decorations. But I really want to go for a stroll."

"You don't go for a stroll Carter," She said as she found a blank page, grabbed a pen and began to write. "You leap through other systems and zoom through the academy's data signal. Need I remind what you're capable of when I'm not here to keep an eye on you?"

She paused, stopped writing, thought for a bit then went back to scribbling. As she did so, she looked at the screen with a very stern look.

"The last time you did that," She picked up her pen and waved it warningly at the screen, "You shorted out building A's computer system. So until I figure out why they get fried every time you visit, you're staying here with me while I keep running diagnostics."

"For the record and in my own defense. If the school committee will even listen to a lowly AI," Carter replied smugly, "The computer servers in building A are very faulty and was already undergoing difficulties anyway when I happened to pass by."

"Yes but the month before that incident, your other trip to the Dean's office slowed their performance down by sixty percent. That added to the problem a month later. You're lucky that you were dad's A.I. and the Academy has a lot of respect for him and his equipment."

She knew she had hit a mark because the screen suddenly flashed a bright red. Carter definitely had a very good knack of associating colors to whatever he was feeling. Unfortunately it was even more difficult to get a read on him since he was not built like the modern AIs.

"They can't prove that!" Carter spoke indignantly as the red line in the center of the screen bounced all over the place. "I only stopped by to make sure your email made it safely to the correct departments without hitting a firewall."

Aubrey chuckled and shook her finger at the screen. The screen suddenly went still as Carter became silent.

"Uh-uh," Audrey said teasingly, "Actually they DID prove it. All they had to do was scan the interior system of the damaged components and they found residual computations left by a foreign A.I. of your specifications. Specifications built by my father. The only reason why I haven't faced suspension was thanks to my parent's status."

At these words, Carter shut up. He flashed a bright greenish color. Audrey wasn't sure whether it was lime or neon green.

"Well it's hard to camouflage myself when I visit," He muttered electronically through the speaker. Audrey rolled her eyes as he continued, "Your dad designed me to be different from the other computers. He tried to take an old model A.I. and upgrade it. The end result was me. A very corrupt and badly enhanced A.I. that's clumsy and damages systems."

"No," Aubrey said as she finished her journal entry, "Dad designed you to be different because he felt your model was more reliable. As a computer expert for the military, he knew your specs back and forth and decided to make you one of a kind. He believed that you could do great things when he gave you to me as a birthday gift too. Every time I would ask about you, my dad would always praise you and say what great progress you were making whenever he taught you how to socialize like a living person. So be grateful for how you are now. Forgetting about the damage you've done so far up to now that is."

"I just don't understand why I should be confined when I was originally designed to adapt to the world before me. I admit, it has been a wonderful three years since I was put under your care but it's really disappointing," Carter said flatly, "I mean, my time could be spent better than monitoring your computer. Speaking of which, when will you finish the final designs for my visual representation?"

Aubrey closed her notebook and put it away. She had just begun work on creating a visual representation for Carter last week but there had been some slight complications.

"I'll finish it when I can Carter," Said Audrey, "Why are you in such a hurry to get your own body? It's not even a body for that matter, it's just a hologram of a body that modern AIs use."

"I just thought that it would allow you more distraction from..."

"I know Carter," She interrupted. "I've just... it hasn't really been motivating for me recently."

"I understand. Pardon me for almost bringing it up," Carter said flashing light pale blue. "I just figured you might be bored speaking to a squiggly line on a computer all day."

"Well unfortunately," She said patting the top of the screen with her hand, "I can't finish it until I get approval from the lab. It's really hard to find equipment for your model since there aren't that many of your type in service. You were custom retro-fit so it has to be just right otherwise you might go from a tall blond to a short dimply red head. If I did have it though, I could finish it in no time and you could design yourself however you like. The other option is to keep waiting patiently for my request from A.I. Industries for the equipment but they keep to themselves a lot when it comes to sharing information. I hear that the female A.I.'s at Amborg Industries are very attractive and they always love meeting new guys. I mean... foreign computer programs of a specific nature."

"I have told you already Miss Wright," Carter flashed Orange on his screen, "I will only give the AIs at Amborg Industries a reason to hate the old generation line of technology. They wouldn't like my presence to crap all over their image. Besides, why should I work there when I serve no one but you and your immediate family members or friends?"

"Aww. No one appreciates that bit of sentiment more than me," Audrey chuckled. "You'll always be the sweetest A.I. I know. Unless... someone invented a better version of you. Then I wouldn't mind tossing you in the garbage."

"I know that was a joke but if it weren't for the confines of this monitor, I'd throw something at you."

"Looks like you'll just have to talk me to death," Audrey said smiling at the screen. "Learn to take jokes like a program."

Their conversation was interrupted when a beeping sound went off overhead. A voice over the P.A. in her room spoke.

"Sophomore Audrey Wright," One of the secretaries announced. "Please report to Building one dash A: Military Administration and Tactical Science Offices. Someone will be there to see you shortly."

Audrey sighed, stood up and adjusted her uniform so it was straight and presentable. As she shut down the computer and straightened out her things, she bid a quick farewell to Carter.

"Oh boy," She sighed, "I wonder what happened now... Hence I am summoned to face the legends of old and will be persuaded again to take part in the campaign of upholding my heritage."

"Pure poetry ma'am," Carter blinked a few times as his screen powered down, "Would you like me to take notes and record your wise words of dissent against the chain of command? It would be a great rallying cry to the rebels of this country."

"Stamp date and time. The usual please," She said sarcastically and walked out of the room.

"Your sarcasm is noted Miss Wright," Carter replied as the door shut. "I'll be here. Stuck in the same place..."

"Of course Carter," Audrey winked at the screen before closing the door. "Where else are you going to go?"

The campus was bustling with activity when Audrey took the elevator down to the ground floor. As she stepped outside, she heard many of her friends greeting her. Briefly saying a fast greeting, she made her way across campus. However, Audrey couldn't help but feel that something was wrong. To get to building one, she had to walk by one of the security entrances but the guards stationed there weren't as friendly as they were before. Or rather, that's what she thought. Instead of the usual greeting, the guard nodded and motioned for her to move quickly. As soon as she was out of earshot, she failed to hear the order that followed out of the radio set. An order that had never been uttered on the grounds before. As she walked away, she failed to notice a group of transports approaching the entrance.

But she hadn't heard it so her short walk continued. What she also noticed was that the skies were very clear which was unusual. Normally there were birds in the air. Today however, she couldn't hear them singing at all. What she did hear was the roar of an engine which caused her to look up with a startled look. A large aircraft flew overhead and she followed it with her eyes. A few other students nearby also had looked up but they didn't think much of it. Before the craft flew out of view, she saw the rectangular shapes and the logo on the underbelly.

"A transport craft at this time of day?" She wondered. Those were the transports that normally shipped troops across certain distances. Couldn't match the deployment pods from Amborg Industries but they could definitely get the job done. "New students probably," she muttered and kept going.

She had never been more wrong though. As she approached building one, she stopped and took one last glance at the courtyard and saw something else that was puzzling. Four soldiers were walking around the corner and quick-marching into the center. A uniformed officer came out from behind the pillar and greeted them. It was one of the commanders. She saw her logistics professor point once in a direction behind the soldiers and then to the left. All of them nodded and they all split up and took positions in different parts of the courtyard. Audrey wasn't the only one baffled. Many other students saw the soldiers with confused looks but kept to their business. If she had been just a few minutes slower, she thought, maybe she could have stopped at the right time to ask what was going on. However, she remembered her appointment and quickly ran inside.

Minutes later, she was waiting in the lobby of the building.

"Sophomore Audrey Wright."

Audrey quickly stood up when her name was called, straightened her back and placed her hands at her side. One of the secretaries walked up, acknowledged her, and led her to another room. Something caught her eye and she glanced to the right and noted someone she had never seen before. With her vision, she made out the name, Palmer T, on the man's uniform before walking into the other room. New military instructor, Audrey guessed as she sat down in a seat in the middle of the office.

"You were summoned here because the school board has recommended you for a commendation. You performed excellently in the military exercise earlier today, Cadet," The officer read a file and looked up at her. She nodded quietly and the officer adjusted his glasses and read on, "Excellent combat scores that we haven't seen for over fourteen years, class grades... all perfect, medical tests all green despite what happened months ago...what else?"

Audrey smiled, nodded again and waited for the question she knew he was about to ask. The officer closed the file and smiled back.

"Well Miss Wright, it would appear that everything in your file says that you qualify and can pursue whatever job you want in the military or as a civilian in a high level government position," He said. "However that is partially why I called you here."

"Yes sir," She said calmly. She was beginning to understand where this was going. "I assumed that that would be the case."

"You definitely are a model student," The man said, "The first thing we'd like to ask you is…"

"I'll take it from here captain."

The officer looked, stood up and immediately saluted. Audrey, confused, turned to see who had interrupted. She instantly shot out of her seat and saluted as well when she recognized who it was but then awkwardly dropped her hand remembering she wasn't actually a member of the military.

"At ease, you two," The woman walked in saluting the two of them. "Captain, I'd like to speak to Cadet Wright alone please. May I borrow your room for a minute?"

He nodded, uttered a quick 'yes ma'am' and immediately walked out. Audrey almost had the urge to sigh in relief. She was looking at one of the most decorated officers in the military. Her mother had worked alongside this woman for a long time.

"Were you the one that wanted to see me Colonel?" She asked as the Colonel took a seat and perused the file. The woman stared back and smiled.

"Yes Audrey," She nodded, "I take it your file was already read back to you. Notice any surprises or concerns?"

Audrey shook her head but the stern look from the Colonel stopped her and she slowly nodded nervously. Biting her lower lip, she looked casually out the window, thought about what she wanted to say next and then opened her mouth but then stopped.

"I am referring to your sudden and surprising performance in that last combat exercise earlier," The colonel picked the file up from the table. "Your maneuver surprised well… all of the staff recording the simulation. I wasn't however."

"Colonel? I don't understand," Audrey said nervously. The colonel began to chuckle and held the file to her chest.

"The reason why I wasn't surprised," She tapped Audrey's forehead, "…is because I know you've been paying attention in my classes. Just like your mother used to. You scored perfectly in all of your testing and studies even after all you and your brother have been through. I expected some problems to occur but it would seem that you are coping well."

"Permission to speak freely?"

"For my oldest friend's daughter? Of course," The colonel smiled.

"You aren't going to ask me if I should enlist in the military?"

"No," The colonel sighed. "I believe too many people have pestered you about your career options enough."

She stepped around the desk and had Audrey follow her to the window.

"Every student comes here as a civilian," She explained. "You and your brother both did and definitely proved to many people here that you are your parent's children. With the way I've watched Thomas, it's clear he wants to pursue your father's line of work. But he pretty much camouflaged your progress with his optimistic views for seven months. It would appear you aren't the person I saw come to this school with such a bright gleaming expression anymore. It has come to the attention of most of my staff and the other professors here that you have lost the motivation to go the highest point reachable."

"I'm sorry Colonel," Audrey admitted it. She couldn't lie to a woman her mother trusted. "I just have a lot to think about. I always find myself questioning myself whenever my parents are brought up. Some days I feel like I want to do more but other times I want to just stick to the corner of the room and never be noticed."

"You're young," The colonel replied. "Lots of others go through this phase too. I can't really be too supportive otherwise there are some who will consider it as favoritism. Also I haven't had to go through what happened with you so I'm afraid my knowledge of the subject is limiting."

"Even limited knowledge from the right people helps," Audrey replied. "I think."

"Well," The Colonel nodded as the sun shined brightly through the curtains. "I just wanted to check up on you. Had to do it in a setting where it wouldn't look suspicious. I am in my uniform more days than I can count and being the head of the military forces on school ground, I hardly have time to get away. I know I should have done this many more times over the last few months but..."

"With all due respect ma'am," Audrey replied. "Thank you. I'm sorry I haven't been putting more consideration towards what I wanted to do lately."

"From an academic perspective," The Colonel said. "I will say that is an acceptable answer. From a military perspective, you've got a lot of fight in you that would definitely make me swear you in right now. As your mother's friend, I wouldn't hold it past you if you felt this way. You take as much time as you need."

"I don't suppose you know if A.I. Industries is hiring?" Audrey asked.

"I'll see if Dr. Kendrick will take my calls."

The two women suddenly broke into quiet fits of laughter.

Later Audrey looked over the list of career choices on a sheet of paper as she left the building. All her life, she knew that she would go to the Academy for her higher education but after a year, she realized that she didn't know what she wanted to do specifically. She wondered what her father would say now that her schooling was halfway done. He always knew how to make her see the right way but now, there wasn't really much of an option. The Academy wanted every student to push for settling on their education choices as soon as possible. But for her, the timing was just off. Audrey quickly looked at her watch and realized it was time for lunch.

Later, she sat in the cafeteria with the rest of her dorm mates. As they chattered away, she kept thinking about what Thomas and the Colonel had said to her earlier. Trying to focus on other stuff, Audrey looked up at one her friends and watched what he was doing. Her fellow sophomore, Joey, was watching a small television screen which he held in his arms.

"Joey? What's that you're watching?" Audrey asked which made him huddle the screen to his chest tightly. He looked up, pushed his glasses up the rim of his nose and replied.

"Oh just some private communiques that the science lab intercepted. We think it's a really awesome video."

He held the screen up for her to see. Audrey looked and saw the emblem of Amborg Industries. Choking on her food, she leaned forward and dropped to a whisper.

"What are you doing?!"

If there was one thing that Audrey knew, the science lab had a reputation for 'accidently' achieving access to classified material among government databases.

"You could get in big trouble Joey for looking at that!" She whispered frantically. "Any material from A.I. Industries is especially monitored! They're probably looking for this information now and are this close to locking you out!"

"What's the big deal?" Joey replied, "When I see something highly encrypted, I got to take a peek. Don't worry, no one will know."

Sarah looked at her screen as it continued to play. She looked up at Mandy with a questioning look.

"With that boy's attitude," She remarked. "We kind of know now... Is there a reason why the story isn't centered on 117 now?"

"You'll see," Mandy replied pointing down at the screen. "As someone who knows the ending, you have no idea how hard it is to contain the spoilers."

"As long you don't get into trouble..." Audrey took a bite out of her sandwich and began to chew really fast as Joey returned a smile.

"Don't worry, I don't think the material is controversial at all," He said. "Even if Dr. Kendrick keeps all materials from A.I. industries classified. This video clip doesn't seem so interesting. All it shows is this weird warehouse fight or something. Check it out. Looks like the amborgs are fighting something."

"That doesn't sound classified," Audrey spoke suspiciously with her mouth full.

"They're fighting some sort of weird giant robot…"

"Never mind, I take that back."

Things were starting to really concern her. Security was a bit more uptight than usual. The staff of the Academy looked slightly more nervous than ever. A.I. Industries classified material intercepted by Joey. Looking around to make sure no one could hear her, she turned to the rest of her friends and asked a question.

"Hey do you guys notice anything strange going on?"

Her question had prompted the exact reactions she was hoping for. The entire table instantly became quiet as everyone leaned and huddled closer. One of the girls quickly spoke first.

"Well, there's a group of soldiers patrolling the outside of the mechanical building complex," She said shrugging her shoulders, "But I figured that they were the new day watch or something. I only noticed because someone in one of the outdoor automobile class was talking about it."

"Something is definitely wrong," Audrey nodded in agreement. "I mean, why send soldiers to various parts of the campus?"

"It could be a training exercise," One of the guys piped up talking with his mouth full. The student next to him nodded in agreement, "They have unscheduled training ops for regular military personnel undergoing urban combat training. Some of the buildings are even used to practice tactics and training in the events of real potential battle scenario."

Everyone else began nodding in agreement but Audrey wasn't convinced. She looked up and noticed one of the school's professors speaking to a soldier. She bid her colleagues a quick farewell and pretended to get in line for more food. As she got closer, she could make out the hushed tones.

"Professor, orders are orders," The soldier was whispering silently as he gripped the shoulder strap. His weapon was hung tightly on the man's back but it looked as if he was ready to whip around and start shooting. "We need to get you out. I technically shouldn't be here in full view of everyone but they told me you'd be here and I was the only one near you to be able to talk to you."

"Alright alright!" The old man said quietly as he began walking away. "Just promise to get the students, all of them, away. The children can't stay here. I will not leave before them. Take that up with your superiors if you have to but I will stay here and fight for them."

"We'll try sir. Evacuation will be commencing soon and we will attempt to get as many people off-campus in order to explain. WE explain now and panic will ensue from those undisciplined from the military classes here. Until they figure out how to disclose this to the students, we need to begin escorting everyone to a safe location."

The soldier stopped. He quickly looked right then turned and looked and saw Audrey staring. She immediately looked away. She got out of line and ducked away. That's it, she thought, something is terribly wrong. Audrey immediately left the cafeteria and ran to look for her brother. If there was going to be trouble, Thomas was someone she needed to check on...fast.

She sped walked across campus to where she knew her brother would be. He wasn't at his class as usual which worried her. Over the next hour and a half, she roamed the campus until finally, she went to where the senior dormitory was and kept a casual face. Obviously, the soldiers didn't want to alarm any of the students and were planning a quiet evacuation so she put on a less than casual show. She practically leaped up the stairs to the building but before she could open the door, someone called her.

"Hey sis, what's up?"

She whirled around instantly and practically leapt into Thomas' arms. Taken aback, he chuckled slightly as he struggled to stand firm and not fall back down the stairs.

"You're ok!" She exclaimed which only made him let out a baffled grunt.

"Should I not be ok?" He asked as he began to laugh and let her go. "Since when are you so huggable? What's wrong? Something up?"

"Yes!" She said in hushed tone, "I think the campus is going to be attacked."

"SHH!"

"Wait you knew?!"

Thomas lifted his hand and pushed her to the side of the entrance. The two of them became silent as a group of soldiers marched past. Audrey instantly became worried. The fact that her brother was in line with whatever was happening began to scare her.

"Yes I did," He said. "A lot of the seniors with military majors were warned and believe it or not, they were asking for volunteers to take up defensive posts to help assist in the evacuation."

"Ok I get there's a giant evacuation," Audrey exclaimed. "But from what? Please tell me you didn't volunteer for a post! Because we're not military. Not yet!"

"They asked me because of our parents," Thomas replied. "Believe it or not, they offered to make us part of the first priority evacuees. THAT was what I turned down. I said I would stay and fight. Our parents' achievements was no reason for them to place our needs above that of our friends and fellow classmates."

"But who would risk an attack on the Academy?" Audrey asked. "You'd need an army to even think of taking a quarter of the grounds."

"I'm afraid there is an army based on recent intelligence."

"How can you be so calm?"

"For one reason," Thomas said with a shrug. "The fact that the academy hasn't been attacked before is already a good enough reason. Whoever has the guts to attack here will need an army like you just told me. It's never going to work successfully if they're trying to take the ground. But I know for a fact that there will be an attack. There are casualty estimates which we don't want to take the chance. You will be evacuated with the transport ships but the main focus is to get the non-military students, civilians and younger people away."

"No!" Audrey said. "I'm staying with you! I'll ask them to get me to stay too."

"Senior students only!" Thomas replied. "They would never allow you or any other dare devils risk their lives!"

"But you'll be left behind."

Her last sentence caught Thomas off-guard. Evidently he had just realized that he wouldn't be going with her. Audrey took in all that she had just heard and breathed slowly. She made an attempt to smile but there was something still worrying her. Before she could continue with her questions, a loud noise sounded across campus, interrupting her thoughts. She had heard it before as a freshman when she came on campus for orientation and had been told what it meant. Now, she was hearing it again and she trembled. It was a siren. The kind used long ago to signal an attack. Thomas was looking towards the noise as well. He wasn't smiling anymore.

"Ok..." He muttered. "That is definitely not the plan. That's not the evacuation signal we determined for the campus and it's a half hour early. It's the air raid signal."

He instantly turned to Audrey and grabbed her shoulders.

"Listen!" He said as several alarmed students were beginning to move. He stared desperately into Audrey's eyes. "I guess the plan's changed! But you listen to me! Get with the rest of your dorm and get out of here ASAP! I'm going to find my assigned team! If the worst should happen though, you go to the nearest armory and dig in and hide! Got it?"

Without a word, Audrey nodded and Thomas smiled.

"Thatta girl," He said as he ran off.

The door to the building flew open as more seniors were pouring out as fast as they could. Many of them were following the path Thomas took while others ran in other directions. Audrey turned and ran back towards her dormitory as the alarm kept ringing in the air.

"Attention all students. Remain calm. Campus wide evacuation underway. Transport ships will be arriving to bring you somewhere safe. This is not a drill. Attack imminent. Proceed to your designated evacuation zone and standby for immediate relocation to a safe zone."

The voice of the automatic evacuation recording was loud and clear. Audrey ran towards the flow of clamoring students and proceeded on the way to the launch pads. It was literally a miniature airport for pilots that was located half a mile from the classrooms. Since the runway was not the closest place to run to, all the students ran to some hallways that connected and led to some old helicopter pads. The entrance to the launch pad Audrey had entered was swarming as the transports landed on the strips of asphalt and lifted off again and again. Audrey looked ahead of the swarm and saw Joey and the rest of her classmates. She sidled in between people and eventually joined up with them. At the end of the tunnel, the corridor split into eight other tunnels leading to a different launch pad. From what she could see, they were halfway to the entrance that her dorm mates had wandered towards.

"Oh man, this is scary," Joey said meekly, "You think that I shouldn't have watched those classified videos? Are they going to get me?"

Audrey placed a hand on his shoulder. She couldn't help but laugh reassuringly at Joey's paranoia.

"No," She said smiling, "This is something else. We'll be fine. We just need to wait a bit longer and we'll be out of here."

As soon as she said these words, a loud whoosh occurred and everyone in the tunnel looked up. The sun was beginning to set. It had roughly been a couple of hours since her appointment with the colonel. Now the afternoon was slowly vanishing as orange light bathed the area. Audrey then saw a transport come in and land at one of the pads. Soon enough, the line of people began moving forward. However, after a few minutes, they stopped as a soldier at the end of the tunnel began to wave and yell.

"Transport's full! Take it away!"

"What?!" Someone nearby yelled in disbelief, "We've barely moved!"

He was quite right. Audrey looked around and saw many of the students show signs of concern. However before anyone could protest, they heard a loud boom.

"LOOK UP THERE!"

Everyone looked up when they heard the student scream and saw a black speck fly across the sky. With lightning speed, something dropped from that speck and landed with a crash in the field outside the tunnel.

"What the hell is that?!" Someone yelled in the middle of all the panicked tones. Audrey looked and saw a tall figure stand up and immediately walk forward, gesture to a few soldiers and disappear out of sight.

"Is that an amborg?" Joey asked with a terrified stare. Someone from the crowd answered, "Yes it is! I saw it wearing a number!"

More booms came from the sky as everyone looked back up to the sky again. More specks were falling from the sky like meteors. Several of them landed in different parts of the campus but they could all hear loud thuds echoing across the ground. Audrey could see more tall figures rise up in the distance from where they landed and leaping instantly out of sight like magic.

"Why would amborgs be dropping here?!"

Audrey already knew the answer before it was even asked.

"Because this attack is worse than we thought," She said breathing slowly to whoever listened. "What if it isn't an attack on the Academy? What if we're being herded right into a kill zone?"

"We're sitting ducks," Joey replied while a few other of the students listened. "Like animals waiting to be slaughtered."

"We don't know that!"

"Let's just wait for the next transport!"

A few fireballs flew into the air as an explosion was heard in the distance. This made several students stare in shock as they attempted to figure what was destroyed from the plume of smoke rising upwards. Automatic gunfire instantly began sounding off in the distance.

A whooshing noise occurred and everyone looked up to see the transport at their launch pad rise slowly up into the air. Audrey watched as the transport began to lift higher and higher until there was a blinding flash of light that ripped right through one of the engines. Audrey watched in horror as the exhaust of the transport blew out and burst into flames. The ship moaned and began to lose altitude. The destroyed engine began to whine and power down. Unable to maintain a level pitch. It plunged out of the sky and headed straight for the tunnel. Right for the long line of gaping students. Realizing how helpless they were, Audrey instantly took a deep breath.

"RUN!" She yelled as loud as she could as the falling wreckage made contact with the corridor several meters ahead.

Everyone in front of her was scrambling to run the opposite direction and she followed suit. A loud tremor and force sent Audrey staggering towards the ground but she maintained a steady sprint while chasing after several retreating students. Dust, concrete, and dirt flew over her head. Another explosion detonated from behind her and a larger shockwave pushed her to the ground. Her ears began ringing and she instantly felt dizziness flow through her head. She opened her eyes and saw dust in the air. Squinting through the smoke, she attempted to try and find Joey. Luckily, he had landed a few feet in front of her and she crawled to his side.

"Joey! Get up! We got to go!" She yelled but her own voice was muffled. Shaking her head, she tried to focus and get her senses back up to speed. Joey lifted his head and pushed himself to a sitting position. He appeared to be alright but then fidgeted as a he realized there was a dead body next to him. Audrey put her hand on his shoulder and shut her eyes and urged that they move away from the crushed student. As they crawled further up the hall, a loud noise made them stop in their tracks.

Both of their attention was diverted to a commotion outside. There was a loud clanging, crashing and sound of metal ringing outside. Listening carefully, they heard some loud whirring thrown into the mix.

"Those are hydraulics," Joey breathed. "On something big too."

"Oh my god, what is that?" Audrey said pointing.

Outside, there was a tall figure flying to the ground. It was an amborg. It was kneeling on the ground and preparing to leap at something.

"There's the something huge," Joey said.

A massive robot began to march towards the amborg. As the two of them peered through the cracked glass, they could hear the loud whirring from the hydraulics. At least there was a machine to put the sounds too.

Audrey watched as the cybernetic teenager didn't wait another second and sprung towards the massive machine. Audrey had never seen anything like it before. She didn't have to ask Joey if he had stumbled upon something as big as that before. The look on his face told her everything. They saw the amborg attempt to punch the giant in what looked like the head. There was a loud bang as their fist made contact.

The robot, unfazed, smacked the amborg so hard in midair as it was falling back to the ground, they flew and hit the window right where Joey and Audrey were watching. Gaping, Audrey saw the amborg fall onto its back. She saw that it was a male amborg. He turned its head towards her and noticed them. Gulping, Audrey and Joey saw the scars and the signs of battle fatigue over the boy's face. She saw the number 35 etched on his chest and the bracelet on his arm flashed. She couldn't hear the voice coming out of the bracelet but the amborg was also mouthing a single word at them.

"Run!" Audrey made out. Right after the amborg gave this command, the robot grabbed him by the leg, threw him into the field, charged forward and with an almighty crash, stomped the helpless figure right into the ground. Horrified, Audrey grabbed Joey and the two of them sprinted out of the tunnel. Debris continued to fall from the ceiling as the tunnel structure deteriorated. Keeping their hands above their heads as they ran, the two of them along with a few stragglers successfully made it outside.

Upon exiting the tunnel, there was no time to stop and ponder the situation. Explosions immediately began to hit all around. Choosing a random direction, Audrey shoved Joey and the two of them ran into the middle of the chaos. The battle was everywhere. Surrounding them.

"What do we do?!" Joey turned and watched as a soldier was hit in the back of the head with a bullet. The soldier collapsed and did not get up. Thinking quickly, Audrey had to find a way to regroup as many others as they could.

"Everyone! Follow me to the armory!" She bellowed as loud as she could. A handful of fleeing cadets turned and immediately began to follow.

She wasn't sure how many people had heard. All she knew was they had to get out of the firefight and quickly get to the nearest building. Perhaps some soldiers would be able to cover them. Hopefully the enemy wouldn't notice their group moving towards one spot. The last thing they needed was attention.

Audrey was leading the group towards the building ahead when an explosion ruptured a pillar close by causing it to fall towards a few soldiers. Her party stopped in their tracks as they heard the tall structure crumbling. Moments before they were crushed however, an amborg instantly leapt towards the pillar and knocked it away. The broken pillar flew in another direction and made contact with a group of enemy troops. Or that's what they looked like to Audrey. She wasn't sure who was fighting who. The recipients of the flying pillar were instantly pulverized from what she saw which made every cadet in the vicinity gape in stunned silence.

"That pillar was over fifty tons..." Someone said meekly. Audrey also stared in complete terror. It wasn't until a rocket flew a few feet away from her face that she remembered that they were still standing in the middle of a battlefield. "RUN! Let's go this way!"

As they continued through the middle of the firefight, objects kept flying over their heads.

"You'd think there be more explosions! But there's a ton of stuff being thrown around instead!"

One of the students dived in order to avoid a large brick slab. It smashed into a wall sending chunks of rock spraying everywhere.

"It's a whole new type of battlefield nowadays..." Audrey muttered as they continued. "Amborgs have a very unique way of fighting."

Along the way, they turned off of the main path to avoid the majority of the fighting. As they ran on one of the side paths which took them in between some buildings for cover. The noise had faded which made them less tense but they were still moving with a sense of urgency as quietly as possible. Nothing remotely happened until they walked past a nearby courtyard near some obelisks.

"Watch out!" One of the girls in the back suddenly screamed. Everyone stopped immediately as something huge crashed into the ground in front of them, blocking the way.

"Ack... take this! Garg! Junkhead!"

Audrey stared as an amborg, pinned to the ground was punching upward into a robot drone's face plate. The fight had stopped everyone in their tracks. The lens allowing the drone to see shattered and sent sparks shooting out everywhere. Groaning, the drone flailed its arms and continued punching the amborg lying on the ground who curled his legs and prepared to spring them outward. With an almighty kick, the drone flew off up into the air and was intercepted by another amborg who intercepted it. The cadets all watched as the second amborg in midair kicked the drone directly in the chest and sent it flying straight down to the ground.

"Thanks a lot," The amborg's bracelet flashed. "Get to cover now! We are losing ground."

"What about you?!" Audrey exclaimed as a loud whistling noise flew over their heads. "What do you mean we're losing ground?!"

"There is insufficient time miss," The amborg replied hastily, "Proceed straight to cover before this part of campus is overrun. Please go inside somewhere where there have been no external explosions on the building infrastructure. You will fare a better rate of survival in the basements."

Without another word, the amborg leaped away and out of sight. Weren't they supposed to help protect us? Audrey stared in shock. What's going on? Were they really losing the fight?

"Keep moving!" Someone yelled and the small group instantly began to make their way to the nearest armory.

Minutes later, Audrey and her party found the nearest building and made their way inside. Everyone crouched against the walls and huddled gasping for air while Audrey pulled the door shut and engaged the locks. Joey rushed to one of the security panels and began to initiate emergency lockdown procedures. The glass windows instantly changed into a dark tinted material. They could see outside but no one could look in. A loud clasping noise indicated that the door was secure.

"We're safe for now," Audrey muttered. She turned to face the group of people still alive and did a head count. Including Joey and herself, there were fourteen of them in total.

"We can't stay here Audrey," Joey whispered as she kneeled down next to him, "We need to get to the weapon lockers."

"I know," She replied firmly, "If my brother made it, he should be here. The armory in the basement here is the closest to the senior dorm rooms. We got to get downstairs."

"I'll go in front," One of the girls stood up raising her hand. Audrey nodded, "Ok. Everyone, file up and follow... what's your name?"

"Deliza," The girl replied.

"Everyone file in behind Deliza. Ready?"

Everyone scrambled into a straight line and hunched over as they heard a muffled explosion occur outside.

"We're heading for the armory. There is a possible group of friendlies inside," Audrey spoke aloud so everyone heard. "I'm operating under the hopes that everyone here has taken the security class and knows how to handle the weapons they have here for emergencies. Without weapons, we're sitting ducks so we need to move as quickly as possible. It's ok to be scared but we need to be brave so let's do this. Everyone ready?"

She looked to the front of the line and to the back. Everyone nodded and held up a thumbs up.

"Then let's go. Deliza, move when you're ready."

"Gotcha," Deliza nodded and held up a fist. Everyone watched silently as the noise outside filled the air until...

"Go!"

The group went down the hallway, took a right turn and then a left. No one spoke but kept their eyes ahead. The people in the back checked to make sure they weren't being followed. Soon, they reached the door to the staircase when Deliza's hand went up. She curled a fist signaling all of them to stop. Immediately after stopping, she knelt down with her fist still in the air. Everyone followed suit and knelt down to the ground. Audrey quickly crouched and sped walked up to the front.

"What is it?" Audrey leaned closer to Deliza and whispered, "Do you hear something?"

"It's coming from down the hall to our left," The redhead replied quietly. "We might have company."

Audrey listened carefully and heard thuds coming from the direction Deliza was pointing. Someone was definitely showing signs of trying to break in.

"Well," She said patting Deliza on the shoulder sympathetically. "Luckily, the staircase is in front of us. Whatever is going on that way," Audrey pointed, "...isn't worth investigating unless if we have weapons or something to fight back with."

All of them silently waited and then Deliza motioned the all-clear sign. She walked up and pushed the door open as quietly as possible. Holding it open, everyone moved forward and moved into the staircase. When they had all made it inside, Audrey signaled to Joey.

"Joey, take point and lead everyone down the stairs," She instructed. He nodded and moved down a few steps to the front. Audrey turned to Deliza and whispered, "Are you ok taking the back? Keeping an eye out for intruders?"

"No problem. Just get everyone down there as fast as you can. At the first sign of trouble, I'll catch up."

"Even if we do get weapons, we need a way to exit this place. Including the way we came in, there are four exits to this building. We may have to work our way back to the entrance we came in if it has to be like that."

"Don't worry, I got it," Deliza said nodding in understanding, "They won't notice me."

Audrey couldn't help but admire Deliza's confidence. As she stepped down the stairs, she had to move fast. Realizing how fast the group had moved ahead, she chose to forget about stealth and ran normally down the concrete steps. Reaching the basement level, she silently opened the door and heard voices the moment she stepped through.

"Please! We're only trying to get weapons for safety!"

Her group had appeared to be stuck. They looked even more scared than before when they were outside.

"Are you crazy?!" Someone from inside the armory door spoke back, "Coming here may have alerted the enemy of our hiding place."

"Open the door and let us in! We'll die if we don't stay with you."

Audrey sprinted up to the group and found Joey arguing with the sealed door. He began breathing in relief when she walked up.

"Thank god Audrey. They won't let us in," Joey said looking over his shoulder and scanning the hall.

"It's ok. Let me try and talk to them."

Audrey knocked on the door once and spoke.

"Please, we need your help," She asked softly. "Open the door and let us in."

"How do we know this isn't a trick?" The same voice Joey argued with spoke again, "You could be an enemy programmed or trained to sound like one of the school personnel or whatever. Or someone might be forcing you to say you're friendlies and make us lower our guard."

"I can assure you it isn't a trick," Audrey spoke calmly, "If you let us in, you'll have reinforcements. Plus, you won't have the deaths of all of us on your conscience."

"I don't believe you," The door then became silent a moment before it spoke again, "We got people in here too and we're not letting anything come in to slaughter us."

Taking a deep breath, Audrey thought for a moment. There was one last option she could think of. It was their last chance.

"Is my brother in there?" She asked through the door. "Senior Thomas Wright? Is he alive?"

"Thomas?" Said the same person's voice. "Who's asking?"

"For heaven's sake, it's his sister, Audrey," She brought a hand up and wiped the sweat off her forehead, "If he's in there, have him talk to me. He'll vouch for me."

"Hey O'Hara. What's going on? I heard my name."

Another voice from behind the door joined the conversation and Audrey's eyes instantly lit up. It was probably the best thing she had ever heard in her whole life.

"Thomas!" She exclaimed at the door.

Immediately, the second voice behind the door replied.

"Audrey! Quick! Open the door! Let them in!"

"Wait a minute! How do we really know it's her?! You're just going to accept that line as clearance?"

"That. Is. My. Sister you dumbass!" Thomas yelled back, "You'd open the door if it was your family too O'Hara. Hurry up!"

As the two seniors behind the door continued to argue, Audrey's group of students all waited nervously. Until...

"Hey guys. What's up?"

Everyone jumped and whirled around. Audrey brought her fists up but lowered them instantly. Deliza had retreated from upstairs and managed to sneak up on all of them very successfully.

"Seriously, is this going to become a thing with you?" Joey stammered as he put a hand on his chest.

"Get used to it four-eyes," Deliza winked. "It may just be the thing that saves your life when you look the wrong way."

She then walked up to Audrey and leaned into whisper.

"Look," she spoke calmly, "If there's any chance we can get inside, it should be now."

Deliza nodded in the direction she came from. Audrey immediately understood the look of concern that developed. Right as this happened, the door hissed and parted open. Two seniors with rifles split up and went a foot in opposite directions down the hall. Both of them covered the hallway as another senior motioned for them to come in.

"Inside now!"

Everyone instantly filed inside as fast as they could.

"Did you get an idea of what's coming?" Audrey asked as Joey ducked in first.

"Meh," Deliza held up a hand and shook it. "I caught a glimpse of them coming down the hall, but they didn't see me. I'm guessing they're in the stairwell now. If they know the layout of the building, then the armory would be a good place to capture. We may have to make a final stand in there."

"Those don't sound like good odds," Audrey muttered.

"Well it's better than dying like pigs in an open hallway with no cover," Deliza replied bluntly. "At least each one of us has a chance to fight back against those cowards."

"Excuse me."

The two of them turned to see Thomas leaning against the door casually with a rifle in hand.

"I'm sure you and your new friend have much to discuss Audrey," He said as he motioned for them to enter, "But I'd much rather duck inside and take my chances holding out in here. Wouldn't you agree?"

The two of them nodded and proceeded inside. The two seniors covered the hallway and backtracked inside allowing Thomas to close the door. The door hissed as it slammed and sealed shut.

"Someone will have heard that most likely," Thomas muttered as he embraced Audrey, "Speaking of which, got any updates from the outside?"

"Total chaos," Audrey replied. "We never made it to the transports. I think some people made it out but they shot down our rides."

Since there wasn't much to do, they all began to catch their breaths. Joey kneeled down and brought out his pad to check for signals. Thomas gestured for them to sit against the wall. Crouching down, Audrey took a breath and leaned her head to the cold metal. Thomas sat next to her and propped his rifle in his lap. He brought up a map of the campus on a three-dimensional pad. It began highlighting green dots on top of some of the roofs.

"We were here," He said pointing at the building next to the one where they were. "We were on the top floor setting up to be ready to assault anyone dropping into the courtyard. Cover for any stragglers. Standard entrapment... except that the enemy didn't send people soldiers..."

"Robots," Audrey replied. "Big huge robots and a drone army."

"Our weapons were useless," Thomas nodded. "We could really use some Jedi right now eh? They sent in those small humanoid defense drones and those were hard to take down. Someone must have hacked in and upgraded their combat programming. If that wasn't enough, the big giant rolie polie looking ones practically blasted the floors we were on to pieces. A lot of seniors got crushed from most of the wreckage in the building than the actual firefight. I got as many people as I could to the armory but it was a death trap wherever we went. I can't remember if we even had time to stop for a breath."

"What about the amborgs?" Deliza asked curiously.

Thomas shrugged and let out a huge sigh.

"They were here and there. Tried helping as many people as they could but from the way I saw it, they were pretty beat up. I took my group of people still alive, grabbed as many people we ran into and huddled here."

"We can probably assume everyone who is hiding in the bunkers or armories are the safest places at this point," Audrey pointed at the map and highlighted red dots on all of the buildings. "Every school building has a place to hide and based on how fast this place has fallen, we're probably going to be targeted next."

A loud bang shook the door. Everyone instantly perked up. Two of the seniors aimed their guns at the door. One of them lifted their hands and signaled Thomas who quickly pulled Audrey and Deliza to a locker.

"Take your pick," He indicated the weapons available as the locker door opened. Deliza grabbed a hand-gun and a knife while Audrey settled with a standard rifle. "Better get in position too."

"What's with the knife?" Audrey asked as she switched the rifle settings to single-shot.

"My parents are close quarters combat instructors in D.C.," Deliza shrugged. "This is the fighting style I'm comfortable with."

"You're a close quarter's expert?" Audrey remarked, impressed at the sight of her classmate.

"You could say that," Deliza smirked. She did grab a rifle but put it around her shoulders. "Long range combat is a bit boring. I'm best when I'm up close to my enemies. Once I'm in range, it's too late for them."

"I doubt that it's going to be a person coming through that door," Audrey said checking the sights of her weapon.

"I'll be ok with whatever. Mom says I'm one tough cookie."

"Everyone grab a firearm and take your positions!" Thomas instructed which ended the girls' conversation. "Joey right? Put the pad down and pick up a gun. Even a science tech needs to fight."

Joey trembled at the thought but instantly sprinted to a locker and grabbed a rifle. There were four aisles in the room. Everyone assembled and pointed their guns at the door. Thomas whistled to the two seniors standing at the door and motioned for them to pull back.

"No sense in you guys getting crushed by the door if it gets bashed in," He muttered. "Too many movie deaths from stationing people at entrances."

Audrey took a position by Thomas and aimed. Deliza moved up the aisle and had her pistol ready. All of them waited silently. Finally, the door shook violently as something outside hit it hard.

Several shots from outside the door rang out and accompanied the thrashing that was inflicted on the door. Muffled yells penetrated through the door causing the students all to glance nervously at each other.

"Steady, everyone," Thomas said reassuringly. Audrey was about to add a little something to encourage everyone when another crash caused the door to fall inside. It landed with a loud thud and there was a lot of noise.

"That was pure grade steel..." Joey whispered loud enough for everyone to hear when it quieted down.

Oddly enough, no one had fired their guns. Audrey looked over the wreckage of the door to see if anyone was coming in.

"I see a foot!"

Immediately after someone spotted movement, everyone opened fire except for a few students. The entire armory was filled with noise as Audrey couldn't hear herself think. Casings, and bullets were flying everywhere and people were yelling at the top of their lungs from either fear or too much adrenaline.

"Cease fire! Stop shooting!"

The gunfire gradually ceased as everyone panted and lowered their weapons. A voice from outside the armory spoke up from around the corner.

"Wow, that was... pleasant," A male voice spoke. Another laughed robotically, "Do you believe they're ready to cease hostilities?"

The first voice spoke again.

"Unsure. You may proceed inside first."

"Afraid of some bullets?"

"No," The first voice replied to the taunt, "But based on all the bullets opposite of the door's entrance, we have been fired upon by at least twenty firearms..."

"They're just scared," A third person spoke reassuringly. "Let me try. This is amborg 297! I am coming in! That being said you two, watch and learn."

Audrey saw a figure step into the entrance way. Just as she lowered her weapon, someone behind opened fire causing everyone else to fire as well. The figure in the doorway immediately ducked out of sight with so much speed.

"HOLD YOUR FIRE!" Audrey yelled as the figure outside yelled as well.

"How rude!" She heard the person outside say.

"Well at least one of them has sense, 297," The other voice said in an amused tone. "Report to me when you have convinced the remaining nineteen people to stop shooting."

"Oh shut up," There were footsteps shuffling around outside, "Cease fire! Students! We are not your enemy! We are amborgs!"

"Oh BULLSHIT!" The senior that had locked the door from earlier yelled back. But one of the other students yelled, "What if they are amborgs?! A regular person would have died from that kind of shooting spree!"

A few more shots rang out at the entrance. There was another moment of silence. From outside, the voices began talking again.

"That went well..." The first voice spoke again but Audrey couldn't hear the one called 297. The second voice spoke again calmly, "He is most likely traumatized. If I may, can I try to calm them down?"

"Go ahead 501," Said the third voice, "But try not to get shot in the head again for the millionth time."

"My head has only been hit six hundred forty two thousand and three hundred seventeen times…"

"Will you just go already before we exaggerate around you again? We are going for an accumulative score of eighteen headshots to 501's calculated total. May we have eighteen please? Maybe seven more for luck?"

Audrey waited but heard no further response from outside. Instead, footsteps were heard as someone stepped into the doorway slowly and were cautiously spaced. This time, a smaller number of the students opened fire. Audrey watched as the figure remained upright as he was riddled with bullets. Everyone stopped firing after a few seconds and stared. Squinting, Audrey saw the numbers 501 labeled on the amborg's jacket. The figure tilted his head down, examined his front and looked back at all of them and smiled casually.

"Greetings," He smiled and walked forward. The damage done by the bullets had only made his clothing dirtier. "Do not be alarmed. My uniform is made of a special synthetic fabric that is bulletproof."

Two more figures entered the room. One of them labeled 297 looked extremely annoyed.

"Really?" His bracelet flashed, "Nineteen of them shoot at me and only four end up shooting Donut."

"Well at least Donut didn't avoid the bullets like you did," The other male amborg, 66, was smiling. ""Plus, he also got them to stop. Talk about taking one for the team."

"Actually," 501 glanced up with a thoughtful look. "That was probably about sixty eight shots for the team to be precise."

"It has been a long day 66 and I am going to kill you 501. Why did he have to pick our team?"

"117 said I should learn to relate with you more," 501 spoke but 297 waved his hand for silence.

"Is everyone alright?" 297 asked as he shifted his attention to all of the students.

Thomas walked up to them and began updating the amborgs about the situation. Audrey looked behind her to check on Joey. He gave a quick thumbs-up and lowered his rifle. She then turned to face the front but realized someone was standing directly in front of her. She jumped and inadvertently pulled the trigger. The shot rang out throughout the entire armory and everyone immediately turned and she felt everyone staring. Gulping, she stared wide-eyed at who she had just fired her gun at.

The amborg, number 117, stood and examined where he had been shot as she stared blankly in shock. Even if they were bullet-proof, what had she done? A very bad first impression. After what felt like the longest three seconds of silence in her life, Audrey then saw his bracelet light up.

"I was," He stated casually, "...going to ask if you were alright, miss. But I believe you have already answered the question... in a direct way."

"I... am... so sorry!" She said meekly, "You startled me. One minute I turn my head and then I see you and... It's a reflex..."

"There is no need for an explanation," His bracelet flashed, "I only wanted to check on you specifically since you hadn't lowered your weapon. You turned your attention to the back and I took it upon myself to inform you that raised weapons may be discharged improperly. It would appear that I was too late."

"I probably won't stop apologizing then," Audrey attempted to force a chuckle but she was beginning to feel tense.

"Take deep breaths. Your heart rate seems to have elevated."

117 nodded and walked to join the other three amborgs. Thomas was looking fairly impressed.

"Wow, four amborgs," He said cheerfully, "I thought at most, only one of you would show up to save our skins. But four is probably an eye-opener."

"All amborgs are currently assisting in rescuing the survivors," 297 spoke, "All of us on campus are probably noticeable. However time is short and we will need to head out after we have taken your group to the evacuation transport."

"I'm all for that," Thomas checked his weapon and shouldered it, "You guys need to be somewhere later?"

"We are on a very short timeline," 66 said, "But I do believe we should at least get acquainted. Keith 66 at your service."

He extended his hand and Thomas shook it. 117 stepped forward.

"David 117 standing by."

"Carter 297," The one labeled 297 waved, "I forgive you all for shooting me."

"Dominique 501. But everyone just calls me Donut."

Audrey's memory immediately began to stir.

"Oh, you're name is Carter? I have an A.I. named..."

She stopped and immediately had a startling revelation.

"Carter! I forgot about him! He's still in my room!"

The four amborgs turned and stared at each other and then at Audrey. 117's bracelet lit up.

"Are you referring to the artificial intelligence with 297's name?"

"There is no need for alarm," 66 added and smiled, "Katie 57 found him transmitting a hidden distress signal and was able to extract him with no trouble."

"Oh thank goodness," Audrey gave a relieved sigh, "Please don't tell him I forgot him. He wouldn't let me hear the end of it."

"It is asking him to maintain silence that is making him extremely difficult," 297 added with an amused look, "57 is having quite the head-ache. But he will be glad to receive word that his owner is alive and well."

"I have a question?"

Everyone stared and Joey lowered his hand sheepishly.

"I just wanted to know why an amborg is named Donut. If you have time," He mumbled.

"It is a very long story for another time I am afraid," 117 spoke up, "One quick reason in particular though, Donut is easier and shorter to say in combat."

"Plus he loves donuts," 66 patted 501 on the shoulder, "In more than one way though. Keep that in mind if you feel like interpreting multiple scenarios."

"I just received word," 117 interrupted. "Transports have been alerted of our situation. Help is coming but we need to leave now."

Not a real people person, Audrey stared inquisitively. For a moment, it seemed like the amborgs had made their troubles disappear but then they were now reminded of their predicament as 297 continued the conversation.

"If we travel as one large group," He said, "We may be highly susceptible to ambush and will sustain maximum casualties. We must split up. Would you mind if everyone revealed themselves for a head count?"

Thomas nodded. He whistled and like a pack of dogs, everyone came out on cue and stepped where the amborgs could see. 66 looked all of them over.

"It would seem that no one here is badly injured," He observed, "Everyone should be capable of quick travel."

"I count thirty-two survivors," 297 looked at everyone, "We shall split into four groups going in different directions. Eight students will be accompanied by one amborg."

"Agreed," 117 nodded. "Is this acceptable?"

He turned and faced Thomas, who was looking at all of the nods and murmurs of approval. He glanced at Audrey. She quickly nodded back with a firm smile.

"Looks like we are," He said with enthusiasm.

"Then divide into groups quickly," 117 acknowledged, "We are leaving this... hell-hole."

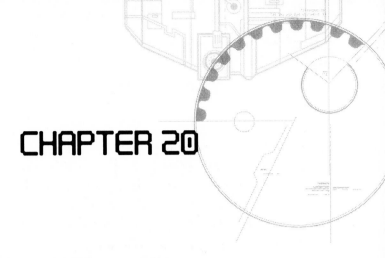

CHAPTER 20

"Do you think 999 would like a scarf?"

"Based on her personality? I seriously doubt that. I even have the math to prove it."

"Hmm, it probably was a stupid thought."

917 and 3 were both standing on sentry duty at the make-shift medical center a couple miles off-campus. They stood on a hill which gave them full view of the Academy. Asides from having random conversations as they watched the columns of smoke rise, 917 and 3 were some of the amborgs experiencing a problem.

"Not necessarily," 3 replied as she staggered a little to the right and 917 caught her with his arms. "It just means... whoa. It just means you're very... thoughtful. Do you feel tired?"

"Not yet," 917 replied pushing 3 back into a more stable stance. "But we need to find a plan quick before we revert to alpha status."

A transmission at that point cut off their conversation and 3 tapped her head in an attempt to focus and get past the haziness. There was a loud whistling noise as the two amborgs looked up. A missile fired from off in the distance landed nearby. The explosion sent mud splattering all over the place. Unfazed, 3 shook her head and attempted to widen the frequency range but it wasn't going as fast as it normally did.

As the lag cleared up. She lifted her other hand to wipe the mud off her face. At that moment, she realized that her hand was dropping back at her side much slowly than normal. Quickly calculating, she shuddered at the numbers that her head finished crunching. Her performance had dropped by seven point two percent.

"Hello? Who is calling? Make it quick before I fall asleep. Literally."

She brightened the tone of her voice to sound as positive as possible. No use feeling pessimistic now, she murmured as she tapped her foot impatiently. Noticing her uneasy mood, 917 was about to say something encouraging but instead felt the immediate urge to sit on the ground. The combat had drained much of his strength and he was leaning on his right arm to stay sitting upright.

"Missy? Is that you?" She suddenly felt relieved and lit up at the voice.

"Johnny!" She exclaimed as she looked towards the academy borders, "Where are you?"

"Just getting a group of survivors out of this place. But it is a bit of a drag."

"Lose any limbs lately?"

"It happened one time. One time."

"I had to make a joke about it at some point," She chuckled to herself. All of a sudden, she felt a pain in her chest and instantly opened her mouth and coughed hard.

"Hey 3!" 5 said with concern. "Are you ok? This is why you were pulled from combat. Because you were low on power. Expend more energy and you will feel a lot more pain."

"Amazing," She whispered.

She could feel 917's confused stare from where he sat and heard nothing from 5 over the comms.

"What?" 5 asked with a confused tone.

"The sensation of it all... coughing," Missy said looking off into the distance. "Pain coming from my esophagus, a reaction to clear mucus from my artificial lungs. It feels so strange, painful but also enlightening as well. The accumulation of whatever I have breathed in intentionally in the past few weeks combined with fatigue from this day has led to pain and a reaction! It has been so long since I coughed."

"3, I'm going to interrupt," 5 spoke up, "As much as I would love to hear you go over the details of what it's like to cough, I have some survivors heading towards your safe zone. Do you think we could have a safe reception?"

3 looked down at 917 who tilted his head with small smirk.

"Right. On our way."

* * *

117 straightened up. He lifted his foot up and stepped away. A drone lay sprawled across the ground in pieces. He bent over and examined the head which had been virtually flattened into the cement.

"All clear."

117 kicked the dead robot body away. The leader of his student group, Thomas peeped from behind the stone wall his group had taken cover behind. Thomas nodded, lowered his rifle, turned to look back and motioned with his arm for the rest of the group to follow. The rest of the students in their group stood up and all of them crept over to 117.

"You may stand," 117 gestured as he turned to face one direction. Nobody stood up at his suggestion. Upon realizing this, 117 added, "I don't hear or detect any other enemies. We are clear until we reach the next checkpoint."

As they continued on, 117 noticed that someone was walking up to his side determinedly. He glanced to his right and recognized the girl that had shot him. This was the sister of Thomas. 117 quickly checked the files of the Academy privately and looked up her name.

"This is obviously the wrong time. Actually, it's definitely the most dangerous time but… I didn't want to waste another moment. I'm sorry," She stuttered.

"Audrey Wright," 117 recited as he looked at her file. "Sophomore. An apology is not presently necessary."

"You're not looking at my records are you?" She said with a surprised look. "It's so strange hearing my name being spoken from an amborg."

"As a matter of fact, I am looking at your records. Superb marksman, honor student, well-balanced tactician, from a strong military lineage alongside your brother, last physical indicated that..."

He stopped immediately and became silent. An incoming alert had just popped up on his HUD. Mandy wanted to talk to him. But to Audrey, she had no idea what was happening.

"Umm, is everything alright? You just cut off." Audrey bit her lip and leaned forward to look at his face. "Did the results of my physical say anything? Oh wait, that should be medically classified..."

"Of course Ms. Wright. There is nothing wrong," He replied swiftly, "I was just having a chat with my technician. Yes Mandy, I will remember your response. I always do."

"Girlfriend?" Audrey blurted. 117 smiled slightly.

"No," He replied, "A friend. Perhaps someone of your age might refer to it as... a B...F...F."

"You do have a sense of humor."

"It would appear you do possess the ability to laugh," 117 patted her on the shoulder as they began moving again, "You were very tense and scared when I first saw you. It looks as if you are feeling slightly better despite the strenuous circumstances."

"Well, if you hadn't shown up, we'd probably be dead by now," Audrey breathed silently.

"Possibly. But I am here now so you may relieve some of your tension."

"As a non-amborg, it's not as easy as you think."

The battle continued in the distance as the group continued their present course. Everyone walked in a single column, hunching over as a group every time there was an explosion on another part of the campsite. It looked like the fighting had shifted and died down elsewhere allowing them a safe and quiet journey towards their evacuation site. It wasn't until after a few minutes that 117 decided to say something reassuring.

"If I may say so, I do believe you and your brother could have successfully ensured your classmates' survival even if the amborgs did not arrive. You possess many qualities that would earn respect from others."

"You seem to know a lot about me and everyone here."

117 casually glanced at her and saw her stare back. He could hear how uneasy and defensive her tone was. He tweaked his head to the left.

"My apologies," He said. "I have not looked at your records again since my technician reminded me of the breach of privacy."

"What did you learn about me?" Audrey asked curiously. She seemed to have lost her apprehension which made it less awkward.

"I don't have to answer if you feel that I'm violating your privacy. Although, you may rest easy since the information I have doesn't feature any lewdness or tidbits of humiliating facts."

"Forget it then," She whispered rather hastily.

"If you insist."

As they walked ahead, Mandy decided to chime in privately at the back of his head.

"Smooth," She said. "Are you trying to make her feel aggravated?"

"It wasn't my intent," 117 transmitted quietly so Audrey couldn't hear him.

"Look just change the subject," Mandy insisted. "Just talk to her normally. Don't bring up her past or anything from her record! That's basically cheating if you're trying to know her better. You just saved her so... keep on her light side."

"So can I ask you something?"

117 ended the conversation with Mandy and returned his attention to Audrey.

"Yes?"

"How fast... I mean I've been curious but... how fast do you calculate... eh... things?"

He wasn't sure if it was just because his energy was low or if it was his basic instinct taking over but 117 couldn't help but chuckle a little.

"What?" Audrey asked, "Was that not a legitimate question?"

"We calculate data," 117 replied with a soft smile. "But 'things' is also appropriate. There are times when we try not to be too judgmental of the English language."

"So I do get an answer?"

"The problem I think," 117 admitted. "Is that you probably do not want to know the exact number. It does fit in the terabytes range though."

"Hundreds of terabytes within a millisecond range perhaps?"

"That is classified but you are surprisingly getting close," 117 replied. "However the real answer might make you jealous."

"Why would I be jealous of the person who rescued us?"

"I haven't rescued you yet," 117 said grimly. "That task is not over yet. When I know you and your colleagues are safe, then we will discuss that topic again."

"I never knew amborgs were so considerate," Audrey said. "I mean, putting your life on the line for people like us must be exhausting at some point. I think that's pretty amazing."

117 stopped and looked her in the eyes with a solemn look. She blinked and looked away.

"I meant that your profession is amazing," She added with a slight fluster in her voice.

"I knew what you meant," 117 sighed. "It is just that in light of recent events, there is no reason for any of us to be considered amazing."

"Why is that?"

But before he could answer her, their conversation was immediately interrupted when someone in the back let out a scream at the same time a gun was fired off in the distance.

In a split-second, Audrey was looking 117 right in the eye and then at nothing. She blinked. All of a sudden he had disappeared. The next thing she knew, she felt something collide with her and was forced to the ground. As she felt her whole front be pushed up into her back, she could hear the start of what sounded like an ambush.

"Get down!" Someone cried out.

Audrey tried to get a grasp of what was happening in her surroundings but she spent most of the start trying to figure out who had pinned her down. As she turned around, she realized the tackler was Deliza. As the two girls rolled off each other, Audrey also realized that Thomas had also been forced down as she craned her neck for a look. Peeping over to her brother, Audrey saw 117 standing five feet away holding onto one of the other members of their party. Bullets were ricocheting all over the amborg's back. Thomas clenched his rifle and moved to the wall. He quickly leaned up and looked up into the distance.

"We got shooters on the roof!" Thomas shouted as he lifted his gun and opened fire. The noise pierced Audrey's ears very sharply and she held her hands to her head.

Crud, she thought, where's my gun?! Hadn't she been carrying it a second ago before being forced to the ground? All of a sudden, she felt something hard hit her rib. Looking down, someone had slid her rifle to her side. She instantly picked it up, joined her brother and aimed at the roof.

"The enemy is firing from an elevated position!"

117 stood upright in front of them while they all stayed behind the wall. Bullets hit him hard but he bravely withstood the impacts. After doing a quick scan, he faced all of them and relayed her instructions.

"There is a modified assault transport approximately forty-seven meters down that path! We will need to secure for evacuation!"

117 indicated down the path and pointed towards an abandoned jeep. It was a military Humvee that had been remodeled with twenty second century tech. Audrey saw its doors hanging open with a body hanging out but incoming fire caused her to duck behind the wall even lower.

"I will draw the enemy fire, stay behind the wall and keep out of the line of sight," She heard 117 shout. "Go now!"

He had grabbed a rifle at some point and leaped onto the wall. He swung it forward and began firing at the roof.

"You heard him! Move!"

Thomas gave Audrey a nudge and the two of them motioned to the others to begin moving. Deliza had snuck to the front and was at the Humvee in less than a few seconds. Someone must have taught her how to move fast, Audrey thought as the bullets pelted the wall.

"Covering fire!!" Deliza yelled. She lifted her rifle and opened fire.

The entire group moved forward as Deliza attempted to suppress their attackers. Thomas fell back to check on the student that had been shielded by 117 making Audrey ahead of everyone. Suddenly, a loud whooshing joined the firefight. Audrey heard the whistling get louder which meant one thing.

An explosion ruptured the wall a few feet ahead of the group. Concrete and small pieces of rock flew outward in every direction. Shaking this off, Audrey found herself crawling and leaning by the gap in the wall. Bullets made their way through the hole causing her to stiffen. Not getting through there without being shot, she thought.

"We gotta move Audrey!!"

Audrey watched in amazement as Deliza ran towards them fast. She dropped and slid on her knees past the hole in the wall and right into Audrey. She looked at Deliza's rifle and realized there was a bullet head lodged right into the loading mechanism.

"Didn't you hear me?!" Deliza asked as she attempted to clean out her weapon. "Come on! Just run and slide!"

"There is no way I could do something like that!" Audrey yelled. "I'd rather not die!"

Having no luck clearing her weapon, Deliza tossed her rifle away. As she drew her knife, she sidled next to Audrey.

"How much ammo do you still have?"

Audrey looked at the meter on the panel behind the scope. She gulped as she read the load out on the light-up display. It was a lot less than she originally thought. But in all the excitement, had she really expended that much ammo?

"Uhh, three shots..." She said calmly, "I think we can panic right about now. We're pinned down and can't move forward..."

"Oh keep it together woman! We're dead if we stay or go! Might as well choose one! Would you rather die sitting or moving as if you were literally running for it?!"

There was a loud clang that drew the girls' attention. They watched as a silver canister flew through the broken section of the wall. Audrey froze in place as it rolled closer and she was sure what it was.

"And that's a grenade..." Audrey gulped as the small canister began beeping.

"Ah dang," Deliza said with a sigh.

"HOLD YOUR BREATH!!" Someone yelled but it was too late.

The cylinder's cap went off. There was loud bang and a bright light. Instantly, Audrey felt herself black out and then there was nothing.

* * *

"I am having second thoughts on what I wish to do when we return home..."

"Really? What did you have in my mind?"

5 sat on the ground sighed. Mud and dirt covered his entire body and he spat out a giant mouthful of it which flew some feet away. 3, 22 and 27 were resting alongside him and were all looking exhausted. They had made it out of the danger zone with their survivors and were now lazily defending the main triage center. Well away from the fighting, all of them were trying to take a break but that was proving to be a little fruitless with their declining energy levels.

"There was a bar that I passed when we were fighting in New York," He said to all of them with his mind. "Maybe I could apply for a job there. Work like a human for a bit. But that is only a small idea."

"Curious," 22 ran a finger through her locks of hair. "Why would you want a job in a bar though? Seems a little miniscule type of occupation."

5 shrugged and rested his head against a crate placed right behind him.

"Thought it would be an interesting idea to learn how to serve drinks," He replied and then smirked. "Maybe I could make drinks better than 3."

"You are so asking for a shot of acid in your next martini."

"Look out, amborg bartender upset," 27 nudged 5 in the head.

All of them laughed. Whether it was from their bracelets or inside the communication frequency they were talking on, they didn't care. As soon as they finished though, 27 suddenly bent and keeled over.

"Agh," He moaned as he clutched his stomach.

"Signal 6 and tell her to get over here now," 5 examined 27 briefly. "Tell her 27 needs a medical examination now."

"Oh man," 27 coughed. "It was that drone that kicked a car into my ribs... It did not cause too much damage but I cannot remember being out for this long... The pain levels are intensifying."

22 stroked her hand across his head and smiled encouragingly. 5 nodded and sat back in relief but made a sighing motion.

"If we are discussing eons of time in the field," 22 brought up cheerfully, "This deployment is definitely not good for my personal hygiene. I am unaware of how the other ladies are doing. But a shower sounds nice right about now."

"You're worried... about personal hygiene at a time like this??" 27 asked raising his eyebrows.

22 shrugged but then suddenly kissed him on the cheek. In response, 27 leapt away and instantly brought his hand up and wiped his cheek furiously.

"Of course," 22 smacked her lips and spit on the ground. "I am a woman after all... Blegh, that was disgusting..."

5 observed with an amused look. He pretended to put on a face and shook his head vigorously in playful disgust.

"THAT," 3 said chuckling to herself, "...is one reason why women are concerned about personal hygiene almost every second."

A loud thud drew their attention to another amborg. Vanessa 6 ran over and scanned 27 quickly. Despite the fact that each amborg was equipped with a database of medical training and self-healing protocols. There was no other amborg that knew medicine better than 6. Her jacket was similar to the design the amborgs wore but she had also added a red-cross patch below her number.

"Looks ok," She said really quickly. She looked him over once and then casually pulled out a needle from her pocket. Ignoring 27's shocked face, she brought it down and with lightning speed, stabbed it into his neck. "How are you 27? Is there a reason you look as if you just drank liquid oxygen?"

Over her shoulder, 27 watched as the 3 and 22 gave each other a fist bump. 6 however, not noticing them went back to her usual routine. Seconds later, 27 instantly calmed down and became quiet. 5 immediately stopped chuckling and stared.

"6," He asked as his eye widened in concern, "What did you give him?"

6 held up the syringe for everyone to see without turning around. She shook her head and whipped her hair out of her face.

"You want to find out?" She asked indifferently. "I have no problems with where I stick this."

"I'm fine," was all 5 muttered in response.

"I'll say this though," She continued without a change in her expression, "Our conditions are deteriorating. Not even my pain killers can stop our power levels from dropping. If we lose power, my pain killers will have more discernable side effects."

"What kind of effects?"

"You just fall asleep for hours... based on the tests I did in the lab and with eager to volunteer personnel back home. It is effective in various scenarios."

"But morphine technically does the same thing though... right?"

6 thought a few seconds before responding.

"Well there is morphine in it," She said.

"Ok then," 3 interrupted. "Perhaps we should discuss less creepy topics and focus more on the catastrophic reality. How long do we have?"

"Well, if it was a normal deployment, we would be able to stay out in the field for months."

6 looked at the back of her hand and noticed it shaking very slowly. They watched as it stopped and she lowered it.

"All of this damage and fatigue has shortened most of our energy... and I mean that physically and metaphorically. For some of us, probably seven to eight hours before our cybernetic parts power down and our performance will completely go down."

"At least in theory," 27 spoke, "We do not necessarily die when our implants power down. But if we do not find energy soon, that theory will be put to the test."

5 looked up at the clouds in the sky.

"Maybe we should stick our arms up and harness the electrical energy of the lightning," He said.

A loud boom sounded in the sky causing all of them to look up. Miraculously, a storm was building up overhead. Bolts of lightning shot and began zipping across the sky as well as bright flashes. Before they could even look up the weather forecast, it began to rain.

"I was being rhetorical!!" 5 yelled out to no one in particular.

"That actually is probably perfect timing," 6 smirked as she suddenly thought of something. "Come on! We need a drop-pod!"

*
**   *
**   *
**

"Audrey! Wake up! Can you hear me? Don't give up!"

Audrey blinked and sat up but hit her head against something and heard a loud clanging noise. She wasn't sure if she was still dizzy from the impact or from what happened while she was blacked out.

"Ouch girl," She heard Deliza say close by, "How many times have you been hit on the head?"

The blow to her head managed to help her regain most of her consciousness. Audrey looked left and stared out of a window. The scenery was flying to the right very fast. She blinked and turned her right to see the scenery whooshing past to the left. It was clear that the group had made it on board the vehicle they had fought towards. But why was she lying down?

"What happened?" Audrey tried to sit up slowly to keep looking around but felt someone force her to lie straight back down. "Are we safe?"

"That grenade that exploded in our face was one of those new shock grenades," Deliza explained as she sat back in her seat. "Sucks the oxygen clean out of the air, makes your brain all fuzzy and forces victims to pass out almost instantly... I guess your breathing training kinda paid off. Otherwise it would have been hard to revive you."

Deliza turned the seat around and was facing the window. She tapped a button on the side and the window went down. She had acquired another rifle and placed the barrel pointing out.

Audrey had only been in the modified Humvees a few times but it was enough that she remembered what it appeared like. Ground vehicles on wheels in the twentieth thru the twenty first century were designed so that the seats all faced forward. One of the perks of the remodeled Humvees were that the driver section was sealed off by steel plating for two people. The back had been expanded outward in width for at least six people. Each person had a chair that could rotate so anyone could get out the door easily and also have easy access to the medical stretchers, like the one Audrey was currently lying on for the medics. Based on what she could remember, it was a lot of doors for a remodel. At least eight exits, or so she thought.

Audrey brought a hand up and rested it on her forehead. The rumbling and vibrations of the wheels seemed to rock her back and forth. This felt soothing and very relaxing.

"I only had like a second to get air..." She groaned. "I really doubt that any of the training they teach us in the emergency classes really prepares you for anything like that..."

"I'll say. You were close to the explosion so that amborg was considerate enough to put you in the stretcher when we made it to the transport. Should have seen how fast he assigned us to our seating and how quickly he set it up for you."

"Really..." Audrey said, "Well where is he? That's another that I owe him. Man, I have got to find a way to save him."

Deliza pointed a finger upwards. Audrey blinked and briefly looked straight up at the steel plating above.

"On the roof," She said casually.

Audrey continued to stare at the transport's ceiling. Without a word, she stared at Deliza and also pointed upwards for clarification. Deliza chuckled and nodded in response.

"I guess amborgs aren't the type to sit in a vehicle in the middle of a danger zone."

"Hey what about Thomas? Is he ok?"

"Oh yeah," Deliza replied with a matter of fact sort of tone. "He's up front driving."

"Nice of you to remember me sis."

Thomas spoke over the small intercom in the Humvee. Audrey smiled in relief and was able to relax a bit more.

"Thanks for getting us out," She said immediately.

"Yeah yeah, love you too sis," Thomas chuckled, "Now be quiet and let me concentrate on driving us out of here."

As they continued on their present course. There was a quick tapping noise that came from the roof. Everyone in the vehicle all became silent and looked at the ceiling.

"We are four minutes from the evacuation zone," 117's voice came through the plating. "Mr. Wright, I suggest slowing down."

"Do you see anything?"

Thomas glanced down the road to attempt to see if there were any upcoming obstacles. What happened next however, rendered him unable to hear 117's next command.

As he looked out into the dirt road, he noticed something fly out into their path. The speed at which he was driving made him realize it was too late to swerve or hit the brakes. A device had been thrown and they were about to become its target. Instinctively, Thomas slammed his foot onto the gas pedal and pushed the needle as far it could go. As the engine roared, he hoped for the best as the Humvee went over the projectile.

There was a thud as an explosion hit the back undercarriage of the Humvee. Because of Thomas' timed acceleration, the explosion did not reach and hit anyone in the passenger section. The shockwave sent the Humvee upwards into a forward flip.

Inside, the passengers were thrown around. In the few seconds they were in the air, Audrey looked out the window and saw the ground flipping on its side and gradually turn completely upside down. The stretcher she laid in had undergone an emergency procedure and activated the straps. They appeared from within the stretcher and whirled around her entire body, tightening and practically pulling her into the stretcher, Audrey safe and secure from her position, watched and rattled around as everything was turning into an experiment from the Vomit Comet. As the Humvee's ceiling dragged and scraped across the ground, there was a loud rattle as Audrey suddenly felt herself falling face-first into the roof. Grimacing in pain, she felt helpless in her predicament. Something had disengaged the magnetic locks that secured the stretcher and she was not enjoying it.

Outside, 117 looked up at the vehicle he had just been crouched on moments earlier. The blast had thrown him clear and into the grass nearby. He watched the now belly-up Humvee slide down the road to a halt and quickly ran after it. Friction eventually brought it to a stop.

Audrey, from her squashed point of view, tried to look around frantically. The straps were preventing her from pushing herself upward. In a frantic attempt to see if anyone was awake, she tried to turn onto the side of the stretcher. Managing to turn at a small angle, she heard people coughing and moaning. Briefly glancing over to her right hand, she saw the panel for the stretcher controls. She reached and extended her hand on the screen and began tapping. It wasn't until her second attempt that the straps finally gave away. They snapped open, releasing her from the harness and she was able to free her arms. Bringing her hands into push up position, she lifted herself upwards and tried to place her feet under her. The tight quarters along with the stretcher on her back made it difficult. She also remembered everyone else was upside down or also trapped like she was so she moved as carefully as she could.

"Is everyone alright?"

It was a bit of a struggle but Audrey managed to crawl to where Deliza's seat was. The explosion had made her seat strap her in just like Audrey's stretcher and she was dangling from the floor of the vehicle like a bat upside down.

"Come on, wake up Deliza!" Audrey cried as she shook the limp body of her friend. "We got to get you and everyone else down! Also we should really complain to whoever designed these stupid harnesses."

"Oh..." She groaned, waking with a start, "That was not cool... I think something hit my head..."

Deliza soon realized that she was looking at Audrey upside down. She bent and reached over attempting to find the manual release located below her seat. Quickly, her straps were also undone and she fell next to Audrey with a thud.

"Isn't the release for your seat straps next to the side of the chair? Why did you reach for your feet?"

"Oh that?"

Deliza crawled and found her rifle and shoved it outside one of the transports windows. Everyone else began to stir from the sudden emergency and the two of them began freeing the rest of their group in the passenger section.

"I was trying to unlock the manual release for the whole chair," Deliza chuckled lazily and shook her head to refocus.

One of the other survivors with them was having trouble with their straps. Audrey took a knife out and cut him free. As he crawled out the window, Deliza prepared to crawl out as well.

"But then I remembered if I did that," She continued, "I'd do more damage to a lot more than my head. Heh. You know what I mean?"

"I think you've been hit on the head far too much today as well. But who am I to talk?"

Audrey chuckled slightly as they made their way out of the wreckage. As she crawled out, she saw a hand reach down for her. Audrey looked up and grabbed 117's hand.

"It would appear that the enemy tossed a very powerful explosive under our vehicle. I have taken care of the ambushers so we should be safe," He reported as the girls straightened up. 117 also began tapping his head and was blinking rapidly. "I couldn't see it at all..."

"What do you mean?" Audrey looked at him with concern.

"I'm very exhausted..." Said 117 with a weary look. "I'm not operating at maximum efficiency otherwise I would have had means to detect traps and inform Thomas to change course. Your brother had the right instinct to speed up otherwise the explosion may have penetrated the passenger compartment."

Audrey looked around and froze. Thomas was not among the group. Immediately, she ran over to the driver's side of the overturned transport and looked inside the cracked glass. She could see Thomas' silhouette upside down in the seat but the cracked glass obscured most of what she could see but she knew that Thomas wasn't moving.

"Someone help me open the door!" She cried frantically as she banged on the door. "Thomas! Thomas wake up! Can you hear me?!"

"Move Audrey!!"

Audrey whirled around when she heard Deliza shout and saw 117 crouch down. Quickly, she moved back and he grabbed onto the door handle. With tremendous force, 117 ripped the door off as if it was paper and set it aside. He reached inside and safely extracted Thomas and the co-driver from their seats.

"Is he alright?!" Audrey asked frantically as 117 carried him and the other student to some grass near the road. He gently set them down and began scanning the two.

"I am transmitting a live feed to amborg 6," He said as he ran a hand over and recorded the damage. "She can quickly relay the results and provide assistance."

"What?" said Deliza, "I thought you amborgs all had medical training?"

117 nodded and began checking for a pulse while he continued to talk.

"Sometimes, it is helpful to have a backup, just to be safe," He said quickly, "6 is our designated medic and so far, she is the only one I know who can help in the events I cannot. If you must trust someone medically, trust her."

"Just help him please..." Audrey begged, "I can't lose him."

117 paused briefly. His eyes flashed a bright green for a moment and then a quick red. Finally, he was able to give a definitive answer.

"He has received physical trauma to his head and glass from the forward window has embedded into his upper abdomen," 117 said as he began to running his hand across the cuts. "He is alive and... waking up. Are you detecting anything else 6?"

Thomas instantly woke up coughing and gasping for air. Audrey breathed a sigh of relief as 117 calmed her brother down. He lifted his head and began scanning the area.

"We must get to the evacuation point and get him aboard the ship. Immediately. We are not safe yet. If we were ambushed here, I suspect more trouble is coming."

"Is he going to be ok?" Audrey asked. She was desperate for an answer. But before she could get one, a loud crash came from behind them. 117 jolted and faced the road from the direction they just came from.

"Is that what I think it was?" Deliza asked aiming her rifle down the road. 117 looked the group over and back down the road. Audrey knew he was assessing the situation.

"There is no time," He stated openly. 117 lifted an arm and pointed off the road and into the trees. "I have stabilized your brother but there is nothing else I can do. You must lead the group into the cover of the forest. Continue in that direction and reach the evacuation ship. Hurry or Thomas' likelihood of survival will perish. Continue on without me and do not stop."

With that being said, 117 proceeded to run back the way they came with his fists clenched. Audrey quickly knelt down and grabbed Thomas' arms. Another student also helped and the survivors quickly moved into the cover of the trees.

"How much ammo do we have?" Deliza quickly asked and all of them searched their pockets.

"Close to nothing!" One of the boys shouted.

"Ok, running is probably the best idea right now," Audrey panted. "We're going to get you to safety Thomas. Just stay with me."

Several thuds could be heard getting closer as everyone made their way into the brush. Just as they entered the tree line, a loud crash diverted their attention. They stared and saw a fallen tree block the road behind them. 117 appeared and jumped onto the tree and leaped onto a massive robot. Audrey recognized it immediately from the start of the battle.

As they saw 117 wrestle and land onto the shoulders of the behemoth, 117 shouted towards their direction.

"I TOLD YOU TO RUN!!!"

Nodding, Audrey checked that Thomas was still awake and began moving forward. While the loud brawl happened behind, everyone moved as fast as they could.

"Come on!! We're not out of this yet."

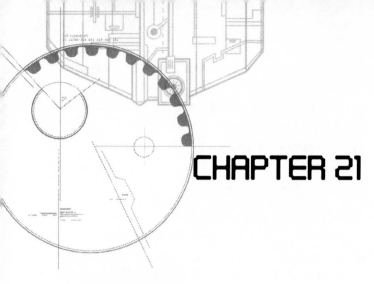

CHAPTER 21

Drop-Pod Landing Zone

"6, this has to be the worst idea you have ever come up with. People have done this in the past. Need I remind you that they didn't exactly survive?"

"You want to check your energy levels again? If you have a better idea, then say so. Otherwise, quit whining and let me work on this."

6 took her hand away from the panel of the drop-pod cluster and pointed a finger in 5's face when he got too close. He lifted his hands up in surrender and backed away with his mouth firmly shut. The rest of the amborgs that had gathered watched in stunned silence.

6 had dragged their drop-pods into a giant horseshoe formation and was setting up wires connecting them all together. By her instructions, they had also managed to acquire a large generator.

"Look 6. I was only trying…"

"That has to be the lowest power level I have seen in your databanks compared to the time you played videogames nonstop for fifteen days," She said observantly and in a very condescending tone. "You want to talk about insanity? Come at me bitch."

6 stopped what she was doing and looked at 5 with an apologetic look.

"Sorry. I didn't mean to curse. I'm tired."

"No apologies are necessary," 5 replied. "But look at this, you have taken several drop-pods, hooked them up together and this is supposed to harness power and refine it so we can properly recharge? We are being struck by lightning."

"Not directly," 6 said. "Have some faith and do something stupid for once in your life 5. It should be in our job requirements."

"It's not a job requirement. It's an occupational hazard."

But she didn't hear his last comment. 6 stepped back away from her pod and admired her handiwork. She had attached some sort of make-shift lightning rod to the roof of the pod. Somehow she had also managed to make twelve kites and they flew in the sky, heavily attached to the roof of the pod and they were now floating and waiting for the storm to hit. 6 turned to look at the amborgs that were currently with her. Her enthusiastic smile faded at their looks of skepticism.

"Oh come on," She protested, "Benjamin Franklin did something like this with one kite in order to experiment with the theory of a lightning rod. That worked didn't it?"

"Yes, that is correct 6," 5 said. He seemed to be the only one willing to speak up from the crowd, "However... we aren't sure if that bit of history is accurate. And another thing..."

He pointed a finger up at the kites as thunder rang out in the sky.

"...You have the lightning rods all ready," He continued, "...and the wires necessary to harness the power into the generator to form a backup power supply for those of us not here. But still, you are asking us to attach ourselves to the ends of those wires from our pods and be the ground rods... we are the receivers. This is not going to work."

"Sure it is!" 6 exclaimed confidently, "LTO is specifically a good conductor for any forms of quick charge and we are designed to run on basic forms of power. Except we can't exactly run on car batteries. And if the technicality of it is not sound for you, it will be fun to have a taste of Zeus' wrath."

"But did we ever test if LTO inside a genetically modified human is capable of withstanding such a large power surge at once?"

5's next question instantly caused them all to shiver.

"Well if we lose power, we won't have any time to return home for a charge," 6 argued as she held up the wire. "If we did, time's still running out and that lunatic who forced us to run this long is still out there. SO I'm going to be electrified whether anyone likes or not!!"

"No you are not!"

6 froze as 1 jumped into the group.

"I will volunteer my life for this..." He said taking the wire from 6's hands. The rest of them moved in and began protesting but 1 waved a hand and they all became silent. The first amborg held the wire tightly. "Be reasonable 6, you're our doctor. What would we do without you if you killed yourself? By accident?"

"Um, every amborg has medical training 1," She said bluntly. "You would all be fine."

"I was being rhetorical..." 1 mumbled. "Anyone of you think that you can do this better than me better pry it from my hands, because I will not let more people risk themselves."

All of them didn't dare try to oppose him. But before anyone could even consider talking this out, lightning flashed across the sky. 1 looked up to the sky and all of sudden, they saw the sparkles of electricity flowing around the kites and down the wires but the charge wasn't powerful enough. Then, a lightning bolt crashed down above them and they saw the rods light up brightly and instantly, power surged down the wires towards them. In that quick moment, 5 put a hand on 1's shoulders.

"What are you doing?!"

5 grinned.

"Two of us have a better chance at this than one. You are not doing this alone. We face Zeus together!!"

"What does that even mean?!"

"Too late..." 5 said gritting his teeth. He slowly gazed up and watched the stream of electricity approach, "Oh this is going to hurt..."

* * *
** ** **

"Give me your head!"

117 had his arms wrapped around the behemoth's head and was not letting go despite its flailing arms hitting him repeatedly in the back. Based on his analysis of the design, the arms weren't built to reach all the way around but it could still strike with it elbows joints based on the damage he was taking. After a few more seconds, 117 almost lost grip until finally, there was a snap and the neck joint was yanked out. Triumphant, 117 dropped to the ground with the head intact in his hands. The behemoth, without its key component powered down and hit the ground as well.

"Mandy," 117 gasped as he dropped the head, "I hid the reading from my own HUD but I think now is a good time to ask. What's my current power level?"

"You are at six percent power David," Her voice replied quietly as 117 began running to find the survivors. It was starting to feel very exhausting just to lift his knee joints. "Why don't you try taking the power reserves from the behemoth?"

"It will not work," 117 replied as he stumbled over a rock, "These things run solely on diesel fuel. The design was elaborate but the fuel tank is heavily armored and protected. At first we almost thought they were electric but they are not compatible with our circuits."

"This bad guy is conveniently and really resourceful..." Mandy said with a worried tone, "First he runs you out of power and strands the amborgs in a place where you can't take it from others."

"Even if we did take power from vehicles per say," 117 said as he leaped over a fallen tree, "Not only would it not be enough, but there are others who need it more than we do. We don't take from the less fortunate."

He tripped and fell into some grass. Dirt stuck to his face as he stood up and kept moving. Ignoring all the mud stains and how dirty he was getting, he desperately made the attempt to ignore the pain in his feet.

"You sure pick a really fine time to be nice David."

"Who am I to claim credit? A long time ago, someone said the needs of the many outweigh the needs of the few."

"Stop quoting Leonard Nimoy and finish the job. We got to be in Pennsylvania yesterday."

117 shrugged and his scans located the survivor's footprints. As he ran towards a small hill, he looked at the heat residue in the ground. It was hard just to maintain infrared vision so he stuck to old fashioned tracking. The students had gone over this area and proceeded to find shelter...

"... that way," He finished his thought out loud.

Eventually, he found a small clearing surrounded by trees. Someone was crying. Adjusting his hearing, 117 found the group clumped together but immediately deciphered what was happening.

"Mandy, stop recording the live feed," 117 spoke softly in his mind. "It is not good. I do not think this should be archived."

"Yeah. I was thinking the same thing. Switching the feed to your own personal drive."

"Thank you Mandy, I accept responsibility for the black out. No one else can see this?"

"Only me," Mandy replied. "As well as whomever we choose to disclose it too."

He walked forward and heard the following conversation. He was close enough now that he didn't have to adjust anymore.

"Audrey, I'm not going to make it out of this one..." He heard someone say.

"Don't say that," Audrey's voice was barely discernible but 117 knew immediately what was happening. "The drop-ship will be here any minute now. Just stay with me please."

117 stopped walking and watched from a distance. He could see Audrey Wright kneeling next to her brother Thomas who was still lying on the ground but awake. There was blood flowing from his lip.

"No Audrey..." He coughed, "Not this time. I got careless... I didn't see that trap when I was driving. I did what I could to save you."

"It isn't your fault," She said as tears flowed down her cheeks, "We're all still alive. We'll make it through this together."

Thomas brought his hand up to his neck and tugged at a chain. It was a necklace with four dog tags and a small lucky charm attached on a silver keychain. 117 looked at the tags with his long vision and recognized the names on the tags from the Academy records but the charm was unfamiliar.

"Take it," Thomas held out the necklace for Audrey, "These were our parent's and... here's my lucky charm. It's yours Sis. It's not lucky if it gets buried and left behind."

"Don't say that! You keep it! Thomas?"

Thomas smiled, breathed once more and spoke softly as she held his hand.

"Mom and dad," He said, "They're proud of you. They always will be... I'll say hi to them for you. I hate to do this Audrey... but you'll need to be tough on your own. Keep believing..."

At that point, 117 returned his hearing level back to normal. He had already heard more than enough. Making his presence known, he stepped into the clearing. None of the other students said anything. A few turned away and looked down. Others tried to offer condolences but they didn't know what to say. Deliza didn't say anything as well. She lowered her rifle to the ground and closed her eyes.

"Thomas?" Audrey whispered but there was no reply. The tears were pouring in a steady stream. Through his head, 117 could hear Mandy also beginning to sniff.

"Oh no," She whispered in his head.

"Man down," 117 replied privately.

117 walked forward. Audrey looked up when she heard his footsteps but kept her gaze fixed on her brother's silent figure.

"I am sorry," 117 knelt down and placed his hand on her shoulder. "He fought well and died peacefully."

Not saying anything, she moved and sunk her head into his chest. He instantly calculated the proper response and slowly held her.

"My condolences for your family," He continued, "I too have lost people I have learned to care for."

Before Audrey could respond however, a loud whoosh appeared overhead. One of the air transports from the Academy was hovering overhead. It all happened in a blur. A couple of soldiers with jet packs stepped off the ramp and landed smoothly next to the group and began to establish a defensive perimeter. Minutes later, the transport touched down in the clearing and two more soldiers walked out and gestured for everyone to get on. As the students began pacing up the ramp, 92, 93 and 18 stepped off and walked over to 117 who was still holding Audrey.

"117," 18 exclaimed as the twins began moving Thomas towards the transport. "Are you alright?"

117 nodded and both he and Audrey stood up. She went on ahead and boarded the transport while he observed the area.

"One casualty," He reported grimly, "Everyone else made it out alright."

"You did what you could," 18 replied reassuringly, "We must return to the drop-pods. 6 has successfully found a way for us to... recharge."

"Why do I feel this is not going to be safe?" 117 replied skeptically.

"When has it ever been safe for us anyway?"

The two of them followed by the rest of the soldiers stepped onboard and the transport rocketed into the sky and began flying. 117 looked around the transport. His group of survivors were sitting in the seats on the starboard side. 92 and 93 sat on the ground, clearly exhausted. Thomas' body was lying among another pair of bodies which turned out to be 35 and 57.

"Are 35 and 57 alright?" 117 asked but before he got an answer, 57 woke up and tried to sit up but instantly clutched her chest in pain.

"Just trying to nap," She muttered. "It's not really easy though without our sleeping tubes back home."

Checking his power levels, 117 sat next to 18 on the floor as the seats were all occupied by the survivors of the school and by the regular soldiers. Two minutes into the flight, the lights of the transport lit up illuminating the whole compartment.

"We are now outside the combat zone," The pilot announced over the P.A. All of the troops breathed a sigh of relief and the students all relaxed. The amborgs however, didn't even move. They all still maintained a battle-worn but strong sense of alertness. It wasn't over yet. 117 sighed but was not smiling, they still had plenty of work ahead of them.

"Thank you."

117 looked up. Audrey had left her seat and sat down in front of him.

"I did lose my brother but you also saved my life many times," She said quietly. "No I meant... You saved all of us and I just wanted to say umm...No I..."

She stopped and looked at the floor. 18, noticing Audrey's loss of words, gently nudged 117 in the shoulder with her dark skinned hand and shot him a private message.

"She has been through quite an ordeal. Assist her."

117 reached a hand out. Audrey looked at it and slowly grabbed his hand in response.

"My name is David 117," He said formally, "If you require any assistance, please... ask. I am here."

Audrey smiled as she shook hands. Her other hand came up and wiped her eyes.

"Thank you..." She whispered, "What did you mean when you said that you lost someone you cared about?"

"Someone I loved," 117 replied casually, "However, this love was probably not the same as the love you had for your brother. I am truly sorry, had the circumstances been different, I would have tried harder to save him."

"I don't blame you," Audrey said empathetically.

All of a sudden, the engines began whining down and the pilot's voice spoke up again.

"We are now landing at the Amborg Drop-pod LZ. Prepare to disembark. Medical teams are standing by and all amborgs onboard are to head over to Amborg 6's drop-pod for... a recharge. Whatever that means."

"Duty calls," 92 exclaimed.

He and 93 both bent down and helped 35 and 57 to their feet and they walked out. 57 paused for a moment and looked back at Audrey. She was about to say something but proceeded without a word after the twins. All of them seemed eager to try out 6's recharging technique. 18 patted 117 on the shoulder and walked out. Deliza patted Audrey on the back and exited as well. 117 turned to give Audrey a farewell when the two of them stepped off the ramp.

"It has been a pleasure Ms. Wright," 117 said, "I apologize for leaving you in these circumstances. On a brighter note, I believe I see several of your classmates."

Audrey turned around to see where he had pointed. In the distance, she recognized a few of her classmates and dorm mates but she also couldn't help but notice how few of them there were. She didn't want to know how many people lost their lives along with Thomas. She wasn't ready for the pain. But in the distance, she could see Joey had made it through the encounter. He was sitting in a wheel chair, under the care of some medical staff. But it looked like he was ok.

117 watched Audrey slowly beginning to smile. The transport lifted off and flew away sending a large current of air in every direction. Unprepared, Audrey felt the air push her forward. 117 immediately stepped in front of her, blocking the wind. She was about to say thank you again but he held up a hand to stop her. The pair then walked towards another group of students. 57, having escaped the grasp of the twins, walked up to 117 and quickly exchanged a few words.

"I'm glad that Joey is alright!" Audrey said happily, while 57 rapidly sent 117 a private message, "He shouldn't have been forced into this. None of us should have."

"And that is also not all," 117 continued as 57 walked in front of Audrey.

She stared up at the tall female brown headed amborg labeled 57. Audrey, watched as she extended her hand out. Puzzled, Audrey looked and saw a standard computer chip in the tall girl's hand. Then she remembered.

"You're Katie 57?"

"You have a very interesting artificial intelligence..."

57 nodded and placed the chip in Audrey's hand. Her tone of voice sounded strained. Being polite was clearly difficult for the female amborg.

"Although he did give me quite a headache, he is very unique," She muttered. "I believe that it is time for him to be returned to his owner. Finally... if you do not mind my hastiness to eject him from my care."

Audrey held the chip in her hand which lit up and Carter's voice spoke out.

"Miss Wright!" His disembodied voice cried out, "It is so delightful to see you! Or to be accurate, perceive you! They told me that you were alive but I couldn't help but worry! When the attack first occurred, I rewrote my programming so that I could provide some sort of defense but you locked me out from all the school servers so I was trapped in your room!! If it hadn't been for this amborg, I wouldn't be here!"

"You're talking?" Audrey stared in amazement. "Without a computer..."

"About that," 57 sighed. "In order to transport him out of the computer he was in, we offered him a ride in one of our own standard computer chips. It has a format that is able to house all known artificial intelligence. We had to reformat his basic structure algorithms and we upgraded him to our own specifications. We are unsure though if this was the best idea."

"It's true!" Carter flashed brightly in Audrey's hand. "This storage unit they let me jump into is amazing! I can talk to you whenever and wherever you go! I was absolutely mortified when the campus was attacked. I worried so much."

"Talked too much is much more accurate," 57 said shaking her head in pained agony.

"CARTER!" Audrey yelled and the chip instantly became quiet. "I'm fine. Calm down. Would you mind speaking slowly?"

"Oh... well you will be happy to know that I am still perfectly in my prime condition," He said normally, "And I got to spend a lovely amount of time with the charming Miss Katie 57. What a darling. I got to be inside an amborg's head. A *female* one's head. It was like a trip to heaven in her brain."

"Great," 57 flatly rolled her eyes and walked away, "Now the A.I. thinks he has a chance with me... What I put up with in this line of work."

Audrey chuckled nervously and pocketed Carter. Suddenly remembering one small detail, she pulled the chip out and muted it at the Carter's protests. 117 looked on with a surprised look.

"You know how to mute an Amborg Industries computer chip?" He asked.

"Uh well," Audrey chuckled. "I did consider working there as an option. You know how schools have you consider all career options right?"

"I am afraid not. I have never been to a real school."

Audrey stopped smiling and realized that 117 was being serious. She had almost forgotten that he wasn't like a normal person. He had a different life from hers. But several instances made him seem exactly like a human. Knowing he had to return to his duties, she felt it was time to properly bid him a farewell.

"You and your amborgs saved me and the only things I have left of my family."

117 had begun to walk away when he felt it had gotten a bit awkward but he stopped when she spoke up. He turned his head briefly to acknowledge her and smiled.

"It is what we do Audrey. I would advise you to not introduce your artificial intelligence to the programs at A.I. Industries. He has an odd bedside manner according to 57. Imagine what the female AIs would say about him."

"And that is what I keep telling him," She chuckled.

As he began to leave, she couldn't help but feel that there was something being taken away from her now that she was safe. She quickly called after him.

"Will I see you again?!"

117 stopped, turned and waved. He kept smiling and replied with a thumbs-up.

"When this is over, I would like to."

Several amborgs who had regrouped with the main group were all commenting about the changes made to 6's drop-pod. As 117 joined with the rest of them, he realized he was the last group to arrive. The battle was ending and the army was able to establish the means to clean up the area. Thankfully, all of the amborgs were alright and surrounding the pod in one large circle. They were all looking towards the center at the pair lying on the ground. 117 stepped into the ring and realized that it was 1 and 5.

"What happened to them?" 117 asked as he stared wide-eyed at the two first group amborgs sprawled across the ground.

6, who was scanning them, looked excited and slightly demonic at the same time.

"Oh this?" She gestured to the two amborgs as if nothing had happened, "Well to be blunt, they were the first ones to try out my charging station. And from what I have found out, it worked wonderfully! Complete and one hundred percent chance of thunderstorm recharge with a generator of energy for everyone with a side of success and additional seasoning of 'called it'!"

"And?" 117 looked at 5's face which was staring wide-eyed towards the sky. "If it was successful, what's wrong with them? Why are they on the ground like that?"

"Their energy levels have spiked!" 6 yelled out triumphantly in a maniacal fashion, "Full power with currents of it evaporating in the air! We just need to wait a few more seconds for the energy to redistribute back to their brains!"

"Hang on!" 297 said sharply. "We shorted out their brains?!"

6 ignored him and kept scanning.

"They should wake up in approximately… three… two… one!"

"YAAAAHHHHH!!!"

Both 5 and 1 instantly bounced to their feet and began running around the group in a frenzy shocking everyone who were unfortunate enough to be in their path.

Everyone else flinched and fell backward, including 117 and 6, at the sight of 5 and 1. For a moment, it looked as if they were ready to go on a rampage until the two smoking amborgs looked around curiously and stopped for second.

"Wow! That was great!!" 5 yelled, "Power levels exceeding to infinity and beyond at one hundred and eighty four percent! Come on where are the robots?! Let me at them! I can fight them all day! All week! All month! For the rest of my life! Oh wow, I think I might barf..."

1 was not as energetic as 5. Instead, he clutched his stomach and also looked as if he was going to hurl. Despite the fact that his energy was emanating like an aura around his body, he didn't look so good even if he had just defied the rules of science.

"That was much needed..." 1 leaned forward but steadied himself. He moaned in pain as he looked ready to burst, "Power at one hundred and seventy two percent. But why do I taste... chimichangas? When did I have those?"

He burped and straightened up. Everyone all looked approvingly at what they were seeing. Despite how sick they looked, everyone was disregarding the second thoughts about the recharging technique. 6 was looking very excited despite her sudden Dr. Frankenstein personality adaptation.

"Heh. They're. They're ALIVE!! Perfect! Who's next?"

She had asked no one specifically but her outburst made several third group amborgs flinch in terror.

"Yikes 117," 6 remarked as she scanned 117's power levels before he could even reply. "Five percent power? You obviously need this. Just stand there, and don't move a muscle. There technically is a line and unfortunately, you do not get to plug into the generator. Just let the machine do the work. Here take this and just think happy thoughts. I want to see if that makes a difference. Ooh here comes another one!"

Before 117 could blink, 6 had placed a wire into his hands and was rapidly briefing him but he could barely comprehend what was going on. The last thing he specifically heard was, "This may sting a little. Have fun!"

"What??" 117 asked in bewilderment.

Everything was going too quickly. He looked at the wire in his hand and followed the trail slowly with his eyes. He saw it was connected to the drop-pods and he subconsciously looked up at the storm clouds surrounding the kites. Before anyone could answer his hysteria, another lightning bolt hit the kites and surged down the wire. 117 saw the electricity coming towards his hands. At the same time, at least three other hands were placed on his shoulders. 117 gulped as everyone latched onto him as a three way battery.

"Oh son of a..."

The electricity hit them all conveniently before he could finish his sentence. All of them yelled out in pain as the energy coursed through all of them.

"Ok, that was good," 5 said watching on in amusement at the sight of his siblings screaming. "However, remind me to give 6 a sedative when we get back. She has gone just a little crazy with this and I'm not feeling ok with it."

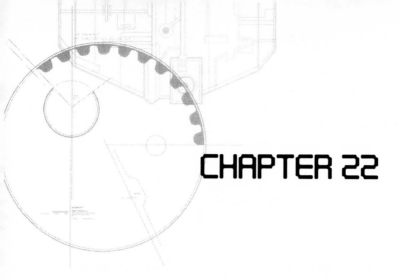

CHAPTER 22

Pennsylvania. Hours after the academy battle.

"You know 6 that was probably a strange but brilliant idea."

"What is your current power level?"

"I am functioning way beyond my normal capacity."

"I can see that 5. Put the car down."

5 immediately shot 6 a look of desperation. He was holding a wrecked car above his head with both hands with no difficulty at all. Although it looked impressive, she wasn't at all amused. 6 was standing alongside him with her arms crossed and staring him down as one would look at a badly behaved dog. Looking around, the streets had never been emptier with trails of destruction in its path. 117 had mentioned earlier that it reminded him a lot of Los Angeles.

Having left the battlefield of the Academy, it was now turning into midday. Only one day earlier, they had been in Texas, Seattle and diverted to the school campus. By the time the battle had wrapped up, it was practically dawn when the U.S. Forces had regained control and the amborgs had been recharged. Unfortunately, the result was that Pennsylvania's defenses had been left vulnerable. A large number of forces hidden in the capital took the military by surprise. With the amborgs stuck west, establishing a foothold was very difficult. They had spent the late hours searching for any student survivors from the surprise attack and when the sun began to peak in the sky, they knew they had been worked to the point that they lost track of time.

The fight at Independence Hall had been a swift and sudden turn of events now that the U.S. Army was no longer fighting alone. The amborgs had arrived here for one thing only. To see the final battle through on the doorsteps of where they knew would be the base of operations for their greatest adversary ever. They had divided up into pairs since they were all functioning at full power but several of them were beginning to feel side-effects to the recharge. 5 in particular was being carefully monitored by 6.

"But I want to throw another car at the bad guys," He whined so loudly that 6 had to hold back a laugh.

She stepped in front of him and placed her arms around his neck.

"A car was actually not what I had in mind."

5 looked back at her in surprise. He dropped the car behind the two of them and put his arms on her waist as it landed with a loud crash.

"You want me to throw you?" He asked raising his eyebrows. She smiled and kissed him on the cheek which meant he had guessed correctly. "Is that really a good idea?"

"Yes. Just make sure not to miss."

5 nodded as he backed up and lifted her by the waist. 6 looked over his head at where she wanted to be thrown. She was already calculating the right trajectory and transmitting the variables to 5. Getting ready for a potential body-slam, she hardened her nerves as he lifted her up.

"What was that kiss for?"

6 looked down at 5 as he was preparing to leap backwards. He lifted an eyebrow with curiosity.

"Just in case I never get the chance to do that again," she replied with a teasing grin. "After all, who else is around for me to give a kiss too?"

"So I was the only one conveniently near you?"

"Well, there is one other reason," She hinted.

"What's that?"

"Sorry 5. But it'll have to wait until next time."

5 smirked.

"Well doc… give them your wrath."

"No… you say, 'give em hell.'"

5 shrugged. He took a few steps back and leaped up into a backflip. In the middle of the flip, he let go of 6 like a catapult, diverting most of his power into his arms. What resulted was him finishing the backflip and 6 flying off in a superman flight towards her target.

Ok, she thought, if that wall is as weak as it looks, breaking through it will be no problem. Gritting her teeth, her fists made contact with the aged cement. Shattering on impact, 6 continued to fly through the wall and then she ended up punching the face of a drone. Taking by surprise, the drone's faceplate was instantly shattered and the rest of the body was lifted off the ground. Gravity began to push 6 and the drone towards the floor. In midair, 6 quickly positioned her feet and extended her legs forcing the robot to land and slide across the ground.

Using her newly acquired surfboard, 6 balanced her weight as her radar identified more targets. Establishing her maneuver, 6 leapt back off of the drone/surfboard and somersaulted across the floor while drawing her guns and aiming them to the left and right.

"This is 6," she said, transmitting to anyone in range and pulling the triggers, "I have broken through the first lines. Could use a lot of help once I am finished here."

But she wasn't able to hear anyone reply to her transmission. She heard the whoosh of a portable anti-tank missile and suddenly, she felt herself flying backwards. It happened in such a blur. Really? A rocket? She thought as she crashed into the ground. Feeling the heat on her clothes and hearing the immediate sizzling of her surroundings, she lifted herself up and threw a knife into the distance with practically no problem. Hearing a distant scream, she wiped her forehead and walked forward. Enemy soldiers appeared and began to charge her down.

"LTO knives, rockets, bullets and a ton of other crap," She muttered angrily as a few bullets also hit her. She ignored them and began moving forward, "I'm not afraid of you anymore."

Disarming the first person that came within reach, she snarled and kicked two of them through a wall. As more of the enemy engaged, the more pissed off she was. It was not a good day.

"You think we show no emotion?!" She yelled grabbing a gangster by the head and forcing him into the mud. "This is for 43!"

Further down the line, there were some amborgs that weren't sharing in 6's luck.

Lieutenant Palmer never dreamed that he would experience what he was currently witnessing. Holding a wounded soldier was one thing. Holding a wounded amborg was not something he saw coming at all. He had been asked by 117 to lead the majority of his troops to support the offensive in Pennsylvania. They barely had time to mobilize since the Academy. He was sure that several of his soldiers had failed to report in to their squads when they had been given orders to move rapidly to one of the nation's historical landmarks. So far, the initial defense troops stationed in Pennsylvania had shown drastic losses and high casualties when the first attacks began. Almost every man and woman had been called in from the reserves but even with all the people fighting, they were getting beaten hard.

"Please stay with me... Listen to my instructions carefully."

Palmer looked into 3's eyes and nodded.

"I won't," He said, "Just tell me what you need. It'll be ok, you'll be just fine."

"I cannot regain the control of my legs..."

No emotion my ass, Palmer thought. This girl was clearly in pain and pleading for her life. He wasn't sure what to worry about. The life of one girl literally in his hands or the entire safety of the country.

"Don't worry 3," He held her tightly as bullets flew overhead. He wouldn't be able to do this alone. He needed to defend the amborgs with his life if necessary, "It was just a rocket. Nothing that Dr. Kendrick can't handle or fix."

3 smiled and nodded. Looking to her left, she pointed over to a pile of wreckage.

"Put me next to that car over there."

"What?"

"297 is in trouble..." She continued, "Put me behind that car and go help him. He is trapped. I will be alright. Just help him! I will see if I can get my legs working again from that location."

"What? 297?"

Palmer carried her straight to the wreckage she had indicated and set her down. She tapped her head and waited a second. An explosion nearby instinctively caused him to leap forward and shield her with his body. 3 however, shoved him away and opened her mouth.

"This is no time for that Lieutenant! Go help him now!" She yelled, "He is requesting artillery to drop right on top of his position!"

"Won't that kill him?!" The lieutenant replied with a look of shock. He had never imagined having to give orders to drop ordnance on their own allies.

"It'll be fine!" 3 nodded in response. "Give me my gun and go now! Don't make me repeat this!"

Nodding, Palmer left 3's "pop" gun, or whatever it was with her and ran off. A soldier, stranded by themselves was sitting with their backs against a wall. Fortunately, he had a radio which eased Palmer's mind at once. Sprinting, he slid across the ground and crawled next to the radioman, identified who he was and grabbed the receiver. This was what I do best, he thought as the radioman kept a sharp eye out as he began calling out orders to whoever could hear him.

* * *
** ** **

466 grabbed 501 and put his arm around her shoulders. A fifty caliber bullet had struck his head, the seventh one and blood was coming out of his mouth. His recharge had helped him greatly but his body had been worn out to the point where he had taken too much damage. The threshold was too much and he had utterly

collapsed into a crater with 466 at his side. Despite the charge up, he could feel the strain in every single one of his muscles. It was a very peculiar sensation which he hadn't felt since before he became an amborg.

"I cannot go on anymore."

"Yes you can," 466 said firmly and with every scrap of confidence she could muster. "Ah!"

She was cutoff as a machinegun opened fire upon them and several bullets struck her in the leg. Taking the bullets head-on, she yelled out a battle cry and she dove with 501 to the ground behind some cover.

"Carolina!" He exclaimed, "Are you ok? Is there a hole in your leg joints?"

"No," she groaned, "No holes but I really felt that one... I do not think I can take this pain anymore..."

"Quick! Just lie down and maybe we can just stay here until we have a plan."

They both crawled and huddled together as the sound of war rang around them. They both put their arms around each other and turned onto their backs. As they laid down for a short break, they both stared upwards at the remnants of the skies. Even though they had been fighting for more than a day, it was still a magnificent sight. Even with all the gunfire and explosions ringing out around them. Still, they both made an attempt to relax.

"Will this ever end?" 466 asked suddenly as she looked at the colors of blue mixing with the white and grey portions of the clouds. 501 shrugged but after a few seconds of deep thought, he began nodding in agreement.

"Yes," he stated firmly, "Because this will end at some point. Whenever that happens, whether or not we live to see the end... All I know is that there will be an end to... just about anything."

"You do know I was referring to the current events of the present time right?"

466 turned her head and gave him a look of sarcasm. 501 returned her gaze and chuckled. He had known exactly what she meant.

"I know," he replied, "I just wanted to give you hope by talking about the good and bad endings that are likely to happen. But we can't speculate on what the future might be. We have to live and proceed with our decisions to make memories and establish the present timeline. Only then will I be able to answer your question."

"Donut," 466 smiled, "Just shut up."

"Just saying," He laughed.

She also began laughing too. In the middle of it, somehow both of them sidled next to each other and continued looking up at the sky. It was a moment no enemy could shatter. That, or they had hidden themselves really well from the gangsters and the drones.

*
**   *
**   *
**

"How many of us are left?"

"Of the seventy-nine of us that left Amborg Industries, thirty four of us still remain in this fight. The rest are incapacitated or trying to hide in order to recuperate."

117 slammed the wall. 35, 57, 1, and 5 were all huddled with him in a group inside the remains of a building. The sun was pouring through, mostly because the roof had been blasted to pieces. All of them were not feeling optimistic considering their updated problem. Their energy levels were all operating their systems perfectly however their morale was low. Physically, they were probably stretched too thin. More than many of them had felt in years since they first became cybernetic.

"None of us are dead though at least," 5 said reassuringly when no one spoke. This caused them to all lift their heads and nod in relief. They were very fortunate not to have lost anyone. 117 shined a light and a map of the area appeared.

"Based on where the enemy has centered and fortified their position, the assassin is hiding inside this five-story building," 117 coughed, "It may look like a warehouse but it is plainly sited here. However he has so many defenses, we are being stopped anywhere we try to hit."

"And every time we do," 35 observed, "Another one of us gets wounded and put out of commission. Now look at us... We had eighty-nine and this crazy challenger has an army and enough tactical capabilities to hurt over two-thirds of us."

"At least none of us are dead remember?" 57 said agreeing with 5's previous statement.

"They just have tight defenses and they are not advancing from their position to kill us. He is running out of resources to make an assault. Instead, what we have managed to do is, all of the wounded amborgs have fortified themselves and hidden themselves in strategic positions. All we need is to come up with a new plan while everyone rests and recovers."

"The U.S. army cannot break through the defenses by itself," 117 said looking at every inch of the map. "Their forces are spread thin from the first waves. And all the reinforcements that were brought with us are in disarray."

Scanning for any sign of a break in the enemy defenses, he was trying to think of a solution to minimize further casualties. The troops currently with them in Pennsylvania were literally detachments of several battalions from all over the country with command attempting to establish a stable chain of control. There was rumors of taking all the soldiers they had and reforming them into one whole battle group but that would consume too much time. The only question was, if they waited now, would the assassin escape undetected? If they went in, they also risked being cut off from outside support at the cost of heavy casualties based on their current status.

"When an eventual assault occurs," He announced, "We will be the spearhead but we cannot do this in our current state. We are at an impasse. There is no way in but… we also can't afford to stop here. There's just no time."

"We've come too far to give up," 1 added, "If this man succeeds here, then the world will be open to him and we will be involved in a prolonged conflict."

"So it really is all or nothing," 5 stated. "But no more ideas on our side."

117 placed a hand on his forehead and shook his head. He tried asking Mandy for help.

"What do I do Mandy? I am not decisive as you… if we wait, this man will find a way to escape and the world will burn. If we go now, are our troops really willing to die for one tyrant? Another amborg could be killed. We have nothing else."

There was no response. 117 tapped his head. The connection was clear but there was no response on the other end. Confused, he looked at the others. They all understood what the expression on his face meant and they instantly began calling and trying to reach their technicians. Everyone soon had a type of answer.

"It would appear that something has preoccupied our own technicians," 5 said with the same confused look that everyone was beginning to display. "All of our technicians by the look of it. How curious."

117, now completely satisfied that it wasn't just Mandy he had lost contact, felt relieved. He didn't have to be nervous but all the same, he was concerned as to what had dragged Mandy from her post.

"Mandy? Please respond," He asked again, "I cannot do this anymore. All of my options are… gone."

"Not all of them."

Mandy finally responded. Out of breath and panting on the other end, the tone in her voice made her sound excited about something in particular.

117 analyzed the sound patterns in her voice. It didn't seem like something was wrong. She was in a very excited mood which was a change to the current situation. He looked at the other amborgs, who apparently were in deep conversation with their own technicians. Apparently there wasn't any bad news at all.

"Is everything ok? Why did you not respond?"

"Because Dr. Kendrick has got an option for you to use!" She shouted so joyfully that 117 had to turn the volume down, "ETA one minute! It's great David! Stand by for our A.I. Industries ace in the hole!"

"One minute? I don't understand."

What happened next answered his question automatically. A blip had appeared on 117's radar. All of the other amborgs all straightened up and began tapping their heads. They were all switching to their radars. They all saw it too. The blip on the radar instantly flashed and a number appeared in the flashing blue light and it was coming towards their position. Everyone instantly gaped towards the sky as they heard a boom ring out. It was the signal from another amborg I.F.F. tag. But it was not who they were expecting at all.

"I do not believe it..." said 1 as a grin spread across his face. "It's really her. I had a feeling she wasn't going stay out of this one."

"Oh yeah, now we're talking," 5 was leaping in the air in short hops at the flying object in the sky. "I am so down with this!"

57 looked up to the sky and smiled with 35.

"Welcome back to the land of the living," She said as she high-fived 35.

117 stood staring at the sky with his mouth agape as he made out a drop-pod flying towards them. Suddenly, it changed trajectory and dropped towards them.

"43? Is that you?"

It fell through the clouds and dropped a few feet into the street in front of them with a loud boom. The pod landed in the street with a crash sending pillars of dirt up into the air. It hit with so much force that anyone nearby probably would have been shaken off their feet. But the amborgs watching stood, unmoving as the door hissed. After a few seconds, the pod opened up and out stepped a familiar face.

"Well? Are you going to stand there gaping or am I going to wait for you to applaud?"

43 stared at all of their dumbstruck expressions with an amused look. No one knew exactly how to greet or say anything to her. They just stared. When 43 didn't get the reception she hoped for, she lowered her arms and sighed. All of them stared at each other but they began smiling.

"Geez you take one knife to the chest and almost miss probably the biggest event we've ever been a part of and no one shows any recognition for when you finally show up. Looks like my dramatic entrance failed."

Not replying to her blunt choice of words, 117 walked forward and extended his arms forward. He didn't dare approach her. Was it a dream? 43 held a look of annoyance across her face at the sight of him.

"That is not going to work David 117," She said, "You lead the biggest operation in amborg history without me and now without any ideas in your calculations, what makes you think I should help you now?"

"If you want me to convince you, I shall. Because I never knew if I would see you awake again. I wanted you back. Now… we can end this."

"Right, and I suppose flattery is your method for making me feel better?"

57 walked forward and interrupted at that point.

"What do you want us to do sis?" She shrugged, "You're alive. I mean… you're awake. That has to be the best news we have received this whole time. You're out of a coma. Would you cut the guy a break and stop acting so uptight and stubborn?"

"Relax Katie, I was kidding."

"Now that you are back," 5 said changing the mood, "I think we can inspire some fear inside those stupid drones."

"You mean the ones that have you currently stumped right now?" 43 replied with a smirk.

"Yep she's back," 5 muttered as he turned away.

"All I know is," 117 interrupted, "I would die by your side anytime. But you are most welcome to help us finish this."

"So I show up and all of you are immediately inspired," 43 observed approvingly, "I guess you did miss my skills. At least you guys haven't forgotten me entirely"

"I have missed more than that," said 117 but 43 put her fingers to his lips.

"I know," she smiled. "But for now, what do you say we beat the man that knifed me and hurry home? Right now, I am in the… mood for just a bit of good old fashioned revenge."

"Well, unless you are carrying ten thousand pounds of explosives," 1 cut-in clearing his throat. 43 and 117 broke apart and they all gathered around the map. She immediately synched up with everyone was instantly brought up to speed with the current situation, "There's no way for us to penetrate the defenses."

"Maybe not ten thousand pounds of explosives," 43 said smiling confidently, "But I have myself, my brain and supplies."

"I take it you have a plan?" 35 asked.

"You might find it a little unorthodox."

"She is alive."

"43 has returned!"

"Now we can give them REAL hell."

Word spread quickly of 43's arrival. Adding herself to the communications of all the amborgs in the vicinity inspired hope. They were ninety again. Every amborg found themselves picking themselves off the ground and preparing to leap back into the fray. Regardless of injury, everyone rallied when 43 sent out a broadcast to everyone.

"I know you've all suffered," 43 spoke out while everyone was gathering at her pod to grab the supplies she had brought.

All the soldiers fighting in the area were tuned into the transmission, all of the technicians, and every single person within reach of a radio were listening as well. 43 had hijacked a radio system and opened it to everyone she could reach.

"All of this has been difficult to bear," 43 tapped her head, "But now I return with a goal in mind. A goal that will affect everyone. Every human, soldier and family member still fighting for their lives and even the amborgs. Everyone knows who the enemy is. He has challenged us and we have met him head-on. Now, he wants to show the world our weakness. He wants to revel in our failure to protect you. We have lost many people and I am sorry for all the innocents who have perished. I say, here and now for everyone to hear, that we do have a weakness. We aren't perfect or invincible. This war has taught us that. This is a message to our allies and the adversary in question, we will never stop fighting until people like you are stopped. The more you try and put us down, we will not give in. Because if we give up now, there is no one left to stand against you. This is not a calculation or an equation anymore. This is about human life, which you assassin, have declared an all-out war upon it. You asked us what gives us the right to fight for people beneath us. You accused the amborgs of being cold and apathetic to all aspects of life."

She looked at 117 and then finished her speech.

"You are wrong," she said deeply, "We fight not for ourselves but for everyone else because it is a gut feeling. It's not complicated to us anymore. It is the human thing to do. Some people do not see us as human anymore but we will continue evolving and living for this planet. Our allegiances will always be against you. Destroyer of life."

At those words, a loud silence occurred. The amborgs were already preparing themselves. Fueled at the inspirational words of 43, they were all prepared to face the biggest battle in their lifetimes. Before anyone could make a move however, there was a loud crackle of electricity in the radio broadcast. A large voice began shouting in the broadcast.

"Destroyer of life? I like the sound of that." The assassin's voice spoke over a megaphone which everyone heard quite clearly. 117 knew it was him from the video that started this.

"So the little girl returns from her wounds," He laughed over the entire battlefield. "What makes you and your little family the advocates for humanity? You are machines! But I do congratulate you on your resolve but why not give up now and save your skins? Why do you think you can stop me? Go on. Answer in the only way you can. As a calculator risking what you can afford to lose to stop me."

"The answer..." 43 replied in the radio transmission, "...I will personally bring to your face. I know I fight because there is no one else like us. Because our feelings are for everyone else. Brace yourself. Because you're going to pay for sticking a knife in me. In all of us."

The radio broadcast ended as 43 cut the signal connection. She turned and faced the small group before her. All of them having regained their morale and confidence. Walking past them, 43 walked back to her drop-pod where they had already pulled a few boxes out.

"Nice speech." 5 grabbed one of the boxes and set it down in the street. "Almost thought you were going to reveal our plans. So what do you plan on doing first?"

"I suggest we use these and bring in the cavalry," 43 replied as she kicked opened one of the boxes and reached inside. Everyone else also did the same.

5 reached in his box and pulled out some shiny stickers. They all recognized what they were. After all, 43 had used one on them a few months ago during her rampage. 1 obviously remembered it.

"I never saw so many arrows before."

35 held up one very carefully.

"What do we do with so many?" He asked nervously even though the answer was plainly obvious.

"Well," 43 replied. "These ones, thanks to Dr. Kendrick, have been calibrated to fly an object at any ... terminal velocity. A lot faster than the original prototypes."

"It would appear we owe Dr. Kendrick our thanks."

117 stuck an arrow onto a broken refrigerator. It instantly shifted and flew towards the wall. Everyone side-stepped it as it landed into the layers of stone with a boom. The wreck stuck to the wall for a few minutes but then, the force became too much and a hole appeared. They watched as the wrecked houseware flew further and further away at tremendous speed out of sight until they could only hear loud crashes. They also heard the cries and crushing sounds of a few enemy drones. Finally there was an explosion off in the distance.

"At least these arrows have a safety distance," 43 said as she looked at the hole with concern. "Otherwise we'd probably be sending up more satellites into space."

"It was a nice shot though," 5 smiled. "Terminal velocity eh? Well that was a perfect demonstration."

"Actually," 117 replied. "I wasn't expecting that to happen."

"Sarcasm dear," 43 said encouragingly as she picked up her box.

117 shrugged but admired his handiwork as a brick fell from the top of the hole.

"What exactly is the distance they travel before they shut off?" He asked.

"Unfortunately, the maximum distance it propels an object is up to three miles," 43 replied. "Give or take."

"Give or take?"

"These arrows don't have infinite power," 43 explained as they all grabbed their boxes and stepped outside. "Once they all fly an object three miles, they are as good as dead. Our best bet when using them is shutting them manually to save their batteries."

117, upon hearing this bit of information, looked in the direction where he remembered the refrigerator had gone. He tried to lock on to the arrow's signal that he had stuck but unfortunately, it was out of range and far too late to send a signal. Everyone else stopped to listen. They could hear yells in the background which meant the fridge missile was still going. 43 chuckled nervously. Everyone turned back to her and ignored the crashing noises which were getting quieter the further it flew.

"Anyway," 43 said. "We give each amborg, wounded or active, one box. I brought a lot. All those modified compartments on my drop-pod aren't just for show. Then, find some pieces of junk. Things big enough to hurtle. Things that add potential property damage to the max."

"Oh," 1 nodded in approval. "Inanimate cavalry. Very ingenious."

43 clambered onto a piece of a billboard.

"Why call an artillery barrage when you can settle on an old fashioned storm from heaven?"

43 gave them a wink as she stuck an arrow onto the board, gave them a wink and off she flew into the air and out of sight. The gravity of the billboard pointed upward and took 43 away as if she was riding a nonexistent winged creature. Faster than anyone could have imagined.

"So I suppose our plan is to find anything that's worthy of destruction, gather it all together, then everyone sticks an arrow on everything heavy, and we ride among the falling debris like fire from the sky and basically kamikaze our way in."

57 looked around clarifying this newly found plan. Everyone was already looking for something suitable to ride on which confirmed her summarization.

"Oh why not," She shrugged as she ripped off a car door and laid it out like a skateboard and looked for a good place to stick the arrow on. "Junk kamikaze. This will be one for the history books."

117 smirked as he found an overturned vending machine, stuck an arrow onto the side and grabbed on for the ride. The arrow, pointing directly upward, lit up and instantly, the gravity of the object changed. Instantly, 117 flew up into the air and was already high up with a bird's eye view of the area. Acting fast, 117 pulled the sticker off and adjusted the direction before the effects wore off. The sticker, now facing a new direction sent the vending machine shooting across the sky instead of upwards. He had to distribute the arrows quickly, he thought, where to land?

Picking a spot fairly close to where 3's location beacon was, 117 sent a signal to the arrow, shutting it off. He felt the vending machine begin to slow down but for some reason, it didn't fall. Curious, 117 pulled the sticker off which seemed to correct the result. Without the sticker, 117 felt real gravity begin to apply to the vending machine. Interesting, he said as he began falling at an uncontrollable speed. The arrow when shut off will stop it moving and keep it suspended. He soon remembered that he was falling and immediately went back to concentrating.

Down below, there was another problem with 3.

"Surrender now Amborg, and your death shall be swift."

"I think I shall avoid the surrender then."

3 was backing away from the drone which had drawn an LTO knife and was advancing menacingly. Listening to 43's message had lifted her spirits but after that, a drone had found her and she was finding it difficult to avoid another slash. The pain in her legs was killing her as she barely side-stepped another jab.

"I could really use some help!"

Suddenly, she saw 117's beacon appear on her radar. But from where?

One minute, there was a beep indicating his arrival, the next, there was a loud massive boom. The drone disappeared under a huge object that fell from the sky. When the dust and dirt cleared, 3 stared as a 117 clung onto the top of… a vending machine where the drone had just been.

"Are you alright 3?" He asked weakly.

"I should ask you the same thing."

3 stared as 117 slowly clambered off his ride.

"A vending machine?" She asked. "You must have had to have been a couple thousand feet in the air to achieve that kind of landing."

"I think I was," 117 replied as he handed her something. She held them and recognized them immediately.

"Arrows!" 3 said happily, "This will be good help. My legs are killing me. But what am I supposed to do with all of these?"

"Well," 117 said clambering back onto the vending machine, "Find something you can ride on, then scrape up all of the junk you can find. We also need 125 and 274's transportation grenades. It can give us more stuff to drop on the enemy."

She watched as he stuck an arrow back on the side of his wreck ride. It was pointing straight upwards. In the few seconds before it shot straight up, he quickly passed on a quick message.

"Saddle up, lock and load, Missy."

117 winked and without a moment to lose, the machine shot straight up into the air. 3 stood in place and scoffed.

"The only time a western analogy works with my first name," She muttered. "He picks now to use it."

3 picked up her pop gun, checked the ammo count, and began looking for something that could carry her.

"If you are going to reference western movie genres *and* use my name at the same time," She muttered to herself, "At least offer a girl a ride will you?"

Homing in on 297's position, she instantly had an idea. Taking one of the arrows, she stuck it on herself. The result was utter chaos. Not prepared for the sudden change in gravity, she immediately felt herself free-falling towards a car! Shifting her weight, she skimmed over the roof feet first with no problem but then found herself flying in a supine position down the street with the speed of a bullet.

Must change the direction of the arrow! She thought fast. Ripping it off, 3 shifted and found herself back in a free-fall. The effects of the arrow was wearing off and she was moving back towards the ground. Sticking the arrow on her stomach on the side and making sure it faced up, she managed to change the direction. As a result, she felt herself falling towards the sky.

"Ok," 3 strained as she flew, "Before I shoot out of the atmosphere, change direction... now!"

Again, she took the sticker off and began flying in a parabola as gravity forced her back towards the ground. Managing to get her bearings, 3 saw that she was not slowing down and the ground was getting closer. Making sure the arrow was pointing in the right direction, she stuck it on her stomach for the third time, punched her fists forward as the direction of her gravity changed, and flew five feet above the ground and zoomed towards 297's beacon in a super-girl pose.

The highlight of 297's day was seeing Missy 3, flying above all things, crashing into a behemoth class robot which was seconds away from crushing him. 3 had approached with what appeared to be an imitation of the caped hero, Superman, but the instant she realized what she was flying at, she had apparently reached for her stomach, pulled something off, flailed her arms in the air desperately as if she couldn't hit the brakes and flew into the robot. Her speed, which was faster than 297 had ever seen before, was enough to cause her to crash and punch straight through the exoskeleton of his attacker leaving a gaping hole in the upper chassis. The robot fell to the ground completely destroyed and so did 3. Several hundred meters away into what was left of a bar.

"Ok now that," 297 said stunned as the behemoth groaned and sparked, "... is falling with style.

He made a reminder to himself to see if he could devise a bar joke after witnessing what he had just seen.

"An amborg fighting a behemoth sees 3 fly into a bar," He thought. "Nah, that might not work."

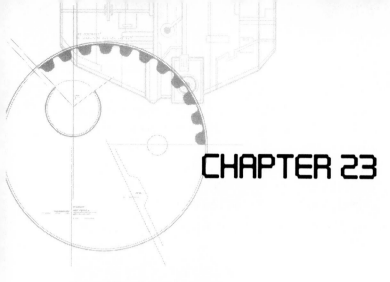

CHAPTER 23

**Enemy Warehouse Perimeter.
Roughly half an hour later.**

("To be accurate, shouldn't it say above the perimeter?")

("Hush, Sarah. Keep watching.")

*** *** ***

"On my mark, disable all power transfers to the Arrows."

"I hope the enemy appreciates the gift we are going to deliver."

Palmer peeped over a wall slab while listening to the radio. The amborgs were planning something huge and it was happening any second. Except, he couldn't see anything remotely resembling a miracle. He swore when one of the enemy drones spotted him and a couple of enemy soldiers began firing at him. Ducking down, he leaned against the wall as bullets hammered behind him. He crawled away from the slab of cover and moved into another crater. Oh I hope the plan happens right about now, he prayed silently as he tried to be as still as possible.

"Well well well," A voice from above spoke tauntingly.

"My men sure don't have that amount of sass," Palmer muttered.

He was right when he looked up and saw a drone and a thug stare down at him. Now he was sure. Definitely not one of his soldiers.

Palmer watched the drone and the soldier point their guns at him and prepared for the worst. This time, he chose not to close his eyes. He wanted to look his enemy in the eye before he went. However, the death he pictured didn't come. Instead, a shadow appeared behind the gangster and the drones. Palmer looked up and saw something large flying... no, falling towards the three of them. By the time they realized a shadow was enveloping overhead, it was too late.

A large crash occurred which made Palmer fall back in terror. There seemed to be a lot of stuff falling everywhere. The place where the drones and the soldier was replaced by a large UAV drone. Palmer stared, in utter shock at the old piece of equipment that had just saved his life. These types of drones were supposed to be out of commission. Where had it come from? Before he could so much as open his mouth, he looked up and saw something amazing.

"How do you like the gift?" A robotic voice asked.

"Yikes! That's pretty scary."

Without taking his eyes off the sky, Palmer barely uttered the words.

Over a hundred different heavy objects were falling from the sky and landing towards the enemy warehouse. He heard the chaotic beeps and roars coming from the enemy position as pieces of rubble and assorted pieces of everything were making contact. A giant ensemble of booms, crashes, thuds mixed with screams filled the air from the fortified warehouse.

"Since when can amborgs not predict weather?" 3 said clapping her hands happily at the sight of their garbage artillery barrage, "I predict a massive downpour of train in about three seconds."

"Train?" Palmer turned and scanned the skies.

She couldn't mean what he thought she meant. He stared and raised both of his eyebrows at Amborg 3 who was pointing a finger upward. Gesturing for him to look in the right direction.

"Well you don't want to miss this part of the show do you?"

Turning around quickly and staring upward, Palmer's mouth dropped again as a freight car fell and crushed some enemy drones at the perimeter of the enemy fortress. At least five or six more cars also fell and landed either on the warehouse or on the enemy position creating massive pandemonium.

"How did you get a freight train?!" Palmer yelled as the loud clanging tore past his ears.

3 smiled and placed a hand on his shoulder. She pulled some earplugs out of her pocket and passed them to him.

"You want to thank 501 and 466 for that," She replied, "It was their idea. Asked nicely at the nearby train yard and well... stuck some arrows. Good thing the train yard had no use for this specific train right?"

"Well that's all nice and good but..." Palmer ran his hands through his sweaty hair. He took the earplugs and immediately drowned out the noise. Over the noise he had to shout in order for her to hear his next question, "How are we supposed to clean all this up?!"

"One step at a time Lieutenant," 3 patted him softly on the shoulder and then stepped away to pick the UAV drone off the ground. "Clean-up is not exactly a priority right now."

"And another thing," Palmer suddenly remembered, "Where did you acquire a vintage twenty first century UAV drone?"

"Well... Let us for the moment say that some of the enemy soldiers broke into the Smithsonian for a treasure hunt. Until yours truly stopped them."

The sheepish grin that 3 gave him made him very uneasy. As she flipped the drone over and checked its condition, it dawned on him.

"You did not..."

"Don't worry, Lieutenant Palmer," Missy said as she picked up the drone and set it against the wreck of a car.

The bodies of the enemy drone and soldier were still crushed flat. Palmer didn't want to know if they had survived but stared at the wrecked piece of military hardware.

"It is a mere replica," She said innocently but Palmer eyed the UAV suspiciously.

"It doesn't look like a replica..." He said cautiously, "Too large and it looks as heavy as the real thing."

"Well..." 3 shrugged for a moment and quickly said, "The original was accidently destroyed."

Concerned, Palmer, stared at the drone and 3 who was forcing a smile. All of sudden, he stared disdainfully at the sudden realization of what she had said.

"What does that mean?" He asked, immediately regretting it.

"It means that once I fix this," 3 promised, "I will put it on display in the Smithsonian personally. No one will tell the difference!"

"That belongs in a museum!!"

"And it will..." 3 climbed back onto the drone and stuck an arrow onto the hardware, "When I have no use for it anymore."

* * *

117 sat down next to 501 and peered around a corner.

Two bullets struck the instant he peeped out causing him to pull his head back to the safety of the wall. Not surprising since the two of them were the volunteers leading the attack from the ground. The plan was simple. Half the amborgs would move their way across the ground slowly, inch by inch. While the other half would find heavy pieces of whatever they could find, throw them in the air with the arrows. The most agile and courageous of this half of the amborgs would ride the debris into the sky, aim them, and send them flying towards the enemy warehouse while they fell down to grab onto the next load of ammo. The plan was working as the amborg ground team managed to slowly push forward as their barrage was forcing the enemy to cower in their holes but it was still moving too slow. The big pieces of junk was mostly expended and now it was a light rain of car doors and bricks. Their numbers had been significantly reduced but enemy drones, shooters and a few giant behemoths were still taking shots at them.

"Afraid one will hit your head?"

117 turned to face 501 who was grinning cheekily. 117 was about to retort but paused. 501 had actually made a very good joke.

"Well actually," He replied as the two of them sat, hunched against the wall, "Based on all of the damage I have taken, I feel as if I could die just from a simple bullet to the head."

501 shook slightly to indicate he was laughing silently.

"Some of them are simple," He said confidently. Then he began to list out the times he had been shot, using his fingers to count. "Others tickle, most of them stick to my face, and rare ones explode. I probably should have died. If I were human, it would have been a total of two hundred and eighty six times that I should have died."

"Well you haven't died yet." 117 said in a very calm and grateful tone. "Look, I admit, you are annoying at times. But that is the 501 I prefer to fight with in combat. In the time I have known you, it does me great pleasure to call you my little brother."

501 nodded in recognition. He silently thanked 117 on a private channel. As he did so, 117 got an idea. He immediately held his hand around the corner and waited. A shot rang out and he caught a bullet instantly in his fingers. Retracting his arm, he examined it carefully. It was red hot.

"Care to take an analysis on this Donut?"

501 stared at the bullet. He took one glance at it and immediately worked his magic.

"Ooh, incendiary tracer," He said cheerfully, "Those are warm when you catch them at least but are very difficult to get out of your skin if you take them head on. For humans, those are designed to melt right through and shred the skin."

"Well if I still had my vending machine," 117 noted as he threw the bullet away, "We would at least have proper shielding."

"Where did you lose it?"

"Oh, in the heavy barrage of junk and miscellaneous artillery," 117 brought up his memory banks and brought up the video replay, "It went through that window on the second floor. Fifth from the right."

501 looked up at the window that 117 had indicated. He looked at the gaping hole that was shaped roughly the size of how large the vending machine was. He turned to ask 117 another question.

"Where is 43? I have not seen her or heard from her since that inspirational broadcast. 466 was really...motivated."

"Just say fired up,"117 muttered, ignoring the question, picked up a pebble and threw it.

"But it is not something I can get used to say," 501 shrugged as the pebble hit the wreckage of a police vehicle. "Especially if they literally aren't in flames..."

He trailed off as they watched where the pebble had landed. The two of them stared at the abandoned law enforcement transport and then glanced at each other briefly. 117 was already transmitting a plan.

"Humor me..." 117 said as he smirked and the two of them stood up, "Just once."

Both of them ran over to the car, lifted it and pulled it to the wall they hid behind. Then slowly, they pushed it out into the open in full view of the warehouse defenders and hid behind it. Bullets riddled the side of the car immediately. Acting fast, the two of them flipped the car onto its right side, grasped the underside and lifted it up.

"I got the idea from what the Greeks did with their shields," said 117.

501 nodded in excitement.

"And we progress forward slowly, footstep by footstep!"

"Wrong," 117 grabbed an arrow, reached up and stuck it onto the door. Pointing it directly at the warehouse. "I have devised a faster version," 117 said as the arrow powered up, "You should hang on 501, I think I set it to full power and it's almost out of juice!"

The car shot straight forward. Screams and yells filled the air along with the bullets pouring into the car-shaped shield. Both 501 and 117's feet were off the ground at high speed. Flying like flags, they flew several feet into a wall which was unable to hold against such force. As it slammed through, 117 shouted to 501.

"Let go!"

The two of them somersaulted into the ground. The car blasted into another wall, and another, and another as they both skidded across the ground. They looked around and realized they had successfully reached the warehouse. The hole was their entrance into the final objective but several of the perimeter guards were charging.

"Quick, shut it down before it gets too far out of range!"

The two of them reached out their hands and transmitted the shut-down codes but weren't sure if the flying police car received the transmission. They quickly engaged the guards when the results of the arrow were unconfirmed. 117 grabbed a charging drone's arm and ripped it off.

"We can only hope it worked!" He said as he smacked another person with the arm.

"You know, how about a warning before you send a car out the other end of the building?!"

Mid-fight, 501 and 117 glanced at the hole the police car had disappeared through only to see it come flying back the way it came. 117 immediately transmitted instructions for 501. Seconds before impact, they leapt in opposite directions and out of the way. The car rolled in and crashed across the ground clearing the area quickly. The arrow was definitely off now. 501 and 117 walked back to each other, looked at where the car landed, and proceeded into the ground floor of the warehouse. They looked across the room to see who had sent their ride back.

"That could have taken my leg out again..."

"5, stop complaining. How many cars have been thrown at you today?"

117 and 501 watched as 5 entered the building from another hole across from them, followed by 1, 7, 8, 13, 19, and 27. 501 stared at all of them and checked his databanks. He counted all of them and added them to a small list he had just started.

"Looks like the first group has made it into the warehouse," 501 said cheerfully looking at 5 who stared back in annoyance. He was still pouting.

"Then we can say that 5 was the first one from the first group," He wrote, "And then 117 was first from the second group."

"Actually 501," 117 replied. "I am not the first from the Second Group."

"What do you mean?" 501 asked pointing at 5 and 117 skeptically.

"Ok, now I want to know too," 1 spoke up from behind 5.

They were interrupted by a loud crumbling noise from above. Unfazed, everyone immediately shifted their attention upwards and watched as a hole in the ceiling opened up. Apart from the rubble, a girl dropped and landed on her back in the middle of the floor a few feet away from the group of amborgs.

"Ok, I didn't see that at all..." 43 coughed as she sat straight up.

117 ran over and helped her to her feet. As the amborgs moved in, another team of amborgs which consisted of 3, 466, 297, 57 and 35 also arrived from where 117 and 501 previously entered.

"43 got here first?" 501 stared. "When did she get here? When did she even go upstairs while we were still breaking the perimeter??"

43 gave a triumphant smile as she greeted 117 with a kiss on the cheek.

"Oh that was easy. You see, we would never have been able to break the enemy perimeter in our current condition," She said staggering a bit but stood straight and shrugged off the fall. "So after everyone got their fair share of arrows, I climbed back inside my drop-pod, flew up with all the debris we collected and flew straight down to the roof of the warehouse. All of the junk we dropped camouflaged my approach."

"A shortcut," 5 observed, "In a fast effort to catch the Assassin."

"Yes," 43 nodded intently. 117 noticed her biting her lip as she said this. Silently, he reached inside his pocket while she continued to talk. "However the warehouse roof was not strong enough for the landing speed and weight of my pod so I fell two stories to the second floor."

"Then you fell three stories and here you are now," 1 added humorously.

"This assassin is cunning. The entire floor I landed in was a large maze. Several corridors, twists and turns, and multi-colored doors. It sounds impossible but I was lost in there several times."

"Why not destroy the walls?" 3 asked, looking up at the hole that 43 had fallen from. "Create more shortcuts? Would that not make it simpler?"

"There's a lot of strange material in the walls," 43 reported. "Otherwise I'd still be up there and not here."

43 began walking towards the stairs at one end of the warehouse.

"Also, the instant I turned to backtrack, an explosive detonated under my feet and that is why I am down here with all of you guys. I get the feeling that we won't be solving this without being angry."

"Well how about we map out the floors? Work the maze together?"

"The instant you are on the floor and in the maze, there is no signal for us to communicate with each other," 43 called back to them and began climbing the stairs. "He has constructed this warehouse to his specifications. If we get to him by cheating and shortcuts, we don't know what he will do. He is forcing us to play by his rules and I intend to finish it."

At these words, she immediately ran up the stairs. The rest of the amborgs in the area began to follow suit. While everyone began discussing their puzzle solving tactics, 117 grabbed 501 by the shoulder, stopping him from moving.

"Not you. You will stay here, Donut," 117 said sternly on a private channel.

501 stared back, looked at 117's expression, and almost began to protest. But he nodded when 117 stared him down and obediently listened for instructions.

"Take Carolina… and when the rest of the amborgs make their way here, you tell them what to expect when they climb up to the upper levels. But there is something else."

"Why are we on a private channel?" 501 asked curiously looking around to make sure no one was observing them. 117 put his arm around 501, saw more amborgs enter and with his other arm waved for them to join. "Listen 501, something is not right, 43 is lying."

501's eyes widened. This was definitely an attention grabber. The only issue 501 was having trouble comprehending was the fact that amborgs do not lie. But before he could question this any further, 117 waved at 466, who had just arrived, for her to join them.

"Take Carolina 466 and any other members of the third group specifically the ones you trust and guard this area."

"What do you mean 43 is not telling the truth?" 501 asked.

He had spoken outside of the private channel which was heard by 466. As she joined them with a confused look, 117 opened the channel to her as well. Almost immediately, 117 replayed the whole conversation that he had started with 501. Quickly, he brought her onto the same page.

"She lied, right in front of us," 117 said sternly to the two of them, "She defied her ethical programming in her implants. We are not programmed to lie, our conduct has always been to the truth and what is right and wrong. So why did the girl I love lie to my face?"

"But that does not have any bearing to any form of truth 117," 466 replied. "Hang on. Let me catch up on the full conversation."

"Think for a moment 466," 117 replied. "Is the 43 in this recording of us just now the same one that taught you all that you know now so far?"

"Well she could just be occupied."

"So occupied to abandon our own coordinated efforts and pursue the objectives by herself?"

501 stopped to think for a moment but when he spoke again, he sounded slightly convinced by what 117 was saying.

"She did seem very eager about ending this," He replied thinking about her responses. "117 does also have a point. She has not been contributing alongside us like she used to. It did feel different but I assumed it was because of her condition."

"She recovered from her coma right?"

466 looked at the two of them but then she realized what she had just said.

"Or… recovered from a coma that was already declared terminal," she muttered.

"More or less," 117 replied. "I find it very convenient that when a solution was needed, 43 was provided to us and now we seem to be on a straight path to the finish. There is something else behind this."

"Actually, what I also noticed is that she seems to have abandoned all aspects of teamwork," 466 reported. "The one thing that has changed about her is that she seems to be driven solely by the motive of revenge."

"Also," 501 added. "It does not seem like her to pursue the mission without her own partner. I mean, 117 and 43 have been inseparable. I mean in the field that is. For example, if they were on two separate missions, they obviously would not be together. But every time they are deployed and working together, they always work as partners. She ditched him. No offense 117."

501 looked at 117 who was nodding.

"She is hiding something," 117 guessed. "For some reason, she has the means to end this but… at the same time, it does not feel right. The truth is, when we first set out, I calculated… or to be accurate, I considered the possibility of apprehending this assassin. Capture but not kill."

At these words, he immediately had to signal for the two third group amborgs to be silent. He knew this would not sit well with them. 501 and 466 were giving him looks of apprehension which was not surprising. 117 was probably the only person to even think of putting a man in prison despite the entire country being set aflame.

"I know this possibility is unsettling to the rest of us but we can't just kill him."

"He has massacred hundreds of people," 466 protested silently. She looked around. A few amborgs walked by but they didn't hear anything. Without giving too many signs of trouble to the other amborgs, the trio slowly began to make their way to the stairs, "Why does he not deserve death?"

"That is the human side arising in you 466," 117 replied calmly, "Anger, confusion, prejudice. It's what he wants. You say you want to kill him in cold blood but if it was down to you, would you actually do it? That isn't how the system works. In my time studying human behavior, it is true that I have been slow but I personally say that we would be better off doing the right thing and turn him over to a jury. Sure they will probably give him the death penalty anyway for his crimes but I would rather beat him to the point where he knows pain. This way… if he has any remorse or any scrap of guilt, I want to make sure he has time to live with it until his dying day. He tortured our emotions in such a short time, then we should make him endure that in the long-run. Truthfully, I won't be the one to kill him. Think for a moment, calculate with your implants and not with your human side. The sole purpose of what we have faced these past days was to drive us to the breaking point."

117 turned to 501 and looked him in the eye.

"Do you see how blood thirsty we have become lately? We have been pushed to the primitive roots of our human personalities. And we may be cybernetic but we still have the mentalities of young adults. He can manipulate us before we even realize it. If we kill him, we prove his point exactly. That the amborgs can be corrupted, murderers and vigilantes disregarding the law and what is right and wrong. Kill him, and we become him. People will see us not as their protectors but they will fear us. That is the point of this entire challenge, to bring down the amborgs no matter how we finish his game. He's so self-destructive that he doesn't care if he dies. He wants us to sink to the bottom after this is over. Look at the destruction that has happened across the country. Maybe after this is over, someone will find a way to blame us for this. The right thing to do is to capture and turn him over to the authorities. This way, he will answer for his crimes and the people will know who really started this war. The more we deal with him, he enjoys having fun out of it. I want to stop him but not in a way where we kill off the only link that completely explains this mess. Everyone is so eager to kill in war that it isn't until later in life when they suffer."

He was expecting the two young amborgs to completely disagree with his plan. But to his surprise, 501 and 466 both looked at each other and they slowly nodded.

"That does make sense," 501 replied. "But there may be a lot of discord from the rest of us. There are already a ton of us almost at the end."

"That is why as a family," 117 replied. "I know we can trust each other. Ranting personal opinions was a bit of a waste of time but our objective is to also stop 43. She has the most motive out of all of us and if she were to kill this man, we would probably face more trouble than actual victory."

"I get it," The young amborg smiled. "You should know by now that you were the big brother I never really had. I know you think of the right stuff."

"I know you want him dead Donut," He said patting him on the shoulder. "I want him to pay for what he did to 43 but if we stoop to his level, then no one will trust us again. When we finish this, we need to do everything we can to rebuild and do what we were created to do. Thus, we do this the right way."

"Are you sure that was a calculation? Or was it the human side of you speaking David 117?"

117 looked at 466. She had barely spoken in the conversation but the two boys could tell that she was already in agreement.

"I am afraid I'll have to tell you later."

All three of them smiled but then 466's instantly gazed wide-eyed at 117.

"But if that's the case, I think this means we better hurry!" She exclaimed.

"Right. If I do not make it out," 117 said. "It is your job to remind the other amborgs who arrive of our new mission. The reason for our existence rests in you."

"We have to stand guard?" 501 sighed. "Man…"

"If we die up there," 117 replied, "Someone has to lead us. 501, I am entrusting that to you and 466."

"Cool," 466 chuckled. "We get to run the show. But wait 117, why did you not warn the rest of the amborgs when they followed 43?"

"If I stopped all of the amborgs from following after her, it would have made her suspicious," 117 called back. He was already heading towards the stairs, "How would you like to fall victim to a 43 attack again? It is possible she is already suspicious of my behavior. Especially since I didn't follow her up the stairs immediately. Put simply, fingers crossed."

He held up his hand and crossed his index and middle fingers just like the way Mandy taught him. She had once told him even he would have to hope and wish for luck. He remembered he had told her that computers didn't need it. He set a reminder to himself to apologize sincerely if he made it out alive afterwards.

Stepping up the stairs, 117 spoke to Mandy as quickly as possible. With every step he climbed, the signal began to go hazy. What is this place built of? He wondered as he tried to clear the communication line. It wasn't until he placed his hand on the wall that he recognized where he had encountered this material. It was exactly like the conditions in Texas when they couldn't detect the signals of the explosives in certain places. If they maze was built like this, then that really did mean no outbound or oncoming signals. They each had to rely on their own self-mapping tech. If he ran into the others, he hoped that they could have the chance to coordinate.

"Mandy," He said trying to send out one last transmission. "Did you hear the whole thing?"

"David... The signal is starting to get hazy," She informed him, "Once you get in there, I can't provide you with a second pair of eyes. The feed could go out and you will go dark. David, what are you going to do about Serina?"

"I have to get to the Assassin before her," 117 said as he arrived at a door at the top of the stairs, "43 isn't going to apprehend him. Don't argue, scan my memory banks and analyze her expression. It is the truth. She is planning to kill him for what he did to her as revenge and that is not what Dr. Kendrick made her to be. Something is definitely not right. Anticipate a trap because it has been far too convenient. 43's arrival, a clear shot to the warehouse, it is not right. There is never a smooth way out with this guy. If I were him, I would calculate all the possible strings to pull. That means he probably has something planned for us."

"Hmm," Mandy replied through the static. "It does feel strange. I feel a tingling in my shoulders. Once you drop out of contact, I'll inform Dr. Kendrick. There is definitely something suspicious that makes this too convenient. You go get her David. And this guy too. I think you're absolutely right that it never turns out like this. If you believe this is the right thing then hurry. Before it's too late.

"Understood Mandy."

And he took a step through the door. The connection cut off completely as the door swung shut.

"All I have to do is stop the woman I love who happens to be capable of killing me," 117 muttered as he looked around a corner, "...and save the life of the man who declared a one man war on the entire United States, ended the life of the aforementioned woman, put us through the biggest amborg operation in history, and happens to be the one that everyone hates and wants to kill. Just what I needed, extra challenges. Oh no."

117 backtracked but did not recognize which way he had come from. He could have sworn this was the only way but he had stumbled into a path with three different halls. He had already been sidetracked? There was a flash of light and he blinked. When he looked again, the hall became dark but then he saw a light at the far end. Not a good idea to go that way, he thought as he felt his way towards the hall that was on his right but felt a smooth wall. Had that been there before?

"Even more extra challenges," He said nervously, "I think I'm lost."

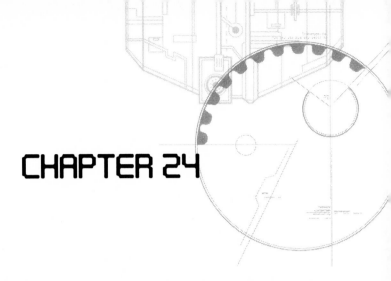

CHAPTER 24

"Ok that was four rights, two lefts, and another right. And then one more left."

"Stop trying to map this place 917. We know we're on the third floor… At least I still hope so. But every time we try remembering the way, it is not the same and we go back down one floor with every screw up."

"The maze is bound to give soon. But yes, this is really unfair. How long have we been at this?"

"Two hours and twenty-six minutes. Hey 917. Look! A door."

917 and 999 opened the door and stepped through. The instant they did, the door slammed shut behind them as expected. Turning around sharply, 917 instantly grabbed the door handle, turned and pulled as hard as he could. It was stuck.

"Great…" He muttered angrily while 999 looked around. "Another newly discovered dead end… Now we are currently stuck. Time to go back to the second floor."

"Maybe not," She replied urging him to let go of the handle, "We haven't fallen yet. Maybe we're on the right track now."

She pointed and 917 realized that there was a hallway. It wasn't a dead end after all.

"Shall we?" 917 muttered as he released the door handle and the two of them began walking down the hallway. As they continued, the hallway became narrower and narrower causing them to turn and sidle through. They wondered what would come next.

"There is no communication from anyone on the outside."

"917, in our current state, please worry about the fact that... urgh... it's getting much more difficult to squeeze through..."

"I was only trying to make conversation... supposedly it is good for passing time."

"Well if you want to talk, try talking about something other than the obvious."

"What do you suggest dear sister?"

"Ok buster," 999 stopped and turned her head to look back at him. "When this is over, you bring two cans of ice cream and we hunker down in the cafeteria for a few hours."

917 stared.

"That is not a very common request coming from you," He replied.

"I'm tired alright? Damn. I'm saying stuff I don't normally say."

917 bumped into her. She was apparently moving much slower now. 999 turned to give him an annoyed look before continuing.

"You wouldn't believe the stuff I have been saying to people these last couple days," She said. "It's almost like someone intoxicated me and now I am drunk with vulnerabilities."

"Asides from how much I want to decipher whatever that means," 917 said. "There is one important thing we need to clear the air about."

"What?"

"You like ice cream?"

"Of course I like ice cream!" 999 snapped. "I'm lactose intolerant but I eat it because it's great! What is so surprising about that?"

"But the last time we had ice cream," 917 replied thoughtfully. "You turned it down when I offered you a scoop."

"I'm perfectly capable of getting my own," 999 sighed. "I believe I said that at the time too."

"You didn't have to slap it out of my hand at the time either," 917 muttered. "I waited an hour to get that for you."

"I usually acquire what I need whenever everyone isn't looking."

As they continued to sidle for a few more minutes, 917 began to wonder how far they had gone. Finally 999 stopped for a second to catch her breath. It was fortunate that neither of them were claustrophobic.

"This corridor is definitely reminding me about my figure..."

999 suddenly stopped and didn't finish her sentence. Before 917 could say another word, she turned her head to look back and glared at him. He immediately looked into her eyes but it was too late. She had already caught him staring down.

"Do not say another word," She muttered respectfully.

917 smirked as she turned her head and continued down the narrow corridor. Casually, he glanced and stared before pointing his eyes upward.

"Is it my fault that the walls are conveniently showing off how nice your b..."

He wasn't able to finish the sentence when her fist suddenly punched him in the head.

In another part of the maze. There were other obstacles that the other amborgs were facing.

"You are not my father!"

297 was on his knees and holding his arm over his eyes. In front of him stood a a man resembling him but was older.

"There isn't anything ahead for you, Carter," His father spoke calmly, "Put an end to this quest and turn back. It's over!"

"My father is dead!" Carter snarled looking up, "Furthermore, he never told me to surrender. When he still walked the earth, I know that he didn't raise me to quit. If you think you can prevent me from progressing, you are surely mistaken!"

"Can you really remember? You were only a small boy when your mother and I left you on the streets. You have nothing ahead. Go back while you can."

"Get up 297. I believe it's my turn."

297 turned sharply and saw 57 walk past. She faced 297's father with a face of utmost fury but made no hostile movement. Instead, she lifted a hand and reached for a shoulder but felt thin

air. 297 then realized what was happening. His father was actually a holographic projection. But how did the Assassin manage to find information to construct 297's father?

"This isn't real," 57 said flatly. "Leave my brother alone."

Finally, 297 stood and walked past his father. Despite its protests, both he and 57 proceeded to the end of the room and exited through a door. After the door closed, 297 curled his fingers into fists. Before he could slam them into the wall, 57 was one step faster. She dropped to her knees and began hammering the ground. Startled, 297 immediately bent down and put his hands on her shoulders.

"It was... tzzt... my sister..." 57 spoke out loud. 297 looked back at the closed door.

"What do you mean?" He asked curiously. All thoughts about his fake father immediately went to the back of his mind. He rubbed his hands up and down her shoulders in an attempt to console her.

"That hologram showed you an image of your father," she explained, "But what I saw was my sister. You remember her... right?"

At a loss for words, 297 became silent and he sat on the ground next to her. How could he forget? 57's sister hadn't survived the enhancement process. He had met her before augmentation but it was very brief. Everything that made amborgs what they were had taken the lives of several others who volunteered. 297 looked ahead as 57 kept describing what she had seen.

"She was lying on that table... All personnel and Dr. Kendrick tried everything but she realized she was already dying. I made the attempt to speak to her with my voice but it was gone. Altered by my becoming advanced... She failed to hear a proper farewell from my own mouth."

"You saw her again? How are these holograms becoming things in our past?" 297 looked further down the hall.

It was completely identical to the other hallways they had been through. The repetition of the structure was really starting to stretch out to where he wanted to nuke the place. All of this is designed to break us, he thought. We have already been broken over and over.

"She said she blamed me for not having the opportunity to survive," 57 bit her lip and shut her eyes. "My sister accused me of murdering her and that the life we have as amborgs was not rightfully mine."

"You should not believe that," He instantly spoke up, "You saw through that and pulled me with you past it. You got me away from that thing pretending to be my father. It was also not your sister. Yet you beat it with all the mental strength you had."

"But would she really be angry that I am alive and she is not?"

"No one can answer that!" 297 replied immediately. "I mean, if we had the resurrection stone from the Deathly Hallows, it might be worth a shot but... there is nothing we can do about it."

Carter nudged her and wrapped his arms around her. He motioned for her to stand and he practically had to pull her to her feet. As they stood up, she took a few deep breaths.

"That is not how your sister was when she lived," He said firmly. "All of us understood the risks, and we ALL chose to pursue this life. Your sister would be proud of everything you have done. And I know that because she believed in everything you do now and that is why you carry her memories as a part of you. Pain is natural. Just endure it for a while longer. Continue and finish the fight, then her memory will be at peace. Do not let that fake hologram haunt you."

Both of them reached an intersection which broke into three directions. On the left corridor wall, the number twelve had been written. The center corridor had thirteen scratched into the wall and the corridor on the right was displaying the number fourteen. Supposedly, amborgs 12, 13, and 14 had been this way already. Before they could choose a direction, 57 trembled and backed against the wall. 297 stood next to her for a few moments. Seeing his father had completely thrown him off-guard which was probably bearing down in a similar way on 57 and anyone else who would eventually pass through that room.

"That hologram..." She spoke after a few moments of silence. "It was my sister to me but it was your father to you, 297?"

"It terrified me when my father reappeared. It has been so long since my parents were killed," 297 bowed his head, "It must have been programmed to simulate memories in order to stop us."

"It was multi-actual..."

"What?"

57 faced 297 with a shocked look.

"It was two different holograms at the same time," She exclaimed. "I saw my sister, you saw your father. Hologram technology being able to simulate two completely different people is close to impossible."

"The Assassin must have also found a way to infiltrate our records," 297 said thinking back to how his father had materialized and how accurately he looked. "Our records should not be that easy to infiltrate."

57 trembled even more.

"Those were our memories that were accessed," she shuddered, "It manifested into something we once cared about and that program turned our memories against us. The Assassin knows how to break us. He has brought back something we lived with for years and stamped it deep in our hearts. I do not know if I can continue."

"117 has not surrendered yet," 297 said quietly, "We cannot stop now. We have to fight with him until this is over. Because if he does this to others, then there will be even bigger atrocities."

"And that is exactly why I ask you to keep fighting."

117 had arrived from behind them so fast that both of them jumped but felt relieved instantly and relaxed.

"Boy, in this maze," 57 said, "I sure am glad to see another friendly face."

"We have been pushed to the brink," 117 said grabbing each of their hands. "I am not ordering you to fight with me. Our programming has always been to the right things. But these past few days have wreaked havoc on all of us. So, despite your exhaustion, despite all of the problems that we have faced and the trials, I ask if you will fight with me."

57 and 297 grasped his hands tighter at these words. Both of them already knew what their answer was. 117 pulled both of them to their feet and the three of them all nodded.

"Oh and for good measure, in the possibility that we die today," He added, "This may as well be the last time that I shake your hands. And this is also the last time that I ask you to make one last push."

"Damn it 117," said 297, "You had to jinx it."

"I always did love a challenge," 57 shrugged. All of them let go of each other's hands and stepped into the intersection, looking at each direction. "As long as we do this together."

"There is one thing," 297 spoke. "No matter what happens, we are still the same people we were before we changed. That is something I will never forget. And if the Assassin decides to use that to his advantage, I will personally send him to hell. He is definitely going to pay for bringing my father back desecrating his memory."

"Speaking of that," 57 remembered, "117, what did you see when you encountered the hologram? You did not appear to be as fazed as we were."

"Oh that?" 117 shrugged, "Well if it is designed to be manifesting our memories and preventing us from proceeding by corrupting our memories, then it made a big mistake."

"Who did it reveal itself as to you?"

"The stupid program turned into 43," 117 chuckled, "It made a poor choice in selecting an antagonist."

"Especially since she's the one who really wants to kill the guy that designed this madhouse."

All three of them laughed at 297's observation. But they stopped when 117 gave him a firm look. 297 had spoken to 501 about 117's opinion for the assassin earlier and although he resented the idea of placing the enemy in custody, he was in agreement to the plan.

They ended up continuing further down the maze. Finally they reached some stairs. But before they ascended it, they all paused for a moment. They had lost track of time during the big push in the maze. Was this really the end? Luckily, they knew how many floors it had been.

"Last floor," 57 noted, looking up at all the stairs, "I am ready to end this."

"This is most likely the end of the maze," 117 said firmly.

"How do you know?" 297 said as they started climbing up.

"We are close. I can tell."

All of them, stuck mid step, turned when the wall nearby burst outwards. A large hole was blown out and they all turned in defensive stances to see what the commotion was all about. They watched as 1, 3, and 5 stepped through the hole. All of them looked exhausted as they practically fell down at the bottom of the stairs.

"How on earth..." 117 started but 1 held up a hand for silence.

"Trust me," He said, "Give us a moment and we might tell you."

"That would really be nice," 3 said running her hands through her hair.

Her clothing looked disheveled and they all saw that she was painted multiple colors. 5 and 1 also had different splatters of paint but she seemed to have taken the most of it. 5 pulled his left hand off with his right and turned it outward. Several coins dropped from inside and fell on the ground with a series of metallic pings.

"How did someone put *coins*..." 297 started but 5 waved his hand less arm.

"I really do not wish to discuss that," He sighed. "It was a gas room. Something that our air filters could not withstand. We began to feel intoxicated so we tried to find a quick exit."

"Remember to tell them about the music too," 3 added. "There were speakers in there that blasted music at volumes that would have probably made normal humans deaf. Even with our hearing off though, it still burst in our heads."

"When we shut off our hearing," 1 finished, "We could not coordinate and had a hard time locating each other because the lights went out as well. 3 eventually began charging through the walls. We triggered another trap when we fell into another room and that is why we are covered in paint."

"Well that explains the colors," 297 observed, "What about 5? He seems to be running on high fumes. Also, where did the coins come from?"

"Not been the same since the recharge," 3 shrugged, "His temper has been on a short circuit. In the darkness, there was music, then a wall bursting, the sound of paint spraying, and then I heard the sound of coins clinking. But I do not know as to why they ended up inside 5. He will have to tell you himself after it is over."

"Like I said," 5 muttered, "I really would rather not say how. Sorry for snapping at you guys. I have been very restless."

"Under those conditions, sounds perfect for the ending. By my calculations, it is the last floor," 1 said looking up the stairway. "Shall we?"

"Let us finish this," 117 said firmly.

"I got some complaints that I believe this guy's customer service needs to know about right away," 5 muttered as he cracked his knuckles.

* * *

"This is kind of boring."

"We have a job to do. 117 told us to stay here and we are staying here."

501 and 466 stood in the middle of the first floor of the warehouse. Everyone was already upstairs figuring out how to get past the maze except for them. 466 was circling on the spot, pouting. It had been thirty minutes since the last amborg stepped up the stairs.

"What are we supposed to stay here for?" She asked looking up at the ceiling.

"What do you mean?"

466 looked at him and shrugged.

"It seems pointless to stand here you know?" She said. "The military is watching the perimeter but we should be there. This guy is probably not going to try and escape by running down the stairs. The probability of that happening is ridiculous."

"But not an unlikely one," 501 replied.

Glancing briefly at the various holes, she then turned to 501 who crossed his arms.

"As much as I would love to go up there and help, 117 asked us to stay down here for another reason as well," He said casually but 466 could hear how uneasy he was, "But... he did not tell us what it was we were waiting for specifically. I think we should wait to see what it is."

"He always did have a very good sense of judgement. But why would he not be more specific of what to wait for?"

"It probably has something to do with this button," 501 lifted his hand and opened it.

466 looked at the button sitting in his palm and knew that it was 117's. She had thought however that it was just a useless old thing he just carried around like a charm. Now 501 had it.

"Did you press it?" She asked, never having seen it in use.

"117 did before he gave it to me but I have no explanation why. I am also unaware of the purpose of the device."

"It is probably safe to say it is not a detonator," 466 said thoughtfully.

"In a way kids, it is the detonator to the lock of a cage. Once the padlock is blown away, the door opens and releases a terrible beast..."

466 whirled around but someone struck her in the head, disorienting her, then she felt her feet swept from underneath. She fell to the ground, landing hard on her back. 501 also didn't have time to react. Someone had kicked him from behind sending him staggering forward. Before he could straighten up, someone had hit him hard on the back and he fell onto his stomach. Slightly dazed, he felt himself being rolled sideways and forced onto his back next to 466. A hooded figure was standing above the two of them flanked by even more strangers they didn't recognize.

"...Me," Said the first figure with a smile.

501 looked up and saw an old man based from what he saw. That could not be correct, he thought. An old man had taken two amborgs down? Impossible.

"You are silent, swift and strong..." 501 said bluntly, "Even we could not hear you. Who are you?"

"Who do you think? I assume this is an unconditional surrender? I've always wanted to keep an amborg as a pet."

"Look," 466 said calmly, "If you let us go, perhaps we can propose an alternative solution that satisfies both of our goals."

501 threw up his hand immediately at the sound of the word surrender.

"Yes, there is no need to capture us," He said as loudly as possible to whoever could hear. "We kind of have things to do."

The old man turned his head towards 501's hand and stared at it.

"Relax kid," He said. "I'm not with the man you're trying to hunt down. What I do know is, my grandson called me here and he isn't here to welcome little old me."

The old man's tone became less aggressive and he began chortling which caused 501 and 466 to peer nervously at each other. The hooded figures were now backing away slowly. The old man extended a hand to 501 and 466.

"117 told me about you two," He said, "But honestly. You guys are that bad at fighting? Always have the skills to protect yourself even when you think you're safe. Especially if it's only you two guarding a place like this. I definitely expected better."

The two of them stood and faced the strange arrivals. The old man pulled his hood back and stared at the two third group amborgs.

"Do you know who I am?" He asked 501 and 466.

501 only could guess based on rumors he had heard. Still, he and 466 shook their heads. The old man sighed.

"Well, I wouldn't expect 117 to be so open about me but for a quick introduction, I'm his old man's old man. Call me Mark. Only 117 gets to call me Grandpa mind you. I don't care if you kids are all self-proclaimed brothers and sisters. He kinda forfeited that right when he became so lovey-dovey to 43."

"What?" 466 frowned.

"That was a joke… oh never mind. I forgot how you kids haven't updated your sense of humor."

Both 501 and 466 gaped at the old man. They could not believe their ears. 117 had a relative? An actual living relative? Now it made sense to 501.

"117 mentioned someone who called himself his grandfather during a mission in Los Angeles," He recalled. "It was the night he got stabbed. That was you?"

"Excellent deduction," The old man chuckled. "Now would you two tell me where my grandson is? And also how you have his method of contacting me?"

"I guess 117 wanted me to give it to you," 501 replied, "There has been a new development in which 117 needs help."

"I kind of put two and two together kid."

"Four."

"Excuse me?"

466 stared when Mark turned and frowned at her. She blushed.

"Two and two is four," she muttered.

"I'm not senile. This isn't the time to be literal," Mark snapped.

He then looked back towards 501.

"What were David's exact instructions?" He asked in an urgent tone of voice.

"He ordered both of us to stay down here to wait," He spit out, "I believe he meant to wait for you. He is up in the maze attempting to stop 43."

Grandpa Mark listened but instantly, 501 could tell he had confused him.

"Hang on," Mark said putting a hand to 501's face, "Let me do a download. It's faster but this might feel weird."

501 felt a power surge going to his head and then nothing. Staring at Mark's hand, 501 and 466 noticed he had some sort of electrical brace. Grandpa Mark pulled something out of a socket in the arm brace and put it in his ear. A holo-screen let up creating a type of visor around his eyes.

501 stared in admiration at what he was doing. He is re-watching my own memories, he thought, wow he is good. The visor shined for a few more seconds before dissipating.

"Ok I think I understand now what David wants me to do," He said taking the earpiece out and sticking it back into the arm brace.

"You are also cybernetic?" 466 stared in amazement.

"Not as advanced as you kids but I know the basic upgrades to speed things along," Mark winked. "Alright, now that I'm to speed, let's figure out what to do."

"You do not have a plan?" 466 asked in surprise. Grandpa Mark stared back and nodded.

"Yes, my grandson didn't have time to actually leave a distinct blueprint for me but he needs help and we need ideas. First let's make a safety chute."

"What do we require a safety chute for?" 501 asked curiously. Mark gestured for him to be quiet.

"A back-up plan!" He corrected, "If I am right, this assassin is about to drive your amborg friends to the point of insanity. Hasn't that been the whole point of this entire war? 117 showed me the challenge video shortly before Texas. This guy says he's doing this because he can. Reminds me of the Joker but there is nothing to support that. Let's assume he actually does have an ulterior motive for doing all of this. He has resources, military strength and enough power to blitz the entire country in a short period of time. And he seems to get a kick out of causing the amborgs the most trouble. He has been quick to make your lives miserable from day one and I think it is going to affect everyone badly. The question is, why does he hate you so much and what would killing innocent people do? If I had to guess, he's trying to make you lose in front of the people you're working to save. This sort of logic and personality... it is consistent with someone on a path to destruction. He wants to die knowing his mission has succeeded and make others clean up or inspire more to commit more atrocities. He's proving that the amborgs can lose. You two, 501 and 466. Take groups of my people around the outside of the building and catch anyone who tries to jump out the side. Forget killing them and apprehend on sight."

"Why would anyone escape that way?"

"If this guy makes it to a window, we have to make sure he doesn't succeed in killing himself. Everything he has done these last two days is enough for the death penalty but there will be more trouble if nobody sees him answer for it. They will see only the amborgs failing to catch the man responsible. He wants chaos and you kids to pay for all the damage."

"That does not make sense," 466 replied.

"It does to me," Mark replied. "It's what I would do. A criminal of his type has no remorse and no guilt at all. He declared war knowing full well of the end result. Eventually we would catch up to him. He did the impossible. He started a war on the U.S. and created enough destruction and mayhem to scare millions of people. Now he has nowhere to run except death itself. By uniting all the crime syndicates and deploying those robots across the place, it becomes total anarchy and people are paying the price. If he was able to drain your power and exhaust you to the point of giving up, he not only shattered the people's last line of defense but stepped on your reputation. 43 is definitely a pawn, whether she knows it or not. If she kills him before we can take him in, endless possibilities could happen."

"What is that?" 501 said nervously.

"For starters," Mark replied. "It shows that the amborgs aren't as cool-headed as everyone knows you all are. Are you really cold-blooded killers? You were made to protect people because of the right thing and knowing when to stop. 43 will sink to a very dangerous level and that's what 117 believes must be stopped. Kill off the mastermind behind all of this and who knows what'll happen? People hate you for not giving them the man responsible, then over time, someone decides to shift the cause of this whole war on the amborgs. I don't know. Either way, whatever happens, there is nothing good that'll happen. Just go under the impression that everything bad might happen regardless of what we do. 117 thinks that taking this enemy in is the best method for generating the least amount of bad results. There's still going to be heat out of this but it's the best plan than what 43 is planning. Got it?"

501 and 466 nodded immediately.

"Good," Mark said in relief. "Because I doubt I can repeat that rant again…"

"We recorded it," 466 replied. "You are all set."

"First off, I'm betting you kids are in serious trouble," Mark muttered. "He asked me to come all the way over here after all."

"There is very little difference," 501 replied. "We cannot even formulate a plan to help 117. They are up in the maze and by the time we get through it, it could be too late."

"Ok so we find a way to get there early."

"What?"

"My son," Mark said as he closed his eyes and leaned into his hand. "117's father always used to say that if you supposedly weren't going to make it in time, think about ways to be there sooner."

He opened his eyes to see 501 and 466 staring at him with concern.

"Anyway," Mark continued. "The real question is exactly that. Why me?"

"Took the words from our mouths," 466 sighed.

"And I thought you were the literal one. Sassy little… Look the point is… Wait let me think. Go watch the perimeter."

Mark's guards all moved out rapidly and swiftly. 466 and 501 all watched as Mark shook his finger as if he was just about to find the last piece to the puzzle.

"He wouldn't call Dr. Kendrick here," He muttered. "Too obvious and much to tempting of a target in a battlefield. Why didn't he call in one of his military friends? Someone in the chain of command may be smarter than me… supposedly. Why would he ask the last of his family…"

He then looked at 501 and grinned.

"That's exactly why he called me," Mark said as his eyes lit up. "Family!"

"What does that mean?" 501 asked.

"Bear with me just a second," Mark said. "What is it that humans typically do most of the time? They think outside of the box. Now that's typical for a basic plan. 117 tackles the maze while everyone else outside figures out other ways."

"Like the time that 18 cheated?" 466 asked.

"What do you mean?"

"Well when we were initially being trained as amborgs," 466 explained. "Dr. Kendrick built a series of mazes for us to solve. It was 18 that eventually got fed up with the last one that he spent months building. So, after several days of being stuck in there, she created her own shortcuts. Dr. Kendrick did mention we could use whatever methods we could to finish. She argued that cheating was one way."

"Then that's what we do," Mark nodded in approval. "We cheat. Your amborg programming usually prevents you from pursuing certain parameters. So this guy exploited that and basically forced all of you to enter the maze."

"How can we cheat?" 501 asked. "We can't get an accurate reading of the interior of the maze. We do not know where the end of it is. There is no other way. A military demolitions group is on the roof right now but the report is that they cannot use too much otherwise they risk destroying the whole building. There is too much reinforcement to accurately determine how much explosive we need to break through."

"43 already tried remember?" Mark replied. "She used her drop-pod and made it to the second floor from the sky. We just need to do the math and try landing on the fourth floor based on that data."

"We can use our drop-pods to try but even with the two of our pods, we could risk making one hole too many."

"Wait a minute," Mark replied. "Didn't 43 already make a hole in the roof? Wait don't tell me. Let me guess. The hole resealed itself with some sort of extra barricade? Some sort of blast shield?"

The two of them nodded.

"For crying out loud," Mark sighed. "Fine, I'll do it. You stay here and watch the floor. Make sure no one tries skipping out on us. All of the amborgs have tried to take this maze from the right way. 117 is telling me, I think, to meet him at the finish by destroying the assassin's rules. I'm not going to question why you kids didn't think of going in through the roof from the start but it might just take someone not designed like you to help finish this. Now where did 117 park his drop-pod?"

"I am afraid that is another problem," 501 said sheepishly, "Drop-pods only operate specifically to the amborg they are calibrated to. It would never run for you."

"Fortunately, I knew his father 501," Mark replied. "And I know that the drop-pods have another security feature which I know will help me. If you'll excuse me, I'm going to hot-wire a drop-pod."

"Hot-wire... A term for an electrical instrument depending on the expansion of a wire when heated or on a change in the electrical resistance of a wire when heated or cooled," 501 recited questioningly, "But I fail to see the relevance..."

"Or..." 466 added, "It means to start the engine of a vehicle by bypassing the ignition system, typically in order to acquire/steal it."

"Thank you sweetheart," Mark stated as sarcastically as he could, "Now let's move! I think I know who this bad guy is. I just need to call Kendrick."

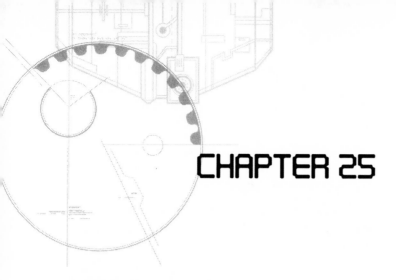

CHAPTER 25

The Fourth Floor (Hopefully)

117 looked back at the small number of worn-out amborgs. 3 was showing a bit of concern by the expression on her face. Everyone else, despite their fatigue, were looking up to him for one last briefing. 117 nodded in understanding as he led them forward. Finally, it was over. As they approached a double door, they knew what was at stake. They were going in with just them. They didn't have time to wait for any stragglers to come after them. It was time to make the last push.

"Status?" 117 asked. Everyone checked their power levels and damaged systems. Everyone had had their share of battle damage but they all nodded. "I want everyone to know that we have the strength. Enough for this last fight. I would like to make one simple request."

"David 117, the outcome I envisioned has been the same since this incident first started," 5 interrupted angrily. "We should not be apprehending someone who has committed acts of mass genocide."

"Well, 5," 1 replied. "I partially agree with you but unfortunately, that is why all eighty nine of us participated in a vote. You and twelve others agree to execute him on the spot but the rest of us have spoken otherwise."

"I have told you the truth," 117 replied firmly. He knew that there were would be at least more than a few people arguing against him. This was the last opportunity he had to try and convince the team in front of him now. "But we are amborgs. If we kill, then the last rule of human nature will fall and the enemy will win. I do not deny the lives that we have taken on the field whenever we set out on an operation. But those were moments when I personally did not feel. People told me I had to kill these criminals because they deserved to die and we said that it was war and they were casualties of it. The roots of my humanity have been dug deep during this incident and I am sure the rest of you have felt a great change as well. But I know that I will regret it if this mastermind, this evil person has his way. We have to take him in. If he dies, then we may even become like him. Stop looking at me like that 5. It is rude to roll your eyes. I know that in our cybernetics, we are designed… we volunteered to do the right things for life. You may hate me for a long sense of time but I learned that sometimes, I do not have to care. I just need to do what I believe to be ok. Of course the system has flaws. We make it right though no matter what. All that matters now is we finish this."

117 looked at 5 who had a serious look.

"Can I at least break his face?" He said after what seemed like a good deal of an awkward silence.

Everyone stared at 5 but then they saw that he had said another joke. One by one everyone began to chuckle slightly.

"Just in case it is not clear though," 1 spoke up.

1 stood in between 5 and 117. The whole team looked at the first amborg.

"I will only say this once more because for the record, it deserves to be said out loud. I agree with the both of you."

He made his statement very firm and grounded that none of them even replied. Both 5 and 117 looked at each other and then guiltily down at the floor. Their prides had clashed and for amborgs, that was emotionally unstable. 1 motioned for the two of them to look at him.

"Yes, I believe that 5 is right. We should not allow this murderer to live," He explained. "Under societal traditions and the wishes of basic human personality traits, the death of this assassin is the fulfillment of justice people want. But as 117 has said where very few would have the courage to for fear of being abused, I think he is right as well. We have been blinded so much by anger of all emotions that we lost the very sense of purpose for why we chose to agree to this life. I agreed to fight death in the face because I was afraid. I had nothing to lose and I wanted to have reason to keep living my life. If I had to have a CPU installed in my brain, then ok, that was what I agreed to and here I am. Like 117 said, I wanted to fight for the right thing and as 5 said, I want nothing more than to destroy the very evil that hurts the good and bad people that drove us to this lifestyle. But what matters now is what we decide to do that makes us who we are. Do people believe in us or should they fear us after this? We figure that out then but as 117, we should not care. And as 5 said, we should also act out our anger on someone in a way. So can we please stop with all the philosophical, moral judgement crap already? We are badass cyborgs. We are taking this guy in because if he is laughing at us, then we break his face but keep him alive so we can have millions of people look at him and he will be held responsible. No way to hide from it."

Everyone silently pondered over what had just been said. 5 looked down to the ground and gave a small nod to show he was beginning to agree. 117 couldn't speak, 1 was repeating his words to 501 differently but more effectively than he could have ever thought of.

"I can do that," 5 said.

"Agreed," 117 remarked.

"Also," 1 added. "To hell with a plan. It is such a pain to come up with something and then it gets really screwed up. I say we wing it."

"Then let's do it already," 57 replied. "After all, how many times have we ever improvised?"

"Including this time?" 297 asked. "Zero."

"Then we find out," 117 said as he lifted his leg and kicked the door in.

"At least let us have time to get ready with an awesome entrance," 57 said. "Oh well."

The doors flung inward easily. For a second, 117 thought he had sprung a trap. But since there wasn't anything, they all began marching in. All of them saw 43 standing a couple feet away from the assassin. Both were standing very still. Why though? 117 wondered. This was not what he was expecting to see, which probably meant that their arrival was not just good timing. There were no windows so the entire room was lit up from the ceiling lights and the computer monitors behind the assassin. Just the amborgs and their illusive adversary.

"You're under arrest."

43 whipped around and gaped at them all. Everyone except her along with a reluctant 5 had said the command simultaneously. They all turned at each other quickly before staring back at the Assassin.

"Ok so we are arresting him," 5 said humorously when everyone gave him concerned stares. "Just making sure."

"What?!" 43 exclaimed.

The assassin, saying nothing stared back. The visor blocked his face, but 117 knew he had his attention fixated on the amborgs. Or at least, he assumed he was looking their way. An eerie silence fell over everyone. The only sounds remaining came from the cracking noises from the monitors behind the assassin. Finally, their adversary stood, walked forward, reached his hand to his face and took the visor off. 117 and the rest of them stared.

It was a man probably older than Dr. Kendrick by a few years. Many decades younger than 117's grandfather at least. There were a few scars across his face but it didn't hide the look he gave them. He frowned at the amborgs and his gaze cut deeply from across the room. 117 had mostly seen military personnel look in that way. This man was not to be underestimated above all else.

"Arrest me?" He said in a very flat tone. He smirked a little and scoffed. "I wonder what sparked such change. Yet... Not all of you seem to be on the same side. I can tell by how different the looks of anger are spread across your faces."

The man's voice deepened. There was a sinister chuckle following his words. 117 glanced at 43 who was curling her fists. He knew exactly what was about to happen. As discreetly as he could, he set up a private channel to everyone except 43.

"We will not fall for your plan," 117 snarled back as he stepped forward. The assassin stood his ground and faced him. "It's over."

"Look at you, the leader of this grand story," He sneered, "The age of a man but the body of a boy. A robot who tries to be what he isn't! You were given the opportunity to be greater. It was Kendrick who had all of you evolved! Yet you help and fight for people who left you for dead."

"We evolved physically beyond this world," 1 spoke in a challenging tone. "People die all the time but we never leave our own foundations. Our humanity is what makes us who we are. WE are not robots. Not now, and not ever!"

"The original one! How bout that?" The assassin exclaimed, "What an honor. How does it feel to be the alpha? The one who holds the highest power?"

"Coming from a mass-murderer," 3 piped up, "You have done far too much to even ask that sort of question."

The assassin gazed at Missy who shrunk back instantly. They were all trying to be tough but it was no surprise that they were nervous about trying to start a fight. But 117 spoke again, breaking the tension a bit.

"We were never put in a position of power."

"Ha!" The assassin lifted his hands and shrugged. "Kendrick has been holding you back! Why do you think he created you? He wanted an army, people who would listen and be unstoppable! Yet you chose this meager lifestyle. Why did you children get this opportunity? What on earth makes you special?!"

"You speak with so much disgust and hate," 117 observed. Maintaining a close watch on 43, who looked ready to pounce, he understood immediately. "Who are you?"

"Yeah, what happened?" 3 said sarcastically, "Dr. Kendrick turned you down?"

"Yes."

"Oh shit," 3 replied with wide eyes. "I was being rhetorical."

"Ok… that makes sense," 5 muttered.

Everyone glanced at 5 who shrugged.

"What? A guy challenges us and declares all-out war because a long time ago, he got rejected from being an amborg and hates that we did and he did not. Is that right?"

"Well," The assassin sighed. "It's not like I wrote and prepared a whole monologue for it. So good job."

"There's no need for any condescension," 1 replied.

"Actually, I am condescending because it ticks me off," The man replied. "I offered Kendrick money... literally, I wanted to pay for his research and have your cybernetics as a reward for being one of the few individuals willing to believe in his futuristic crap. He decided to make it on his own without my help. So in response, well, I set out to destroy everything."

"Man, you do not take rejection well," 57 spoke.

"You probably offered Dr. Kendrick something he did not want to be a part of," 117 said bravely. "A mercenary with a quest for power and an upgrade was not what he wanted. There was a reason he picked us."

"Well, why don't you ask your dear Dr. Kendrick? He never told you about me. Did he? Amazing. You'd think he would have at least mentioned about the actual rejects. Why were you chosen? What did all of you kids have?"

"That is a simple answer. Nothing," 117 said, "Absolutely nothing at all. Dr. Kendrick looked at the unfortunate and made us better."

"ENOUGH!"

All of them, including the assassin turned their heads sharply and stared. 43 seemed to have entered a new stage of rage. Much different than when 117 saw her last. 117 had expected this but unfortunately, every second she was withheld from her prey was apparently making her turn into... something really bad.

"Is it just me or is she even crazier than when we saw her as we came in?" 297 asked nervously.

"This man has taken so much from this world," She exclaimed. Outraged, she shook her hand and pointed at the assassin. "It is our job to extinguish him from this life."

"So how come you have not already done this?"

It was 1 that took a step forward and stood next to 117 cautiously. He transmitted a private message to 117 and together, everyone began to inch forward.

"If you reached this place before us," 1 said slowly, "How come you have not killed him yet. What held you back? Why were you just standing there when we stepped through the door? How long did you stand there and hesitate? What is going on 43?"

43 looked down. The net of questions thrown at her had practically stunned her. On the private channel, 1 transmitted to the rest of them that he hadn't expected that sort of response.

Perhaps it is internal damage, 1 transmitted to all of them. Stand by to respond.

Suddenly, it made sense to 117. Her cybernetics was in a state of chaos which was why she was acting abnormally. They just needed to subdue the assassin and 43. He needed to get close for a few seconds. Making sure everyone else was updated about the plan, they got ready to make their next move.

"43, you are blinded by anger. Don't do this! If you actually held out until we got here then that means you know this is not what you want!"

"I... I... uh... I... need," 43 stammered. "No! I have to do... the right...agh. Must... fulfill... secondary objectives!"

"Finish the job amborg 43," The Assassin replied. "I didn't give all of my best resources for you to fail now. Come at me!"

Finally, it was enough.

"Take them now!" 117 shouted.

They split into two groups. 117, 3, 5, leapt at 43 while 1, 57, and 297 went for the assassin. Both groups engaged in combat. Out of the corner of his eye, 117 saw that the man was fast. He has cybernetic implants as well, 117 thought as he diverted his attention back to 43.

117 faced 43 with 5 and 3 on his flanks as they surged forward. He threw two punches which were easily blocked. 43 grabbed his arms and kicked him into 3. 5 leapt forward and swung a right cross. As she lifted her left arm to defend, 5 threw his left fist towards her head. She grabbed it and forced him to his knees.

"You would really hit a girl like that Johnny?" She said cunningly.

117 and 3 got themselves untangled and leapt back towards the pair. 117 lifted a leg and kicked 43 in the stomach causing her to

bend over slightly. Just as he suspected, she had not made a full recovery. 3 crouched and also dove for 43's lower waist but she lifted her leg in response and 3 was kneed in the face. She fell and clutched her nose as 117 took his chance and immediately grabbed 43 by the neck, holding her in an arm-lock.

"We do not require oxygen," She said unaffected by the chokehold. 117 held his ground as she elbowed him rapidly in the stomach. "This is the best you got?"

"No," 117 replied. "This is!"

117 instantly diverted energy into his palms and initiated a power surge. This briefly stunned 43 as he began running diagnostics on her systems. That however was also not what happened. 117 felt as if his mind was moving down his neck into his arms and into the connection he initiated with 43.

* * *

"Where am I?"

"Well, well, well, David 117. Nice of you to join in."

117 blinked and found himself in a completely different location. This was not the warehouse. Instead, he found himself standing inside of a home. One he recognized very well. He turned however at a disturbing sight. 117 saw 43 sitting on a sofa unconscious. In front of her, to his surprise was the assassin.

"When did you realize I had broken into 43's system?"

"It was just the second I made contact and did a diagnostic," 117 replied. "I had suspicions. Her sudden reappearance even after Dr. Kendrick tried everything. The way she pushed herself and fought so hard to rejoin us just to get to you. It was obsessive behavior. That wasn't 43. I guessed something else had taken over her entirely but I couldn't confirm it. To be honest, I only wanted to stun her but then... I found myself... here. Now the question is, what are you?"

"Isn't it obvious?" The assassin chuckled. There was a faint red glow coming from his clothing. As if his clothing was leaking tar into the atmosphere. As 43 feebly stirred his body suddenly blitzed and phased in and out of form. Just like a computer glitch. "I'm just a program with a single purpose. Do everything necessary to fix this host and kill my creator. All for the goal of making the amborgs appear as power-hungry monsters. I do that and my mission is over and I'm supposed to erase myself from existence."

"You have failed," 117 said confidently, "We discovered your presence and now we can free 43 from your control. The instant her system restarts, you will vanish without a trace."

"Just try it, I'd like to see what happens when you destroy your beloved woman trying to get me out. Kill me, and I will make sure her artificial consciousness here dies forever. Her implants will fail and she will permanently stay dead. Are you sure you want your beloved Serina 43 to go through that? Because this is the part where you make your choice. Surrender and she dies. Or, make a move and she still dies."

"I like the third choice," 117 replied with a smirk. "Distract you so she can do that."

"What?"

"I'm tougher than I look you jerk!"

43 suddenly leapt from the sofa and grabbed the assassin by the neck. She kicked hard into the back of his leg forcing him to kneel. 117 also moved forward and brought his fist into the program's face. The body shattered and red traces of it fragmented and flew all over the room. He kept his fists clenched as 43 kneeled back to the ground. The red particles then disappeared and light shone in from the window.

"He came in," She said as she tried to keep calm. "I remember I was monitoring 43's cybernetics. You know? Fixing myself. And then... I tried to fight him but he subdued me and took over! I don't understand how..."

117 looked around the room and scanned it.

"But I can't sense him here anymore," 43 said as she nervously looked around. "Is it over?"

"Yes."

117 smiled warmly as he embraced her.

"Remember? It's me Serina," He cradled her and spoke to her as she looked around the room.

"This place," 43 said softly, "It was where we hid waiting for our parents to return. It was our home and then it became so dark."

"I know, but it's over now," David 117 smiled, "You fought for long enough. Finally you can live the rest of your life how you want and not by another's dictation. You're safe now and once you're up to speed, we'll fight together. We end this..."

"...The right way," She finished, "I know. He took over my whole system but I heard all of you. Please forgive me. I hurt you and our brothers and sisters. I hoped that you would see that I didn't mean to. I did so much to try and prevent myself from becoming a blood-thirsty killer but that program... he wanted me to do it and I couldn't stop it from happening. I tried so hard to fight."

"It doesn't matter," 117 spoke clearly, "I have you back now. And then I'll take care of you."

"It isn't simple, I'm dying 117."

"Then we find a way to help. I won't give up on you."

"I know but... stop. It's not meant to be forever. Not in this way. We have to return to the real world and... I'm afraid that my cybernetics can only keep me alive for only a little while longer. That program revived me but it's only temporary."

"I won't lose you," He said desperately.

"My soul may be dying 117," 43 replied. "But we always will have an artificial conscious of ourselves living in the digital world. That and our memories will always be together. You need to let me go though. I'm afraid too but I had to accept it."

117 held her even tightly as she soothingly rubbed his back.

"We were built for great things David 117. You just have to do all of that for me ok?"

"I promise."

"Now go get him. I'm restarting my system. Go. You still got one job left to finish."

With a great flash of light, the system restored itself and 117 felt himself being blinded until everything became dark. He felt himself being pulled away and into the darkness. But as he drifted back, he heard 43 say one last thing.

"Go home and live."

* * *

"117!"

117 blinked and looked around. 43 was still being held in his arm lock but he realized she had stopped fighting him and was still. 5 was trying to hold the two of them up.

"How long was I out?" 117 asked as he and 5 lowered 43 to the ground.

"A few seconds. What happened?"

"Uhh, I'll explain later."

The two of them laid 43 on the ground and checked on the other fight. A loud crash grabbed their attention. He and 5 watched as 57 and 297 were thrown across the room to the door.

"NOO!"

3 screamed so loud that it practically highlighted what 5 and 117 were about to say. The assassin was holding 1 by the throat. As he struggled to free himself, the assassin had drew an LTO blade and drove it into 1's rib. 1 choked and thrashed harder. 117 and 5 immediately leaped to the rescue. The assassin, with his free arm threw a punch when 5 came into range. 5 deflected it but the assassin swung his other arm which was still clinging onto 1's dangling body. 1's body crashed into 5 and the two of them went into the wall leaving 117 charging alone. Without taking his eyes off his adversary, he quickly scanned and checked the condition of his team. 57, 297, and 5 were all beat up. 3 was taking care of 43 and 1 was badly wounded. While he calculated this, a punch got through and 117 felt sharp pain in his head. I am losing, he thought, defeat imminent.

"Come on! Where's that spirit of yours? Still want to arrest me?" The assassin mocked as they continued fighting. "Maybe I'll have you kill me since you took care of my scapegoat!"

117, out of pure annoyance, raised his voice.

"I really wish you'd shut up," He said in between punches.

"You can't stop me by yourself! Even if the rest of your friends make the maze, they still have to deal with me! You have seen what I've done to your team. What makes you think you can stop me now?"

"Then I just need to keep fighting until all of us get here!"

117 was kicked in the chest hard causing him to roll onto his back. 117 somersaulted backward and crouched onto his feet. He needed to think fast otherwise he was dead. This had to end.

"Run out of those ideas kid?" The man laughed and placed his hands on his hips.

"Fun fact about 'cough'...amborgs, we are never out of ideas. We calculate one thousand ideas for every second. But yeah, I guess I am out of ideas."

Before anything else could happen, there was a loud thud that caused the entire room to shake. Plaster and pieces of cement fell from the ceiling as the wall collapsed. Cement and debris flew everywhere. A hole roughly the size of a car opened up and a large object had shot through the hole. Sunlight and wind flowed in, drawing everyone's attention. A drop-pod had landed a few feet from the computer monitors. It was 117's drop-pod. They stared as the door opened and out came his Grandpa Mark.

"There you are David!" He coughed. "You won't believe how many holes I've made in the roof and sides of this place. Boy, am I glad to have finally found you. They told me I was going to bring the whole place down if I wasn't too careful. I don't know what they're so worried... I mean the place is still..."

He paused and stared at the scene before him. Even the Assassin was silently staring along with everyone else.

"...standing," Mark finished. "I guess I interrupted something epic?"

He gaped at 57 and 297 helping each other to their feet. 3 was holding 43 tightly. And 5 was attempting to take care of 1's wound. Finally he stared at 117 and the assassin standing in the center. 117 looked relieved whereas the assassin appeared only slightly discomforted.

"Who the hell are you?" He yelled.

Grandpa Mark smirked and walked up to David's side.

"I'm this boy's father's father," he said bravely.

"So you aren't an amborg? What makes you think this old man can help?!"

At these words, Grandpa Mark, put on a very grim face, glanced over at David who stared back and nodded. Both of them using non-verbal communication, cracked their fists and stepped forward in unison.

"Let me guess," Mark asked 117. "Ex-military rogue mercenary with a lot of time on his hands? Maybe a max security cell will give him time to think about his life until he rots. Shall we, David, my boy?"

"By all means Grandpa."

Both of them lunged. Even with 117's fatigue, his grandfather was making up for it triple-fold. The tide had turned miraculously. 117's grandfather had not spent the last two days fighting. He was fresh as a newly laundered drone off the manufacturing line. The assassin began to falter under the blows and speed of the elder.

"I AIN'T AS YOUNG AS YOU THINK JACKASS!!" Mark roared as he punched again and again.

Eventually, 117 began stepping out of the way for his grandfather who appeared to be dropping everything on their adversary. The two men, both fitted with implants engaged in a massive duel. But the assassin was on the defensive completely. It was hard to believe that an old man was doing the work that the amborgs couldn't. But 117's team didn't care one bit. They were gaining satisfaction at the sight of their biggest adversary getting beat by an old man with superhuman cybernetic implants. Finally, Mark threw a punch so hard that when the assassin made the attempt to block it, there was loud crack as the assassin's arms were both broken from the massive force.

"Agh!" He cried. The assassin backed against a wall, unable to lift a finger.

"If there's one thing you should know," 117's grandfather said, "There's usually always someone better and older who can kick your ass. And if I can't do that job, then next time, the amborgs will do it. So old coots like me can retire."

The assassin panted and spat on the ground. He was beaten.

"Then finish me off already!"

"It sure ain't my call," Mark said cheekily, "He's all yours kid!"

And then 117 swooped in and punched the assassin right in the face. There was a loud smack as the full force of the punch went right into his unguarded face.

"Hey hey hey! I thought we weren't killing him!" Shocked, Grandpa Mark stared as the Assassin crumpled and slumped to the ground. 117 pulled his arm back.

"He's fine."

Both of them kneeled and checked for life-signs.

"Huh. Nicely done," Mark sighed in relief when they found the assassin was still alive. "You are learning more and more."

"Still learning though," 117 sighed. "I hope this was the right thing."

"Well, your father would have agreed. Come on, let's get you kids patched up and turn this guy in. You want to figure out who he is right?"

"There is still so much to repair. I can't stop…"

"Focus on those later, you can do those important bits after you've rested or repaired... if you kids do that sort of thing. Let the humans fix things for a change. You've saved us so get some R&R."

"We are humans," 117 groaned.

The waves of fatigue were suddenly catching up as the adrenaline instantly faded and waves of pain traveled up his arms. Mark chuckled.

"I know David. But let's face it. Not really."

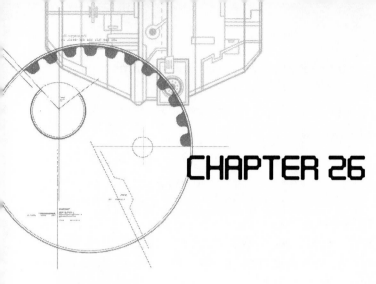

CHAPTER 26

Classroom 312

"So what do you think so far?"

Sarah looked up from her screen and paused the playback.

"Amborgs." She said observingly. "They aren't what they appear to be."

"Go on," Mandy leaned forward with interest. Sarah noticed this and continued to give her observations.

"As the war progressed with each hour," She recalled. "I did not see the amborgs as numbers anymore. I saw them as soldiers and I also saw them as... human."

"That is what I tried teaching 117 over a long period of time," Mandy nodded in agreement. "Now let me ask you this, why do you think the war was such a bad reason for the original amborgs to evolve as humans?"

"The more exhausted they were," Sarah replied, "The less energy they had, it made many of them reverted back to a basic human instinct. Almost a violent one."

Sarah looked at her teacher for confirmation. Mandy only stared back with a pained expression and was silent.

"That was the point wasn't it?"

Sarah looked through the footage of the Dominoe Incident and within seconds, recapped all that she had seen.

"The amborgs were Dr. Kendrick's symbol for the tools to rebuild and lead humanity onto a better path. When the war happened, it was a fight to destroy everything the amborgs stood for. And 117 led all of them on the defensive and by arresting the man responsible, he avoided a potential catastrophe? I cannot confirm this query though."

"That is almost very accurate Sarah," Mandy smiled. "A lot of people questioned why the amborgs had to study to be like humans again. David 117 and the original family of amborgs were all advanced beyond physical and mental abilities that people could only dream of. Yet, they were kind and helped people. They fought for the homes that left them for dead and they gave hope back to people that needed it. But the Dominoe Incident happened because eventually, one man, in this case the assassin, wanted to destroy all of that. Fortunately, he didn't succeed because 117 found it in his heart to continue showing pity and respect and chose not to act out in violence. The amborgs became more human in a way when they were faced with probably one of the worst encounters they've ever dealt with in the first time of their entire cybernetic lifestyles."

"But it caused an emotional stir that almost led to violence," Sarah said. "Johnny 5 almost seemed ready to fight against his own brother."

"Let's just say that the amborgs learned a lot more than they bargained for," Mandy explained. "The assassin did succeed but not in the way he originally intended. Instead of destroying the amborgs by subjugating them to violence, they found a way to adapt and accept that into their lifestyles."

"Wait," Sarah replied. "You approve of the fact that we still have emotional tendencies towards violence?"

"It's always in us Sarah," Mandy replied. "The seed of violence is always waiting to bloom. How we demonstrate or show self-control is how we always have good judgement. But when we live to a point in time where we forget about certain parts of ourselves, then we are capable of destroying our own humanity. The amborgs worked so hard for a peaceful life that eventually, they learned the hard way that our primitive roots always focus on violence and aggression. From that though, they learned a great deal about emotion. Many of them after the incident learned how to blend in exactly like the rest of the population and some decided to continue on without emotion. The discoveries and self-sacrifices the amborgs of the First, Second, and Third group became the most remarkable stories I have the pleasure of witnessing."

"Is there any more I should be watching?" Sarah asked gesturing back to the screen, "I believe there was more you wanted to show me."

"Yes indeed Sarah," Mandy smiled. "And you'll see now the ultimate decision the amborgs made as a family in order to truly go out into the world and really be a part of it."

"Please," Sarah looked back to her screen more enthusiastically than before. "Computer, begin the playback."

"Look who's so excited to see the ending," Mandy replied with a chuckle. "And when we began, you had no idea what I'd be teaching."

"I am merely... imitating... appropriate behavior at an only mildly interesting story," The young amborg replied sternly.

"Sure. Sure you were."

* * *
** ** **

2128, July
Warehouse exterior. An hour later.

"News crews aren't a good idea right now, ma'am."

"If you just let me have a few minutes with them, Lieutenant, we can show the public our heroes. The ones who put a stop to this once and for all. Seriously, you got to let me have the first shot at talking to them!"

"How about after you give them a break? They just saved us from the biggest maniac ever to appear this side of the world and I'm in charge of making sure no one bothers them. You aren't going to die from getting this exclusive."

"If I don't get a couple of words at least, I might be. You have no idea how angry my boss is."

Palmer was arguing with the news-woman Ashley Jenkins that had been rescued earlier by the amborgs. Apparently, she suddenly had developed feelings of extreme gratitude for her timely rescue and had pestered one of the soldiers at the edge of the combat zone for access. How she had ended up walking to the army command center, he would never know. Lack of security wasn't a surprise since everyone was scattered all over resting easy with the fact that the battle was over. All that mattered was, his orders were to keep the warehouse evacuated of all personnel and no one was to enter until it was examined thoroughly and carefully. While the security teams were preparing to investigate the area, he was also making sure no one tried anything with the amborgs. They deserved to be left alone after all the work they had accomplished.

A little ways away, the amborgs were all huddled together privately under armed guard from A.I. Industries security in a closed off area in the military zone. To be exact, it was a blown out dance hall that all of them picked as the perfect spot to relax. The government and the army officially gave them that spot for some well-earned laziness. They had definitely been through enough alongside all the people of the country.

"Boy, I wish I could get some privacy myself," He muttered silently as the news-woman began talking about heroism in knights of shining armor.

Wonder what Mandy is thinking right now? He thought and let out a sigh. I really need to spend a great deal of time with her after this...

Back at Amborg Industries, Mandy was actually feeling very uneasy after the debriefing. An hour ago, she and the rest of the technicians received word from their amborgs in Pennsylvania. 466 and 501's technician had maintained full contact with the pair when they had been assigned by 117 to remain on the ground floor. All the other technicians and Mandy sat for a long time in the dark. Completely cut-off from their cybernetic partners. Finally, when the first amborgs evacuated out with word that it was over, everyone rejoiced. The thought that the battle was ending made everyone rest easy.

Except for Mandy who was still concerned. There was something out of place with what she heard from 117's report specifically. He had only sent that report along with all the recordings that took place inside the maze. One scene in particular replayed over and over when his team had made the final confrontation.

"43 was not herself..." She muttered as she walked into a hallway intersection. "Oh I really wish what I'm about to do next is wrong."

Deciding where to go next, she proceeded left down the hallway towards the medical bay. All the while, she failed to notice a figure hiding behind a corner, watching her walk away. Mandy lifted her wrist and activated her communicator.

"Security," She said, "This is technician Mandy. Can you please send some guards to meet me at the medical bay?"

She stopped and looked behind her, checking to see if she was alone. The hall was silent except for the buzz from her bracelet and the head of security responded.

"Of course, Ms. Mandy," A male voice spoke, "But I haven't received any signs or any indication for such a response. Do you have clearance for this?"

"Security," She said as she uneasily began walking, "Call it a hunch, I think we have a potential saboteur."

"I see," The man replied, "Notifying security."

She began fast-walking until finally, she reached the medical bay. Without waiting for anyone, she stepped inside. All of the hospital beds and stations were empty. Except for one person.

"Mandy! What a surprise!" Dr. Wildman stepped out of his office and greeted casually. "How are you doing? Isn't it good that this is over?"

"I don't know Dr. Wildman, I think I have a problem which only you can help me with," Mandy said smiling curtly and sitting in a chair along the wall. Dr. Wildman glanced curiously at her. "There's been a violation of human rights."

Wildman stared, showing no change in emotion. He raised an eyebrow and stared inquisitively. Mandy looked around briefly as he spoke.

"Oh really?" He said calmly, "I'm pretty sure that one of the therapists or counselors here would be more helpful. I'll go and get one."

He began walking towards the door. As he was about the pass Mandy, she stood up and quickly stepped in the way of his path, stopping him. There was definitely something making him nervous and she already confirmed her suspicions.

"The more you talk doctor," Mandy said as she took a few deep breaths. "It only makes me know more about what you did."

Dr. Wildman returned her gaze with a puzzled look. Mandy decided to firmly stand her ground as she spoke again.

"I'm pretty sure this violation needs to be solved with your expertise," She leaned her head forward, hardened her tone and stared deep into Wildman's eyes even though she was terrified. She could see that he was trying to avoid her gaze. "I learned something very interesting from my debriefing with 117. It would appear that after closer examination of 43's systems, there was a small corruption. You see, you're the only one who probably has the information I need."

Dr. Wildman took a breath and stared.

"What can I help with? I'm only the head of the medical staff," He replied as casually as possible. But Mandy only chuckled confidently.

"Well you see doctor. Someone here at A.I. industries was hired to carry out an act of sabotage."

"I see. But shouldn't this be a security matter?"

"Funny you mention that," Mandy spoke. The smile on her face was gone now and Dr. Wildman couldn't bear to look her in the eye. She then decided to throw the last card she had. "Perhaps you'd like to explain to them why you were the one that infected amborg Serina 43 with that corruptive AI. You were the only one supervising her condition at all times based on 117's quick look through the security system here. Then hours before they were about to give up in Pennsylvania, you just clear her for active duty? You should admit it right now and lower the consequences now while you still can. There's obviously a reason you keep trying to leave."

Dr. Wildman stared but then began to sigh.

"Alright," He said softly. "I might as well... I left a video for John explaining my actions. I was going to end my life to be honest."

"I'm listening."

"The amborgs were always bright and I knew it'd be suspicious the instant I told Kendrick that 43 woke from the death sleep," Dr. Wildman said. "I was the one who introduced an artificial program into her system which evaded scans."

The door opened and two security guards came in. They both held their rifles menacingly but did not take aim at anyone. Instead they looked around with very curious looks. Mandy turned to acknowledge them and then faced the doctor again who was slowly settling into a chair.

"He killed my wife..."

"What?"

Mandy instantly crouched down and looked at the doctor who had begun shedding tears.

"He made me do it," Wildman gasped in between sobs. "During the battle of New York, he sent me an encrypted message saying he had taken my wife and daughter. I never knew they would pay with their lives just because I was stupid not to live here at the facility with them."

"He got to them?" Mandy asked sympathetically.

"After 43's incident, Kendrick suggested that all personnel move their families someplace safe. Many relatives were moved directly here to A.I. Industries but I moved my family elsewhere. I told John to make sure others were safe until it was over you see? He sent me a video and killed my wife on camera as a warning. And he told me my daughter would suffer the same fate if I didn't do it. He baited me you see? He knew I was not the type of person to do his work so he tortured my daughter. After witnessing that, all he wanted me to do was what he wanted and he would let her go."

"You had no choice," Mandy said. "But you still could have fought him."

"He had access to my office," Wildman said quietly. "Every time he contacted me, he always knew what I was doing, what I wore, which staff I had. I don't know how but when I received his first message, it opened a link for him to see what was going on in med-bay. I was always under his watch... I couldn't tell anyone when I wanted to."

"Your daughter Dr. Wildman," Mandy asked urgently. "She wasn't in Pennsylvania? Do you know where we can find her? It would help the amborgs make it a priority."

"After 43 arrived in Pennsylvania, he sent my daughter to the LA police with her legs broken," He continued after a long pause. One guard walked behind him and handcuffed his hands. "She had been abused to the point where she couldn't walk, talk or even say what happened. The LA police found out who she was through a fuzzy facial recognition and fingerprints. Just had to look past her scarred bruised face. He hurt her anyway even after I did what he asked... What monster does that to a little girl? My little baby daughter? Killing my wife and scarring my daughter for the rest of her life. I almost lost my mind."

"We can help you Doctor," Mandy said reassuringly, "Kendrick will do anything for you. He will always help you. You're always going to be his friend and since it's all over and you told someone, then that's that. You can still correct the wrong. So we're just going to keep you confined with company ok? We'll bring your daughter home."

"I'm sorry, I'm so sorry..." Wildman sobbed as the security guards led him out. Mandy followed closely. As they left the med bay, they found Stan putting floor wax all over the floor.

"Stan, what are you doing?" Mandy asked suspiciously, "Didn't you clean a few hours ago?"

"Well, you looked troubled from that secret debriefing, Ms. Mandy," He replied cheerfully, "When you called security, it was enough to get my ticker going. So I followed you. It looked like you were on the path of catching someone guilty so I thought I'd lay a trap if he tried to run so I waxed the floor with extra wax."

"That's really thoughtful of you Stan," Mandy laughed calmly.

The security guards, stared at each other, gripped Dr. Wildman harder and proceeded cautiously over the slippery floor.

"It would appear that we were attacked on our home territory."

Mandy and Stan turned to find Dr. Kendrick walking towards them. He watched grimly at Dr. Wildman's receding back and removed his spectacles. He had also heard the whole thing at the wrong time. He didn't look it, but he was also in shock.

"When one focuses on one thing with a passion," He said, "We forget the little things during the heat of the moment. And even that, can bring down the house. How could I have let this happen?"

"How could you have known Doctor?" Mandy asked in an effort to motivate Kendrick. "You thought you were doing the right thing. Refusing to turn that man into an amborg. Clearly you saw that he was no good."

"I did see that," Kendrick nodded, "But I failed to see what he was capable of at the time. I saw a man seeking power. But the reason I saved all the candidates I picked for the amborg procedures. It was because I saw children and people the world had turned and thrown away. The ones who didn't get to understand what it was like to be on top. I wanted to give them a new life where they fought for the right thing. But how many people paid the price for it?"

"All we can do is grieve for a time," Stan replied. "But eventually, we all got to move on. After all, I shine these floors so I can see hope for my children's future. You're doing the exact same thing Kendrick."

Kendrick pulled a bracelet from his pocket and clicked it. It lit up and began projecting images of smiling teenagers and young adults.

"This is what I saw in my candidates even when I told them of the risks," He said, "With nothing to lose, all of them risked their lives to become my creations. The courage to do that is in everyone. You just need to see that instead of trying to calculate it. They have evolved far greater than I ever thought possible. And I couldn't be more proud. I just… it shouldn't have had to end like this. It was a terrible tragedy."

"Are you trying to sound guilty for what happened or you trying to say something motivational? Just move on and make sure all the floors have been cleaned for good. We don't have time for sentimental bullshit. Go back to work you two. It's what I'm going to do. I'm not disrespecting anything, I'll just clean with sadness until I have reason to smile again."

Without another word, Stan dragged the mop across the floor and began humming loudly.

"Your children are coming home John," He said softly. "They want you to be there when they come back. What's done is done. Now get your ass back to work and do some more good. All anyone cares about is the people still going and keeping optimistic about their hopes and dreams of a better place."

Stan then moved down the hall humming a song. Dr. Kendrick stopped for a moment to register what he had heard and was hearing. It was probably the most peaceful sound he had heard in ages.

* * *

If anyone had never seen something worth looking at before, then they were definitely missing out. In this case, ninety amborgs were spread out across a closed down area in the middle of the U.S. Capital. Completely sealed and isolated from the real world for some much needed rest. Although it was a temporary situation, none of them cared. Everyone was either lying motionless on the ground or sitting with their backs to the walls. Some were even seeking comfort in each other's arms and laps. Most of all, the one thought running across all of their minds was the fact that they could finally stop and relax.

"Dr. Kendrick says we may seek out our own achievements."

117 stared at 1 who sat across from him. 5 was massaging his own shoulder to his right and 6 was resting her head on 1's left shoulder. 3 who had been lying on the ground, perked up. 43 merely blinked as she cuddled next to 117. Everyone stared at 1 who nodded to confirm what he had just said.

"The topic has been discussed between the two of us for over a year now," 1 said as 6 lifted her head off his shoulder and looked inquisitively at him. "He believes to understand the world we live on, we should actually move out and live in it. The subject we talked about was… what we would do if we were not on active duty as amborgs. I said I would think about it and find the right time to pass on that subject to everyone else."

"What on earth is that supposed to mean?" 5 asked. "Amborgs will still be needed. Why would we leave?"

"It is not a directive Johnny," 1 spoke clearly, "It is a suggestion. Dr. Kendrick believes that amborgs can do normal things. See things from multiple perspectives as possible."

"He wants the people of the world to correct the world's mistakes on their own? While what? We go backpacking in Tibet?" 3 asked pushing her elbows into the ground and leaning up. "Without us?"

"We would still be around to help," 1 said, "Dr. Kendrick says he is not going to stop finding more people to be amborgs. I mean people do not always have to rely on just us right? I kind of want to have a vacation to myself instead of constantly answering every burglary every day. Dr. Kendrick said… 'I will make the newbies do the work until we decide to return home.' End quote."

"If we blended in…" 117 spoke, "We could covertly change the world. Look at what this incident has taught us. Our large successes brought out an evil to combat us and we almost failed."

"Are you saying because of this one-time thing," 5 asked, "We should just disappear? Be vigilantes and hide ourselves?"

"I am guessing that the decision is yours 5," 6 chimed happily, "I like the idea a lot. It makes me think about settling somewhere and becoming a doctor or something. If we decided to immerse ourselves into normal society, we can fully test ourselves as regular humans. Where we should belong now that this is over. Let the police and army have their jobs back. It could be fun. Meeting doctors and understanding different cultures with certain practices."

"And… if something like this happens again," 43 sighed cheerfully, "We can always find each other and bring the family back. We are amborgs. How hard could it be to have all of us come running home?"

"Yeah, I do not believe any of us will be going out of this world anytime soon," 3 said looking up at the sky, "Besides, looking for each other on Earth is easy if your brain is technically a computer."

117 looked at 43 who snuggled closer.

"You know," he said, "We don't have to say goodbye so soon. I think a celebration is in order. After that, we can come and go as we please."

5 nodded. His lifted his arm and gave a thumbs-up. No sooner did he lift it, his wrist popped and the hand dropped to the dirt.

"After I get my hand repaired," He said with an embarrassed look, "Who am I to argue with the concept of a great party?"

1 stood up and stretched his arms. He relayed a signal to all the other amborgs who responded. Three words were all he needed to transmit before walking off to find where his drop-pod had crash-landed. Every amborg, eager to go back to their charging stations and the cafeteria, stretched and all slowly got up.

"Amborgs, return home."

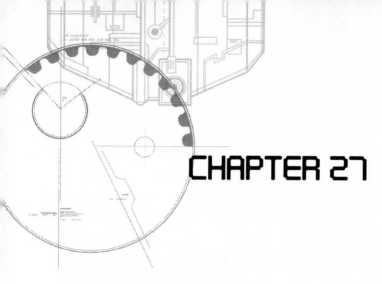

CHAPTER 27

2128, August, Amborg Industries

"Well the assassin has been placed into deep custody, the evidence will keep him there for the rest of his life. That is... until his execution which I have been invited and they've requested an amborg escort. All of his assets are being frozen and seized by the government and used to rebuild what was destroyed. Compared to my money, it's pretty good... The three groups have all contributed to repairs all across the country. I'm currently searching for candidates for the fourth and fifth groups. All should be relatively safe. The U.N. is asking me to be a permanent advisor should something out of hand happen again whereas the Supreme Court wants me to attend of a hearing debating whether we really need the amborgs... And let's see, oh yes, my children are leaving to take on the real world. Just an ordinary day I guess."

"Can you repeat all of that in one breath Dr. Kendrick?"

"Don't test me David 117."

117 was in Dr. Kendrick's office. Through the walls, the party was loudly resonating in the walls but their conversation went on uninterrupted. Out of all the amborgs that had posted something, whether it be big or small, 117 had not actually talked with Dr. Kendrick about his future plans. He knew the moment he had returned to the facility, he expected a conversation with his "father" about the subject would come up.

"So 117, what's your plan?"

Although it was a fairly simple question, 117 shrugged anyway. His life before becoming cybernetically enhanced was one he chose not to remember. After he became an amborg, he never thought of doing anything else even though Mandy had consistently taught him about individuality.

"I don't have any plans that I wish to fulfill at the moment," He replied after a few seconds of calculating. "Being an amborg is the best thing that I know how to do. If you ask me about the future, I am uncertain what I want. But I would like to request temporary leave to the Academy for a period of twenty four hours."

"The Academy?" Dr. Kendrick looked up from his daily report. He hadn't expected 117 to make such a request like that before. "What business draws your attention there?"

"A promise that I intend to see through," Said 117 firmly. He promptly chose to look away from Kendrick's curious gaze. "I want to inform someone of my safety and honor the pact I made in words with her."

"Well, take all the time you need David," Kendrick smiled, "You're free to find out what it is you want to do. It's not like I'm forcing you to choose a career on the spot. I just asked you here because I want to know what you want to do now that we foresee a time of peace. Supposedly."

"I plan to return here after my leave of absence," 117 smiled, "I am compelled to continue operating under your command. Besides, I am one amborg who would wish to remain at the place I call home. I want to continue being here, being your son, and carrying out what needs to be done."

"You do know that you aren't the only amborg staying right?" Dr. Kendrick removed his spectacles and stared at 117. "I happen to know 1 wishes to stay after he has seen the world. 999 wants to have nothing to do with freedom. She is more accustomed to a system where she can follow it but I swear that girl just hates the words 'bikini' or 'holiday'. Almost felt like she'd rip my throat out if I even mentioned her taking time off again. And there are at least ten others asides from that. Heh heh. Not everyone is making the choice to stay out there. I'll still have a capable team."

"I have no clue what I wish to do if I chose to hide myself amongst the world," 117 spoke honestly, "I just want to remain here where I can be the best I can be. To help and do the right things for people. Even if humanity is left to deal with their own issues, we still need to be on hand."

"If you're sure 117," The doctor said, "Then I could put you down for a new program I'm developing for those that are staying and for future amborgs. If you're interested of course."

He held up a data-pad for 117 to see. It was tagged as a new protocol that 117 did not recognize. It was red flagged and meant that Dr. Kendrick had marked it for revision before sending it out. 117 briefly perused it instead of uploading it to his brain which caught Dr. Kendrick by surprise.

"What do I need to do?"

Medical Bay

"Do not tell anyone."

"Of course, doctor-patient confidentiality. But 117 knows. He is waiting for you to tell him. Or at least, he wants to be able to talk with you and prepare for the inevitable."

43 sat on one of the beds while 6 was uploading examination results into her data-pad. As they were being uploaded to the main screen, 6 looked at 43's tired but calm face. Dr. Wildman had been relieved of his duties and the rumors were that Dr. Kendrick was doing everything he could for his family but he did need to face punishment for what he did. Fortunately, since he didn't have a choice, many of the amborgs were contributing their support for him, especially 6. The medical facility was now temporarily under her command who decided to postpone her own vacation.

"I plan to tell him," 43 said confidently, "I just... Yikes. How do I even tell him in an easy way? 'Hi 117. I am dying. We should probably make out my will?' Oh that's terrible... If only I had not been hurt in the first place. I mean, how do you tell someone you might die at any time?"

"I don't know little sis," 6 sighed. "Not necessarily at any time soon. From what I can see in the test results from your physical and cybernetic evaluation, at least a few months to go. Granted it still is pretty bad but at least you won't be in a coma."

43 took a breath and looked to see that they were alone. A nurse carrying some fluids walked past. Immediately understanding 43's expression, 6 turned and the two of them smiled at the nurse encouragingly. The nurse continued on, unsuspecting a thing. 6 immediately stopped smiling and stared at 43 with a serious look.

"But I also seem to have the feeling," She said to her patient. "You plan on doing something ridiculously crazy. I know that look. What are you up to?"

43 clapped her hands together and grinned happily. Checking again to see if they were alone, she bounced up once on the bed as 6 pulled the curtains shut. They both leaned in closer to each other and switched to a private channel.

"I am asking you to help change the results on that pad," 43 requested silently. 6 stared back with a look of concern. "It is not serious at all, just do not tell anyone about this plan. Keep telling them I am dying."

"But that is the truth. You really are dying," 6 stared in confusion. "Unless you want me to defy the laws of nature, then it's not possible. Just so you know 43, I'm a doctor... not a miracle max."

"Nice Trekkie and Princess Bride reference. Why don't I show you what I managed to crack?"

43 nodded and immediately blinked her eyes. Tapping her forehead, 6 immediately began receiving data schematics on the private channel. Slowly, 6's expression became less annoyed and more inquisitive. She looked at 43 who was smirking and then looked away to contemplate what she had seen. Finally, 6 smiled in amazement.

"Where did you learn how to do this?" She asked with her mouth hanging open.

"Let's just say, I took some info from that A.I. and I learned how to do something awesome. But I need another amborg's help. I need your help."

"For what? The procedure seems straight forward. Years ahead of what we already know but definitely plausible. Is that the multi-actual hologram tech from the maze? Why would you ask me for help if you've already got... all this... illegally obtained software?"

"Well there is a risk that if I do this, I only have one shot. I have to do one last download," 43 replied which made 6 stare. "I need to do another download and I need someone to be willing to accept me as a temporary house guest. There is a risk my plan could fail but if I borrowed a healthy amborg's computer system, then it would be a great back up plan."

"You have got to be kidding me," 6 stated bluntly, "You do know what kind of download you're talking about right? You know about those computer viruses? I feel like I'm seconds away from clicking the 'ok' button to disaster."

"Just do something impulsive for once in your life 6!" 43 exclaimed. "What could go wrong?"

"I have done impulsive stuff before! And that's not a safe question to throw around."

"Oh really? Name one thing you've done in your perfect life that was impulsive."

"Dang it. Alright fine, you got me there," 6 sighed with a huff. "I suppose I should have been more careful when I discussed doctor/patient confidentiality with you. Now it would seem I have no choice at this point... Fine. I'll do it."

"Thank you Vanessa."

"It's just going to be weird..." 6 looked up when she heard something. Realizing it was nothing, she looked back to 43." A project of this scale, I cannot imagine keeping it a secret. Especially when the words, 'consciousness transfer' is written in your rough draft."

"Look on the bright side, it will all be between just you and well... after we're done, you."

43 gave the biggest smile which made 6 even more worried. For the amborg doctor, she felt the biggest amount of chills shooting around her CPU. Oh 117, your girlfriend has the biggest guts ever, she thought.

"Ok 43... What do I need to do? What kind of timeframe are we looking at?"

43 instantly reached an arm out and grabbed 6's arm. Alarmed, she looked directly into her patient's eyes.

"Immediately," 43 replied with a smug smile.

"What?!" 6 exclaimed. Going over the instructions 43 had told her just seconds earlier, she was shocked at the idea of initiating the procedure right now.

"You're probably going to experience split-personality disorder during this part."

Cafeteria

"Are you really leaving?"

Despite the large round puffy eyes that the little toddler was giving, 501 and 466 had to resist giving into so much cuteness. They were the selected volunteers to try and persuade Thalia that their going away was a good thing.

"How come we were picked to tell Thalia about our going away plans?" 501 asked 466.

"I volunteered us this time actually," She replied.

"Miss Thalia, it is our time to live as humans," 501 tried to say as reasonably as possible as he switched to a public channel. He had to avoid direct eye contact though since Thalia had begun to sniffle on purpose which wasn't making the job any easier. "But we will be around. I promise."

Saying goodbye to 501 and 466 was not what Thalia had envisioned when the party was reaching its end. They had suddenly decided that they were leaving on their own adventure. Without her! Only a small handful of the third group amborgs had decided to leave but this didn't sit well with Mr. Ramirez's daughter at all.

"But all of you won't be here to work together again!" Thalia cried on the verge of tears. 466 kneeled in front of her and picked her up. Several onlookers were on standby in the events the amborgs couldn't calm the girl down. "You always stay together. That's what a family does. Mommy always said that before she left."

"Miss Thalia, we are not leaving forever," 466 said reassuringly as she hugged the little girl, "We will always help for the right reasons. We just need time for ourselves. We want to take this opportunity to be the best humans we could be."

"But you already are! You don't have to prove to the world that you're human by hiding yourself," Thalia protested. "You are the best human beings ever."

501 and 466 glanced at each other. Thalia, still buried in 466's arms, suddenly began to cry. George, immediately smiled reassuringly as he grabbed Thalia from 466 and cradled her. First he had to check whether or not they were fake tears or not. When they were all sure that Thalia wasn't faking it, they all smiled as happily as they could. Except for 501. He was also beginning to tear up and mimic Thalia.

"She's just having a tantrum," Mr. Ramirez said reassuringly to the pair, "She always wanted an amborg to call as her big brother or sister. Now that most of you are leaving, well, goodbye is hard for her. She doesn't want this change to happen. No child likes that sort of thing."

"We will return Thalia," 501 said encouragingly. He was desperately trying not to let the tears drop. He was saved the trouble when 466 nudged him in the ribs, "If you're in trouble, look to the sky and watch for shooting stars. A brother or sister will always be there for you."

466 looked up and turned to stare at 501.

"What on earth are you referencing that from?" She asked stifling a giggle as 501 merely shrunk back.

"Nothing... I was trying to come up with my own personal catchphrase," He mumbled.

"Do you mean it?" Thalia asked.

"About my catchphrase? Well you see... ow!"

"Yes, he means it," 466 said after she slapped him.

"Of course! We always keep a promise," 501 said happily ignoring the fact that his face was stinging a little. "It's kind of in our programming so we have no choice!"

Thalia laughed.

"I'll miss you Donut! Can we have a tea party again sometime?"

"Well we don't have to leave now," 501 glanced at 466 who nodded, "Why don't have that party now?"

Both he and Carolina made sure to record Thalia's face as it lit up with joy in the bright sunlight. They had another happy moment to remember for their memories. One more thing to do before they left.

"Tell us what to do, little princess," George Ramirez called after her daughter who was already bounding away.

Amborg Residential Area, 999's quarters. Rechristened as "Angel's home."

"Boy, this was such a good idea."

297 lifted his spoon and looked at the melting ice cream drooping from the utensil. He shrugged and took a bite as 57 kept taking mouthfuls very happily. 92 and 93 were both conveying their gratitude at the desserts.

"It's true I did request ice cream," 999 replied with a very annoyed look. "But do you all have to eat in MY room?"

"Relax Angel," 917 replied as he ate a spoonful of strawberry. "Learn how to have more than one person for company in your room for once. I heard that maybe there was going to be a videogame tournament later. It could be fun."

999 looked at him with a look of pure and utter hatred. However without arguing, she stuck her spoon into the cookie dough flavor and continued eating.

"I am not comfortable with so many people in my room..." She muttered stubbornly.

"I will take the blame for that one," 917 replied as the amborgs all switched ice cream containers. "I mean, it's hard to raid the freezer by myself and carry all this ice cream. You never specified a flavor and fortunately, I was caught by the rest of these party goers instead of the kitchen staff."

"And now we can have our own special party," 57 replied waving her spoon. "Ooh! Pass me the rainbow sherbet!"

"It all tastes good," 297 muttered. "But it feels wrong. Did we manage to cover our tracks?"

"If I was by myself," 999 replied. "I'd have been able to do it without getting caught. Hey 92. Pass me the quadruple layer chocolate can."

"If we do get caught," 93 spoke up. "What are they going to do? Ground us?"

"Our ice cream privileges might get revoked for a couple years," 917 smirked. "Ah… French vanilla."

"This tastes so damn good," 999 muttered as she frowned. "I literally am battling between trying to be angry but this sugar is just so… dang refreshing.

"Only Angel can taste something so sweet and still not even crack a smile," 93 joked. "I would pay big money just once to see her smile."

"Not even with all of Dr. Kendrick's fortune," 999 replied flatly.

"But what about that time shortly after the Dominoe Incident ended?" 297 asked. "57, didn't you say something about seeing 999 actually smiling?"

"Sorry boys," 57 replied cheekily eating another mouthful of ice cream. "But Angel actually gave me money to keep that a secret."

"What? How much?"

"About ten grand…"

"Wait a minute," 92 said angrily. "It would have cost me all of Dr. Kendrick's fortune just to see you smile. But when 57 says different, you only paid ten thousand? That isn't fair!"

"Since when was I fair with my brothers?" 999 asked.

It wasn't until after they had consumed all twenty eight flavors that 999 finally made them clean up and leave. 917 offered to help out in case she still needed anything but she wanted to rest for a while which was definitely something she never thought she'd ever find herself saying to anyone else.

When she was sure she was alone, she reached a hand underneath her pillow and pulled out a small box. Opening it, she took the contents out and walked over to her desk.

"57," 999 sighed. "I do not know the purpose for what you were trying to capture, but regardless, I will not turn away this gift."

It was a printed picture 57 had taken of her and 917 shortly after the Dominoe incident had ended. What made it interesting to look at was that both she and 917 were smiling in the photo. For some reason, she harbored no anger or disgust towards it.

"I guess one photo of me smiling is not the end of the world."

She left the picture on display at the head of her desk and then left her quarters to go think.

"I wonder though…" 999 looked down at the floor. "What else can I do other than what I do now? I should ask 917. He might be able to come up with something."

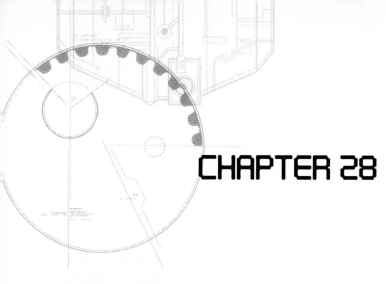

CHAPTER 28

Amborg personnel files: Transitional Period.
Subject: Missy Three
Two weeks after leaving A.I. Industries.

"I have never seen such good credentials. So you say that the restaurant you previously worked for was blown up during the battle of New York?"

3 nodded curtly. The head chef was sitting across from her, reading the resume that she had sent. He didn't remember seeing any job postings being sent out to the public. Yet there it was, a very spectacular looking resume on his desk. At the time he didn't have much to do, since everyone was working to repair all the damage from the war. So he figured he might as well read it. Very interested in the applicant, he gave her a call and here they were.

"Oh yes," She spoke out-loud as clearly as possible.

There were some parts of her throat that felt scratchy but 3 was slowly getting used to it. She had practiced using her real voice for days in an attempt to sound as authentically human as possible. Minus the fact that her identity had been completely forged.

"I have been looking for work since what happened in New York and then this whole crazy deal with the amborgs in Pennsylvania was just so terrifying!"

"I can imagine," The chef said in agreement, "Well, I don't see why you can't be a part of this place. Your accomplishments here is pretty incredible. I have never seen anyone who looks so young but has also accomplished all of... Well. This."

"You should put more salt on that!" 3 said sharply.

"What?"

The waiter she had snapped at jumped but the chef waved him away. Carefully balancing the tray of food, the waiter walked away muttering under his breath. 3 immediately bit her lip and turned off her visual analysis program. I'm supposed to be human. Human. Human. Human. She thought to herself. No super vision allowed.

"Oops," She muttered. Chuckling nervously as the head chef went back to the interview. "Sorry, I ehhh, I just have this passion for food and... uhh, I can just tell."

The chef stared but nodded slowly as he stood up and walked away. She hoped she hadn't accidently scared him away.

"Who knows," He said waving her resume for her to see, "You just might teach me something. Ms..."

He stared back at the application to try and remember her name.

"Melissa Carson," 3 said confidently. "Thank you for accepting me."

"It's nice to meet a fellow chef who's polite in a city like this. You start next Monday," The chef joked as he walked away. This however confused 3, now newly christened with her new name.

"People in New York aren't polite?" Melissa asked out loud but the chef had disappeared into the back.

"Ever been to Jersey?" A customer from behind asked rhetorically. "Get used to the area quick otherwise all those leeches are going to eat your nice personality up like demons."

3 turned and gave the customer a smile.

"I think I'll get along just fine here."

File subject: Katie 57
Location: Los Angeles Police Department Precinct 18

"Hey Harrison, did you meet any of the rookies that just transferred here?"

Lewis peeped his head into the newly repaired cubicle belonging to his partner. Harrison brought his head up from his arms. He stared at Lewis with a look of annoyance. From the look of disappointment and shame, Lewis could tell that Harrison already had.

"I don't have to Lewis," He groaned, "I can tell you everything you need to know about the new rookie even without having met her... Of course I met her already..."

"Her? What do you mean? I was talking about the new group."

"I know. And one of them impressed me... a lot... Made me realize I'm getting too damn old."

Now that the war was over, several officers of the precinct were looking forward to a little bit more time off than their usual duties before. Even after the brutal conditions suffered from the Dominoe Incident, Harrison was surprised at how the police camps and academies were still sending eager new volunteers their way. The spike in recruitment rates was skyrocketing and lots of new officers seemed to be flooding in every day.

"You're not that old Harrison," Lewis replied. "Come on! We got to give orientation to some of these newbies."

"No thanks," Harrison muttered. "Let Captain Bradley deal with that. She knows how to whip kids into shape."

"I'm going to take that as a compliment Harrison."

Harrison and Lewis both turned to see Captain Bradley who was walking by.

"Get ready for a new world you two," She replied. "Kids with college degrees and years of schooling are heading our way. Now they'll be taking it easy since they won't have to worry about being shot at every day for the foreseeable future. Means more paperwork for a lot of us vets."

As she walked away from the other two, she closed the folder she was carrying. Bradley didn't want to show it but she was also feeling the pain that Harrison was going through. Apparently one of the new recruits that had arrived was already making an impression which was distracting a lot of the staff. She followed all of the rumors and implied directions down to the firing range where it sounded like a party was taking place. Each person she passed by instantly put on serious faces and wandered off.

Watching the large crowd of officers gathering around one single booth, she raised an eyebrow. Luckily she managed to make it to the back of the crowd without anyone noticing. Peering over the mass of shoulders, she looked to see who was practicing.

"Man she is so hot..." One officer was saying. Another one instantly interrupted, "No way dude, I called dibs."

"Dream on… Both of you are way too old for her," One of the female officers said in a very blunt but cheerful tone, "She looks barely into her twenties."

Captain Bradley, annoyed at the conduct she was hearing, cleared her throat. Everyone all froze and realized her presence was among them. They instantly turned around.

"Evidently there's going to be a line if I'm hearing everyone correctly," She said loudly, "Now give the new girl space, let her be, or I'll make everyone here wear slings where they don't want to wear them."

The men all immediately straightened up and began walking off at these words. The women all laughed at the sudden ego change in all off their male compatriots. A few of them stayed behind while most of the officers walked out. Sergeant Johnson remained the only male officer still gathered at the booth.

"Don't you have a report to fill out Johnson?" Bradley asked suspiciously. Was he also going to be distracted by the rookie as well?

"No Captain," Johnson replied. "I finished it early when I learned we were getting new recruits. I was curious as to why this rookie was getting so much attention. I felt it'd be nice to show them that not all of us are indecent. I'd much rather be friends and get to know her decently as I do have the time."

"Think you're real smooth Johnson? You expecting this particular rookie to suddenly trust you like that?"

"Didn't cross my mind ma'am, but now I am glad I finished my work early. The other men might have tried much more indecent things."

One of the female officers giggled.

"What's wrong Johnson? Can't handle me?" She teased as two other officers began laughing. "But you might have a point, this rookie sure is making me question my own sexuality."

Bradley finally looked over their heads at the rookie who was not paying attention to any of them. She wore earmuffs and evidently didn't hear any of their conversations. Instead, she was firing the standard issue fire-arm down the range. Bradley looked closely to see that the target was set all the way at the end of the room. Shooting a target that far, Bradley stared in amazement, I must be getting old.

"Alright, clear off now," She ordered.

As Johnson and the remaining officers left, the captain tapped the rookie on the shoulder. She instantly stopped firing the weapon and turned around.

"I'm afraid I have to apologize for the conduct of my officers," Captain Bradley said irritably, "You'd think they never seen a rookie before."

"It's no problem ma'am," The rookie replied taking off her earmuffs and setting the firearm down on the table. "I… didn't… 'Ahem'…really mind. Just here to do my job and well, I always try to do my best. My father always said I took after my mother… And that I should be aware of the people I might attract when I joined the police corps."

"You attracted them alright," Bradley replied. "Now everyone's going to want to be your partner."

"Thank you Captain Bradley," The young woman replied. "Until then, I can take care of myself until I get settled. If I may say so, your reputation is… well… epic."

"So I've been told."

The truth was, Bradley had never heard anyone describe her in that manner before. The rookie sounded curious and showed so much optimism as if she was an energetic infant. Quick, clear and on point. Clearly this new recruit was one to look out for. Good thing too, she thought, I don't want to look after another babyish kid anyway. For some reason, she felt as if this recruit was already mentally fine. Too fine.

"Well. Good for you. Officer...?"

The rookie turned and stood so her name plate shone brightly in the light.

"Denton," She said with a smile and a salute. "Casey Denton."

"As you were then."

As Bradley walked away, she briefly glanced back to watch Casey fire her gun again. As she left the shooting range, she found some male officers hanging around the entrance. Trying to sneak a peek no doubt, she thought grimly. After she told them off, she went back to her office and sat down at her desk. Part of her desk hadn't been repaired so she was stuck with a piece of the corner missing.

As she sifted through her files, she found herself looking at past operations with the amborgs. Many of them needed to be formally drafted and submitted by the end of the week but Captain Bradley for some reason, felt slightly troubled. The sudden appearance of a new recruit who was developing quite a name for herself was too much of a good thing to happen in one day. She did like the new girl but unfortunately, she couldn't remember the last time she had thought considerably about a new recruit before.

"It feels…" She muttered. "No. Denton's presence seems really familiar… I wonder…"

She reached her hand over to the phone and picked it up. Racking her brain quickly, she rang up the number for her own newly acquired emergency hotline to A.I. Industries.

"Hello? May I speak to Kendrick please? This is Captain Marsha Bradley of the L.A.P.D."

File subject: Carter 297
Location: Ramstein Airforce Base

"It sucks man, what happened back home. You know?"

297 watched the young soldier ahead of him breath in and out. Observing him carefully, 297 ran a quick background check just

to have an idea of who he was listening to. This soldier had been overseas for a while now based on his record.

"You have family? To return home to?" He asked inquisitively.

The soldier looked at him with a depressed look and nodded.

"I joined just so I could fight against the enemies threatening home," He replied. "But then a blitz war happens on our own territory and I'm not there when my family needed me the most."

297 nodded. He had a faint idea of what many of the troops on base felt when the Dominoe Incident occurred. To be so far from the action was agonizing to say the least. He expected the mood to be gloomy since his arrival just a few minutes earlier. Luckily, he was sure that he had successfully inserted himself covertly into the U.S. Special Forces teams. Relief groups and many squadrons were tasked with rotating many members of the military overseas. Many of them had families and command was flooded with requests to go home. Only volunteers were now selecting duties based out of the U.S.

"It almost seems like the entire military is disbanding around the world," 297 said observingly.

"Ain't that the truth? Spend a whole tour defending a base in Germany against supposed terrorists or insurgents takes weeks to process. But then one moron destroys half the cities back there and now everyone wants to go back and find out what's going on. As soon as I know how my family is doing, I'll wait until the traffic back home dies down. Got a lot of good soldiers here even considering going A.W.O.L. just to take regular commercial flights home too. Ain't that something?"

"I'm sure it must be difficult," 297 replied.

"I'm not worried," The man replied. "My relatives are all military so they know how to handle their problems. When the first attacks happened, they got as many neighbors and friends out of the neighborhood and left Pennsylvania. But man, let's talk about you! It must be difficult volunteering to be here instead of home! I mean, true. The military needs people out here but isn't it harder to leave your home to fight battles that might not even happen here? Why would you want to be posted here?"

"It's all about perspective I guess," 297 shrugged. "I do have a home but it is safe now. Still got a job out here to do right?"

"I guess..."

"With me here," 297 added, "It means one more of you gets to go home and that's good right?"

"I don't think it works like that but I kinda see what you're getting at. Anyway, you can call me Dennis."

Dennis led 297 away from the tarmac. The transport ships that had dropped him off with several other squads were beginning to lift off. Carter looked back as a couple of them were already airborne.

He knelt down to clean out his rifle. He had wanted to take more time to clean it properly but decided to let it degrade naturally by about five percent in order to make it look convincing. The last thing he needed was to be a perfectionist in front of special-forces soldiers and get noticed. Be as authentic and convincing as possible, he thought. Don't stand out. How hard is that for an amborg?

"You know you're right? About the amborgs?"

297 flinched slightly and looked at Dennis casually.

"What about them?"

"What you said about home being safe right now?" Dennis smiled. "It's cuz we got the amborgs fighting at home too. I think there'd be a lot of worse things happening there if we didn't have them."

"Yeah," 297 replied with a little relief. "No kidding!"

"Yeah," Dennis spoke thoughtfully. "I'd trust those guys with my family if I'm not there. They can fight and really know how to make the bad guys think twice about their actions. I owe them a lot. Wish I could tell them thanks."

"I'm sure they'd appreciate the support."

"I know right? Screw all those people that think the amborgs started the war. I mean seriously, why would you try blaming a bunch of cyborgs after they just helped stop the whole incident? They fought for us and with us and they caught the guy who did all of it. I mean that's some damn good work at the end of all of it. Moderate damage across the whole country but at least it's not completely devastated. Some of the public just eats that stuff up without even knowing how crappy it is. The amborgs take more heat than we do here at Ramstein and some people are just using them as scapegoats. I'd rather be back home fixing things up instead of complaining and doing nothing."

"You are a very well-tempered soldier," 297 replied. "It definitely sounds like you do deserve a pass back home."

"Well," Dennis sighed. "It doesn't matter how nice or cool I be. Still stuck here from the looks of it. Thank god they opened the communication lines for the barracks though. At least I'll be able to talk to my folks tonight."

Suddenly, Dennis stopped. Noticing, 297 politely stood still as the other soldier began to laugh.

"Man! I am so stupid!"

"About what?" 297 asked.

"I haven't asked your name! I've been rambling this whole time and I don't even know who I'm escorting!"

"Ah well," 297 shrugged. "You've had a lot on your mind and well it happens."

"So what do I call you then?"

"Richardson," 297 spoke. "But you can call me Carter. That's easier to say in the heat of the moment."

"Hey that's cool," Dennis nodded. "What's it like being in Special Forces?"

"Oh well," 297 replied. "Uhh..."

"Ha ha I get it."

"Get what?" 297 asked curiously.

"Special Forces can't talk about what their up to right?" Dennis said as they stopped. "It's all classified and you can't tell me?"

"That's right... I guess," 297 sighed.

297 hadn't thought about his responses carefully. He picked a cover in the Special Forces because he figured that it'd be the perfect position where he didn't have to be social too often. Especially since he had planned on being alone seeking

perspective about what it was like to lead in his opinion, a very brave but independent lifestyle. To Dennis, he was probably not acting very well based on what he decided to do as a human.

"Well," Dennis said with a very reserved sigh. "If you can't talk, then I'll do the talking. I mean, the Spec ops soldiers are so uptight and meanish. You're probably the first one I've met not ordering me to go away."

"Rivalry in the military does give a sense of friendly competition if it doesn't do anything stupid," 297 spoke. "We may be in a different branch but I don't see any reason we can't be friends. It is better for soldiers to know more people right?"

"I like you man," Dennis smiled. "Yeah. More friends the better."

297 suddenly turned his head sharply. His cybernetics were sending alarms in his head and his spine was aflame with tingling.

"What's that?" He said alarmingly.

Dennis looked at him and around the area. Several troops were marching around and there was still loud noises coming from the transports. The two of them stood while 297 raised his rifle and lifted his left index finger. Dennis, a little concerned, moved towards 297 with his hand raised.

"Hey man," Dennis said reassuringly. "Just be calm ok? Seriously. What do you think you're doing? Lower your rifle before someone sees you. You're going to scare somebody. Alright? Hell you're scaring me a little. Just tell me what's going on."

297 clenched his rifle with both hands and instantly felt very worried.

"Trouble," He said in a harsh tone.

An explosion detonated behind them. 297 and Dennis turned sharply to see one of the grounded transports in flames and a large plume of flames bursting outward. Several troops around were falling on the ground. Some were diving for cover or actually being shot as 297 heard several bursts of automatic fire enter the mix. Yelling and loud cries filled the air. Listening carefully, he could hear their own troops desperately crying out in the chaos but another group of yells grabbed his attention.

"It's an attack!" 297 yelled. "On your feet Dennis! We got company!"

"Christ! The tarmac's being bombed!" Dennis yelled. "Where's it coming from?!"

297 turned about and had his back to the tarmac and saw the source of the yells. Somehow, in the middle of the airbase, there was a group of people charging guns blazing at them with guns, missile launchers and giant behemoth robots.

"Oh my god, who the hell...?!" Dennis yelled. "It's those big bots that attacked the U.S.! They're here too?!"

"Contact!" 297 yelled as he disabled the safety on his weapon and began firing. "Watch the enemies with missile launchers! Cover me!"

"You got it! But what are we going to do Carter?!" Dennis cried as he stood alongside as 297 thought up a plan.

"We got to move now Dennis! Focus fire and move over to that emplacement! See if you can call for help! I'll get in touch with whoever I can on my end!"

The two of them began firing back at the enemies in the distance as they ran and sprinted towards an anti-air emplacement under fire. The soldiers there were in deep cover.

"Alright Dennis!" 297 yelled. "Did you get anyone on your radio!"

"I'm trying to filter all this crap! Can't figure out if we're in the middle of a shitstorm or just a minor skirmish! This is Staff Sergeant Dennis of second platoon based near the tarmac! Is anyone there?!"

"This is Special Forces operator Richardson reporting!" 297 spoke into his radio as he stood and fired at two targets that fell. "Under heavy attack! Looks like uniformed bogeys with automatic assault gear, Pee-Em-Els, and a bunch of behemoth class drones! We need whatever support there is! We've lost a few transports... they are in flames! They hit a lot of people during the off-loading!"

"Roger that Richardson," Someone replied over the radio. "This is the tower. We confirm! Several targets on the tarmac. They're moving towards the transports. You got to cut them off before they get to all of them! Incoming missile! Get down!"

297 and Dennis looked up and turned to view the tower just in time to see a missile streak towards it. It detonated and turned the building into an explosive pillar.

"There goes our bird's eye!" Dennis yelled as he stood up and motioned for 297 to follow. "Come on! I know the best way to get to the hangar! My team will be there!"

"Dennis! Get down now!"

297's commands came too late as he heard several thumps strike Dennis. He saw his comrade crumple to the ground with a loud scream. 297 instantly lowered his rifle on the ground, crawled over to Dennis who was clutching his chest in pain and pulled him closer to the emplacement.

"Hang in there Dennis!" He yelled as he inspected the wounds. "Stay focused on my voice!"

Exactly six shots had struck Dennis. Two had hit his left shoulder and the rest were centered directly in his chest. However, one had struck in a place where 297 knew the impeding results.

"Damn it," Dennis coughed as he held a hand over the hole in his heart. "This… 'cough' is going to ruin my day."

"Stay with my voice Dennis. Focus on me," 297 said as he listened to the gunfire. Some of it died down but the battle was not over. "Just take it easy and stay calm."

297, remembering his medical training from 6 grabbed a syringe from his back pocket marked with the Red Cross emblem and injected it into Dennis' arm. The wounded soldier's breathing instantly became much more relaxed and slower thanks to the pain killer but there was nothing he could do to heal the wounds or any time to get him out.

"Damn it," Dennis choked. "I messed up bad."

297 tried applying pressure to Dennis to stop the flow of blood but there was slow steady stream soaking through his chest armor. He watched as Dennis lifted his hands for one of his pockets on his waists.

"This is for my parents," He said as he pulled a data card from his pocket. 297 recognized it as special video message mail. "Make sure they get this. I sent them a letter two days ago but this was... me telling them I was coming home. I need them to get this."

"Give it to them yourself," 297 said bravely. "Tell me about your parents. What are they like? Keep talking. Just keep talking."

"The...best...k-kuh-kind any person... could have," Dennis rasped slowly. "Hey Carter... do you think you can do me one more favor... tuh-tuh too?"

"Sure Dennis," 297 replied as he put Dennis' video mail into his satchel. "Name it."

"You think maybe you could go to the amborgs and tell them I said thanks?"

"What?"

297 looked down at Dennis with surprised tone.

"Just hear me out..." Dennis coughed. "I have one regret and that is when I decided to be stupid enough to leave home to fight a battle that ended like this. The amborgs... they did more than just save my family. They help hundreds of thousands a week and look what I've done... Ran away from home to... fight nothing and to die like this... and yet, people find ways to put the heat on them."

"You did what many other people could only say or dream of," 297 replied. "You put on a uniform when they didn't and you fought when they couldn't because like the amborgs, you chose to volunteer your life for the duty of protecting innocent lives. You have nothing to regret."

"You sound like you... know them," Dennis smiled with tears beginning to stream in down his eyes.

"I do," 297 smiled. "I'll tell them about you. You have fought bravely."

Dennis lifted his hand which 297 held onto tightly. Moments later, he took one last breath and then shut his eyes. 297 looked at his readings and confirmed it. Dennis' life signs disappeared.

"I'll make sure you don't get left behind," He declared as he grabbed his rifle and stood.

Turning around, 297 sighted his next target and ran.

"I need to find out how this happened."

File subject: Kiden 18
Location: Livorno, Italy

The streets were extremely dark under the Tuscany sky. Antique gas lanterns were lighting up the area as 18 looked left and right down the street. Should be clear, she thought. Finally she walked down the path and into a back alley. There was a man standing outside. Although she was now supposed to be human, she stepped forward bravely and downloaded the Italian language.

"Buena sera," She greeted as the database fixed to her brain almost instantaneously. The man looked up and merely nodded back.

"Salve," He said indifferently.

He sounded quite menacing and cold but she supposed it was his job. 18 could tell that the man had concealed weapons on under his jacket but perhaps if she got on his good side, perhaps he could be friendly.

"May I go in?"

The man stared but then he began to laugh.

"English huh?" He said observingly, "You are one crazy girl if you think you're getting in. Why don't you do both of us a favor, save some trouble and just go home?"

18 smirked and pulled some money out of her pocket. The man instantly became silent as he looked at the wad of bills. He gulped and shifted closer to the door. Hmm, she thought, I thought it'd be harder.

"You can't," He said firmly. "The boss is trying to relax and he'll kill me if I let anyone disturb him. He's been moody these past few weeks. He's not about to change his mind just because a child like you said so."

She tossed the money with a flick of her wrist which he caught easily.

"Count it."

Taken aback, the doorman instantly flicked through the bills. It took a few minutes for him to sift through the money. The longer he counted, the nervous he became. She saw his hands shake until he finished at the last bill. For a minute, Kiden wondered if she even needed to talk the man down. He almost looked like he was having a panic attack. Finally, the guard gulped at the amount that he had counted.

"Take your money stranger," He said.

He had really good resolve, 18 noted. The man stood there, feet planted, holding the money in his outstretched hand.

"Tell you what," She said, "You keep that and... I make sure your boss stays happy for both our sakes. Cap-ire?"

"You're a crazy cagna," The man muttered in response.

Still nervous, he made this fact as clear as possible in a final attempt to sway 18. Not planning on being turned down, she stood her ground. Finally, he slowly unlatched the door.

"Grazie," She said as politely and cheerfully as she entered.

"I pray and hope that we both don't have to go to our funerals... A shame to see someone as young as you standing up to the head of the Italian mob."

"I'm not as young as you think."

"Mercy."

The hall was lit up brightly. Art hung from the walls as 18 progressed to the door at the end of the hall. She opened it gently and stepped inside. There were men sitting at tables, drinking, playing cards and smoking. Just as she expected of a modern mob scenario. Bits of it looked nothing like the movies however. There were tons of hit men and women in the main room. No dancers, or any forms of entertainment other than casino style card games and alcohol. The bartender looked suspiciously at Kiden but went back to polishing shot glasses. She noticed one of his hands reach below the bar, grab something and put it on top of the counter. It was a new experimental rifle. Can't they ever stop bringing up ways to shoot people? She wondered. Oh wait, we all know the answer to that. Wow, vintage glass, she observed as she winked at the man behind the counter. Taken slightly aback, the bartender put a hand on the rifle and tapped his fingers on his weapon as if he hadn't made his point clear enough. 18 walked past the bar and approached the table at the far corner. Suddenly, she felt eyes from every direction turning to get a look and the noise was dying down.

"I don't have any scheduled visits from anyone today so you better talk quick... and it looks like I'm getting a new doorman. Although… I do admire the fact he was able to say no so many times to you even though you're as persistent as the temptations of the devil. I will spare you two since I'm now extremely curious."

18 smiled.

"Thank you for your time," She bowed her head which caused every person in the room to instantly become silent and slowly fidget.

One wrong move and the room would light up faster than a roman candle, she thought, let's hope these guys actually like being reasonable every other day.

"Actually, would you believe me if I said I have a gift for you?"

The head boss of the Italian mafia leaned forward. He eyed her suspiciously and with two fingers, took the cigar out of his mouth and pointed it in her direction.

"Look miss, I am not doing too well. And there isn't a damn thing a pretty girl such as yourself can do to make me feel good," He said menacingly in English. However, she continued smirking which made him even more annoyed. "I told you to be quick miss. Otherwise I give the signal and in this case, only you die."

The men sitting on the boss' flank shifted and their arms went for the pockets on the insides of their jackets. 18 stared back at the two men with raised eyebrows. She made sure they saw her expression clearly. Sighing, she immediately reached in her jacket and pulled a bag out of her pocket and threw it onto the table.

"I heard you got into a fit of trouble from one of your partners," She said ignoring the flinching movements from the guards but the boss merely lifted his hand, commanding them to freeze. "So… basically I went and stole back what he took from you. If you want to keep that bag however, you stop terrorizing innocents who had nothing to do with what's in there."

She pointed at the bag with a stern look. The boss, raised an eyebrow and leaned forward to grab the bag. He peered inside to see what was in it. After a moment, he waved the guards down and put the bag back on the table. One of his henchmen, at his command, immediately took the bag and removed himself from the room.

"Alright, young lady, you have my attention..." He muttered calmly. There was less hostility in his voice which made the tension in the air practically float away. Everyone not near the main table turned and went back to what they were doing. The boss then leaned forward casually smiled, "Do I want to know how you managed to... acquire my diamonds back? What was it you demanded? My hearing is not as good as it was in my younger days."

"That you leave civilians alone," 18 repeated a bit louder. The boss leaned back, as if she had just lunged at him with a whip. "I know that you've been intimidating them. I know about the thief that thought it'd be ok to challenge your rule by robbing you. But he shielded himself behind poor innocent people. When you went looking for him, you did so by stepping on good people. People that are making this thief a martyr and thinking it's time to fight back while you sit here thinking you're safe."

"Careful, girl," The boss snarled, "You keep talking like that, I might change my mind about what I already think about you."

"It's all about ego to you isn't it?" 18 replied. "Do you want the thief or not?"

"You stole back the diamonds from this elusive volpe," The boss spoke. "Why is this man not here before me?"

"Oh he'll be here," 18 smiled. "I'm having him shipped to your door in a few minutes. But here's what I'm telling that you need to know. This part is free."

"Go on..."

"This volpe, you say?" 18 said. "He was obsessed. You could say, he was a fan who idolized someone who did the impossible. The mastermind of Incidente Dominoe."

"A tragedy my child," The boss nodded his head respectfully. "A blitz that shattered the hearts of millions even those who did not live on the same continent. You sound as if you were in the heart of it. But now you are here in the land of my ancestors bringing down a thief that idolized the one they call the Assassino?"

"People who idolize their 'heroes' can do great things," 18 spoke. "Terrible, yes. But great things. He stole from you because he wanted you to make the mistake of hurting people in your search for him. I caught him rallying and distributing weapons to many people willing to fight back. But if I'm correct, more bloodshed and needless killing is not what we all want."

"If the damage has been done," The boss said with conviction. "What good is catching the man? If the people want to fight, what can I do?"

"You can do something they won't expect but it will make them realize that you made a mistake. You tell them it was a misunderstanding by lowering your weapons first and showing them compassion. That's something I'm sure your pride can afford to give up. It'll give the people the opportunity to see that you do care about them while maintaining your system that has been in place for a long time. The man who initiated the Dominoe Incident proved that there can be others who will rise up because of their obsessive idolization to continue his infamous work. But it is actions of people like you with power and reason who can show that we can also fight by not falling victim to this game of risk with human lives."

Everyone who heard her was silent. The boss listened intently and looked at his guards. Now, 18 wasn't sure what was going to happen. It was a big risk that she was taking making demands with the Italian mob especially since it was her first time going in alone. Finally, the boss stood up.

"That was probably the bravest thing you've had to do up to now in your life," The boss spoke. "If I do everything you say, what's in it for the long run for both of us?"

"It's really not that complicated signore," She continued, "I help you, and you do something small for me every time I finish the work. And I'll only ask for ten percent of the profits for every job I do. Basically, I'm offering you my strictly professional services, taking very little, and I'm one of the best. Speaking modestly of course. Oh and… it doesn't matter if you refuse or not. Because I prefer to have my voice spoken in every simple thing."

"No one has ever done work for me and asked for so little," The boss observed suspiciously. It had to be the strangest offer he had ever heard in his entire life. "What's your angle?"

"The right thing. Take it or leave it."

"You know," He said, "Part of me wants to throw you out but the rest of me wants to keep you around just so you could be clearer about what it is your supposed angle is. But since you brought back my diamonds, I'll consider it an entry fee and no questions asked for now. But I'm watching you… understood? Any funny business, then you know what I'm capable of."

"I assumed you would. A piacere to be working for you."

"Young lady," The boss spoke again, "You do know you're willing to work for a mob right? This is ridiculous to a certain extent. I do hope you're taking my warnings seriously."

"Oh don't worry about me. This is exactly what I'm ready for. Just as long as you respect me, then I respect you in the same aspect. It's safer that way until we learn or decide to trust one another."

CHAPTER 29

2135, Amborg Industries

"I trust you enjoyed your stay?"

Brad nodded. He probably had spent the entire day learning more than he had ever thought was possible. To hear things from another perspective felt invigorating. He had suddenly developed a whole new respect to what it was that the amborgs had done or were still doing in the present. After all of that information, he immediately began to feel exhausted from the amazing story. However that was the end of it and he was going back home. Dr. Kendrick and 117 were escorting him to a transport which was preparing to take him home.

"Absolutely," Brad exclaimed excitedly, "It's amazing listening to a whole new perspective about the Domino Incident, the amborgs, and their individual disappearances following that war. Everyone I knew just wondered why they disappeared. We thought the government exiled them or something."

"Yes, and you can also see why I'm reluctant to let someone like you become an amborg," Dr. Kendrick said, "Because you would be burdened with a new life that sounds like it is filled with freedom but in reality, it may not at times. Not only that, you'd also need to be able to withstand any pain that they undergo as a family. Remember, they grew up without their real parents, their homes, no education but the sheer determination to live. Only one of the best possible caliber would be capable of helping to nullify the kinds of trauma we have faced. In some situations, we still have certain stages of relapses or even the occasional physical or mental breakdown."

"And as a precaution," 117 interrupted. "We would advise against you taking this rejection seriously and offer you several promotions to boost your welfare and morality."

"What?" Brad asked incredulously.

"Oh," Dr. Kendrick chuckled sheepishly. "That's just a little note of warning we like to say to our rejected applicants. You know er… Please don't try to declare one man wars anywhere please and we'll give you cookies."

"Oh gotcha," Brad chuckled. "No, I won't try to idolize and start another Dominoe Incident. That happened when I was young. But because of this, I guess it wouldn't hurt to consider different careers."

"Remember," 117 said informatively. "Our lives are not technically suitable career prospects. We instead prefer to think of them as adequate ways of living. You'd be surprised at what kind of jobs several of us have successfully held over the last few years."

"Maybe I'll hear about those stories some other time," Brad smiled. "I'm already thinking of coming again after all."

"You'll always be welcome," Dr. Kendrick nodded as he patted the student on the shoulder. "You're very lucky you know, especially to hear about such a critical story."

"There is one more question though. Whatever happened to 43 and her condition? I don't think we covered that."

117 nodded casually. They stopped in the middle of the hall and 117 looked around.

"I believe I can trust you for some reason Brad," The amborg said quietly. "It is true that 43 was slowly dying after the Dominoe Incident. But what happened to her is essentially a leap in scientific endeavors. I ask that the following information be kept a secret."

Brad nodded in agreement. 117 looked at Dr. Kendrick who smiled and the two of them continued escorting Brad down the hall. 117's bracelet activated and projected an image of 43.

"Two years after the incident, her condition worsened obviously," He explained, "Everyone onsite struggled to find a solution to repair the damage and she admired our determination even when there was no hope. It was amazing how she fought strongly for her life. 6 managed to minimize the pain but in 2130, her system finally failed completely and she passed on."

Horrified, Brad felt that the question he asked had been uncalled for but Dr. Kendrick seemed to know exactly what he was thinking because he received another sympathetic pat on the shoulder.

"It's a legitimate question, Brad," He said smiling, "43's condition was never really fixable in the first place. We just had to let that part of her go."

"I'm sorry," Brad said bowing his head a bit, "She meant a lot to both of you. It's just not easy losing someone who's gone forever."

"From my experiences, never apologize for something you didn't participate or do," 117 replied. "Also, a minor correction Brad. She is not gone forever."

"What?"

Dr. Kendrick looked at Brad in surprise. Then he began to laugh. He had definitely missed something.

"You didn't know? Or to be accurate, you didn't figure it out?"

Brad, now beginning to be confused, stared. Had he missed something in the whole story? One slight tidbit? The agony was starting to be too suspenseful. Finally, before he could ask, Dr. Kendrick pressed a button and a light flew across the panel on the wall. Seconds later, there was another flash and the projector lit up and the lovely figure of Serina appeared and floated next to the image of 43 from 117's bracelet.

"Yes Dr. Kendrick?" She asked curiously.

She then saw the floating image of 43 and then leapt in horror.

"Oh goodness," She exclaimed. "Is that what my hair looks like? Yikes."

Silently, her holographic hand reached up to her head and she quickly began to readjust her holographic hair. Brad stared in surprise. The two women looked completely identical. 117 couldn't help but smile when he saw the look on Brad's face.

"A miracle as you would say Brad," He said as he shut down his bracelet. Serina, still floating in the air, stopped fiddling with her hair and then straightened up, chuckling nervously. "That is what happened."

"Brad," Dr. Kendrick chuckled, "I'm amazed you didn't realize it. Especially when we told you the part of the story where 43 elaborated her plans to 6."

"Well, I just assumed that they just happened to have the same name," Brad kept eye-balling Serina who giggled. She suddenly disappeared and then flashed over to 117. She perched on his shoulder like a parrot and then sat down, "But I never guessed that they were the same... She's an artificial intelligence! Without a human body? I mean, the A.I. inside her CPU manifested into a holographic one? Wait... What??"

Serina nodded to everything that Brad had blurted out. She floated off 117's shoulder and moved across the air over towards Brad.

"When I lived," She said happily, "I was Serina 43. Now, I just float around doing my own thing. My real body has been kept nicely preserved here. Just because someday someone in the unending future might find a way to bring it back to life. Pfft, that might take a few centuries but at least I lived and well, that's a nice possibility to have on my mind. Nice to formally meet you again. But it would be nice if you didn't let anyone know about my particular background."

"Why is that?"

"Well you see," She said, "When I was dying, I told Vanessa 6 how to help keep my mind and data intact. When I was originally infected, I learned about the enemy A.I. inside me. He shut me up so well but at some point, I was able to spy and learn a few things about the programming. Despite its really bad and poorly design, it had a very advanced schematic. Really mind-blowing tech. The secrets I acquired from the assassin's program allowed me the opportunity to continue living but since my body was dying, I needed time to fully preserve myself. It wasn't easy to make myself the way I am now which is why 6 allowed me to borrow her less damaged CPU for my work."

"When 43 basically approached 6 with the idea," Dr. Kendrick explained. "Vanessa accepted but then she started to act strange which led to a lot of misdemeanors. I never knew that 43 was transferring her consciousness into 6 on a regular basis. But a few weeks before her body failed, 6 uploaded 43's mind and data into hers for the final touch and Serina was created. An exact identical copy of her former persona. It had never been done before and 43 cracked the key to making herself compatible as an artificial intelligence without us knowing. The science behind it all is incredible but also dangerous. It's a relatively new breakthrough in the grounds of science."

"Dangerous indeed. It did explain why 6 acted strangely like 43 for a year," 117 added in a very amused tone. Serina nodded and smiled silently as he continued, "I could never understand why 6 all of a sudden became so affectionate towards me. We assumed that she was making an attempt to comfort me but as it turns out, it was only Serina working out the kinks of adjusting to a new lifestyle. You could say she forced 6 to develop certain qualities of a multiple personality syndrome."

Serina stuck out her tongue.

"Sorry, it was difficult keeping myself hidden," She protested, "Some of my original personality quirks kept trying to leap out when I wasn't expecting it. After a year inside the hospitality of 6, I was able to create myself as an A.I. Not perfectly but I do have unique qualities compared to most of the artificial intelligence programs in use today."

"And that brings us to why we should keep this between us," Dr. Kendrick said warningly. Everyone huddled closer together, "All of the amborgs know about Serina but to the world and anyone else who knows, Serina 43 is dead. The ability to create yourself as an artificial intelligence is not just amazing but it is out of this world. Speaking modestly, this is something that I cannot and won't be able to do for years, no matter how smart I am. In the wrong hands, everyone would try to unlock the methods that Serina here underwent in her transformation. Serina here is... to be frank, an historical achievement in the eyes of artificial intelligence research. Decades beyond what we're capable of. Serina was born as a human who then underwent the transformation process from cyborg to a program. Literally, she rewrote herself into a program. Untouched and unassisted by human hands. An A.I. of that caliber born already self-aware is the most tempting piece of work out there. It's also Serina's right though to keep it to herself though."

117 held out a hand and Serina leapt out it and sat down peacefully. She yawned and rocked back and forth. Brad stared and hung onto every word that Kendrick was disclosing.

"An amborg truly is an amazing thing isn't it?" He asked. Dr. Kendrick smiled and nodded. "Doing impossible things because… Well. Who knows what circumstances can bring?"

"Yes I agree. They amaze me every day," Brad said in amazement.

"Do I have your word that Serina's secret remains with you now that we've fully determined that we can trust you?"

Brad watched as Serina began doing cartwheels on 117's hand.

"Of course."

"I suppose you and 6 have resolved the issues?" Brad asked curiously.

117 smiled.

"She still gets embarrassed every time she gives me a check-up but it is amusing. Besides, I already have someone else to worry about. Excuse me Dr. Kendrick, Serina, I have to get ready to leave."

As he walked away, Serina waved wildly as if she was catching flies. Brad stared.

"What does that mean?"

Serina chuckled and flashed a bright blue.

"It means my old flame is going on a date with one lucky human," She said happily.

"I think he's serious about this one too," Dr. Kendrick nodded in agreement. "I'm still amazed that you and 117 are alright with the circumstances."

"Well I'm made out of numbers," Serina sighed cheekily, "I can only state or express myself with words only. I can't provide any form of physical contact for any of those categories of relationships. Besides, as long as he's happy, then that's ok with me."

"You could make technical fireworks or pretty much generate algorithmic computations for romance?" Brad suggested.

Serina giggled.

"I could," she admitted. "But I don't have what I used to have. Instead, I managed to find a better life for myself. Well... one where I can live on. Hehe. The circumstances may be strange but I really am happy."

After saying a few short goodbyes, Brad was taken to the transport for a quick ride home. Dr. Kendrick had to practically force Brad onto his own private jet. Which was, in his humble opinion, one of the few aircraft in the world that could travel at incredible speeds. Serina and Dr. Kendrick waved as the transport lifted off safely and whooshed away.

"I think that boy has a bright future ahead of him," Dr. Kendrick observed happily. "He'll contribute heavily in the world's needs. Especially what he doesn't know yet."

"Why do you think that?" Serina asked curiously as the transport only became a bright orange light in the distance.

Dr. Kendrick, beckoned for her to follow. She blinked once and reappeared on his shoulder.

"Everyone who knows what they can do always begin forging a path to making the world a better place," He said, "The journey is the most enlightening part when one tries to work for the end game. It always starts with one."

As they turned around and stepped back inside the facility. Dr. Kendrick remembered another important detail.

"Serina," Dr. Kendrick asked curiously, "In any part of that story, did... did we tell or mention any indication to Brad about... that particular event?"

Serina stared but silently began shaking her head.

"Looking at all the security footage, audio logs and the entire time Brad was here, references to the event you're talking about is... a zero count."

Dr. Kendrick nodded with a sigh of relief.

"Good because that incident is not ready to be revealed. Soon it will but for now, we keep it just within the scientific communities."

"Now then, I believe next week, we're paying a visit to the Apogee station Serina," He continued normally, "Do you know which amborgs would be interested in a trip?"

"I'll start asking," Serina said excitedly and whizzed away.

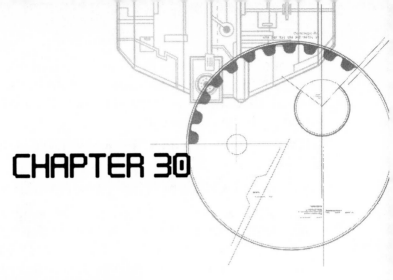

CHAPTER 30

2136, Los Angeles, One year A.B. (After Brad).

* * *
** ** **

("Mandy, I know this is an annoying question. But when will the lesson end?")

("Almost Sarah. This part was actually given to me by 117's grandfather. Turns out he thinks it is footage everyone should see.")

("Is there really a historical timeline marking that says 'after Brad'?")

("In our historical files, yes. Now shush.")

* * *
** ** **

"So are you in or out?"

"I don't know."

"All I'm saying is that if we could end up teaching them, it'd be a great skill set to have! You're going to have to deal with your insecurities of watching over children soon."

From the top of a very tall skyscraper, fourth group amborgs, Alex 280 and Ally 113 were both sitting on the edge of a rooftop overlooking the city. From their vantage point, they had begun to talk about personal details while they waited patiently for their next set of orders. Lately they had been told to try having off-topic small talk in order to pass the time. Both of them made sure their internal chronometers were shut off. They were apparently not supposed to be too precise.

"Ok, I guess we can do it," He said as he stretched his arms above his head.

113 smiled and brought out her notepad from her waist pocket.

"Great!" She said as she flipped the pages and scanned the names written on the page. "I'll call... Diane and we'll be official volunteer chaperones for the school's field trip. As friends to the local schools and helpful subjects of volunteer programs for kids, they will be very happy to hear of our support."

"I like babysitting kids," 280 spoke as he scratched his head, "But thirty four kids on a trip to the zoo is a bit much isn't it 113?"

"Well, confidentially speaking, we are evolved humans and we can handle it."

"Not so loud!" He said urgently, "You want to blow our cover?"

"What's the big deal?" She replied gesturing to the lights of the city, "If we're blown, we just disguise ourselves and go dark. Do the death protocol and ta dah. There is no cause to be alarmed. We are figments of the human mind."

Before he could respond, a small beeping noise began sounding off. If anyone else had been around, they wouldn't have heard it. Both amborgs perked up and instructions were feeding straight into their brains from a private message.

"All members standby," A voice spoke in their heads, "Everyone has reached their positions. Prepare for phase two of the operation. Objectives are now being prioritized to each one of you. Secondary directives will apply. As always, anyone caught slacking or compromising the objective is in charge of garbage duty or something they will hate doing for a month. Now then, proceed."

"That's our cue," 280 said calmly as he stood up on the ledge. 113 stood and looked over the edge.

"Right behind you," She said as he leaped off the roof. Taking a breath, she also stepped off the ledge. "I love this part."

* * *
** ** **

From inside the building, Marsha Bradley stared out the window. She had had a very quiet day which was a completely different change than a year ago. She couldn't remember the last time she had gone seventy-two hours without firing a gun. The idea of peace was definitely not what she expected. In Los Angeles, it wasn't normal at all. Shrugging the idea out of her head, she immediately took another bite of her fish with her fork and looked back out the window. The city actually looked like a beautiful sight which was another surprise to her. It was strange looking out and not seeing buildings with holes in them. Then again, it was even stranger that she was having a fancy dinner in a skyscraper.

"You seem different. Some dessert for your thoughts?"

She turned her head back sharply. She had forgotten who she was eating with of all people.

"What makes you say that?" She said sharply at Mark who was smiling.

In the back of her head, she thought about how odd it was to see the grandfather of an amborg, and the head of a group of vigilantes wearing a casual dinner suit. The fact that she was actually on a dinner date with him kept giving her goosebumps. Mark chuckled and leaned forward.

"Well, for starters, you aren't complaining about your food like the last time," He observed. "And also, I think this is the first time I've seen you wear a skirt. But I don't think this particular one counts."

"Hey, I haven't got time to wear all that fashionable crap," She snapped. She lowered her volume when a few customers turned in their direction. It wasn't the time to raise her voice which was annoying. "And my dress uniform from the force counts. I put a lot of thought into wearing this uniform and you're going to find some way of being ok with that."

"Well. At least you put some thought into considering a skirt," Mark said approvingly as he lifted his wine glass and took a sip, "That's definitely something different about you today. Reminds me when we were a lot younger back in our school days."

Before she could come up with a retort, a black shape flew downwards outside of their window catching their attention. It was gone so quickly that Bradley thought she had almost imagined it.

"Did you see that?" She asked quietly.

Mark nodded. No sooner did she ask, a second shape flew down following the first. This time, both of the adults were already looking out the window to catch a clear glimpse of the second one.

"Was that a person??" Bradley set her silverware down and immediately prepared to get up but was waved down by Mark. "Did two people just fall past our window?"

Mark lifted his hand for silence and they waited. Activity in the restaurant continued around them normally. No one else appeared to have noticed what they had seen. After a few more seconds went by, Mark then went back to his food casually as if nothing had happened.

"Well?" Bradley asked under breath. "Why are you so calm about it?"

"They were probably Kendrick's amborgs," He muttered reassuringly.

"What?"

"Marsha honey," He said in between chews, "If two people really just committed suicide by jumping off a building, then someone down there would be calling somebody like you for help and you'd be on the way down already. Besides, since that hasn't happened in the last two seconds and I don't hear any screaming, there's probably nothing to worry about."

Bradley paused and thought for a moment. The old man was right. There was absolutely nothing to be worried about. Nothing but good signs seemed to flow continuously in the atmosphere. Her years of experience as an officer had almost ruined their dinner date.

Might as well try being normal, she thought grimly. If she knew what the word meant.

"What's Tinhead been up to these days? I hardly hear from him," She asked in an attempt to change the subject.

"You miss him eh?"

"No," Bradley scoffed. "He hasn't made headlines that much lately. Well, at least the amborgs that do make news… they aren't ones I recognize or know of too well."

"Last I heard," Mark said as took another large bite. "They all decided to take a sabbatical… which most of them are still on considering that decision was made years ago. Also… Tinhead? Really? That's your nickname for him?"

"It just stuck I guess."

"It must have," Mark smiled as he grabbed his wine glass. "You really do miss having him around?"

"Look," Bradley sighed. "You don't have to be so condescending about it. Just explain it to me. Why would he just get up and leave? Isn't he good at his job?"

"Being good at their job is precisely why they've gone."

Mark grabbed the napkin from his setting and wiped his mouth.

"I mean, I'd like some decent vacation time after all the crap they went through. Saving the country and all that," He said smiling. "117's interpretation of it is, he believes that there are enough believers out there that can take care of the world's problems without the amborgs. People like you, captain dear, who have the ability to accomplish a lot."

"I can't just find time for a vacation," Bradley muttered as she began eating again. "I got to have something to do."

"What do you think this is?" Mark gestured to the dinner table. "I mean, it's not an ideal resort but you did decide to come to dinner with me. Why? Because I'm betting that you felt empty sitting at your peace-time desk with the same old work you do every day now."

"That's not… I suppose…" Bradley wasn't fully convinced, "It just doesn't make sense that with all their power, they could have everything but instead, they choose to be hidden among us."

"They do have everything," Mark said bluntly, "Or rather, they have the capacity to achieve everything but instead, they don't want to. That's the thing, at the same time, they also hate having a lot at their disposal. They're only trying to be human after all. But, on occasion, how you feel about them is relatable. I've seen kids looking up at the skies. Watching and waiting for those streaks of light to soar above them. They're heroes to those kids. I guess some people really want them back."

"With them gone and things kinda settling, my officers haven't been dying than how they used to. I mean that's a good thing but at the same time, they're going way too soft. Sometimes, I kind of want to follow an amborg in the field again. I just hope they don't go too far. I miss a little action."

"I think they just don't want to do your job for you," Mark chuckled, "Speaking in a practical way. They'd be putting you and thousands of others out of a job if they weren't hiding right now. That's just a probability."

"Quiet you," Bradley said annoyed. "Or you aren't getting any tonight. Oh man, I have been drinking tonight… Can't watch my own mouth."

"Not as feisty," Mark said flirtatiously, "Peace time has changed you way too much."

**   **   **

The White House

"Excuse me, Mr. President?"

"What is it? Unless another crisis has been declared, don't wake me."

The president was not accustomed to calls very early in the morning. Especially when he wasn't even at his desk. He knew however when he saw one of his military commanders standing in the entrance to his bedroom that something important had come up. He knew that the First Lady would instantly want to make sure he was already sitting up. Unfortunately, his wife was not at home though. Right, the president thought, she's doing a campaign in Europe. Disgruntled, he slowly got up from his mattress and looked for his bathrobe.

"Oh my god, there hasn't actually been another crisis… has there? I seriously don't need this now," He asked as he scrambled towards the door almost instantly. The commander shook her head calmly.

"No sir," She said reassuringly, "Urgent call from the U.N. An alpha priority thirteen message. It would appear that every leader in the country has been requested to be a part of this meeting. Despite their sleep schedules. My apologies."

"Fine. Fine."

Now he was definitely feeling that something bad was happening no matter how calm the commander looked. Soldiers were bred to be brave. The president couldn't help but admire their resolve. He nodded curtly at his subordinate.

"I'll get dressed right away," He sighed. "Better get a move on."

Roughly ten minutes later, he was sitting at his desk with guards covering the entrances and exits. An alpha thirteen only meant one thing to the U.N. Complete secrecy which unfortunately was uncomforting to a lot of people. The president pressed a button and armor plating descended from outside and covered the windows. The guards began closing all the doors and locking the place down. Finally, one soldier gave the thumbs up after they did a quick sweep of the room and everyone except for the president and two of his military advisors were in the room. With all their security procedures finished, the president was allowed to continue.

"Room secure sir," The commander confirmed. "Connecting to the call."

She stepped forward and placed an advanced laptop on his desk. She entered an access code and then the screen opened up. The president leaned forward placing his left hand on the pad and shutting his left eye. He spoke the passcode.

"Betamax was at its peak. But all that rises will eventually come down in some form or another. Where I sit right now, may there be mercy on the brave souls daring to join our adventure."

"Passcode, retinal scan and biological confirmation clearance acknowledged and secure," The computer replied. "Alpha thirteen message feed is clear and running. Welcome Mr. President of the United States."

The president made sure his face was in direct line of sight to the camera on the computer. He quickly readjusted his tie as the computer rang and the green light signaled that he was connected.

Many other faces began to appear on his screen. He recognized most of them as members of the U.N. council. To his amazement, there were many leaders of other countries also appearing. He had never seen a huge gathering of leaders on a computer screen before. Then again, no one had. If a hacker stumbled upon this heavily encrypted system, they'd probably wet their own brains out. Many of them looked as if they also had been woken up like he had. Others were all displaying confused looks.

"Mr. President," The Russian Leader said graciously bowing his head, "It is good to see you. Seeing you here is enough to make me feel secure. Especially when the number on this alpha is thirteen."

"Likewise Veniamin," The president replied, "Does anyone have any idea what's up? I apologize for my lack of formalities, I was woken up at a very inconvenient time."

"Based on this large gathering at this hour..." The Prime Minister from Britain grumbled, "I can definitely sympathize with the President. I hope it is worthwhile. I am eager to go back to sleep so I hope this will be over soon."

"I agree," The leader of the Germany spoke, "I do not like being interrupted and pulled away from the affairs of my homeland."

"Trust me this is beyond the capabilities of any of your countries."

Everyone became silent. The President stared at his screen and saw a face join the faces of the world. It was Dr. John Kendrick. Everyone, disoriented from lack of sleep or waiting curiously, all straightened up at his sudden appearance.

"Dr. Kendrick," The Russian President spoke, "It was you who issued the alpha message? A pleasure as always my friend."

"Indeed it was I who had to wake a portion of you from your beds. For that I apologize," Dr. Kendrick replied casually.

Before he could continue however, the French leader suddenly interrupted.

"Doctor, if this is another one of your pranks, let me remind you that most of us are at least three seconds away from hanging up on this call. I still haven't forgotten the time one of your... daughters accidently dialed my emergency landline."

"I know that in the past, my bedside manner has not always been respectful of authority but in this case, I actually have made a breakthrough so unless you want to drop behind in world-wide phenomenal technology, I suggest you listen. With respect."

Sensing a bit of hostility now building based on the French leader's silent expression, the U.S. President immediately took charge.

"Please doctor, I happen to agree with my colleague," He interrupted graciously before his French colleague could spit out an insult, "I was just woken up because of something urgent so we'd like for you to get to the point. Please. The majority of the world's leaders are watching because you called us. Give them something to listen to."

"Very well then," Kendrick spoke over the monitors, "Esteemed leaders from around the globe, we at Amborg Industries have made an incredible discovery regarding the incident that occurred in the year of 2128. Within the halls of my installation itself."

Everyone became silent and stared.

"You mean, you've figured it out? The portal?" The Prime Minister asked absolutely stunned.

He wasn't the only one. Every other person involved in the call were all exclaiming in wonder and great fascination.

"I have indeed," Kendrick said with a gleam, "And you are all invited to A.I. industries for a more detailed look into what we're doing. Covertly is the preferred medium of travel to my facility for this discovery."

"Nonsense," The leader of France said smugly, "It's impossible. I feel as if you are overstepping your bounds again Kendrick. No matter how big of a genius you are."

"Hold on now," The U.S. President spoke up, "I have had no reason to ever doubt Dr. Kendrick despite his quirks considering the fact that it was his amborgs that saved my daughter only a few months ago. Before, it can be argued that he saved the country during the Dominoe Incident. If he says he's done it, then I believe him."

"Thank you Mr. President," Dr. Kendrick said in gratitude, "I always knew you were sensible enough. One of the reasons I voted for you."

Many of the other leaders were also nodding and murmuring agreement. Finally, one of the U.N. council members spoke.

"It would appear that all of us are in agreement. I hope?"

The French Leader merely nodded silently but the President could tell he was still cheesed off.

"Then it's settled."

"Good," Dr. Kendrick smiled. "I have a few more notes to run through but it shouldn't take up too much of your time. You'll be back to living normally in a few minutes."

Everyone agreed very quickly and soon, after another ten minutes of Dr. Kendrick's presentation, the call was over. As the laptop was shut down and put away, all the guards reentered the room and immediately began restoring the Oval Office to the way it originally was. The President sighed heavily as he leaned back in his chair.

"Can I get you anything sir?" His commander asked.

"Nothing for now..." He sighed, "Maybe some coffee or something to eat. Looks like the world is changing. In a few years, assuming I'm still president, we could be looking at something big. Oh and commander, remember that for the record, this meeting is off the books and it didn't happen. As I'm supposed to say in order to conform to standard procedure. Et cetera, et cetera, you know the drill."

"Of course sir. Took the words right out of my mouth."

"This is going to be the most exciting thing to ever happen, or the world's worst nightmare. And billions of people won't know which is which until it's happening right in front of them."

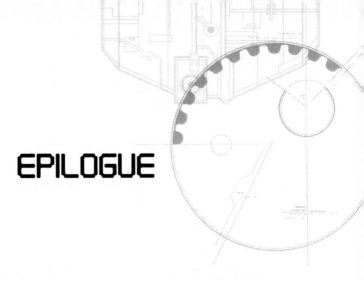

EPILOGUE

"This concludes the complement of subject material and all known informative files compiled by Instructor Mandy Walker, relating to inquiries and learning materials of Amborg 117 and the Domino Incident. Thank you for watching a product of visual learning experiences."

Sarah watched as the screen powered down. Mandy stretched her arms above her head.

"Well what did you think?" She asked when she lowered her arms.

Sarah thought for a moment. As an amborg, she felt that this was a relatively simple answer. But David 117's former technician was well known for her reputation as a teacher of basic human etiquette. So complex calculations would always be overruled.

"I don't know Mrs. Mandy," She replied, "I understand the motives of all the amborgs, leading up to and after the great Domino Incident. They all went their own ways and learned about their humanity by immersing themselves in what they wanted to do on their sabbaticals. And then one thing led to them joining together again to deal with bigger threats in the future after that. History is a fascinating subject but why did this particular lesson require that I learn about 117?"

Mandy placed a hand on the girl's shoulder and sighed.

"Like I said before," She explained. "You remind me of him a lot. You aren't fully aware of what human emotion is like. After augmentation, you seemed to struggle with adapting to the amborg's way of living. It almost felt like you were lost. Just like he was when I was his technician. David 117 was a unique and smart individual that fully developed into a proper human being in a way that can't be taught. He learned and evolved to be himself. That is how human emotion or exposure to the basic instincts of humanity shapes you properly. Which is why I figured showing you direct footage of this self-made lesson plan would give you some new perspective."

"What was David 117 to you when you first met him? Did you have a feeling that you just knew he was the one who would be best mentored by you?"

"Good question."

Mandy stood and walked over to a shelf where she kept some of her belongings for her classroom to see. She grabbed a photo and showed it to Sarah. It was Mandy and 117 from a long time ago. He was merely smiling whereas she looked to be laughing about something in particular.

"The best mentor or teacher," Mandy instructed, "Is always yourself. I only remember small tidbits about David 117. At first, he just seemed so lost compared to all the other amborgs I had read about or met already. I ventured a guess that he'd be the one who needed a slight push. There are other amborgs who have definitely made an impact on the world and countless lives but I don't believe I regret choosing him."

Mandy handed Sarah another photo. It was a large group of amborgs and technicians all posing at what appeared to be some sort of celebratory barbecue.

"This was taken a few days before many amborgs disappeared into society after the Dominoe Incident," Mandy said pointing herself out in the photo. "There I am."

"I'm afraid I don't seem to have particularly good experiences when it comes to gatherings like these," Sarah said with a mournful look. "Perhaps I am as socially awkward as you say."

"That's not true," Mandy said as Sarah handed the pictures back. "The Domino Incident, the high school student Brad, David 117 and Serina 43. Those were great factors that brought out the best in him. It took a lot of perspective in order for him to learn. Many of the older amborgs look back and reference some of these events as life lessons. They don't always work for everyone but for people who struggle, they can be used as examples of how to find a new meaning in life. 117 isn't the only one by the way. There are other stories too. 917's sacrifices, the destiny of Katie 57, 999 as the lone wolf as well as her call sign 'Angel', and even the one of Johnny 5's leg."

"May we learn more about these types of stories?" Sarah asked with a hint of curiosity in her voice.

Her modern bracelet was flashing wildly as she attempted to try and use her real voice. She couldn't understand why older amborgs had wanted to regain the use of their vocal chords when speaking with their minds and bracelets was easier. However, she was naturally curious about her predecessors. The siblings that were out there changing things and following their programming. Siblings that she grew up hearing stories about and now she was one of them.

Mandy restarted the computer and accessed the database. There were countless files to scroll through. It had taken her a few days to organize the video files and records about 117 and the Domino Incident for this private tutoring session. But she figured another small story wouldn't be such a big deal. It'd have to be extremely short since it was getting late if her clock was right. She gestured and waved her hand for the young amborg to choose.

"Well, we have time," Mandy spoke cheerfully, "But why don't you choose one story specifically? It will make your natural curiousness more satisfying if I didn't choose for you."

"Can we learn about Angel 999?" Sarah asked selecting 999's personal profile. "What's this story about her joining the S.C.E.?"

"Ah, well a lot of amborgs had a choice during that time," Mandy replied. "I'll give you a basic intro but you'll have to give me time to compile another video session."

"Ok. 999 is one of my favorite amborgs."

"Alright. Well, let's take a look at what's easier to understand."

"Thank you Ms. Mandy."

"You're welcome Sarah 117."

END SESSION.
Amborg Industries thanks you for your patronage and support.